DP&F

Before Adam

& Other Stories

Other Jack London titles published by Leonaur

The Iron Heel & Other Stories
The Star Rover & Other Stories

Before Adam
& Other Stories

Jack London

The Collected Science Fiction & Fantasy of Jack London: Volume 1

Before Adam & Other Stories by Jack London

FIRST EDITION

Published by Leonaur Ltd

ISBN (10 digit): 1-84677-015-7 (hardcover)
ISBN (13 digit): 978-1-84677-015-9 (hardcover)

ISBN (10 digit): 1-84677-008-4 (softcover)
ISBN (13 digit): 978-1-84677-008-1 (softcover)

http://www.leonaur.com

Publisher's Notes

In the interests of authenticity, the spellings, grammar and place names used by the author have been retained.

The views expressed in this book are not necessarily those of the publisher.

Contents

Before Adam

Chapter 1

Pictures! Pictures! Pictures! Often, before I learned, did I wonder whence came the multitudes of pictures that thronged my dreams; for they were pictures the like of which I had never seen in real wake-a-day life. They tormented my childhood, making of my dreams a procession of nightmares and a little later convincing me that I was different from my kind, a creature unnatural and accursed.

In my days only did I attain any measure of happiness. My nights marked the reign of fear -- and such fear! I make bold to state that no man of all the men who walk the earth with me ever suffer fear of like kind and degree. For my fear is the fear of long ago, the fear that was rampant in the Younger World, and in the youth of the Younger World. In short, the fear that reigned supreme in that period known as the Mid-Pleistocene.

What do I mean? I see explanation is necessary before I can tell you of the substance of my dreams. Otherwise, little could you know of the meaning of the things I know so well. As I write this, all the beings and happenings of that other world rise up before me in vast phantasmagoria, and I know that to you they would be rhymeless and reasonless.

What to you the friendship of Lop-Ear, the warm lure of the Swift One, the lust and the atavism of Red-Eye? A screaming incoherence and no more. And a screaming incoherence, likewise, the doings of the Fire People and the Tree People, and the gibbering councils of the horde. For you know not the peace of the cool caves in the cliffs, the circus of the drinking-places at the end of the day. You have never felt the bite of the morning wind in the tree-tops, nor is the taste of young bark sweet in your mouth.

It would be better, I dare say, for you to make your approach, as I made mine, through my childhood. As a boy I was very like other boys -- in my waking hours. It was in my sleep that I was different. From my earliest recollection my sleep was a period of terror. Rarely were my dreams tinctured with happiness. As a rule, they were stuffed with fear -- and with a fear so strange and alien that it had no ponderable quality. No fear that I experienced in my waking life resembled the fear that possessed me in my sleep. It was of a quality and kind that transcended all my experiences.

For instance, I was a city boy, a city child, rather, to whom the country was an unexplored domain. Yet I never dreamed of cities; nor did a house ever occur in any of my dreams. Nor, for that matter, did any of my human kind ever break through the wall of my sleep. I, who had seen trees only in parks and illustrated books, wandered in my sleep through interminable forests. And further, these dream trees were not a mere blur on my vision. They were sharp and distinct. I was on terms of practised intimacy with them. I saw every branch and twig; I saw and knew every different leaf.

Well do I remember the first time in my waking life that I saw an oak tree. As I looked at the leaves and branches and gnarls, it came to me with distressing vividness that I had seen that same kind of tree many and countless times in my sleep. So I was not surprised, still later on in my life, to recognize instantly, the first time I saw them, trees such as the spruce, the yew, the birch, and the laurel. I had seen them all before, and was seeing them even then, every night, in my sleep.

This, as you have already discerned, violates the first law of dreaming, namely, that in one's dreams one sees only what he has seen in his waking life, or combinations of the things he has seen in his waking life. But all my dreams violated this law. In my dreams I never saw *anything* of which I had knowledge in my waking life. My dream life and my waking life were lives apart, with not one thing in common save myself. I was the connecting link that somehow lived both lives.

Early in my childhood I learned that nuts came from the grocer, berries from the fruit man; but before ever that knowledge was mine, in my dreams I picked nuts from trees, or gathered them and ate them from the ground underneath trees, and in the same way I ate berries from vines and bushes. This was beyond any experience of mine.

I shall never forget the first time I saw blueberries served on the table. I had never seen blueberries before, and yet, at the sight of them, there leaped up in my mind memories of dreams wherein I had wandered through swampy land eating my fill of them. My mother set before me a dish of the berries. I filled my spoon, but before I raised it to my mouth I knew just how they would taste. Nor was I disappointed. It was the same tang that I had tasted a thousand times in my sleep.

Snakes? Long before I had heard of the existence of snakes, I was tormented by them in my sleep. They lurked for me in the forest glades; leaped up, striking, under my feet; squirmed off through the dry grass or across naked patches of rock; or pursued me into the tree-tops, encircling the trunks with their great shining bodies, driving me higher and higher or farther and farther out on swaying and crackling branches, the ground a dizzy distance beneath me. Snakes! -- with their forked tongues, their beady eyes and glittering scales, their hissing and their rattling -- did I not already know them far too well on that day of my first circus when I saw the snake-charmer lift them up? They were old friends of mine, enemies rather, that peopled my nights with fear.

Ah, those endless forests, and their horror-haunted gloom! For what eternities have I wandered through them, a timid, hunted creature, starting at the least sound, frightened of my own shadow, keyed-up, ever alert and vigilant, ready on the instant to dash away in mad flight for my life. For I was the prey of all manner of fierce life that dwelt in the forest, and it was in ecstasies of fear that I fled before the hunting monsters.

When I was five years old I went to my first circus. I came home from it sick -- but not from peanuts and pink lemonade. Let me tell you. As we entered the animal tent, a hoarse roaring shook the air. I tore my hand loose from my father's and dashed wildly back through the entrance. I collided with people, fell down; and all the time I was screaming with terror. My father caught me and soothed me. He pointed to the crowd of people, all careless of the roaring, and cheered me with assurances of safety.

Nevertheless, it was in fear and trembling, and with much encouragement on his part, that I at last approached the lion's cage. Ah, I knew him on the instant. The beast! The terrible one! And on my inner vision flashed the memories of my dreams, -- the midday sun shining on tall grass, the wild bull grazing quietly, the sudden parting of the grass before the swift rush of the tawny one, his leap to the bull's back, the crashing and the bellowing, and the crunch, crunch of bones; or again, the cool quiet of the water-hole, the wild horse up to his knees and drinking softly, and then the tawny one -- always the tawny one! -- the leap, the screaming and the splashing of the horse, and the crunch, crunch of bones; and yet again, the sombre twilight and the sad silence of the end of day, and then the great full-throated roar, sudden, like a trump of doom, and swift upon it the insane shrieking and chattering among the trees, and I, too, am trembling with fear and am one of the many shrieking and chattering among the trees.

At the sight of him, helpless, within the bars of his cage, I became enraged. I gritted my teeth at him, danced up and down, screaming an incoherent mockery and making antic faces. He responded, rushing against the bars and roaring back at me his impotent wrath. Ah, he knew me, too, and the sounds I made were the sounds of old time and intelligible to him.

My parents were frightened. "The child is ill," said my mother. "He is hysterical," said my father. I never told them, and they never knew. Already had I developed reticence concerning this quality of mine, this semi-disassociation of personality as I think I am justified in calling it.

I saw the snake-charmer, and no more of the circus did I see that night. I was taken home, nervous and overwrought, sick with the invasion of my real life by that other life of my dreams.

I have mentioned my reticence. Only once did I confide the strangeness of it all to another. He was a boy -- my chum; and we were eight years old. From my dreams I reconstructed for him pictures of that vanished world in which I do believe I once lived. I told him of the terrors of that early time, of Lop-Ear and the pranks we played, of the gibbering councils, and of the Fire People and their squatting places.

He laughed at me, and jeered, and told me tales of ghosts and of the dead that walk at night. But mostly did he laugh at my feeble fancy. I told him more, and he laughed the harder. I swore in all earnestness that these things were so, and he began to look upon me queerly. Also, he gave amazing garblings of my tales to our playmates, until all began to look upon me queerly.

It was a bitter experience, but I learned my lesson. I was different from my kind. I was abnormal with something they could not understand, and the telling of which would cause only misunderstanding. When the stories of ghosts and goblins went around, I kept quiet. I smiled grimly to myself. I thought of my nights of fear, and knew that mine were the real things -- real as life itself, not attenuated vapors and surmised shadows.

For me no terrors resided in the thought of bugaboos and wicked ogres. The fall through leafy branches and the dizzy heights; the snakes that struck at me as I dodged and leaped away in chattering flight; the wild dogs that hunted me across the open spaces to the timber -- these were terrors concrete and actual, happenings and not imaginings, things of the living flesh and of sweat and blood. Ogres and bugaboos and I had been happy bed-fellows, compared with these terrors that made their bed with me throughout my childhood, and that still bed with me, now, as I write this, full of years.

Chapter 2

I have said that in my dreams I never saw a human being. Of this fact I became aware very early, and felt poignantly the lack of my own kind. As a very little child, even, I had a feeling, in the midst of the horror of my dreaming, that if I could find but one man, only one human, I should be saved from my dreaming, that I should be surrounded no more by haunting terrors. This thought obsessed me every night of my life for years -- if only I could find that one human and be saved!

I must iterate that I had this thought in the midst of my dreaming, and I take it as an evidence of the merging of my two personalities, as evidence of a point of contact between the two disassociated parts of me. My dream personality lived in the long ago, before ever man, as we know him, came to be; and my other and wake-a-day personality projected itself, to the extent of the knowledge of man's existence, into the substance of my dreams.

Perhaps the psychologists of the book will find fault with my way of using the phrase, "disassociation of personality." I know their use of it, yet am compelled to use it in my own way in default of a better phrase. I take shelter behind the inadequacy of the English language. And now to the explanation of my use, or misuse, of the phrase.

It was not till I was a young man, at college, that I got any clew to the significance of my dreams, and to the cause of them. Up to that time they had been meaningless and without apparent causation. But at college I discovered evolution and psychology, and learned the explanation of various strange mental states and experiences. For instance, there was the falling-through-space dream -- the commonest dream experience, one practically known, by first-hand experience, to all men.

This, my professor told me, was a racial memory. It dated back to our remote ancestors who lived in trees. With them, being tree-dwellers, the liability of falling was an ever-present menace. Many lost their lives that way; all of them experienced terrible falls, saving themselves by clutching branches as they fell toward the ground.

Now a terrible fall, averted in such fashion, was productive of shock. Such shock was productive of molecular changes in the cerebral cells. These molecular changes were transmitted to the cerebral cells of progeny, became, in short, racial memories. Thus, when you and I, asleep or dozing off to sleep, fall through space and awake to sickening consciousness just before we strike, we are merely remembering what happened to our arboreal ancestors, and which has been stamped by cerebral changes into the heredity of the race.

There is nothing strange in this, any more than there is anything strange in an instinct. An instinct is merely a habit that is stamped into the stuff of our heredity, that is all. It will be noted, in passing, that in this falling dream which is so familiar to you and me and all of us, we never strike bottom. To strike bottom would be destruction. Those of our arboreal ancestors who struck bottom died forthwith. True, the shock of their fall was communicated to the cerebral cells, but they died immediately, before they could have progeny. You and I are descended from those that did not strike bottom; that is why you and I, in our dreams, never strike bottom.

And now we come to disassociation of personality. We never have this sense of falling when we are wide awake. Our wake-a-day personality has no experience of it. Then -- and here the argument is irresistible -- it must be another and distinct personality that falls when we are asleep, and that has had experience of such falling -- that has, in short, a memory of past-day race experiences, just as our wake-a-day personality has a memory of our wake-a-day experiences.

It was at this stage in my reasoning that I began to see the light. And quickly the light burst upon me with dazzling brightness, illuminating and explaining all that had been weird and uncanny and unnaturally impossible in my dream experiences. In my sleep it was not my wake-a-day personality that took charge of me; it was another and distinct personality, possessing a new and totally different fund of experiences, and, to the point of my dreaming, possessing memories of those totally different experiences.

What was this personality? When had it itself lived a wake-a-day life on this planet in order to collect this fund of strange experiences? These were questions that my dreams themselves answered. He lived in the long ago, when the world was young, in that period that we call the Mid-Pleistocene. He fell from the trees but did not strike bottom. He gibbered with fear at the roaring of the lions. He was pursued by beasts of prey, struck at by deadly snakes. He chattered with his kind in council, and he received rough usage at the hands of the Fire People in the day that he fled before them.

But, I hear you objecting, why is it that these racial memories are not ours as well, seeing that we have a vague other-personality that falls through space while we sleep?

And I may answer with another question. Why is a two-headed calf? And my own answer to this is that it is a freak. And so I answer your question. I have this other-personality and these complete racial memories because I am a freak.

But let me be more explicit.

The commonest race memory we have is the falling-through-space dream. This other-personality is very vague. About the only memory it has is that of falling. But many of us have sharper, more distinct other-personalities. Many of us have the flying dream, the pursuing-monster dream, color dreams, suffocation dreams, and the reptile and vermin dreams. In short, while this other-personality is vestigial in all of us, in some of us it is almost obliterated, while in others of us it is more pronounced. Some of us have stronger and completer race memories than others.

It is all a question of varying degree of possession of the other-personality. In myself, the degree of possession is enormous. My other-personality is almost equal in power with my own personality. And in this matter I am, as I said, a freak -- a freak of heredity.

I do believe that it is the possession of this other-personality -- but not so strong a one as mine -- that has in some few others given rise to belief in personal reincarnation experiences. It is very plausible to such people, a most convincing hypothesis. When they have visions of scenes they have never seen in the flesh, memories of acts and events dating back in time, the simplest explanation is that they have lived before.

But they make the mistake of ignoring their own duality. They do not recognize their other-personality. They think it is their own personality, that they have only one personality; and from such a premise they can conclude only that they have lived previous lives.

But they are wrong. It is not reincarnation. I have visions of myself roaming through the forests of the Younger World; and yet it is not myself that I see but one that is only remotely a part of me, as my father and my grandfather are parts of me less remote. This other-self of mine is an ancestor, a progenitor of my progenitors in the early line of my race, himself the progeny of a line that long before his time developed fingers and toes and climbed up into the trees.

I must again, at the risk of boring, repeat that I am, in this one thing, to be considered a freak. Not alone do I possess racial memory to an enormous extent, but I possess the memories of one particular and far-removed progenitor. And yet, while this is most unusual, there is nothing over-remarkable about it.

Follow my reasoning. An instinct is a racial memory. Very good. Then you and I and all of us receive these memories from our fathers and mothers, as they received them from their fathers and mothers. Therefore there must be a medium whereby these memories are transmitted from generation to generation. This medium is what Weismann terms the "germplasm." It carries the memories of the whole evolution of the race. These memories are dim and confused, and many of them are lost. But some strains of germplasm carry an excessive freightage of memories -- are, to be scientific, more atavistic than other strains; and such a strain is mine. I am a freak of heredity, an atavistic nightmare -- call me what you will; but here I am, real and alive, eating three hearty meals a day, and what are you going to do about it?

And now, before I take up my tale, I want to anticipate the doubting Thomases of psychology, who are prone to scoff, and who would otherwise surely say that the coherence of my dreams is due to over study and the subconscious projection of my knowledge of evolution into my dreams. In the first place, I have never been a zealous student. I graduated last of my class. I cared more for athletics, and -- there is no reason I should not confess it -- more for billiards.

Further, I had no knowledge of evolution until I was at college, whereas in my childhood and youth I had already lived in my dreams all the details of that other, long-ago life. I will say, however, that these details were mixed and incoherent until I came to know the science of evolution. Evolution was the key. It gave the explanation, gave sanity to the pranks of this atavistic brain of mine that, modern and normal, harked back to a past so remote as to be contemporaneous with the raw beginnings of mankind.

For in this past I know of, man, as we to-day know him, did not exist. It was in the period of his becoming that I must have lived and had my being.

Chapter 3

The commonest dream of my early childhood was something like this: It seemed that I was very small and that I lay curled up in a sort of nest of twigs and boughs. Sometimes I was lying on my back. In this position it seemed that I spent many hours, watching the play of sunlight on the foliage and the stirring of the leaves by the wind. Often the nest itself moved back and forth when the wind was strong.

But always, while so lying in the nest, I was mastered as of tremendous space beneath me. I never saw it, I never peered over the edge of the nest to see; but *I knew* and feared that space that lurked just beneath me and that ever threatened me like a maw of some all-devouring monster.

This dream, in which I was quiescent and which was more like a condition than an experience of action, I dreamed very often in my early childhood. But suddenly, there would rush into the very midst of it strange forms and ferocious happenings, the thunder and crashing of storm, or unfamiliar landscapes such as in my wake-a-day life I had never seen. The result was confusion and nightmare. I could comprehend nothing of it. There was no logic of sequence.

You see, I did not dream consecutively. One moment I was a wee babe of the Younger World lying in my tree nest; the next moment I was a grown man of the Younger World locked in combat with the hideous Red-Eye; and the next moment I was creeping carefully down to the water-hole in the heat of the day. Events, years apart in their occurrence in the Younger World, occurred with me within the space of several minutes, or seconds.

It was all a jumble, but this jumble I shall not inflict upon you. It was not until I was a young man and had dreamed many thousand times, that everything straightened out and became clear and plain. Then it was that I got the clew of time, and was able to piece together events and actions in their proper order. Thus was I able to reconstruct the vanished Younger World as it was at the time I lived in it -- or at the time my other-self lived in it. The distinction does not matter; for I, too, the modern man, have gone back and lived that early life in the company of my other-self.

For your convenience, since this is to be no sociological screed, I shall frame together the different events into a comprehensive story. For there is a certain thread of continuity and happening that runs through all the dreams. There is my friendship with Lop-Ear, for instance. Also, there is the enmity of Red-Eye, and the love of the Swift One. Taking it all in all, a fairly coherent and interesting story I am sure you will agree.

I do not remember much of my mother. Possibly the earliest recollection I have of her -- and certainly the sharpest -- is the following: It seemed I was lying on the ground. I was somewhat older than during the nest days, but still helpless. I rolled about in the dry leaves, playing with them and making crooning, rasping noises in my throat. The sun shone warmly and I was happy, and comfortable. I was in a little open space. Around me, on all sides, were bushes and fern-like growths, and overhead and all about were the trunks and branches of forest trees.

Suddenly I heard a sound. I sat upright and listened. I made no movement. The little noises died down in my throat, and I sat as one petrified. The sound drew closer. It was like the grunt of a pig. Then I began to hear the sounds caused by the moving of a body through the brush. Next I saw the ferns agitated by the passage of the body. Then the ferns parted, and I saw gleaming eyes, a long snout, and white tusks.

It was a wild boar. He peered at me curiously. He grunted once or twice and shifted his weight from one foreleg to the other, at the same time moving his head from side to side and swaying the ferns. Still I sat as one petrified, my eyes unblinking as I stared at him, fear eating at my heart.

It seemed that this movelessness and silence on my part was what was expected of me. I was not to cry out in the face of fear. It was a dictate of instinct. And so I sat there and waited for I knew not what. The boar thrust the ferns aside and stepped into the open. The curiosity went out of his eyes, and they gleamed cruelly. He tossed his head at me threateningly and advanced a step. This he did again, and yet again.

Then I screamed...or shrieked -- I cannot describe it, but it was a shrill and terrible cry. And it seems that it, too, at this stage of the proceedings, was the thing expected of me. From not far away came an answering cry. My sounds seemed momentarily to disconcert the boar, and while he halted and shifted his weight with indecision, an apparition burst upon us.

She was like a large orang-utan, my mother, or like a chimpanzee, and yet, in sharp and definite ways, quite different. She was heavier of build than they, and had less hair. Her arms were not so long, and her legs were stouter. She wore no clothes -- only her natural hair. And I can tell you she was a fury when she was excited.

And like a fury she dashed upon the scene. She was gritting her teeth, making frightful grimaces, snarling, uttering sharp and continuous cries that sounded like "kh-ah! kh-ah!" So sudden and formidable was her appearance that the boar involuntarily bunched himself together on the defensive and bristled as she swerved toward him. Then she swerved toward me. She had quite taken the breath out of him. I knew just what to do in that moment of time she had gained. I leaped to meet her, catching her about the waist and holding on hand and foot -- yes, by my feet; I could hold on by them as readily as by my hands. I could feel in my tense grip the pull of the hair as her skin and her muscles moved beneath with her efforts.

As I say, I leaped to meet her, and on the instant she leaped straight up into the air, catching an overhanging branch with her hands. The next instant, with clashing tusks, the boar drove past underneath. He had recovered from his surprise and sprung forward, emitting a squeal that was almost a trumpeting. At any rate it was a call, for it was followed by the rushing of bodies through the ferns and brush from all directions.

From every side wild hogs dashed into the open space -- a score of them. But my mother swung over the top of a thick limb, a dozen feet from the ground, and, still holding on to her, we perched there in safety. She was very excited. She chattered and screamed, and scolded down at the bristling, tooth-gnashing circle that had gathered beneath. I, too, trembling, peered down at the angry beasts and did my best to imitate my mother's cries.

From the distance came similar cries, only pitched deeper, into a sort of roaring bass. These grew momentarily louder, and soon I saw him approaching, my father -- at least, by all the evidence of the times, I am driven to conclude that he was my father.

He was not an extremely prepossessing father, as fathers go. He seemed half man, and half ape, and yet not ape, and not yet man. I fail to describe him. There is nothing like him to-day on the earth, under the earth, nor in the earth. He was a large man in his day, and he must have weighed all of a hundred and thirty pounds. His face was broad and flat, and the eyebrows over-hung the eyes. The eyes themselves were small, deep-set, and close together. He had practically no nose at all. It was squat and broad, apparently without any bridge, while the nostrils were like two holes in the face, opening outward instead of down.

The forehead slanted back from the eyes, and the hair began right at the eyes and ran up over the head. The head itself was preposterously small and was supported on an equally preposterous, thick, short neck.

There was an elemental economy about his body -- as was there about all our bodies. The chest was deep, it is true, cavernously deep; but there were no full-swelling muscles, no wide-spreading shoulders, no clean-limbed straightness, no generous symmetry of outline. It represented strength, that body of my father's, strength without beauty; ferocious, primordial strength, made to clutch and grip and rend and destroy.

His hips were thin; and the legs, lean and hairy, were crooked and stringy-muscled. In fact, my father's legs were more like arms. They were twisted and gnarly, and with scarcely the semblance of the full meaty calf such as graces your leg and mine. I remember he could not walk on the flat of his foot. This was because it was a prehensile foot, more like a hand than a foot. The great toe, instead of being in line with the other toes, opposed them, like a thumb, and its opposition to the other toes was what enabled him to get a grip with his foot. This was why he could not walk on the flat of his foot.

But his appearance was no more unusual than the manner of his coming, there to my mother and me as we perched above the angry wild pigs. He came through the trees, leaping from limb to limb and from tree to tree; and he came swiftly. I can see him now, in my wake-a-day life, as I write this, swinging along through the trees, a four-handed, hairy creature, howling with rage, pausing now and again to beat his chest with his clenched fist, leaping ten-and-fifteen-foot gaps, catching a branch with one hand and swinging on across another gap to catch with his other hand and go on, never hesitating, never at a loss as to how to proceed on his arboreal way.

And as I watched him I felt in my own being, in my very muscles themselves, the surge and thrill of desire to go leaping from bough to bough; and I felt also the guarantee of the latent power in that being and in those muscles of mine. And why not? Little boys watch their fathers swing axes and fell trees, and feel in themselves that some day they, too, will swing axes and fell trees. And so with me. The life that was in me was constituted to do what my father did, and it whispered to me secretly and ambitiously of aerial paths and forest flights.

At last my father joined us. He was extremely angry. I remember the out-thrust of his protruding underlip as he glared down at the wild pigs. He snarled something like a dog, and I remember that his eye-teeth were large, like fangs, and that they impressed me tremendously.

His conduct served only the more to infuriate the pigs. He broke off twigs and small branches and flung them down upon our enemies. He even hung by one hand, tantalizingly just beyond reach, and mocked them as they gnashed their tusks with impotent rage. Not content with this, he broke off a stout branch, and, holding on with one hand and foot, jabbed the infuriated beasts in the sides and whacked them across their noses. Needless to state, my mother and I enjoyed the sport.

But one tires of all good things, and in the end, my father, chuckling maliciously the while, led the way across the trees. Now it was that my ambitions ebbed away, and I became timid, holding tightly to my mother as she climbed and swung through space. I remember when the branch broke with her weight. She had made a wide leap, and with the snap of the wood I was overwhelmed with the sickening consciousness of falling through space, the pair of us. The forest and the sunshine on the rustling leaves vanished from my eyes. I had a fading glimpse of my father abruptly arresting his progress to look, and then all was blackness.

The next moment I was awake, in my sheeted bed, sweating, trembling, nauseated. The window was up, and a cool air was blowing through the room. The night-lamp was burning calmly. And because of this I take it that the wild pigs did not get us, that we never fetched bottom; else I should not be here now, a thousand centuries after, to remember the event.

And now put yourself in my place for a moment. Walk with me a bit in my tender childhood, bed with me a night and imagine yourself dreaming such incomprehensible horrors. Remember I was an inexperienced child. I had never seen a wild boar in my life. For that matter I had never seen a domesticated pig. The nearest approach to one that I had seen was breakfast bacon sizzling in its fat. And yet here, real as life, wild boars dashed through my dreams, and I, with fantastic parents, swung through the lofty tree-spaces.

Do you wonder that I was frightened and oppressed by my nightmare-ridden nights? I was accursed. And, worst of all, I was afraid to tell. I do not know why, except that I had a feeling of guilt, though I knew no better of what I was guilty. So it was, through long years, that I suffered in silence, until I came to man's estate and learned the why and wherefore of my dreams.

Chapter 4

There is one puzzling thing about these prehistoric memories of mine. It is the vagueness of the time element. I do not always know the order of events, nor can I tell, between some events, whether one, two, or four or five years have elapsed. I can only roughly tell the passage of time by judging the changes in the appearance and pursuits of my fellows.

Also, I can apply the logic of events to the various happenings. For instance, there is no doubt whatever that my mother and I were freed by the wild pigs and fled and fell in the days before I made the acquaintance of Lop-Ear, who became what I may call my boyhood chum. And it is just as conclusive that between these two periods I must have left my mother.

I have no memory of my father than the one I have given. Never, in the years that followed, did he reappear. And from my knowledge of the times, the only explanation possible lies in that he perished shortly after the adventure with the wild pigs. That it must have been an untimely end, there is no discussion. He was in full vigor, and only sudden and violent death could have taken him off. But I know not the manner of his going -- whether he was drowned in the river, or was swallowed by a snake, or went into the stomach of old Saber-Tooth, the tiger, is beyond my knowledge.

For know that I remember only the things I saw myself, with my own eyes, in those prehistoric days. If my mother knew my father's end, she never told me. For that matter I doubt if she had a vocabulary adequate to convey such information. Perhaps, all told, the Folk in that day had a vocabulary of thirty or forty sounds.

I call them *sounds*, rather than *words*, because sounds they were primarily. They had no fixed values, to be altered by adjectives and adverbs. These latter were tools of speech not yet invented. Instead of qualifying nouns or verbs by the use of adjectives and adverbs, we qualified sounds by intonation, by changes in quantity and pitch, by retarding and by accelerating. The length of time employed in the utterance of a particular sound shaded its meaning.

We had no conjugation. One judged the tense by the context. We talked only concrete things because we thought only concrete things. Also, we depended largely on pantomime. The simplest abstraction was practically beyond our thinking; and when one did happen to think one, he was hard put to communicate it to his fellows. There were no sounds for it. He was pressing beyond the limits of his vocabulary. If he invented sounds for it, his fellows did not understand the sounds. Then it was that he fell back on pantomime, illustrating the thought wherever possible and at the same time repeating the new sound over and over again.

Thus language grew. By the few sounds we possessed we were enabled to think a short distance beyond those sounds; then came the need for new sounds wherewith to express the new thought. Sometimes, however, we thought too long a distance in advance of our sounds, managed to achieve abstractions -- dim ones I grant -- which we failed utterly to make known to other folk. After all, language did not grow fast in that day.

Oh, believe me, we were amazingly simple. But we did know a lot that is not known today. We could twitch our ears, prick them up and flatten them down at will. And we could scratch between our shoulders with ease. We could throw stones with our feet. I have done it many a time. And for that matter, I could keep my knees straight, bend forward from the hips, and touch, not the tips of my fingers, but the points of my elbows, to the ground. And as for bird-nesting -- well, I only wish the twentieth-century boy could see us. But we made no collections of eggs. We ate them.

I remember -- but I out-run my story. First let me tell of Lop-Ear and our friendship. Very early in my life, I separated from my mother. Possibly this was because, after the death of my father, she took to herself a second husband. I have few recollections of him, and they are not of the best. He was a light fellow. There was no solidity to him. He was too voluble. His infernal chattering worries me even now as I think of it. His mind was too inconsequential to permit him to possess purpose. Monkeys in their cages always remind me of him. He was monkeyish. That is the best description I can give of him.

He hated me from the first. And I quickly learned to be afraid of him and his malicious pranks. Whenever he came in sight I crept close to my mother and clung to her. But I was growing older all the time, and it was inevitable that I should from time to time stray from her, and stray farther and farther. And these were the opportunities that the Chatterer waited for. (I may as well explain that we bore no names in those days; were not known by any name. For the sake of convenience I have myself given names to the various Folk I was more closely in contact with, and the "Chatterer" is the most fitting description I can find for that precious stepfather of mine. As for me, I have named myself "Big-Tooth." My eye-teeth were pronouncedly large.)

But to return to the Chatterer. He persistently terrorized me. He was always pinching me and cuffing me, and on occasion he was not above biting me. Often my mother interfered, and the way she made his fur fly was a joy to see. But the result of all this was a beautiful and unending family quarrel, in which I was the bone of contention.

No, my home-life was not happy. I smile to myself as I write the phrase. Home-life! Home! I had no home in the modern sense of the term. My home was an association, not a habitation. I lived in my mother's care, not in a house. And my mother lived anywhere, so long as when night came she was above the ground.

My mother was old-fashioned. She still clung to her trees. It is true, the more progressive members of our horde lived in the caves above the river. But my mother was suspicious and unprogressive. The trees were good enough for her. Of course, we had one particular tree in which we usually roosted, though we often roosted in other trees when nightfall caught us. In a convenient fork was a sort of rude platform of twigs and branches and creeping things. It was more like a huge bird-nest than anything else, though it was a thousand times cruder in the weaving than any bird-nest. But it had one feature that I have never seen attached to any bird-nest, namely, a roof.

Oh, not a roof such as modern man makes! Nor a roof such as is made by the lowest aborigines of today. It was infinitely more clumsy than the clumsiest handiwork of man -- of man as we know him. It was put together in a casual, helter-skelter sort of way. Above the fork of the tree whereon we rested was a pile of dead branches and brush. Four or five adjacent forks held what I may term the various ridge-poles. These were merely stout sticks an inch or so in diameter. On them rested the brush and branches. These seemed to have been tossed on almost aimlessly. There was no attempt at thatching. And I must confess that the roof leaked miserably in a heavy rain.

But the Chatterer. He made home-life a burden for both my mother and me -- and by home-life I mean, not the leaky nest in the tree, but the group-life of the three of us. He was most malicious in his persecution of me. That was the one purpose to which he held steadfastly for longer than five minutes. Also, as time went by, my mother was less eager in her defence of me. I think, what of the continuous rows raised by the Chatterer, that I must have become a nuisance to her. At any rate, the situation went from bad to worse so rapidly that I should soon, of my own volition, have left home. But the satisfaction of performing so independent an act was denied me. Before I was ready to go, I was thrown out. And I mean this literally.

The opportunity came to the Chatterer one day when I was alone in the nest. My mother and the Chatterer had gone away together toward the blueberry swamp. He must have planned the whole thing, for I heard him returning alone through the forest, roaring with self-induced rage as he came. Like all the men of our horde, when they were angry or were trying to make themselves angry, he stopped now and again to hammer on his chest with his fist.

I realized the helplessness of my situation, and crouched trembling in the nest. The Chatterer came directly to the tree -- I remember it was an oak tree -- and began to climb up. And he never ceased for a moment from his infernal row. As I have said, our language was extremely meagre, and he must have strained it by the variety of ways in which he informed me of his undying hatred of me and of his intention there and then to have it out with me.

As he climbed to the fork, I fled out the great horizontal limb. He followed me, and out I went, farther and farther. At last I was out amongst the small twigs and leaves. The Chatterer was ever a coward, and greater always than any anger he ever worked up was his caution. He was afraid to follow me out amongst the leaves and twigs. For that matter, his greater weight would have crashed him through the foliage before he could have got to me.

But it was not necessary for him to reach me, and well he knew it, the scoundrel! With a malevolent expression on his face, his beady eyes gleaming with cruel intelligence, he began teetering. Teetering! -- and with me out on the very edge of the bough, clutching at the twigs that broke continually with my weight. Twenty feet beneath me was the earth.

Wildly and more wildly he teetered, grinning at me his gloating hatred. Then came the end. All four holds broke at the same time, and I fell, back-downward, looking up at him, my hands and feet still clutching the broken twigs. Luckily, there were no wild pigs under me, and my fall was broken by the tough and springy bushes.

Usually, my falls destroy my dreams, the nervous shock being sufficient to bridge the thousand centuries in an instant and hurl me wide awake into my little bed, where, perchance, I lie sweating and trembling and hear the cuckoo clock calling the hour in the hall. But this dream of my leaving home I have had many times, and never yet have I been awakened by it. Always do I crash, shrieking, down through the brush and fetch up with a bump on the ground.

Scratched and bruised and whimpering, I lay where I had fallen. Peering up through the bushes, I could see the Chatterer. He had set up a demoniacal chant of joy and was keeping time to it with his teetering. I quickly hushed my whimpering. I was no longer in the safety of the trees, and I knew the danger I ran of bringing upon myself the hunting animals by too audible an expression of my grief.

I remember, as my sobs died down, that I became interested in watching the strange light-effects produced by partially opening and closing my tear-wet eyelids. Then I began to investigate, and found that I was not so very badly damaged by my fall. I had lost some hair and hide, here and there; the sharp and jagged end of a broken branch had thrust fully an inch into my forearm; and my right hip, which had borne the brunt of my contact with the ground, was aching intolerably. But these, after all, were only petty hurts. No bones were broken, and in those days the flesh of man had finer healing qualities than it has today. Yet it was a severe fall, for I limped with my injured hip for fully a week afterward.

Next, as I lay in the bushes, there came upon me a feeling of desolation, a consciousness that I was homeless. I made up my mind never to return to my mother and the Chatterer. I would go far away through the terrible forest, and find some tree for myself in which to roost. As for food, I knew where to find it. For the last year at least I had not been beholden to my mother for food. All she had furnished me was protection and guidance.

I crawled softly out through the bushes. Once I looked back and saw the Chatterer still chanting and teetering. It was not a pleasant sight. I knew pretty well how to be cautious, and I was exceedingly careful on this my first journey in the world.

I gave no thought as to where I was going. I had but one purpose, and that was to go away beyond the reach of the Chatterer. I climbed into the trees and wandered on amongst them for hours, passing from tree to tree and never touching the ground. But I did not go in any particular direction, nor did I travel steadily. It was my nature, as it was the nature of all my folk, to be inconsequential. Besides, I was a mere child, and I stopped a great deal to play by the way.

The events that befell me on my leaving home are very vague in my mind. My dreams do not cover them. Much has my other-self forgotten, and particularly at this very period. Nor have I been able to frame up the various dreams so as to bridge the gap between my leaving the home-tree and my arrival at the caves.

I remember that several times I came to open spaces. These I crossed in great trepidation, descending to the ground and running at the top of my speed. I remember that there were days of rain and days of sunshine, so that I must have wandered alone for quite a time. I especially dream of my misery in the rain, and of my sufferings from hunger and how I appeased it. One very strong impression is of hunting little lizards on the rocky top of an open knoll. They ran under the rocks, and most of them escaped; but occasionally I turned over a stone and caught one. I was frightened away from this knoll by snakes. They did not pursue me. They were merely basking on flat rocks in the sun. But such was my inherited fear of them that I fled as fast as if they had been after me.

Then I gnawed bitter bark from young trees. I remember vaguely the eating of many green nuts, with soft shells and milky kernels. And I remember most distinctly suffering from a stomach-ache. It may have been caused by the green nuts, and maybe by the lizards. I do not know. But I do know that I was fortunate in not being devoured during the several hours I was knotted up on the ground with the colic.

Chapter 5

My vision of the scene came abruptly, as I emerged from the forest. I found myself on the edge of a large clear space. On one side of this space rose up high bluffs. On the other side was the river. The earth bank ran steeply down to the water, but here and there, in several places, where at some time slides of earth had occurred, there were run-ways. These were the drinking-places of the Folk that lived in the caves.

And this was the main abiding-place of the Folk that I had chanced upon. This was, I may say, by stretching the word, the village. My mother and the Chatterer and I, and a few other simple bodies, were what might be termed suburban residents. We were part of the horde, though we lived a distance away from it. It was only a short distance, though it had taken me, what of my wandering, all of a week to arrive. Had I come directly, I could have covered the trip in an hour.

But to return. From the edge of the forest I saw the caves in the bluff, the open space, and the run-ways to the drinking-places. And in the open space I saw many of the Folk. I had been straying, alone and a child, for a week. During that time I had seen not one of my kind. I had lived in terror and desolation. And now, at the sight of my kind, I was overcome with gladness, and I ran wildly toward them.

Then it was that a strange thing happened. Some one of the Folk saw me and uttered a warning cry. On the instant, crying out with fear and panic, the Folk fled away. Leaping and scrambling over the rocks, they plunged into the mouths of the caves and disappeared...all but one, a little baby, that had been dropped in the excitement close to the base of the bluff. He was wailing dolefully. His mother dashed out; he sprang to meet her and held on tightly as she scrambled back into the cave.

I was all alone. The populous open space had of a sudden become deserted. I sat down forlornly and whimpered. I could not understand. Why had the Folk run away from me? In later time, when I came to know their ways, I was to learn. When they saw me dashing out of the forest at top speed they concluded that I was being pursued by some hunting animal. By my unceremonious approach I had stampeded them.

As I sat and watched the cave-mouths I became aware that the Folk were watching me. Soon they were thrusting their heads out. A little later they were calling back and forth to one another. In the hurry and confusion it had happened that all had not gained their own caves. Some of the young ones had sought refuge in other caves. The mothers did not call for them by name, because that was an invention we had not yet made. All were nameless. The mothers uttered querulous, anxious cries, which were recognized by the young ones. Thus, had my mother been there calling to me, I should have recognized her voice amongst the voices of a thousand mothers, and in the same way would she have recognized mine amongst a thousand.

This calling back and forth continued for some time, but they were too cautious to come out of their caves and descend to the ground. Finally one did come. He was destined to play a large part in my life, and for that matter he already played a large part in the lives of all the members of the horde. He it was whom I shall call Red-Eye in the pages of this history -- so called because of his inflamed eyes, the lids being always red, and, by the peculiar effect they produced, seeming to advertise the terrible savagery of him. The color of his soul was red.

He was a monster in all ways. Physically he was a giant. He must have weighed one hundred and seventy pounds. He was the largest one of our kind I ever saw. Nor did I ever see one of the Fire People so large as he, nor one of the Tree People. Sometimes, when in the newspapers I happen upon descriptions of our modern bruisers and prizefighters, I wonder what chance the best of them would have had against him.

I am afraid not much of a chance. With one grip of his iron fingers and a pull, he could have plucked a muscle, say a biceps, by the roots, clear out of their bodies. A back-handed, loose blow of his fist could have smashed their skulls like egg-shells. With a sweep of his wicked feet (or hind-hands) he could have disembowelled them. A twist could have broken their necks, and I know that with a single crunch of his jaws he could have pierced, at the same moment, the great vein of the throat in front and the spinal marrow at the back.

He could spring twenty feet horizontally from a sitting position. He was abominably hairy. It was a matter of pride with us to be not very hairy. But he was covered with hair all over, on the inside of the arms as well as the outside, and even the ears themselves. The only places on him where the hair did not grow were the soles of his hands and feet and beneath his eyes. He was frightfully ugly, his ferocious grinning mouth and huge down-hanging under-lip being but in harmony with his terrible eyes.

This was Red-Eye. And right gingerly he crept out of his cave and descended to the ground. Ignoring me, he proceeded to reconnoitre. He bent forward from the hips as he walked; and so far forward did he bend, and so long were his arms, that with every step he touched the knuckles of his hands to the ground on either side of him. He was awkward in the semi-erect position of walking that he assumed, and he really touched his knuckles to the ground in order to balance himself. But oh, I tell you he could run on all-fours! Now this was something at which we were particularly awkward. Furthermore, it was a rare individual among us who balanced himself with his knuckles when walking. Such an individual was an atavism, and Red-Eye was an even greater atavism.

That is what he was -- an atavism. We were in the process of changing our tree-life to life on the ground. For many generations we had been going through this change, and our bodies and carriage had likewise changed. But Red-Eye had reverted to the more primitive tree-dwelling type. Perforce, because he was born in our horde he stayed with us; but in actuality he was an atavism and his place was elsewhere.

Very circumspect and very alert, he moved here and there about the open space, peering through the vistas among the trees and trying to catch a glimpse of the hunting animal that all suspected had pursued me. And while he did this, taking no notice of me, the Folk crowded at the cave-mouths and watched.

At last he evidently decided that there was no danger lurking about. He was returning from the head of the run-way, from where he had taken a peep down at the drinking-place. His course brought him near, but still he did not notice me. He proceeded casually on his way until abreast of me, and then, without warning and with incredible swiftness, he smote me a buffet on the head. I was knocked backward fully a dozen feet before I fetched up against the ground, and I remember, half-stunned, even as the blow was struck, hearing the wild uproar of clucking and shrieking laughter that arose from the caves. It was a great joke -- at least in that day; and right heartily the Folk appreciated it.

Thus was I received into the horde. Red-Eye paid no further attention to me, and I was at liberty to whimper and sob to my heart's content. Several of the women gathered curiously about me, and I recognized them. I had encountered them the preceding year when my mother had taken me to the hazelnut canyons.

But they quickly left me alone, being replaced by a dozen curious and teasing youngsters. They formed a circle around me, pointing their fingers, making faces, and poking and pinching me. I was frightened, and for a time I endured them, then anger got the best of me and I sprang tooth and nail upon the most audacious one of them -- none other than Lop-Ear himself. I have so named him because he could prick up only one of his ears. The other ear always hung limp and without movement. Some accident had injured the muscles and deprived him of the use of it.

He closed with me, and we went at it for all the world like a couple of small boys fighting. We scratched and bit, pulled hair, clinched, and threw each other down. I remember I succeeded in getting on him what in my college days I learned was called a half-Nelson. This hold gave me the decided advantage. But I did not enjoy it long. He twisted up one leg, and with the foot -- or hind-hand -- made so savage an onslaught upon my abdomen as to threaten to disembowel me. I had to release him in order to save myself, and then we went at it again.

Lop-Ear was a year older than I, but I was several times angrier than he, and in the end he took to his heels. I chased him across the open and down a run-way to the river. But he was better acquainted with the locality and ran along the edge of the water and up another run-way. He cut diagonally across the open space and dashed into a wide-mouthed cave.

Before I knew it, I had plunged after him into the darkness. The next moment I was badly frightened. I had never been in a cave before. I began to whimper and cry out. Lop-Ear chattered mockingly at me, and, springing upon me unseen, tumbled me over. He did not risk a second encounter, however, and took himself off. I was between him and the entrance, and he did not pass me; yet he seemed to have gone away. I listened, but could get no clew as to where he was. This puzzled me, and when I regained the outside I sat down to watch.

He never came out of the entrance, of that I was certain; yet at the end of several minutes he chuckled at my elbow. Again I ran after him, and again he ran into the cave; but this time I stopped at the mouth. I dropped back a short distance and watched. He did not come out, yet, as before, he chuckled at my elbow and was chased by me a third time into the cave.

This performance was repeated several times. Then I followed him into the cave, where I searched vainly for him. I was curious. I could not understand how he eluded me. Always he went into the cave, never did he come out of it, yet always did he arrive there at my elbow and mock me. Thus did our fight transform itself into a game of hide and seek.

All afternoon, with occasional intervals, we kept it up, and a playful, friendly spirit arose between us. In the end, he did not run away from me, and we sat together with our arms around each other. A little later he disclosed the mystery of the wide-mouthed cave. Holding me by the hand he led me inside. It connected by a narrow crevice with another cave, and it was through this that we regained the open air.

We were now good friends. When the other young ones gathered around to tease, he joined with me in attacking them; and so viciously did we behave that before long I was let alone. Lop-Ear made me acquainted with the village. There was little that he could tell me of conditions and customs -- he had not the necessary vocabulary; but by observing his actions I learned much, and also he showed me places and things.

He took me up the open space, between the caves and the river, and into the forest beyond, where, in a grassy place among the trees, we made a meal of stringy-rooted carrots. After that we had a good drink at the river and started up the run-way to the caves.

It was in the run-way that we came upon Red-Eye again. The first I knew, Lop-Ear had shrunk away to one side and was crouching low against the bank. Naturally and involuntarily, I imitated him. Then it was that I looked to see the cause of his fear. It was Red-Eye, swaggering down the centre of the run-way and scowling fiercely with his inflamed eyes. I noticed that all the youngsters shrank away from him as we had done, while the grown-ups regarded him with wary eyes when he drew near, and stepped aside to give him the centre of the path.

As twilight came on, the open space was deserted. The Folk were seeking the safety of the caves. Lop-Ear led the way to bed. High up the bluff we climbed, higher than all the other caves, to a tiny crevice that could not be seen from the ground. Into this Lop-Ear squeezed. I followed with difficulty, so narrow was the entrance, and found myself in a small rock-chamber. It was very low -- not more than a couple of feet in height, and possibly three feet by four in width and length. Here, cuddled together in each other's arms, we slept out the night.

Chapter 6

While the more courageous of the youngsters played in and out of the large-mouthed caves, I early learned that such caves were unoccupied. No one slept in them at night. Only the crevice-mouthed caves were used, the narrower the mouth the better. This was from fear of the preying animals that made life a burden to us in those days and nights.

The first morning, after my night's sleep with Lop-Ear, I learned the advantage of the narrow-mouthed caves. It was just daylight when old Saber-Tooth, the tiger, walked into the open space. Two of the Folk were already up. They made a rush for it. Whether they were panic-stricken, or whether he was too close on their heels for them to attempt to scramble up the bluff to the crevices, I do not know; but at any rate they dashed into the wide-mouthed cave wherein Lop-Ear and I had played the afternoon before.

What happened inside there was no way of telling, but it is fair to conclude that the two Folk slipped through the connecting crevice into the other cave. This crevice was too small to allow for the passage of Saber-Tooth, and he came out the way he had gone in, unsatisfied and angry. It was evident that his night's hunting had been unsuccessful and that he had expected to make a meal off of us. He caught sight of the two Folk at the other cave-mouth and sprang for them. Of course, they darted through the passageway into the first cave. He emerged angrier than ever and snarling.

Pandemonium broke loose amongst the rest of us. All up and down the great bluff, we crowded the crevices and outside ledges, and we were all chattering and shrieking in a thousand keys. And we were all making faces -- snarling faces; this was an instinct with us. We were as angry as Saber-Tooth, though our anger was allied with fear. I remember that I shrieked and made faces with the best of them. Not only did they set the example, but I felt the urge from within me to do the same things they were doing. My hair was bristling, and I was convulsed with a fierce, unreasoning rage.

For some time old Saber-Tooth continued dashing in and out of first the one cave and then the other. But the two Folk merely slipped back and forth through the connecting crevice and eluded him. In the meantime the rest of us up the bluff had proceeded to action. Every time he appeared outside we pelted him with rocks. At first we merely dropped them on him, but we soon began to whiz them down with the added force of our muscles.

This bombardment drew Saber-Tooth's attention to us and made him angrier than ever. He abandoned his pursuit of the two Folk and sprang up the bluff toward the rest of us, clawing at the crumbling rock and snarling as he clawed his upward way. At this awful sight, the last one of us sought refuge inside our caves. I know this, because I peeped out and saw the whole bluff-side deserted, save for Saber-Tooth, who had lost his footing and was sliding and falling down.

I called out the cry of encouragement, and again the bluff was covered by the screaming horde and the stones were falling faster than ever. Saber-Tooth was frantic with rage. Time and again he assaulted the bluff. Once he even gained the first crevice-entrances before he fell back, but was unable to force his way inside. With each upward rush he made, waves of fear surged over us. At first, at such times, most of us dashed inside; but some remained outside to hammer him with stones, and soon all of us remained outside and kept up the fusillade.

Never was so masterly a creature so completely baffled. It hurt his pride terribly, thus to be outwitted by the small and tender Folk. He stood on the ground and looked up at us, snarling, lashing his tail, snapping at the stones that fell near to him. Once I whizzed down a stone, and just at the right moment he looked up. It caught him full on the end of his nose, and he went straight up in the air, all four feet of him, roaring and caterwauling, what of the hurt and surprise.

He was beaten and he knew it. Recovering his dignity, he stalked out solemnly from under the rain of stones. He stopped in the middle of the open space and looked wistfully and hungrily back at us. He hated to forego the meal, and we were just so much meat, cornered but inaccessible. This sight of him started us to laughing. We laughed derisively and uproariously, all of us. Now animals do not like mockery. To be laughed at makes them angry. And in such fashion our laughter affected Saber-Tooth. He turned with a roar and charged the bluff again. This was what we wanted. The fight had become a game, and we took huge delight in pelting him.

But this attack did not last long. He quickly recovered his common sense, and besides, our missiles were shrewd to hurt. Vividly do I recollect the vision of one bulging eye of his, swollen almost shut by one of the stones we had thrown. And vividly do I retain the picture of him as he stood on the edge of the forest whither he had finally retreated. He was looking back at us, his writhing lips lifted clear of the very roots of his huge fangs, his hair bristling and his tail lashing. He gave one last snarl and slid from view among the trees.

And then such a chattering as went up. We swarmed out of our holes, examining the marks his claws had made on the crumbling rock of the bluff, all of us talking at once. One of the two Folk who had been caught in the double cave was part-grown, half child and half youth. They had come out proudly from their refuge, and we surrounded them in an admiring crowd. Then the young fellow's mother broke through and fell upon him in a tremendous rage, boxing his ears, pulling his hair, and shrieking like a demon. She was a strapping big woman, very hairy, and the thrashing she gave him was a delight to the horde. We roared with laughter, holding on to one another or rolling on the ground in our glee.

In spite of the reign of fear under which we lived, the Folk were always great laughers. We had the sense of humor. Our merriment was Gargantuan. It was never restrained. There was nothing half way about it. When a thing was funny we were convulsed with appreciation of it, and the simplest, crudest things were funny to us. Oh, we were great laughers, I can tell you.

The way we had treated Saber-Tooth was the way we treated all animals that invaded the village. We kept our run-ways and drinking-places to ourselves by making life miserable for the animals that trespassed or strayed upon our immediate territory. Even the fiercest hunting animals we so bedevilled that they learned to leave our places alone. We were not fighters like them; we were cunning and cowardly, and it was because of our cunning and cowardice, and our inordinate capacity for fear, that we survived in that frightfully hostile environment of the Younger World.

Lop-Ear, I figure, was a year older than I. What his past history was he had no way of telling me, but as I never saw anything of his mother I believed him to be an orphan. After all, fathers did not count in our horde. Marriage was as yet in a rude state, and couples had a way of quarrelling and separating. Modern man, what of his divorce institution, does the same thing legally. But we had no laws. Custom was all we went by, and our custom in this particular matter was rather promiscuous.

Nevertheless, as this narrative will show later on, we betrayed glimmering adumbrations of the monogamy that was later to give power to, and make mighty, such tribes as embraced it. Furthermore, even at the time I was born, there were several faithful couples that lived in the trees in the neighborhood of my mother. Living in the thick of the horde did not conduce to monogamy. It was for this reason, undoubtedly, that the faithful couples went away and lived by themselves. Through many years these couples stayed together, though when the man or woman died or was eaten the survivor invariably found a new mate.

There was one thing that greatly puzzled me during the first days of my residence in the horde. There was a nameless and incommunicable fear that rested upon all. At first it appeared to be connected wholly with direction. The horde feared the northeast. It lived in perpetual apprehension of that quarter of the compass. And every individual gazed more frequently and with greater alarm in that direction than in any other.

When Lop-Ear and I went toward the north-east to eat the

stringy-rooted carrots that at that season were at their best, he became unusually timid. He was content to eat the leavings, the big tough carrots and the little ropy ones, rather than to venture a short distance farther on to where the carrots were as yet untouched. When I so ventured, he scolded me and quarrelled with me. He gave me to understand that in that direction was some horrible danger, but just what the horrible danger was his paucity of language would not permit him to say.

Many a good meal I got in this fashion, while he scolded and chattered vainly at me. I could not understand. I kept very alert, but I could see no danger. I calculated always the distance between myself and the nearest tree, and knew that to that haven of refuge I could out-foot the Tawny One, or old Saber-Tooth, did one or the other suddenly appear.

One late afternoon, in the village, a great uproar arose. The horde was animated with a single emotion, that of fear. The bluff-side swarmed with the Folk, all gazing and pointing into the northeast. I did not know what it was, but I scrambled all the way up to the safety of my own high little cave before ever I turned around to see.

And then, across the river, away into the northeast, I saw for the first time the mystery of smoke. It was the biggest animal I had ever seen. I thought it was a monster snake, up-ended, rearing its head high above the trees and swaying back and forth. And yet, somehow, I seemed to gather from the conduct of the Folk that the smoke itself was not the danger. They appeared to fear it as the token of something else. What this something else was I was unable to guess. Nor could they tell me. Yet I was soon to know, and I was to know it as a thing more terrible than the Tawny One, than old Saber-Tooth, than the snakes themselves, than which it seemed there could be no things more terrible.

Chapter 7

Broken-Tooth was another youngster who lived by himself. His mother lived in the caves, but two more children had come after him and he had been thrust out to fend for himself. We had witnessed the performance during the several preceding days, and it had given us no little glee. Broken-Tooth did not want to go, and every time his mother left the cave he sneaked back into it. When she returned and found him there her rages were delightful. Half the horde made a practice of watching for these moments. First, from within the cave, would come her scolding and shrieking. Then we could hear sounds of the thrashing and the yelling of Broken-Tooth. About this time the two younger children joined in. And finally, like the eruption of a miniature volcano, Broken-Tooth would come flying out.

At the end of several days his leaving home was accomplished. He wailed his grief, unheeded, from the centre of the open space, for at least half an hour, and then came to live with Lop-Ear and me. Our cave was small, but with squeezing there was room for three. I have no recollection of Broken-Tooth spending more than one night with us, so the accident must have happened right away.

It came in the middle of the day. In the morning we had eaten our fill of the carrots, and then, made heedless by play, we had ventured on to the big trees just beyond. I cannot understand how Lop-Ear got over his habitual caution, but it must have been the play. We were having a great time playing tree tag. And such tag! We leaped ten or fifteen-foot gaps as a matter of course. And a twenty or twenty-five foot deliberate drop clear down to the ground was nothing to us. In fact, I am almost afraid to say the great distances we dropped. As we grew older and heavier we found we had to be more cautious in dropping, but at that age our bodies were all strings and springs and we could do anything.

Broken-Tooth displayed remarkable agility in the game. He was "It" less frequently than any of us, and in the course of the game he discovered one difficult "slip" that neither Lop-Ear nor I was able to accomplish. To be truthful, we were afraid to attempt it.

When we were "It," Broken-Tooth always ran out to the end of a lofty branch in a certain tree. From the end of the branch to the ground it must have been seventy feet, and nothing intervened to break a fall. But about twenty feet lower down, and fully fifteen feet out from the perpendicular, was the thick branch of another tree.

As we ran out the limb, Broken-Tooth, facing us, would begin teetering. This naturally impeded our progress; but there was more in the teetering than that. He teetered with his back to the jump he was to make. Just as we nearly reached him he would let go. The teetering branch was like a spring-board. It threw him far out, backward, as he fell. And as he fell he turned around sidewise in the air so as to face the other branch into which he was falling. This branch bent far down under the impact, and sometimes there was an ominous crackling; but it never broke, and out of the leaves was always to be seen the face of Broken-Tooth grinning triumphantly up at us.

I was "It" the last time Broken-Tooth tried this. He had gained the end of the branch and begun his teetering, and I was creeping out after him, when suddenly there came a low warning cry from Lop-Ear. I looked down and saw him in the main fork of the tree crouching close against the trunk. Instinctively I crouched down upon the thick limb. Broken-Tooth stopped teetering, but the branch would not stop, and his body continued bobbing up and down with the rustling leaves.

I heard the crackle of a dry twig, and looking down saw my first Fire-Man. He was creeping stealthily along on the ground and peering up into the tree. At first I thought he was a wild animal, because he wore around his waist and over his shoulders a ragged piece of bearskin. And then I saw his hands and feet, and more clearly his features. He was very much like my kind, except that he was less hairy and that his feet were less like hands than ours. In fact, he and his people, as I was later to know, were far less hairy than we, though we, in turn, were equally less hairy than the Tree People.

It came to me instantly, as I looked at him. This was the terror of the northeast, of which the mystery of smoke was a token. Yet I was puzzled. Certainly he was nothing; of which to be afraid. Red-Eye or any of our strong men would have been more than a match for him. He was old, too, wizened with age, and the hair on his face was gray. Also, he limped badly with one leg. There was no doubt at all that we could out-run him and out-climb him. He could never catch us, that was certain.

But he carried something in his hand that I had never seen before. It was a bow and arrow. But at that time a bow and arrow had no meaning for me. How was I to know that death lurked in that bent piece of wood? But Lop-Ear knew. He had evidently seen the Fire People before and knew something of their ways. The Fire-Man peered up at him and circled around the tree. And around the main trunk above the fork Lop-Ear circled too, keeping always the trunk between himself and the Fire-Man.

The latter abruptly reversed his circling. Lop-Ear, caught unawares, also hastily reversed, but did not win the protection of the trunk until after the Fire-Man had twanged the bow.

I saw the arrow leap up, miss Lop-Ear, glance against a limb, and fall back to the ground. I danced up and down on my lofty perch with delight. It was a game! The Fire-Man was throwing things at Lop-Ear as we sometimes threw things at one another.

The game continued a little longer, but Lop-Ear did not expose himself a second time. Then the Fire-Man gave it up. I leaned far out over my horizontal limb and chattered down at him. I wanted to play. I wanted to have him try to hit me with the thing. He saw me, but ignored me, turning his attention to Broken-Tooth, who was still teetering slightly and involuntarily on the end of the branch.

The first arrow leaped upward. Broken-Tooth yelled with fright and pain. It had reached its mark. This put a new complexion on the matter. I no longer cared to play, but crouched trembling close to my limb. A second arrow and a third soared up, missing Broken-Tooth, rustling the leaves as they passed through, arching in their flight and returning to earth.

The Fire-Man stretched his bow again. He shifted his position, walking away several steps, then shifted it a second time. The bow-string twanged, the arrow leaped upward, and Broken-Tooth, uttering a terrible scream, fell off the branch. I saw him as he went down, turning over and over, all arms and legs it seemed, the shaft of the arrow projecting from his chest and appearing and disappearing with each revolution of his body.

Sheer down, screaming, seventy feet he fell, smashing to the earth with an audible thud and crunch, his body rebounding slightly and settling down again. Still he lived, for he moved and squirmed, clawing with his hands and feet. I remember the Fire-Man running forward with a stone and hammering him on the head...and then I remember no more.

Always, during my childhood, at this stage of the dream, did I wake up screaming with fright -- to find, often, my mother or nurse, anxious and startled, by my bedside, passing soothing hands through my hair and telling me that they were there and that there was nothing to fear.

My next dream, in the order of succession, begins always with the flight of Lop-Ear and myself through the forest. The Fire-Man and Broken-Tooth and the tree of the tragedy are gone. Lop-Ear and I, in a cautious panic, are fleeing through the trees. In my right leg is a burning pain; and from the flesh, protruding head and shaft from either side, is an arrow of the Fire-Man. Not only did the pull and strain of it pain me severely, but it bothered my movements and made it impossible for me to keep up with Lop-Ear.

At last I gave up, crouching in the secure fork of a tree. Lop-Ear went right on. I called to him -- most plaintively, I remember; and he stopped and looked back. Then he returned to me, climbing into the fork and examining the arrow. He tried to pull it out, but one way the flesh resisted the barbed lead, and the other way it resisted the feathered shaft. Also, it hurt grievously, and I stopped him.

For some time we crouched there, Lop-Ear nervous and anxious to be gone, perpetually and apprehensively peering this way and that, and myself whimpering softly and sobbing. Lop-Ear was plainly in a funk, and yet his conduct in remaining by me, in spite of his fear, I take as a foreshadowing of the altruism and comradeship that have helped make man the mightiest of the animals.

Once again Lop-Ear tried to drag the arrow through the flesh, and I angrily stopped him. Then he bent down and began gnawing the shaft of the arrow with his teeth. As he did so he held the arrow firmly in both hands so that it would not play about in the wound, and at the same time I held on to him. I often meditate upon this scene -- the two of us, half-grown cubs, in the childhood of the race, and the one mastering his fear, beating down his selfish impulse of flight, in order to stand by and succor the other. And there rises up before me all that was there foreshadowed, and I see visions of Damon and Pythias, of life-saving crews and Red Cross nurses, of martyrs and leaders of forlorn hopes, of Father Damien, and of the Christ himself, and of all the men of earth, mighty of stature, whose strength may trace back to the elemental loins of Lop-Ear and Big-Tooth and other dim denizens of the Younger World.

When Lop-Ear had chewed off the head of the arrow, the shaft was withdrawn easily enough. I started to go on, but this time it was he that stopped me. My leg was bleeding profusely. Some of the smaller veins had doubtless been ruptured. Running out to the end of a branch, Lop-Ear gathered a handful of green leaves. These he stuffed into the wound. They accomplished the purpose, for the bleeding soon stopped. Then we went on together, back to the safety of the caves.

Chapter 8

Well do I remember that first winter after I left home. I have long dreams of sitting shivering in the cold. Lop-Ear and I sit close together, with our arms and legs about each other, blue-faced and with chattering teeth. It got particularly crisp along toward morning. In those chill early hours we slept little, huddling together in numb misery and waiting for the sunrise in order to get warm.

When we went outside there was a crackle of frost under foot. One morning we discovered ice on the surface of the quiet water in the eddy where was the drinking-place, and there was a great how-do-you-do about it. Old Marrow-Bone was the oldest member of the horde, and he had never seen anything like it before. I remember the worried, plaintive look that came into his eyes as he examined the ice. (This plaintive look always came into our eyes when we did not understand a thing, or when we felt the prod of some vague and inexpressible desire.) Red-Eye, too, when he investigated the ice, looked bleak and plaintive, and stared across the river into the northeast, as though in some way he connected the Fire People with this latest happening.

But we found ice only on that one morning, and that was the coldest winter we experienced. I have no memory of other winters when it was so cold. I have often thought that that cold winter was a fore-runner of the countless cold winters to come, as the ice-sheet from farther north crept down over the face of the land. But we never saw that ice-sheet. Many generations must have passed away before the descendants of the horde migrated south, or remained and adapted themselves to the changed conditions.

Life was hit or miss and happy-go-lucky with us. Little was ever planned, and less was executed. We ate when we were hungry, drank when we were thirsty, avoided our carnivorous enemies, took shelter in the caves at night, and for the rest just sort of played along through life.

We were very curious, easily amused, and full of tricks and pranks. There was no seriousness about us, except when we were in danger or were angry, in which cases the one was quickly forgotten and the other as quickly got over.

We were inconsecutive, illogical, and inconsequential. We had no steadfastness of purpose, and it was here that the Fire People were ahead of us. They possessed all these things of which we possessed so little. Occasionally, however, especially in the realm of the emotions, we were capable of long-cherished purpose. The faithfulness of the monogamic couples I have referred to may be explained as a matter of habit; but my long desire for the Swift One cannot be so explained, any more than can be explained the undying enmity between me and Red-Eye.

But it was our inconsequentiality and stupidity that especially distresses me when I look back upon that life in the long ago. Once I found a broken gourd which happened to lie right side up and which had been filled with the rain. The water was sweet, and I drank it. I even took the gourd down to the stream and filled it with more water, some of which I drank and some of which I poured over Lop-Ear. And then I threw the gourd away. It never entered my head to fill the gourd with water and carry it into my cave. Yet often I was thirsty at night, especially after eating wild onions and water-cress, and no one ever dared leave the caves at night for a drink.

Another time I found a dry gourd, inside of which the seeds rattled. I had fun with it for a while. But it was a play thing, nothing more. And yet, it was not long after this that the using of gourds for storing water became the general practice of the horde. But I was not the inventor. The honor was due to old Marrow-Bone, and it is fair to assume that it was the necessity of his great age that brought about the innovation.

At any rate, the first member of the horde to use gourds was Marrow-Bone. He kept a supply of drinking-water in his cave, which cave belonged to his son, the Hairless One, who permitted him to occupy a corner of it. We used to see Marrow-Bone filling his gourd at the drinking-place and carrying it carefully up to his cave. Imitation was strong in the Folk, and first one, and then another and another, procured a gourd and used it in similar fashion, until it was a general practice with all of us so to store water.

Sometimes old Marrow-Bone had sick spells and was unable to leave the cave. Then it was that the Hairless One filled the gourd for him. A little later, the Hairless One deputed the task to Long-Lip, his son. And after that, even when Marrow-Bone was well again, Long-Lip continued carrying water for him. By and by, except on unusual occasions, the men never carried any water at all, leaving the task to the women and larger children. Lop-Ear and I were independent. We carried water only for ourselves, and we often mocked the young water-carriers when they were called away from play to fill the gourds.

Progress was slow with us. We played through life, even the adults, much in the same way that children play, and we played as none of the other animals played. What little we learned, was usually in the course of play, and was due to our curiosity and keenness of appreciation. For that matter, the one big invention of the horde, during the time I lived with it, was the use of gourds. At first we stored only water in the gourds -- in imitation of old Marrow-Bone.

But one day some one of the women -- I do not know which one -- filled a gourd with black-berries and carried it to her cave. In no time all the women were carrying berries and nuts and roots in the gourds. The idea, once started, had to go on. Another evolution of the carrying-receptacle was due to the women. Without doubt, some woman's gourd was too small, or else she had forgotten her gourd; but be that as it may, she bent two great leaves together, pinning the seams with twigs, and carried home a bigger quantity of berries than could have been contained in the largest gourd.

So far we got, and no farther, in the transportation of supplies during the years I lived with the Folk. It never entered anybody's head to weave a basket out of willow-withes. Sometimes the men and women tied tough vines about the bundles of ferns and branches that they carried to the caves to sleep upon. Possibly in ten or twenty generations we might have worked up to the weaving of baskets. And of this, one thing is sure: if once we wove withes into baskets, the next and inevitable step would have been the weaving of cloth. Clothes would have followed, and with covering our nakedness would have come modesty.

Thus was momentum gained in the Younger World. But we were without this momentum. We were just getting started, and we could not go far in a single generation. We were without weapons, without fire, and in the raw beginnings of speech. The device of writing lay so far in the future that I am appalled when I think of it.

Even I was once on the verge of a great discovery. To show you how fortuitous was development in those days let me state that had it not been for the gluttony of Lop-Ear I might have brought about the domestication of the dog. And this was something that the Fire People who lived to the northeast had not yet achieved. They were without dogs; this I knew from observation. But let me tell you how Lop-Ear's gluttony possibly set back our social development many generations.

Well to the west of our caves was a great swamp, but to the south lay a stretch of low, rocky hills. These were little frequented for two reasons. First of all, there was no food there of the kind we ate; and next, those rocky hills were filled with the lairs of carnivorous beasts.

But Lop-Ear and I strayed over to the hills one day. We would not have strayed had we not been teasing a tiger. Please do not laugh. It was old Saber-Tooth himself. We were perfectly safe. We chanced upon him in the forest, early in the morning, and from the safety of the branches overhead we chattered down at him our dislike and hatred. And from branch to branch, and from tree to tree, we followed overhead, making an infernal row and warning all the forest-dwellers that old Saber-Tooth was coming.

We spoiled his hunting for him, anyway. And we made him good and angry. He snarled at us and lashed his tail, and sometimes he paused and stared up at us quietly for a long time, as if debating in his mind some way by which he could get hold of us. But we only laughed and pelted him with twigs and the ends of branches.

This tiger-baiting was common sport among the folk. Sometimes half the horde would follow from overhead a tiger or lion that had ventured out in the daytime. It was our revenge; for more than one member of the horde, caught unexpectedly, had gone the way of the tiger's belly or the lion's. Also, by such ordeals of helplessness and shame, we taught the hunting animals to some extent to keep out of our territory. And then it was funny. It was a great game.

And so Lop-Ear and I had chased Saber-Tooth across three miles of forest. Toward the last he put his tail between his legs and fled from our gibing like a beaten cur. We did our best to keep up with him; but when we reached the edge of the forest he was no more than a streak in the distance.

I don't know what prompted us, unless it was curiosity; but after playing around awhile, Lop-Ear and I ventured across the open ground to the edge of the rocky hills. We did not go far. Possibly at no time were we more than a hundred yards from the trees. Coming around a sharp corner of rock (we went very carefully, because we did not know what we might encounter), we came upon three puppies playing in the sun.

They did not see us, and we watched them for some time. They were wild dogs. In the rock-wall was a horizontal fissure -- evidently the lair where their mother had left them, and where they should have remained had they been obedient. But the growing life, that in Lop-Ear and me had impelled us to venture away from the forest, had driven the puppies out of the cave to frolic. I know how their mother would have punished them had she caught them.

But it was Lop-Ear and I who caught them. He looked at me, and then we made a dash for it. The puppies knew no place to run except into the lair, and we headed them off. One rushed between my legs. I squatted and grabbed him. He sank his sharp little teeth into my arm, and I dropped him in the suddenness of the hurt and surprise. The next moment he had scurried inside.

Lop-Ear, struggling with the second puppy, scowled at me and intimated by a variety of sounds the different kinds of a fool and a bungler that I was. This made me ashamed and spurred me to valor. I grabbed the remaining puppy by the tail. He got his teeth into me once, and then I got him by the nape of the neck. Lop-Ear and I sat down, and held the puppies up, and looked at them, and laughed.

They were snarling and yelping and crying. Lop-Ear started suddenly. He thought he had heard something. We looked at each other in fear, realizing the danger of our position. The one thing that made animals raging demons was tampering with their young. And these puppies that made such a racket belonged to the wild dogs. Well we knew them, running in packs, the terror of the grass-eating animals. We had watched them following the herds of cattle and bison and dragging down the calves, the aged, and the sick. We had been chased by them ourselves, more than once. I had seen one of the Folk, a woman, run down by them and caught just as she reached the shelter of the woods. Had she not been tired out by the run, she might have made it into a tree. She tried, and slipped, and fell back. They made short work of her.

We did not stare at each other longer than a moment. Keeping tight hold of our prizes, we ran for the woods. Once in the security of a tall tree, we held up the puppies and laughed again. You see, we had to have our laugh out, no matter what happened.

And then began one of the hardest tasks I ever attempted. We started to carry the puppies to our cave. Instead of using our hands for climbing, most of the time they were occupied with holding our squirming captives. Once we tried to walk on the ground, but were treed by a miserable hyena, who followed along underneath. He was a wise hyena.

Lop-Ear got an idea. He remembered how we tied up bundles of leaves to carry home for beds. Breaking off some tough vines, he tied his puppy's legs together, and then, with another piece of vine passed around his neck, slung the puppy on his back. This left him with hands and feet free to climb. He was jubilant, and did not wait for me to finish tying my puppy's legs, but started on. There was one difficulty, however. The puppy wouldn't stay slung on Lop-Ear's back. It swung around to the side and then on in front. Its teeth were not tied, and the next thing it did was to sink its teeth into Lop-Ear's soft and unprotected stomach. He let out a scream, nearly fell, and clutched a branch violently with both hands to save himself. The vine around his neck broke, and the puppy, its four legs still tied, dropped to the ground. The hyena proceeded to dine.

Lop-Ear was disgusted and angry. He abused the hyena, and then went off alone through the trees. I had no reason that I knew for wanting to carry the puppy to the cave, except that *I wanted* to; and I stayed by my task. I made the work a great deal easier by elaborating on Lop-Ear's idea. Not only did I tie the puppy's legs, but I thrust a stick through his jaws and tied them together securely.

At last I got the puppy home. I imagine I had more pertinacity than the average Folk, or else I should not have succeeded. They laughed at me when they saw me lugging the puppy up to my high little cave, but I did not mind. Success crowned my efforts, and there was the puppy. He was a plaything such as none of the Folk possessed. He learned rapidly. When I played with him and he bit me, I boxed his ears, and then he did not try again to bite for a long time.

I was quite taken up with him. He was something new, and it was a characteristic of the Folk to like new things. When I saw that he refused fruits and vegetables, I caught birds for him and squirrels and young rabbits. (We Folk were meat-eaters, as well as vegetarians, and we were adept at catching small game.) The puppy ate the meat and thrived. As well as I can estimate, I must have had him over a week. And then, coming back to the cave one day with a nestful of young-hatched pheasants, I found Lop-Ear had killed the puppy and was just beginning to eat him. I sprang for Lop-Ear, -- the cave was small, -- and we went at it tooth and nail.

And thus, in a fight, ended one of the earliest attempts to domesticate the dog. We pulled hair out in handfuls, and scratched and bit and gouged. Then we sulked and made up. After that we ate the puppy. Raw? Yes. We had not yet discovered fire. Our evolution into cooking animals lay in the tight-rolled scroll of the future.

Chapter 9

Red-Eye was an atavism. He was the great discordant element in our horde. He was more primitive than any of us. He did not belong with us, yet we were still so primitive ourselves that we were incapable of a cooperative effort strong enough to kill him or cast him out. Rude as was our social organization, he was, nevertheless, too rude to live in it. He tended always to destroy the horde by his unsocial acts. He was really a reversion to an earlier type, and his place was with the Tree People rather than with us who were in the process of becoming men.

He was a monster of cruelty, which is saying a great deal in that day. He beat his wives -- not that he ever had more than one wife at a time, but that he was married many times. It was impossible for any woman to live with him, and yet they did live with him, out of compulsion. There was no gainsaying him.

No man was strong enough to stand against him.

Often do I have visions of the quiet hour before the twilight. From drinking-place and carrot patch and berry swamp the Folk are trooping into the open space before the caves. They dare linger no later than this, for the dreadful darkness is approaching, in which the world is given over to the carnage of the hunting animals, while the fore-runners of man hide tremblingly in their holes.

There yet remain to us a few minutes before we climb to our caves. We are tired from the play of the day, and the sounds we make are subdued. Even the cubs, still greedy for fun and antics, play with restraint. The wind from the sea has died down, and the shadows are lengthening with the last of the sun's descent. And then, suddenly, from Red-Eye's cave, breaks a wild screaming and the sound of blows. He is beating his wife.

At first an awed silence comes upon us. But as the blows and screams continue we break out into an insane gibbering of helpless rage. It is plain that the men resent Red-Eye's actions, but they are too afraid of him. The blows cease, and a low groaning dies away, while we chatter among ourselves and the sad twilight creeps upon us.

We, to whom most happenings were jokes, never laughed during Red-Eye's wife-beatings. We knew too well the tragedy of them. On more than one morning, at the base of the cliff, did we find the body of his latest wife. He had tossed her there, after she had died, from his cave-mouth. He never buried his dead. The task of carrying away the bodies, that else would have polluted our abiding-place, he left to the horde. We usually flung them into the river below the last drinking-place.

Not alone did Red-Eye murder his wives, but he also murdered for his wives, in order to get them. When he wanted a new wife and selected the wife of another man, he promptly killed that man. Two of these murders I saw myself. The whole horde knew, but could do nothing. We had not yet developed any government, to speak of, inside the horde. We had certain customs and visited our wrath upon the unlucky ones who violated those customs. Thus, for example, the individual who defiled a drinking-place would be attacked by every onlooker, while one who deliberately gave a false alarm was the recipient of much rough usage at our hands. But Red-Eye walked rough-shod over all our customs, and we so feared him that we were incapable of the collective action necessary to punish him.

It was during the sixth winter in our cave that Lop-Ear and I discovered that we were really growing up. From the first it had been a squeeze to get in through the entrance-crevice. This had had its advantages, however. It had prevented the larger Folk from taking our cave away from us. And it was a most desirable cave, the highest on the bluff, the safest, and in winter the smallest and warmest.

To show the stage of the mental development of the Folk, I may state that it would have been a simple thing for some of them to have driven us out and enlarged the crevice-opening. But they never thought of it. Lop-Ear and I did not think of it either until our increasing size compelled us to make an enlargement. This occurred when summer was well along and we were fat with better forage. We worked at the crevice in spells, when the fancy struck us.

At first we dug the crumbling rocks away with our fingers, until our nails got sore, when I accidentally stumbled upon the idea of using a piece of wood on the rock. This worked well. Also it worked woe. One morning early, we had scratched out of the wall quite a heap of fragments. I gave the heap a shove over the lip of the entrance. The next moment there came up from below a howl of rage. There was no need to look. We knew the voice only too well. The rubbish had descended upon Red-Eye.

We crouched down in the cave in consternation. A minute later he was at the entrance, peering in at us with his inflamed eyes and raging like a demon. But he was too large. He could not get in to us. Suddenly he went away. This was suspicious. By all we knew of Folk nature he should have remained and had out his rage. I crept to the entrance and peeped down. I could see him just beginning to mount the bluff again. In one hand he carried a long stick. Before I could divine his plan, he was back at the entrance and savagely jabbing the stick in at us.

His thrusts were prodigious. They could have disembowelled us. We shrank back against the side-walls, where we were almost out of range. But by industrious poking he got us now and again -- cruel, scraping jabs with the end of the stick that raked off the hide and hair. When we screamed with the hurt, he roared his satisfaction and jabbed the harder.

I began to grow angry. I had a temper of my own in those days, and pretty considerable courage, too, albeit it was largely the courage of the cornered rat. I caught hold of the stick with my hands, but such was his strength that he jerked me into the crevice. He reached for me with his long arm, and his nails tore my flesh as I leaped back from the clutch and gained the comparative safety of the side-wall.

He began poking again, and caught me a painful blow on the shoulder. Beyond shivering with fright and yelling when he was hit, Lop-Ear did nothing. I looked for a stick with which to jab back, but found only the end of a branch, an inch through and a foot long. I threw this at Red-Eye. It did no damage, though he howled with a sudden increase of rage at my daring to strike back. He began jabbing furiously. I found a fragment of rock and threw it at him, striking him on the chest.

This emboldened me, and, besides, I was now as angry as he, and had lost all fear. I ripped a fragment of rock from the wall. The piece must have weighed two or three pounds. With my strength I slammed it full into Red-Eye's face. It nearly finished him. He staggered backward, dropping his stick, and almost fell off the cliff.

He was a ferocious sight. His face was covered with blood, and he was snarling and gnashing his fangs like a wild boar. He wiped the blood from his eyes, caught sight of me, and roared with fury. His stick was gone, so he began ripping out chunks of crumbling rock and throwing them in at me. This supplied me with ammunition. I gave him as good as he sent, and better; for he presented a good target, while he caught only glimpses of me as I snuggled against the side-wall.

Suddenly he disappeared again. From the lip of the cave I saw him descending. All the horde had gathered outside and in awed silence was looking on. As he descended, the more timid ones scurried for their caves. I could see old Marrow-Bone tottering along as fast as he could. Red-Eye sprang out from the wall and finished the last twenty feet through the air. He landed alongside a mother who was just beginning the ascent. She screamed with fear, and the two-year-old child that was clinging to her released its grip and rolled at Red-Eye's feet. Both he and the mother reached for it, and he got it. The next moment the frail little body had whirled through the air and shattered against the wall. The mother ran to it, caught it up in her arms, and crouched over it crying.

Red-Eye started over to pick up the stick. Old Marrow-Bone had tottered into his way. Red-Eye's great hand shot out and clutched the old man by the back of the neck. I looked to see his neck broken. His body went limp as he surrendered himself to his fate. Red-Eye hesitated a moment, and Marrow-Bone, shivering terribly, bowed his head and covered his face with his crossed arms. Then Red-Eye slammed him face-downward to the ground. Old Marrow-Bone did not struggle. He lay there crying with the fear of death. I saw the Hairless One, out in the open space, beating his chest and bristling, but afraid to come forward. And then, in obedience to some whim of his erratic spirit, Red-Eye let the old man alone and passed on and recovered the stick.

He returned to the wall and began to climb up. Lop-Ear, who was shivering and peeping alongside of me, scrambled back into the cave. It was plain that Red-Eye was bent upon murder. I was desperate and angry and fairly cool. Running back and forth along the neighboring ledges, I gathered a heap of rocks at the cave-entrance. Red-Eye was now several yards beneath me, concealed for the moment by an out-jut of the cliff. As he climbed, his head came into view, and I banged a rock down. It missed, striking the wall and shattering; but the flying dust and grit filled his eyes and he drew back out of view.

A chuckling and chattering arose from the horde, that played the part of audience. At last there was one of the Folk who dared to face Red-Eye. As their approval and acclamation arose on the air, Red-Eye snarled down at them, and on the instant they were subdued to silence. Encouraged by this evidence of his power, he thrust his head into view, and by scowling and snarling and gnashing his fangs tried to intimidate me. He scowled horribly, contracting the scalp strongly over the brows and bringing the hair down from the top of the head until each hair stood apart and pointed straight forward.

The sight chilled me, but I mastered my fear, and, with a stone poised in my hand, threatened him back. He still tried to advance. I drove the stone down at him and made a sheer miss. The next shot was a success. The stone struck him on the neck. He slipped back out of sight, but as he disappeared I could see him clutching for a grip on the wall with one hand, and with the other clutching at his throat. The stick fell clattering to the ground.

I could not see him any more, though I could hear him choking and strangling and coughing. The audience kept a death-like silence. I crouched on the lip of the entrance and waited. The strangling and coughing died down, and I could hear him now and again clearing his throat. A little later he began to climb down. He went very quietly, pausing every moment or so to stretch his neck or to feel it with his hand.

At the sight of him descending, the whole horde, with wild screams and yells, stampeded for the woods. Old Marrow-Bone, hobbling and tottering, followed behind. Red-Eye took no notice of the flight. When he reached the ground he skirted the base of the bluff and climbed up and into his own cave. He did not look around once.

I stared at Lop-Ear, and he stared back. We understood each other. Immediately, and with great caution and quietness, we began climbing up the cliff. When we reached the top we looked back. The abiding-place was deserted, Red-Eye remained in his cave, and the horde had disappeared in the depths of the forest.

We turned and ran. We dashed across the open spaces and down the slopes unmindful of possible snakes in the grass, until we reached the woods. Up into the trees we went, and on and on, swinging our arboreal flight until we had put miles between us and the caves. And then, and not till then, in the security of a great fork, we paused, looked at each other, and began to laugh. We held on to each other, arms and legs, our eyes streaming tears, our ,sides aching, and laughed and laughed and laughed.

Chapter 10

After we had had out our laugh, Lop-Ear and I curved back in our flight and got breakfast in the blueberry swamp. It was the same swamp to which I had made my first journeys in the world, years before, accompanied by my mother. I had seen little of her in the intervening time. Usually, when she visited the horde at the caves, I was away in the forest. I had once or twice caught glimpses of the Chatterer in the open space, and had had the pleasure of making faces at him and angering him from the mouth of my cave. Beyond such amenities I had left my family severely alone. I was not much interested in it, and anyway I was doing very well by myself.

After eating our fill of berries, with two nestfuls of partly hatched quail-eggs for dessert, Lop-Ear and I wandered circumspectly into the woods toward the river. Here was where stood my old home-tree, out of which I had been thrown by the Chatterer. It was still occupied. There had been increase in the family. Clinging tight to my mother was a little baby. Also, there was a girl, partly grown, who cautiously regarded us from one of the lower branches. She was evidently my sister, or half-sister, rather.

My mother recognized me, but she warned me away when I started to climb into the tree. Lop-Ear, who was more cautious by far than I, beat a retreat, nor could I persuade him to return. Later in the day, however, my sister came down to the ground, and there and in neighboring trees we romped and played all afternoon. And then came trouble. She was my sister, but that did not prevent her from treating me abominably, for she had inherited all the viciousness of the Chatterer. She turned upon me suddenly, in a petty rage, and scratched me, tore my hair, and sank her sharp little teeth deep into my forearm. I lost my temper. I did not injure her, but it was undoubtedly the soundest spanking she had received up to that time.

How she yelled and squalled. The Chatterer, who had been away all day and who was only then returning, heard the noise and rushed for the spot. My mother also rushed, but he got there first. Lop-Ear and I did not wait his coming. We were off and away, and the Chatterer gave us the chase of our lives through the trees.

After the chase was over, and Lop-Ear and I had had out our laugh, we discovered that twilight was falling. Here was night with all its terrors upon us, and to return to the caves was out of the question. Red-Eye made that impossible. We took refuge in a tree that stood apart from other trees, and high up in a fork we passed the night. It was a miserable night. For the first few hours it rained heavily, then it turned cold and a chill wind blew upon us. Soaked through, with shivering bodies and chattering teeth, we huddled in each other's arms. We missed the snug, dry cave that so quickly warmed with the heat of our bodies.

Morning found us wretched and resolved. We would not spend another such night. Remembering the tree-shelters of our elders, we set to work to make one for ourselves. We built the framework of a rough nest, and on higher forks overhead even got in several ridge-poles for the roof. Then the sun came out, and under its benign influence we forgot the hardships of the night and went off in search of breakfast. After that, to show the inconsequentiality of life in those days, we fell to playing. It must have taken us all of a month, working intermittently, to make our tree-house; and then, when it was completed, we never used it again.

But I run ahead of my story. When we fell to playing, after breakfast, on the second day away from the caves, Lop-Ear led me a chase through the trees and down to the river. We came out upon it where a large slough entered from the blueberry swamp. The mouth of this slough was wide, while the slough itself was practically without a current. In the dead water, just inside its mouth, lay a tangled mass of tree trunks. Some of these, what of the wear and tear of freshets and of being stranded long summers on sand-bars, were seasoned and dry and without branches. They floated high in the water, and bobbed up and down or rolled over when we put our weight upon them.

Here and there between the trunks were water-cracks, and through them we could see schools of small fish, like minnows, darting back and forth. Lop-Ear and I became fishermen at once. Lying flat on the logs, keeping perfectly quiet, waiting till the minnows came close, we would make swift passes with our hands. Our prizes we ate on the spot, wriggling and moist. We did not notice the lack of salt.

The mouth of the slough became our favorite playground. Here we spent many hours each day, catching fish and playing on the logs, and here, one day, we learned our first lessons in navigation. The log on which Lop-Ear was lying got adrift. He was curled up on his side, asleep. A light fan of air slowly drifted the log away from the shore, and when I noticed his predicament the distance was already too great for him to leap.

At first the episode seemed merely funny to me. But when one of the vagrant impulses of fear, common in that age of perpetual insecurity, moved within me, I was struck with my own loneliness. I was made suddenly aware of Lop-Ear's remoteness out there on that alien element a few feet away. I called loudly to him a warning cry. He awoke frightened, and shifted his weight rashly on the log. It turned over, sousing him under. Three times again it soused him under as he tried to climb out upon it. Then he succeeded, crouching upon it and chattering with fear.

I could do nothing. Nor could he. Swimming was something of which we knew nothing. We were already too far removed from the lower life-forms to have the instinct for swimming, and we had not yet become sufficiently man-like to undertake it as the working out of a problem. I roamed disconsolately up and down the bank, keeping as close to him in his involuntary travels as I could, while he wailed and cried till it was a wonder that he did not bring down upon us every hunting animal within a mile.

The hours passed. The sun climbed overhead and began its descent to the west. The light wind died down and left Lop-Ear on his log floating around a hundred feet away. And then, somehow, I know not how, Lop-Ear made the great discovery. He began paddling with his hands. At first his progress was slow and erratic. Then he straightened out and began laboriously to paddle nearer and nearer. I could not understand. I sat down and watched and waited until he gained the shore.

But he had learned something, which was more than I had done. Later in the afternoon, he deliberately launched out from shore on the log. Still later he persuaded me to join him, and I, too, learned the trick of paddling. For the next several days we could not tear ourselves away from the slough. So absorbed were we in our new game that we almost neglected to eat. We even roosted in a nearby tree at night. And we forgot that Red-Eye existed.

We were always trying new logs, and we learned that the smaller the log the faster we could make it go. Also, we learned that the smaller the log the more liable it was to roll over and give us a ducking. Still another thing about small logs we learned. One day we paddled our individual logs alongside each other. And then, quite by accident, in the course of play, we discovered that when each, with one hand and foot, held on to the other's log, the logs were steadied and did not turn over. Lying side by side in this position, our outside hands and feet were left free for paddling. Our final discovery was that this arrangement enabled us to use still smaller logs and thereby gain greater speed. And there our discoveries ended. We had invented the most primitive catamaran, and we did not have sense enough to know it. It never entered our heads to lash the logs together with tough vines or stringy roots. We were content to hold the logs together with our hands and feet.

It was not until we got over our first enthusiasm for navigation and had begun to return to our tree-shelter to sleep at night, that we found the Swift One. I saw her first, gathering young acorns from the branches of a large oak near our tree. She was very timid. At first, she kept very still; but when she saw that she was discovered she dropped to the ground and dashed wildly away. We caught occasional glimpses of her from day to day, and came to look for her when we travelled back and forth between our tree and the mouth of the slough.

And then, one day, she did not run away. She waited our coming, and made soft peace-sounds. We could not get very near, however. When we seemed to approach too close, she darted suddenly away and from a safe distance uttered the soft sounds again. This continued for some days. It took a long while to get acquainted with her, but finally it was accomplished and she joined us sometimes in our play.

I liked her from the first. She was of most pleasing appearance. She was very mild. Her eyes were the mildest I had ever seen. In this she was quite unlike the rest of the girls and women of the Folk, who were born viragos. She never made harsh, angry cries, and it seemed to be her nature to flee away from trouble rather than to remain and fight.

The mildness I have mentioned seemed to emanate from her whole being. Her bodily as well as facial appearance was the cause of this. Her eyes were larger than most of her kind, and they were not so deep-set, while the lashes were longer and more regular. Nor was her nose so thick and squat. It had quite a bridge, and the nostrils opened downward. Her incisors were not large, nor was her upper lip long and down-hanging, nor her lower lip protruding. She was not very hairy, except on the outsides of arms and legs and across the shoulders; and while she was thin-hipped, her calves were not twisted and gnarly.

I have often wondered, looking back upon her from the twentieth century through the medium of my dreams, and it has always occurred to me that possibly she may have been related to the Fire People. Her father, or mother, might well have come from that higher stock. While such things were not common, still they did occur, and I have seen the proof of them with my own eyes, even to the extent of members of the horde turning renegade and going to live with the Tree People.

All of which is neither here nor there. The Swift One was radically different from any of the females of the horde, and I had a liking for her from the first. Her mildness and gentleness attracted me. She was never rough, and she never fought. She always ran away, and right here may be noted the significance of the naming of her. She was a better climber than Lop-Ear or I. When we played tag we could never catch her except by accident, while she could catch us at will. She was remarkably swift in all her movements, and she had a genius for judging distances that was equalled only by her daring. Excessively timid in all other matters, she was without fear when it came to climbing or running through the trees, and Lop-Ear and I were awkward and lumbering and cowardly in comparison.

She was an orphan. We never saw her with any one, and there was no telling how long she had lived alone in the world. She must have learned early in her helpless childhood that safety lay only in flight. She was very wise and very discreet. It became a sort of game with Lop-Ear and me to try to find where she lived. It was certain that she had a tree-shelter somewhere, and not very far away; but trail her as we would, we could never find it. She was willing enough to join with us at play in the day-time, but the secret of her abiding-place she guarded jealously.

Chapter 11

It must be remembered that the description I have just given of the Swift One is not the description that would have been given by Big-Tooth, my other self of my dreams, my prehistoric ancestor. It is by the medium of my dreams that I, the modern man, look through the eyes of Big-Tooth and see.

And so it is with much that I narrate of the events of that far-off time. There is a duality about my impressions that is too confusing to inflict upon my readers. I shall merely pause here in my narrative to indicate this duality, this perplexing mixing of personality. It is I, the modern, who look back across the centuries and weigh and analyze the emotions and motives of Big-Tooth, my other self. He did not bother to weigh and analyze. He was simplicity itself. He just lived events, without ever pondering why he lived them in his particular and often erratic way.

As I, my real self, grew older, I entered more and more into the substance of my dreams. One may dream, and even in the midst of the dream be aware that he is dreaming, and if the dream be bad, comfort himself with the thought that it is only a dream. This is a common experience with all of us. And so it was that I, the modern, often entered into my dreaming, and in the consequent strange dual personality was both actor and spectator. And right often have I, the modern, been perturbed and vexed by the foolishness, illogic, obtuseness, and general all-round stupendous stupidity of myself, the primitive.

And one thing more, before I end this digression. Have you ever dreamed that you dreamed? Dogs dream, horses dream, all animals dream. In Big-Tooth's day the half-men dreamed, and when the dreams were bad they howled in their sleep. Now I, the modern, have lain down with Big-Tooth and dreamed his dreams.

This is getting almost beyond the grip of the intellect, I know;

but I do know that I have done this thing. And let me tell you that the flying and crawling dreams of Big-Tooth were as vivid to him as the falling-through-space dream is to you.

For Big-Tooth also had an other-self, and when he slept that other-self dreamed back into the past, back to the winged reptiles and the clash and the onset of dragons, and beyond that to the scurrying, rodent-like life of the tiny mammals, and far remoter still, to the shore-slime of the primeval sea. I cannot, I dare not, say more. It is all too vague and complicated and awful. I can only hint of those vast and terrific vistas through which I have peered hazily at the progression of life, not upward from the ape to man, but upward from the worm.

And now to return to my tale. I, Big-Tooth, knew not the Swift One as a creature of finer facial and bodily symmetry, with long-lashed eyes and a bridge to her nose and down-opening nostrils that made toward beauty. I knew her only as the mild-eyed young female who made soft sounds and did not fight. I liked to play with her, I knew not why, to seek food in her company, and to go bird-nesting with her. And I must confess she taught me things about tree-climbing. She was very wise, very strong, and no clinging skirts impeded her movements.

It was about this time that a slight defection arose on the part of Lop-Ear. He got into the habit of wandering off in the direction of the tree where my mother lived. He had taken a liking to my vicious sister, and the Chatterer had come to tolerate him. Also, there were several other young people, progeny of the monogamic couples that lived in the neighborhood, and Lop-Ear played with these young people.

I could never get the Swift One to join with them. Whenever I visited them she dropped behind and disappeared. I remember once making a strong effort to persuade her. But she cast backward, anxious glances, then retreated, calling to me from a tree. So it was that I did not make a practice of accompanying Lop-Ear when he went to visit his new friends. The Swift One and I were good comrades, but, try as I would, I could never find her tree-shelter.

Undoubtedly, had nothing happened, we would have soon mated, for our liking was mutual; but the something did happen.

One morning, the Swift One not having put in an appearance, Lop-Ear and I were down at the mouth of the slough playing on the logs. We had scarcely got out on the water, when we were startled by a roar of rage. It was Red-Eye. He was crouching on the edge of the timber jam and glowering his hatred at us. We were badly frightened, for here was no narrow-mouthed cave for refuge. But the twenty feet of water that intervened gave us temporary safety, and we plucked up courage.

Red-Eye stood up erect and began beating his hairy chest with his fist. Our two logs were side by side, and we sat on them and laughed at him. At first our laughter was half-hearted, tinged with fear, but as we became convinced of his impotence we waxed uproarious. He raged and raged at us, and ground his teeth in helpless fury. And in our fancied security we mocked and mocked him. We were ever short-sighted, we Folk.

Red-Eye abruptly ceased his breast-beating and tooth-grinding, and ran across the timber-jam to the shore. And just as abruptly our merriment gave way to consternation. It was not Red-Eye's way to forego revenge so easily. We waited in fear and trembling for whatever was to happen. It never struck us to paddle away. He came back with great leaps across the jam, one huge hand filled with round, water-washed pebbles. I am glad that he was unable to find larger missiles, say stones weighing two or three pounds, for we were no more than a score of feet away, and he surely would have killed us.

As it was, we were in no small danger. Zip! A tiny pebble whirred past with the force almost of a bullet. Lop-Ear and I began paddling frantically. Whiz-zip-bang ! Lop-Ear screamed with sudden anguish. The pebble had struck him between the shoulders. Then I got one and yelled. The only thing that saved us was the exhausting of Red-Eye's ammunition. He dashed back to the gravel-bed for more, while Lop-Ear and I paddled away.

Gradually we drew out of range, though Red-Eye continued

making trips for more ammunition and the pebbles continued to whiz about us. Out in the centre of the slough there was a slight current, and in our excitement we failed to notice that it was drifting us into the river. We paddled, and Red-Eye kept as close as he could to us by following along the shore. Then he discovered larger rocks. Such ammunition increased his range. One fragment, fully five pounds in weight, crashed on the log alongside of me, and such was its impact that it drove a score of splinters, like fiery needles, into my leg. Had it struck me it would have killed me.

And then the river current caught us. So wildly were we paddling that Red-Eye was the first to notice it, and our first warning was his yell of triumph. Where the edge of the current struck the slough-water was a series of eddies or small whirlpools. These caught our clumsy logs and whirled them end for end, back and forth and around. We quit paddling and devoted our whole energy to holding the logs together alongside each other. In the meanwhile Red-Eye continued to bombard us, the rock fragments falling about us, splashing water on us, and menacing our lives. At the same time he gloated over us, wildly and vociferously.

It happened that there was a sharp turn in the river at the point where the slough entered, and the whole main current of the river was deflected to the other bank. And toward that bank, which was the north bank, we drifted rapidly, at the same time going downstream. This quickly took us out of range of Red-Eye, and the last we saw of him was far out on a point of land, where he was jumping up and down and chanting a paean of victory.

Beyond holding the two logs together, Lop-Ear and I did nothing. We were resigned to our fate, and we remained resigned until we aroused to the fact that we were drifting along the north shore not a hundred feet away. We began to paddle for it. Here the main force of the current was flung back toward the south shore, and the result of our paddling was that we crossed the current where it was swiftest and narrowest. Before we were aware, we were out of it and in a quiet eddy.

Our logs drifted slowly and at last grounded gently on the bank.

Lop-Ear and I crept ashore. The logs drifted on out of the eddy and swept away down the stream. We looked at each other, but we did not laugh. We were in a strange land, and it did not enter our minds that we could return to our own land in the same manner that we had come.

We had learned how to cross a river, though we did not know it. And this was something that no one else of the Folk had ever done. We were the first of the Folk to set foot on the north bank of the river, and, for that matter, I believe the last. That they would have done so in the time to come is undoubted; but the migration of the Fire People, and the consequent migration of the survivors of the Folk, set back our evolution for centuries.

Indeed, there is no telling how disastrous was to be the outcome of the Fire People's migration. Personally, I am prone to believe that it brought about the destruction of the Folk; that we, a branch of lower life budding toward the human, were nipped short off and perished down by the roaring surf where the river entered the sea. Of course, in such an eventuality, I remain to be accounted for; but I outrun my story, and such accounting will be made before I am done.

Chapter 12

I have no idea how long Lop-Ear and I wandered in the land north of the river. We were like mariners wrecked on a desert isle, so far as concerned the likelihood of our getting home again. We turned our backs upon the river, and for weeks and months adventured in that wilderness where there were no Folk. It is very difficult for me to reconstruct our journeying, and impossible to do it from day to day. Most of it is hazy and indistinct, though here and there I have vivid recollections of things that happened.

Especially do I remember the hunger we endured on the mountains between Long Lake and Far Lake, and the calf we caught sleeping in the thicket. Also, there are the Tree People who dwelt in the forest between Long Lake and the mountains. It was they who chased us into the mountains and compelled us to travel on to Far Lake.

First, after we left the river, we worked toward the west till we came to a small stream that flowed through marshlands. Here we turned away toward the north, skirting the marshes and after several days arriving at what I have called Long Lake. We spent some time around its upper end, where we found food in plenty; and then, one day, in the forest, we ran foul of the Tree People. These creatures were ferocious apes, nothing more. And yet they were not so different from us. They were more hairy, it is true; their legs were a trifle more twisted and gnarly, their eyes a bit smaller, their necks a bit thicker and shorter, and their nostrils slightly more like orifices in a sunken surface; but they had no hair on their faces and on the palms of their hands and the soles of their feet, and they made sounds similar to ours with somewhat similar meanings. After all, the Tree People and the Folk were not so unlike.

I found him first, a little withered, dried-up old fellow, wrinkled-faced and bleary-eyed and tottery. He was legitimate prey. In our world there was no sympathy between the kinds, and he was not our kind. He was a Tree-Man, and he was very old. He was sitting at the foot of a tree -- evidently his tree, for we could see the tattered nest in the branches, in which he slept at night.

I pointed him out to Lop-Ear, and we made a rush for him. He started to climb, but was too slow. I caught him by the leg and dragged him back. Then we had fun. We pinched him, pulled his hair, tweaked his ears, and poked twigs into him, and all the while we laughed with streaming eyes. His futile anger was most absurd. He was a comical sight, striving to fan into flame the cold ashes of his youth, to resurrect his strength dead and gone through the oozing of the years -- making woeful faces in place of the ferocious ones he intended, grinding his worn teeth together, beating his meagre chest with feeble fists.

Also, he had a cough, and he gasped and hacked and spluttered prodigiously. Every time he tried to climb the tree we pulled him back, until at last he surrendered to his weakness and did no more than sit and weep. And Lop-Ear and I sat with him, our arms around each other, and laughed at his wretchedness.

From weeping he went to whining, and from whining to wailing, until at last he achieved a scream. This alarmed us, but the more we tried to make him cease, the louder he screamed. And then, from not far away in the forest, came a "Goek! Goek!" to our ears. To this there were answering cries, several of them, and from very far off we could hear a big, bass "Goek! Goek! Goek!" Also, the "Whoo-whoo !" call was rising in the forest all around us.

Then came the chase. It seemed it never would end. They raced us through the trees, the whole tribe of them, and nearly caught us. We were forced to take to the ground, and here we had the advantage, for they were truly the Tree People, and while they outclimbed us we out-footed them on the ground. We broke away toward the north, the tribe howling on our track. Across the open spaces we gained, and in the brush they caught up with us, and more than once it was nip and tuck. And as the chase continued, we realized that we were not their kind, either, and that the bonds between us were anything but sympathetic.

They ran us for hours. The forest seemed interminable. We kept to the glades as much as possible, but they always ended in more thick forest. Sometimes we thought we had escaped, and sat down to rest; but always, before we could recover our breath, we would hear the hateful "Whoo-whoo!" cries and the terrible "Goek! Goek! Goek!" This latter sometimes terminated in a savage "Ha ha ha ha haaaaa!!!"

And in this fashion were we hunted through the forest by the exasperated Tree People. At last, by mid-afternoon, the slopes began rising higher and higher and the trees were becoming smaller. Then we came out on the grassy flanks of the mountains. Here was where we could make time, and here the Tree People gave up and returned to their forest.

The mountains were bleak and inhospitable, and three times that afternoon we tried to regain the woods. But the Tree People were lying in wait, and they drove us back. Lop-Ear and I slept that night in a dwarf tree, no larger than a bush. Here was no security, and we would have been easy prey for any hunting animal that chanced along.

In the morning, what of our new-gained respect for the Tree People, we faced into the mountains. That we had no definite plan, or even idea, I am confident. We were merely driven on by the danger we had escaped. Of our wanderings through the mountains I have only misty memories. We were in that bleak region many days, and we suffered much, especially from fear, it was all so new and strange. Also, we suffered from the cold, and later from hunger.

It -- was a desolate land of rocks and foaming streams and clattering cataracts. We climbed and descended mighty canyons and gorges; and ever, from every view point, there spread out before us, in all directions, range upon range, the unceasing mountains. We slept at night in holes and crevices, and on one cold night we perched on top a slender pinnacle of rock that was almost like a tree.

And then, at last, one hot midday, dizzy with hunger, we gained the divide. From this high backbone of earth, to the north, across the diminishing, down-falling ranges, we caught a glimpse of a far lake. The sun shone upon it, and about it were open, level grass-lands, while to the eastward we saw the dark line of a wide-stretching forest.

We were two days in gaining the lake, and we were weak with hunger; but on its shore, sleeping snugly in a thicket, we found a part-grown calf. It gave us much trouble, for we knew no other way to kill than with our hands. When we had gorged our fill, we carried the remainder of the meat to the eastward forest and hid it in a tree. We never returned to that tree, for the shore of the stream that drained Far Lake was packed thick with salmon that had come up from the sea to spawn.

Westward from the lake stretched the grass-lands, and here were multitudes of bison and wild cattle. Also were there many packs of wild dogs, and as there were no trees it was not a safe place for us. We followed north along the stream for days. Then, and for what reason I do not know, we abruptly left the stream and swung to the east, and then to the southeast, through a great forest. I shall not bore you with our journey. I but indicate it to show how we finally arrived at the Fire People's country.

We came out upon the river, but we did not know it for our river. We had been lost so long that we had come to accept the condition of being lost as habitual. As I look back I see clearly how our lives and destinies are shaped by the merest chance. We did not know it was our river -- there was no way of telling; and if we had never crossed it we would most probably have never returned to the horde; and I, the modern, the thousand centuries yet to be born, would never have been born.

And yet Lop-Ear and I wanted greatly to return. We had experienced homesickness on our journey, the yearning for our own kind and land; and often had I had recollections of the Swift One, the young female who made soft sounds, whom it was good to be with, and who lived by herself nobody knew where. My recollections of her were accompanied by sensations of hunger, and these I felt when I was not hungry and when I had just eaten.

But to come back to the river. Food was plentiful, principally berries and succulent roots, and on the river bank we played and lingered for days. And then the idea came to Lop-Ear. It was a visible process, the coming of the idea. I saw it. The expression in his eyes became plaintive and querulous, and he was greatly perturbed. Then his eyes went muddy, as if he had lost his grip on the inchoate thought. This was followed by the plaintive, querulous expression as the idea persisted and he clutched it anew. He looked at me, and at the river and the far shore. He tried to speak, but had no sounds with which to express the idea. The result was a gibberish that made me laugh. This angered him, and he grabbed me suddenly and threw me on my back. Of course we fought, and in the end I chased him up a tree, where he secured a long branch and poked me every time I tried to get at him.

And the idea had gone glimmering. I did not know, and he had forgotten. But the next morning it awoke in him again. Perhaps it was the homing instinct in him asserting itself that made the idea persist. At any rate it was there, and clearer than before. He led me down to the water, where a log had grounded in an eddy. I thought he was minded to play, as we had played in the mouth of the slough. Nor did I change my mind as I watched him tow up a second log from farther down the shore.

It was not until we were on the logs, side by side and holding them together, and had paddled out into the current, that I learned his intention. He paused to point at the far shore, and resumed his paddling, at the same time uttering loud and encouraging cries. I understood, and we paddled energetically. The swift current caught us, flung us toward the south shore, but before we could make a landing flung us back toward the north shore.

Here arose dissension. Seeing the north shore so near, I began to paddle for it. Lop-Ear tried to paddle for the south shore. The logs swung around in circles, and we got nowhere, and all the time the forest was flashing past as we drifted down the stream. We could not fight. We knew better than to let go the grips of hands and feet that held the logs together. But we chattered and abused each other with our tongues until the current flung us toward the south bank again. That was now the nearest goal, and together and amicably we paddled for it. We landed in an eddy, and climbed directly into the trees to reconnoitre.

Chapter 13

It was not until the night of our first day on the south bank of the river that we discovered the Fire People. What must have been a band of wandering hunters went into camp not far from the tree in which Lop-Ear and I had elected to roost for the night. The voices of the Fire People at first alarmed us, but later, when darkness had come, we were attracted by the fire. We crept cautiously and silently from tree to tree till we got a good view of the scene.

In an open space among the trees, near to the river, the fire was burning. About it were half a dozen Fire-Men. Lop-Ear clutched me suddenly, and I could feel him tremble. I looked more closely, and saw the wizened little old hunter who had shot Broken-Tooth out of the tree years before. When he got up and walked about, throwing fresh wood upon the fire, I saw that he limped with his crippled leg. Whatever it was, it was a permanent injury. He seemed more dried up and wizened than ever, and the hair on his face was quite gray.

The other hunters were young men. I noted, lying near them on the ground, their bows and arrows, and I knew the weapons for what they were. The Fire-Men wore animal skins around their waists and across their shoulders. Their arms and legs, however, were bare, and they wore no footgear. As I have said before, they were not quite so hairy as we of the Folk. They did not have large heads, and between them and the Folk there was very little difference in the degree of the slant of the head back from the eyes.

They were less stooped than we, less springy in their movements. Their backbones and hips and knee-joints seemed more rigid. Their arms were not so long as ours either, and I did not notice that they ever balanced themselves when they walked, by touching the ground on either side with their hands. Also, their muscles were more rounded and symmetrical than ours, and their faces were more pleasing. Their nose orifices opened downward;

likewise the bridges of their noses were more developed, did not look so squat nor crushed as ours. Their lips were less flabby and pendent, and their eye-teeth did not look so much like fangs. However, they were quite as thin-hipped as we, and did not weigh much more. Take it all in all, they were less different from us than were we from the Tree People. Certainly, all three kinds were related, and not so remotely related at that.

The fire around which they sat was especially attractive. Lop-Ear and I sat for hours, watching the flames and smoke. It was most fascinating when fresh fuel was thrown on and showers of sparks went flying upward. I wanted to come closer and look at the fire, but there was no way. We were crouching in the forks of a tree on the edge of the open space, and we did not dare run the risk of being discovered.

The Fire-Men squatted around the fire and slept with their heads bowed forward on their knees. They did not sleep soundly. Their ears twitched in their sleep, and they were restless. Every little while one or another got up and threw more wood upon the fire. About the circle of light in the forest, in the darkness beyond, roamed hunting animals. Lop-Ear and I could tell them by their sounds. There were wild dogs and a hyena, and for a time there was a great yelping and snarling that awakened on the instant the whole circle of sleeping Fire-Men.

Once a lion and a lioness stood beneath our tree and gazed out with bristling hair and blinking eyes. The lion licked his chops and was nervous with eagerness, as if he wanted to go forward and make a meal. But the lioness was more cautious. It was she that discovered us, and the pair stood and looked up at us, silently, with twitching, scenting nostrils. Then they growled, looked once again at the fire, and turned away into the forest.

For a much longer time Lop-Ear and I remained and watched. Now and again we could hear the crashing of heavy bodies in the thickets and underbrush, and from the darkness of the other side, across the circle, we could see eyes gleaming in the firelight. In the distance we heard a lion roar, and from far off came the scream of some stricken animal, splashing and floundering in a drinking-place. Also, from the river, came a great grunting of rhinoceroses.

In the morning, after having had our sleep, we crept back to the fire. It was still smouldering, and the Fire-Men were gone. We made a circle through the forest to make sure, and then we ran to the fire. I wanted to see what it was like, and between thumb and finger I picked up a glowing coal. My cry of pain and fear, as I dropped it, stampeded Lop-Ear into the trees, and his flight frightened me after him.

The next time we came back more cautiously, and we avoided the glowing coals. We fell to imitating the Fire-Men. We squatted down by the fire, and with heads bent forward on our knees, made believe to sleep. Then we mimicked their speech, talking to each other in their fashion and making a great gibberish. I remembered seeing the wizened old hunter poke the fire with a stick. I poked the fire with a stick, turning up masses of live coals and clouds of white ashes. This was great sport, and soon we were coated white with the ashes.

It was inevitable that we should imitate the Fire-Men in replenishing the fire. We tried it first with small pieces of wood. It was a success. The wood flamed up and crackled, and we danced and gibbered with delight. Then we began to throw on larger pieces of wood. We put on more and more, until we had a mighty fire. We dashed excitedly back and forth, dragging dead limbs and branches from out the forest. The flames soared higher and higher, and the smoke-column out-towered the trees. There was a tremendous snapping and crackling and roaring. It was the most monumental work we had ever effected with our hands, and we were proud of it. We, too, were Fire-Men, we thought, as we danced there, white gnomes in the conflagration.

The dried grass and underbrush caught fire, but we did not notice it. Suddenly a great tree on the edge of the open space burst into flames.

We looked at it with startled eyes. The heat of it drove us back. Another tree caught, and another, and then half a dozen. We were frightened. The monster had broken loose. We crouched down in fear, while the fire ate around the circle and hemmed us in. Into Lop-Ear's eyes came the plaintive look that always accompanied incomprehension, and I know that in my eyes must have been the same look. We huddled, with our arms around each other, until the heat began to reach us and the odor of burning hair was in our nostrils. Then we made a dash of it, and fled away westward through the forest, looking back and laughing as we ran.

By the middle of the day we came to a neck of land, made, as we afterward discovered, by a great curve of the river that almost completed a circle. Right across the neck lay bunched several low and partly wooded hills. Over these we climbed, looking backward at the forest which had become a sea of flame that swept eastward before a rising wind. We continued to the west, following the river bank, and before we knew it we were in the midst of the abiding-place of the Fire People.

This abiding-place was a splendid strategic selection. It was a peninsula, protected on three sides by the curving river. On only one side was it accessible by land. This was the narrow neck of the peninsula, and here the several low hills were a natural obstacle. Practically isolated from the rest of the world, the Fire People must have here lived and prospered for a long time. In fact, I think it was their prosperity that was responsible for the subsequent migration that worked such calamity upon the Folk. The Fire People must have increased in numbers until they pressed uncomfortably against the bounds of their habitat. They were expanding, and in the course of their expanding they drove the Folk before them, and settled down themselves in the caves and occupied the territory that we had occupied.

But Lop-Ear and I little dreamed of all this when we found ourselves in the Fire People's stronghold. We had but one idea, and that was to get away, though we could not forbear humoring our curiosity by peeping out upon the village. For the first time we saw the women and children of the Fire People. The latter ran for the most part naked, though the former wore skins of wild animals.

The Fire People, like ourselves, lived in caves. The open space in front of the caves sloped down to the river, and in the open space burned many small fires. But whether or not the Fire People cooked their food, I do not know. Lop-Ear and I did not see them cook. Yet it is my opinion that they surely must have performed some sort of rude cookery. Like us, they carried water in gourds from the river. There was much coming and going, and loud cries made by the women and children. The latter played about and cut up antics quite in the same way as did the children of the Folk, and they more nearly resembled the children of the Folk than did the grown Fire People resemble the grown Folk.

Lop-Ear and I did not linger long. We saw some of the part-grown boys shooting with bow and arrow, and we sneaked back into the thicker forest and made our way to the river. And there we found a catamaran, a real catamaran, one evidently made by some Fire-Man. The two logs were small and straight, and were lashed together by means of tough roots and crosspieces of wood.

This time the idea occurred simultaneously to us. We were trying to escape out of the Fire People's territory. What better way than by crossing the river on these logs? We climbed on board and shoved off. A sudden something gripped the catamaran and flung it downstream violently against the bank. The abrupt stoppage almost whipped us off into the water. The catamaran was tied to a tree by a rope of twisted roots. This we untied before shoving off again.

By the time we had paddled well out into the current, we had drifted so far downstream that we were in full view of the Fire People's abiding-place. So occupied were we with our paddling, our eyes fixed upon the other bank, that we knew nothing until aroused by a yell from the shore. We looked around. There were the Fire People, many of them, looking at us and pointing at us, and more were crawling out of the caves. We sat up to watch, and forgot all about paddling. There was a great hullabaloo on the shore. Some of the Fire-Men discharged their bows at us, and a few of the arrows fell near us, but the range was too great.

It was a great day for Lop-Ear and me. To the east the conflagration we had started was filling half the sky with smoke. And here we were, perfectly safe in the middle of the river, encircling the Fire People's stronghold. We sat and laughed at them as we dashed by, swinging south, and southeast to east, and even to northeast, and then east again, southeast and south and on around to the west, a great double curve where the river nearly tied a knot in itself.

As we swept on to the west, the Fire People far behind, a familiar scene flashed upon our eyes. It was the great drinking-place, where we had wandered once or twice to watch the circus of the animals when they came down to drink. Beyond it, we knew, was the carrot patch, and beyond that the caves and the abiding-place of the horde. We began to paddle for the bank that slid swiftly past, and before we knew it we were down upon the drinking-places used by the horde. There were the women and children, the water carriers, a number of them, filling their gourds. At sight of us they stampeded madly up the run-ways, leaving behind them a trail of gourds they had dropped.

We landed, and of course we neglected to tie up the catamaran, which floated off down the river. Right cautiously we crept up a run-way. The Folk had all disappeared into their holes, though here and there we could see a face peering out at us. There was no sign of Red-Eye. We were home again. And that night we slept in our own little cave high up on the cliff, though first we had to evict a couple of pugnacious youngsters who had taken possession.

Chapter 14

The months came and went. The drama and tragedy of the future were yet to come upon the stage, and in the meantime we pounded nuts and lived. It -- was a good year, I remember, for nuts. We used to fill gourds with nuts and carry them to the pounding-places. We placed them in depressions in the rock, and, with a piece of rock in our hands, we cracked them and ate them as we cracked.

It was the fall of the year when Lop-Ear and I returned from our long adventure-journey, and the winter that followed was mild. I made frequent trips to the neighborhood of my old home-tree, and frequently I searched the whole territory that lay between the blueberry swamp and the mouth of the slough where Lop-Ear and I had learned navigation, but no clew could I get of the Swift One. She had disappeared. And I wanted her. I was impelled by that hunger which I have mentioned, and which was akin to physical hunger, albeit it came often upon me when my stomach was full. But all my search was vain.

Life was not monotonous at the caves, however. There was Red-Eye to be considered. Lop-Ear and I never knew a moment's peace except when we were in our own little cave. In spite of the enlargement of the entrance we had made, it was still a tight squeeze for us to get in. And though from time to time we continued to enlarge, it was still too small for Red-Eye's monstrous body. But he never stormed our cave again. He had learned the lesson well, and he carried on his neck a bulging lump to show where I had hit him with the rock. This lump never went away, and it was prominent enough to be seen at a distance. I often took great delight in watching that evidence of my handiwork; and sometimes, when I was myself assuredly safe, the sight of it caused me to laugh.

While the other Folk would not have come to our rescue had

Red-Eye proceeded to tear Lop-Ear and me to pieces before their eyes, nevertheless they sympathized with us. Possibly it was not sympathy but the way they expressed their hatred for Red-Eye; at any rate they always warned us of his approach. Whether in the forest, at the drinking-places, or in the open space before the caves, they were always quick to warn us. Thus we had the advantage of many eyes in our feud with Red-Eye, the atavism.

Once he nearly got me. It was early in the morning, and the Folk were not yet up. The surprise was complete. I was cut off from the way up the cliff to my cave. Before I knew it I had dashed into the double-cave, -- the cave where Lop-Ear had first eluded me long years before, and where old Saber-Tooth had come to discomfiture when he pursued the two Folk. By the time I had got through the connecting passage between the two caves, I discovered that Red-Eye was not following me. The next moment he charged into the cave from the outside. I slipped back through the passage, and he charged out and around and in upon me again. I merely repeated my performance of slipping through the passage.

He kept me there half a day before he gave up. After that, when Lop-Ear and I were reasonably sure of gaining the double-cave, we did not retreat up the cliff to our own cave when Red-Eye came upon the scene. All we did was to keep an eye on him and see that he did not cut across our line of retreat.

It was during this winter that Red-Eye killed his latest wife with abuse and repeated beatings. I have called him an atavism, but in this he was worse than an atavism, for the males of the lower animals do not maltreat and murder their mates. In this I take it that Red-Eye, in spite of his tremendous atavistic tendencies, foreshadowed the coming of man, for it is the males of the human species only that murder their mates.

As was to be expected, with the doing away of one wife Red-Eye proceeded to get another. He decided upon the Singing One. She was the granddaughter of old Marrow-Bone, and the daughter of the Hairless One. She was a young thing, greatly given to singing at the mouth of her cave in the twilight, and she had but recently mated with Crooked-Leg. He was a quiet individual, molesting no one and not given to bickering with his fellows. He was no fighter anyway. He was small and lean, and not so active on his legs as the rest of us.

Red-Eye never committed a more outrageous deed. It was in the quiet at the end of the day, when we began to congregate in the open space before climbing into our caves. Suddenly the Singing One dashed up a run-way from a drinking-place, pursued by Red-Eye. She ran to her husband. Poor little Crooked-Leg was terribly scared. But he was a hero. He knew that death was upon him, yet he did not run away. He stood up, and chattered, bristled, and showed his teeth.

Red-Eye roared with rage. It was an offence to him that any of the Folk should dare to withstand him. His hand shot out and clutched Crooked-Leg by the neck. The latter sank his teeth into Red-Eye's arm; but the next moment, with a broken neck, Crooked-Leg was floundering and squirming on the ground. The Singing One screeched and gibbered. Red-Eye seized her by the hair of her head and dragged her toward his cave. He handled her roughly when the climb began, and he dragged and hauled her up into the cave.

We were very angry, insanely, vociferously angry. Beating our chests, bristling, and gnashing our teeth, we gathered together in our rage. We felt the prod of gregarious instinct, the drawing together as though for united action, the impulse toward cooperation. In dim ways this need for united action was impressed upon us. But there was no way to achieve it because there was no way to express it. We did not turn to, all of us, and destroy Red-Eye, because we lacked a vocabulary. We were vaguely thinking thoughts for which there were no thought-symbols. These thought-symbols were yet to be slowly and painfully invented.

We tried to freight sound with the vague thoughts that flitted like shadows through our consciousness. The Hairless One began to chatter loudly. By his noises he expressed anger against Red-Eye and desire to hurt Red-Eye. Thus far he got, and thus far we understood. But when he tried to express the cooperative impulse that stirred within him, his noises became gibberish. Then Big-Face, with brow-bristling and chest-pounding, began to chatter. One after another of us joined in the orgy of rage, until even old Marrow-Bone was mumbling and spluttering with his cracked voice and withered lips. Someone seized a stick and began pounding a log. In a moment he had struck a rhythm. Unconsciously, our yells and exclamations yielded to this rhythm. It had a soothing effect upon us; and before we knew it, our rage forgotten, we were in the full swing of a hee-hee council.

These hee-hee councils splendidly illustrate the inconsecutiveness and inconsequentiality of the Folk. Here were we, drawn together by mutual rage and the impulse toward cooperation, led off into forgetfulness by the establishment of a rude rhythm. We were sociable and gregarious, and these singing and laughing councils satisfied us. In ways the hee-hee council was an adumbration of the councils of primitive man, and of the great national assemblies and international conventions of latter-day man. But we Folk of the Younger World lacked speech, and whenever we were so drawn together we precipitated babel, out of which arose a unanimity of rhythm that contained within itself the essentials of art yet to come. It was art nascent.

There was nothing long-continued about these rhythms that we struck. A rhythm was soon lost, and pandemonium reigned until we could find the rhythm again or start a new one. Sometimes half a dozen rhythms would be swinging simultaneously, each rhythm backed by a group that strove ardently to drown out the other rhythms.

In the intervals of pandemonium, each chattered, cut up, hooted, screeched, and danced, himself sufficient unto himself, filled with his own ideas and volitions to the exclusion of all others, a veritable centre of the universe, divorced for the time being from any unanimity with the other universe-centres leaping and yelling around him. Then would come the rhythm -- a clapping of hands; the beating of a stick upon a log; the example of one that leaped with repetitions; or the chanting of one that uttered, explosively and regularly, with inflection that rose and fell, "A-bang, a-bang! A-bang, a-bang!" One after another of the self-centred Folk would yield to it, and soon all would be dancing or chanting in chorus. "Ha-ah, ha-ah, ha-ah-ha!" was one of our favorite choruses, and another was, "Eh-wah, eh-wah, eh-wah-hah!"

And so, with mad antics, leaping, reeling, and over-balancing, we danced and sang in the sombre twilight of the primeval world, inducing forgetfulness, achieving unanimity, and working ourselves up into sensuous frenzy. And so it was that our rage against Red-Eye was soothed away by art, and we screamed the wild choruses of the hee-hee council until the night warned us of its terrors, and we crept away to our holes in the rocks, calling softly to one another, while the stars came out and darkness settled down.

We were afraid only of the dark. We had no germs of religion, no conceptions of an unseen world. We knew only the real world, and the things we feared were the real things, the concrete dangers, the flesh-and-blood animals that preyed. It was they that made us afraid of the dark, for darkness was the time of the hunting animals. It was then that they came out of their lairs and pounced upon one from the dark wherein they lurked invisible.

Possibly it was out of this fear of the real denizens of the dark that the fear of the unreal denizens was later to develop and to culminate in a whole and mighty unseen world. As imagination grew it is likely that the fear of death increased until the Folk that were to come projected this fear into the dark and peopled it with spirits. I think the Fire People had already begun to be afraid of the dark in this fashion; but the reasons we Folk had for breaking up our hee-hee councils and fleeing to our holes were old Saber-Tooth, the lions and the jackals, the wild dogs and the wolves, and all the hungry, meat-eating breeds.

Chapter 15

Lop-Ear got married. It was the second winter after our adventure-journey, and it was most unexpected. He gave me no warning. The first I knew was one twilight when I climbed the cliff to our cave. I squeezed into the entrance and there I stopped. There was no room for me. Lop-Ear and his mate were in possession, and she was none other than my sister, the daughter of my step-father, the Chatterer.

I tried to force my way in. There was space only for two, and that space was already occupied. Also, they had me at a disadvantage, and, what of the scratching and hair-pulling I received, I was glad to retreat. I slept that night, and for many nights, in the connecting passage of the double-cave. From my experience it seemed reasonably safe. As the two Folk had dodged old Saber-Tooth, and as I had dodged Red-Eye, so it seemed to me that I could dodge the hunting animals by going back and forth between the two caves.

I had forgotten the wild dogs. They were small enough to go through any passage that I could squeeze through. One night they nosed me out. Had they entered both caves at the same time they would have got me. As it was, followed by some of them through the passage, I dashed out the mouth of the other cave. Outside were the rest of the wild dogs. They sprang for me as I sprang for the cliff-wall and began to climb. One of them, a lean and hungry brute, caught me in mid-leap. His teeth sank into my thigh-muscles, and he nearly dragged me back. He held on, but I made no effort to dislodge him, devoting my whole effort to climbing out of reach of the rest of the brutes.

Not until I was safe from them did I turn my attention to that live agony on my thigh. And then, a dozen feet above the snapping pack that leaped and scrambled against the wall and fell back, I got the dog by the throat and slowly throttled him. I was a long time doing it. He clawed and ripped my hair and hide with his hind-paws, and ever he jerked and lunged with his weight to drag me from the wall.

At last his teeth opened and released my torn flesh. I carried his body up the cliff with me, and perched out the night in the entrance of my old cave, wherein were Lop-Ear and my sister. But first I had to endure a storm of abuse from the aroused horde for being the cause of the disturbance. I had my revenge. From time to time, as the noise of the pack below eased down, I dropped a rock and started it up again. Whereupon, from all around, the abuse of the exasperated Folk began afresh. In the morning I shared the dog with Lop-Ear and his wife, and for several days the three of us were neither vegetarians nor fruitarians.

Lop-Ear's marriage was not a happy one, and the consolation about it is that it did not last very long. Neither he nor I was happy during that period. I was lonely. I suffered the inconvenience of being cast out of my safe little cave, and somehow I did not make it up with any other of the young males. I suppose my long-continued chumming with Lop-Ear had become a habit.

I might have married, it is true; and most likely I should have married had it not been for the dearth of females in the horde. This dearth, it is fair to assume, was caused by the exorbitance of Red-Eye, and it illustrates the menace he was to the existence of the horde. Then there was the Swift One, whom I had not forgotten.

At any rate, during the period of Lop-Ear's marriage I knocked about from pillar to post, in danger every night that I slept, and never comfortable. One of the Folk died, and his widow was taken into the cave of another one of the Folk. I took possession of the abandoned cave, but it was wide-mouthed, and after Red-Eye nearly trapped me in it one day, I returned to sleeping in the passage of the double-cave. During the summer, however, I used to stay away from the caves for weeks, sleeping in a tree-shelter I made near the mouth of the slough.

I have said that Lop-Ear was not happy. My sister was the daughter of the Chatterer, and she made Lop-Ear's life miserable for him.

In no other cave was there so much squabbling and bickering. If Red-Eye was a Bluebeard, Lop-Ear was hen-pecked; and I imagine that Red-Eye was too shrewd ever to covet Lop-Ear's wife.

Fortunately for Lop-Ear, she died. An unusual thing happened that summer. Late, almost at the end of it, a second crop of the stringy-rooted carrots sprang up. These unexpected second-crop roots were young and juicy and tender, and for some time the carrot-patch was the favorite feeding-place of the horde. One morning, early, several score of us were there making our breakfast. On one side of me was the Hairless One. Beyond him were his father and son, old Marrow-Bone and Long-Lip. On the other side of me were my sister and Lop-Ear, she being next to me.

There was no warning. On the sudden, both the Hairless One and my sister sprang and screamed. At the same instant I heard the thud of the arrows that transfixed them. The next instant they were down on the ground, floundering and gasping, and the rest of us were stampeding for the trees. An arrow drove past me and entered the ground, its feathered shaft vibrating and oscillating from the impact of its arrested flight. I remember clearly how I swerved as I ran, to go past it, and that I gave it a needlessly wide berth. I must have shied at it as a horse shies at an object it fears.

Lop-Ear took a smashing fall as he ran beside me. An arrow had driven through the calf of his leg and tripped him. He tried to run, but was tripped and thrown by it a second time. He sat up, crouching, trembling with fear, and called to me pleadingly. I dashed back. He showed me the arrow. I caught hold of it to pull it out, but the consequent hurt made him seize my hand and stop me. A flying arrow passed between us. Another struck a rock, splintered, and fell to the ground. This was too much. I pulled, suddenly, with all my might. Lop-Ear screamed as the arrow came out, and struck at me angrily. But the next moment we were in full flight again.

I looked back. Old Marrow-Bone, deserted and far behind, was tottering silently along in his handicapped race with death. Sometimes he almost fell, and once he did fall; but no more arrows were coming. He scrambled weakly to his feet. Age burdened him heavily, but he did not want to die. The three Fire-Men, who were now running forward from their forest ambush, could easily have got him, but they did not try. Perhaps he was too old and tough. But they did want the Hairless One and my sister, for as I looked back from the trees I could see the Fire-Men beating in their heads with rocks. One of the Fire-Men was the wizened old hunter who limped.

We went on through the trees toward the caves -- an excited and disorderly mob that drove before it to their holes all the small life of the forest, and that set the blue-jays screaming impudently. Now that there was no immediate danger, Long-Lip waited for his grand-father, Marrow-Bone; and with the gap of a generation between them, the old fellow and the youth brought up our rear.

And so it was that Lop-Ear became a bachelor once more. That night I slept with him in the old cave, and our old life of chumming began again. The loss of his mate seemed to cause him no grief. At least he showed no signs of it, nor of need for her. It was the wound in his leg that seemed to bother him, and it was all of a week before he got back again to his old spryness.

Marrow-Bone was the only old member in the horde. Sometimes, on looking back upon him, when the vision of him is most clear, I note a striking resemblance between him and the father of my father's gardener. The gardener's father was very old, very wrinkled and withered; and for all the world, when he peered through his tiny, bleary eyes and mumbled with his toothless gums, he looked and acted like old Marrow-Bone. This resemblance, as a child, used to frighten me. I always ran when I saw the old man tottering along on his two canes. Old Marrow-Bone even had a bit of sparse and straggly white beard that seemed identical with the whiskers of the old man.

As I have said, Marrow-Bone was the only old member of the horde. He was an exception. The Folk never lived to old age. Middle age was fairly rare. Death by violence was the common way of death. They died as my father had died, as Broken-Tooth had died, as my sister and the Hairless One had just died -- abruptly and brutally, in the full possession of their faculties, in the full swing and rush of life. Natural death? To die violently was the natural way of dying in those days.

No one died of old age among the Folk. I never knew of a case. Even Marrow-Bone did not die that way, and he was the only one in my generation who had the chance. A bad rippling, any serious accidental or temporary impairment of the faculties, meant swift death. As a rule, these deaths were not witnessed.

Members of the horde simply dropped out of sight. They left the caves in the morning, and they never came back. They disappeared -- into the ravenous maws of the hunting creatures.

This inroad of the Fire People on the carrot-patch was the beginning of the end, though we did not know it. The hunters of the Fire People began to appear more frequently as the time went by. They came in twos and threes, creeping silently through the forest, with their flying arrows able to annihilate distance and bring down prey from the top of the loftiest tree without themselves climbing into it. The bow and arrow was like an enormous extension of their leaping and striking muscles, so that, virtually, they could leap and kill at a hundred feet and more. This made them far more terrible than Saber-Tooth himself. And then they were very wise. They had speech that enabled them more effectively to reason, and in addition they understood cooperation.

We Folk came to be very circumspect when we were in the forest. We were more alert and vigilant and timid. No longer were the trees a protection to be relied upon. No longer could we perch on a branch and laugh down at our carnivorous enemies on the ground. The Fire People were carnivorous, with claws and fangs a hundred feet long, the most terrible of all the hunting animals that ranged the primeval world.

One morning, before the Folk had dispersed to the forest, there was a panic among the water-carriers and those who had gone down to the river to drink. The whole horde fled to the caves. It was our habit, at such times, to flee first and investigate afterward. We waited in the mouths of our caves and watched. After some time a Fire-Man stepped cautiously into the open space. It was the little wizened old hunter. He stood for a long time and watched us, looking our caves and the cliff-wall up and down. He descended one of the run-ways to a drinking-place, returning a few minutes later by another run-way. Again he stood and watched us carefully, for a long time. Then he turned on his heel and limped into the forest, leaving us calling querulously and plaintively to one another from the cave-mouths.

Chapter 16

I found her down in the old neighborhood near the blueberry swamp, where my mother lived and where Lop-Ear and I had built our first tree-shelter. It was unexpected. As I came under the tree I heard the familiar soft sound and looked up. There she was, the Swift One, sitting on a limb and swinging her legs back and forth as she looked at me.

I stood still for some time. The sight of her had made me very happy. And then an unrest and a pain began to creep in on this happiness. I started to climb the tree after her, and she retreated slowly out the limb. Just as I reached for her, she sprang through the air and landed in the branches of the next tree. From amid the rustling leaves she peeped out at me and made soft sounds. I leaped straight for her, and after an exciting chase the situation was duplicated, for there she was, making soft sounds and peeping out from the leaves of a third tree.

It was borne in upon me that somehow it was different now from the old days before Lop-Ear and I had gone on our adventure-journey. I wanted her, and I knew that I wanted her. And she knew it, too. That was why she would not let me come near her. I forgot that she was truly the Swift One, and that in the art of climbing she had been my teacher. I pursued her from tree to tree, and ever she eluded me, peeping back at me with kindly eyes, making soft sounds, and dancing and leaping and teetering before me just out of reach. The more she eluded me, the more I wanted to catch her, and the lengthening shadows of the afternoon bore witness to the futility of my effort.

As I pursued her, or sometimes rested in an adjoining tree and watched her, I noticed the change in her. She was larger, heavier, more grown-up. Her lines were rounder, her muscles fuller, and there was about her that indefinite something of maturity that was new to her and that incited me on. Three years she had been gone -- three years at the very least, and the change in her was marked. I say three years; it is as near as I can measure the time. A fourth year may have elapsed, which I have confused with the happenings of the other three years. The more I think of it, the more confident I am that it must be four years that she was away.

Where she went, why she went, and what happened to her during that time, I do not know. There was no way for her to tell me, any more than there was a way for Lop-Ear and me to tell the Folk what we had seen when we were away. Like us, the chance is she had gone off on an adventure-journey, and by herself. On the other hand, it is possible that Red-Eye may have been the cause of her going. It is quite certain that he must have come upon her from time to time, wandering in the woods; and if he had pursued her there is no question but that it would have been sufficient to drive her away. From subsequent events, I am led to believe that she must have travelled far to the south, across a range of mountains and down to the banks of a strange river, away from any of her kind. Many Tree People lived down there, and I think it must have been they who finally drove her back to the horde and to me. My reasons for this I shall explain later.

The shadows grew longer, and I pursued more ardently than ever, and still I could not catch her. She made believe that she was trying desperately to escape me, and all the time she managed to keep just beyond reach. I forgot everything -- time, the oncoming of night, and my meat-eating enemies. I was insane with love of her, and with -- anger, too, because she would not let me come up with her. It was strange how this anger against her seemed to be part of my desire for her.

As I have said, I forgot everything. In racing across an open space I ran full tilt upon a colony of snakes. They did not deter me. I was mad. They struck at me, but I ducked and dodged and ran on. Then there was a python that ordinarily would have sent me screeching to a tree-top. He did run me into a tree; but the Swift One was going out of sight, and I sprang back to the ground and went on. It was a close shave. Then there was my old enemy, the hyena. From my conduct he was sure something was going to happen, and he followed me for an hour. Once we exasperated a band of wild pigs, and they took after us. The Swift One dared a wide leap between trees that was too much for me. I had to take to the ground. There were the pigs. I didn't care. I struck the earth within a yard of the nearest one. They flanked me as I ran, and chased me into two different trees out of the line of my pursuit of the Swift One. I ventured the ground again, doubled back, and crossed a wide open space, with the whole band grunting, bristling, and tusk-gnashing at my heels.

If I had tripped or stumbled in that open space, there would have been no chance for me. But I didn't. And I didn't care whether I did or not. I was in such mood that I would have faced old Saber-Tooth himself, or a score of arrow-shooting Fire People. Such was the madness of love.....with me. With the Swift One it was different. She was very wise. She did not take any real risks, and I remember, on looking back across the centuries to that wild love-chase, that when the pigs delayed me she did not run away very fast, but waited, rather, for me to take up the pursuit again. Also, she directed her retreat before me, going always in the direction she wanted to go.

At last came the dark. She led me around the mossy shoulder of a canyon wall that out-jutted among the trees. After that we penetrated a dense mass of underbrush that scraped and ripped me in passing. But she never ruffled a hair. She knew the way. In the midst of the thicket was a large oak. I was very close to her when she climbed it; and in the forks, in the nest-shelter I had sought so long and vainly, I caught her.

The hyena had taken our trail again, and he now sat down on the ground and made hungry noises. But we did not mind, and we laughed at him when he snarled and went away through the thicket. It was the spring-time, and the night noises were many and varied. As was the custom at that time of the year, there was much fighting among the animals. From the nest we could hear the squealing and neighing of wild horses, the trumpeting of elephants, and the roaring of lions. But the moon came out, and the air was warm, and we laughed and were unafraid.

I remember, next morning, that we came upon two ruffled cock-birds that fought so ardently that I went right up to them and caught them by their necks. Thus did the Swift One and I get our wedding breakfast. They were delicious. It was easy to catch birds in the spring of the year. There was one night that year when two elk fought in the moonlight, while the Swift One and I watched from the trees; and we saw a lion and lioness crawl up to them unheeded, and kill them as they fought.

There is no telling how long we might have lived in the Swift One's tree-shelter. But one day, while we were away, the tree was struck by lightning. Great limbs were riven, and the nest was demolished. I started to rebuild, but the Swift One would have nothing to do with it. As I was to learn, she was greatly afraid of lightning, and I could not persuade her back into the tree. So it came about, our honeymoon over, that we went to the caves to live. As Lop-Ear had evicted me from the cave when he got married, I now evicted him; and the Swift One and I settled down in it, while he slept at night in the connecting passage of the double cave.

And with our coming to live with the horde came trouble. Red-Eye had had I don't know how many wives since the Singing One. She had gone the way of the rest. At present he had a little, soft, spiritless thing that whimpered and wept all the time, whether he beat her or not; and her passing was a question of very little time. Before she passed, even, Red-Eye set his eyes on the Swift One; and when she passed, the persecution of the Swift One began.

Well for her that she was the Swift One, that she had that amazing aptitude for swift flight through the trees. She needed all her wisdom and daring in order to keep out of the clutches of Red-Eye. I could not help her. He was so powerful a monster that he could have torn me limb from limb. As it was, to my death I carried an injured shoulder that ached and went lame in rainy weather and that was a mark of his handiwork.

The Swift One was sick at the time I received this injury. It must have been a touch of the malaria from which we sometimes suffered; but whatever it was, it made her dull and heavy. She did not have the accustomed spring to her muscles, and was indeed in poor shape for flight when Red-Eye cornered her near the lair of the wild dogs, several miles south from the caves. Usually, she would have circled around him, beaten him in the straight-away, and gained the protection of our small-mouthed cave. But she could not circle him. She was too dull and slow. Each time he headed her off, until she gave over the attempt and devoted her energies wholly to keeping out of his clutches.

Had she not been sick it would have been child's play for her to elude him; but as it was, it required all her caution and cunning. It was to her advantage that she could travel on thinner branches than he, and make wider leaps. Also, she was an unerring judge of distance, and she had an instinct for knowing the strength of twigs, branches, and rotten limbs.

It was an interminable chase. Round and round and back and forth for long stretches through the forest they dashed. There was great excitement among the other Folk. They set up a wild chattering, that was loudest when Red-Eye was at a distance, and that hushed when the chase led him near. They were impotent onlookers. The females screeched and gibbered, and the males beat their chests in helpless rage. Big Face was especially angry, and though he hushed his racket when Red-Eye drew near, he did not hush it to the extent the others did.

As for me, I played no brave part. I know I was anything but a hero. Besides, of what use would it have been for me to encounter Red-Eye? He was the mighty monster, the abysmal brute, and there was no hope for me in a conflict of strength. He would have killed me, and the situation would have remained unchanged. He would have caught the Swift One before she could have gained the cave. As it was, I could only look on in helpless fury, and dodge out of the way and cease my raging when he came too near.

The hours passed. It was late afternoon. And still the chase went on. Red-Eye was bent upon exhausting the Swift One. He deliberately ran her down. After a long time she began to tire and could no longer maintain her headlong flight. Then it was that she began going far out on the thinnest branches, where he could not follow. Thus she might have got a breathing spell, but Red-Eye was fiendish. Unable to follow her, he dislodged her by shaking her off. With all his strength and weight, he would shake the branch back and forth until he snapped her off as one would snap a fly from a whip-lash. The first time, she saved herself by falling into branches lower down. Another time, though they did not save her from the ground, they broke her fall. Still another time, so fiercely did he snap her from the branch, she was flung clear across a gap into another tree. It was remarkable, the way she gripped and saved herself. Only when driven to it did she seek the temporary safety of the thin branches. But she was so tired that she could not otherwise avoid him, and time after time she was compelled to take to the thin branches.

Still the chase went on, and still the Folk screeched, beat their chests, and gnashed their teeth. Then came the end. It was almost twilight. Trembling, panting, struggling for breath, the Swift One clung pitiably to a high thin branch. It was thirty feet to the ground, and nothing intervened. Red-Eye swung back and forth on the branch farther down. It became a pendulum, swinging wider and wider with every lunge of his weight. Then he reversed suddenly, just before the downward swing was completed. Her grips were torn loose, and, screaming, she was hurled toward the ground.

But she righted herself in mid-air and descended feet first. Ordinarily, from such a height, the spring in her legs would have eased the shock of impact with the ground. But she was exhausted. She could not exercise this spring. Her legs gave under her, having only partly met the shock, and she crashed on over on her side. This, as it turned out, did not injure her, but it did knock the breath from her lungs. She lay helpless and struggling for air.

Red-Eye rushed upon her and seized her. With his gnarly fingers twisted into the hair of her head, he stood up and roared in triumph and defiance at the awed Folk that watched from the trees. Then it was that I went mad. Caution was thrown to the winds; forgotten was the will to live of my flesh. Even as Red-Eye roared, from behind I dashed upon him. So unexpected was my charge that I knocked him off his feet. I twined my arms and legs around him and strove to hold him down. This would have been impossible to accomplish had he not held tightly with one hand to the Swift One's hair.

Encouraged by my conduct, Big-Face became a sudden ally. He charged in, sank his teeth in Red-Eye's arm, and ripped and tore at his face. This was the time for the rest of the Folk to have joined in. It was the chance to do for Red-Eye for all time. But they remained afraid in the trees.

It was inevitable that Red-Eye should win in the struggle against the two of us. The reason he did not finish us off immediately was that the Swift One clogged his movements. She had regained her breath and was beginning to resist. He would not release his clutch on her hair, and this handicapped him. He got a grip on my arm. It was the beginning of the end for me. He began to draw me toward him into a position where he could sink his teeth into my throat. His mouth was open, and he was grinning. And yet, though he had just begun to exert his strength, in that moment he wrenched my shoulder so that I suffered from it for the remainder of my life.

And in that moment something happened. There was no warning. A great body smashed down upon the four of us locked together. We were driven violently apart and rolled over and over, and in the suddenness of surprise we released our holds on one another. At the moment of the shock, Big-Face screamed terribly. I did not know what had happened, though I smelled tiger and caught a glimpse of striped fur as I sprang for a tree.

It was old Saber-Tooth. Aroused in his lair by the noise we had made, he had crept upon us unnoticed. The Swift One gained the next tree to mine, and I immediately joined her. I put my arms around her and held her close to me while she whimpered and cried softly. From the ground came a snarling, and crunching of bones. It was Saber-Tooth making his supper off of what had been Big-Face. From beyond, with inflamed rims and eyes, Red-Eye peered down. Here was a monster mightier than he. The Swift One and I turned and went away quietly through the trees toward the cave, while the Folk gathered overhead and showered down abuse and twigs and branches upon their ancient enemy. He lashed his tail and snarled, but went on eating.

And in such fashion were we saved. It was a mere accident -- the sheerest accident. Else would I have died, there in Red-Eye's clutch, and there would have been no bridging of time to the tune of a thousand centuries down to a progeny that reads newspapers and rides on electric cars -- ay, and that writes narratives of bygone happenings even as this is written.

Chapter 17

It was in the early fall of the following year that it happened. After his failure to get the Swift One, Red-Eye had taken another wife; and, strange to relate, she was still alive. Stranger still, they had a baby several months old -- Red-Eye's first child. His previous wives had never lived long enough to bear him children. The year had gone well for all of us. The weather had been exceptionally mild and food plentiful. I remember especially the turnips of that year. The nut crop was also very heavy, and the wild plums were larger and sweeter than usual.

In short, it was a golden year. And then it happened. It was in the early morning, and we were surprised in our caves. In the chill gray light we awoke from sleep, most of us, to encounter death. The Swift One and I were aroused by a pandemonium of screeching and gibbering. Our cave was the highest of all on the cliff, and we crept to the mouth and peered down. The open space was filled with the Fire People. Their cries and yells were added to the clamor, but they had order and plan, while we Folk had none. Each one of us fought and acted for himself, and no one of us knew the extent of the calamity that was befalling us.

By the time we got to stone-throwing, the Fire People had massed thick at the base of the cliff. Our first volley must have mashed some heads, for when they swerved back from the cliff three of their number were left upon the ground. These were struggling and floundering, and one was trying to crawl away. But we fixed them. By this time we males were roaring with rage, and we rained rocks upon the three men that were down. Several of the Fire-Men returned to drag them into safety, but our rocks drove the rescuers back.

The Fire People became enraged. Also, they became cautious. In spite of their angry yells, they kept at a distance and sent flights of arrows against us. This put an end to the rock-throwing. By the time half a dozen of us had been killed and a score injured, the rest of us retreated inside our caves. I was not out of range in my lofty cave, but the distance was great enough to spoil effective shooting, and the Fire People did not waste many arrows on me. Furthermore, I was curious. I wanted to see. While the Swift One remained well inside the cave, trembling with fear and making low wailing sounds because I would not come in, I crouched at the entrance and watched.

The fighting had now become intermittent. It was a sort of deadlock. We were in the caves, and the question with the Fire People was how to get us out. They did not dare come in after us, and in general we would not expose ourselves to their arrows. Occasionally, when one of them drew in close to the base of the cliff, one or another of the Folk would smash a rock down. In return, he would be transfixed by half a dozen arrows. This ruse worked well for some time, but finally the Folk no longer were inveigled into showing themselves. The deadlock was complete.

Behind the Fire People I could see the little wizened old hunter directing it all. They obeyed him, and went here and there at his commands. Some of them went into the forest and returned with loads of dry wood, leaves, and grass. All the Fire People drew in closer. While most of them stood by with bows and arrows, ready to shoot any of the Folk that exposed themselves, several of the Fire-Men heaped the dry grass and wood at the mouths of the lower tier of caves. Out of these heaps they conjured the monster we feared -- *fire*. At first, wisps of smoke arose and curled up the cliff. Then I could see the red-tongued flames darting in and out through the wood like tiny snakes. The smoke grew thicker and thicker, at times shrouding the whole face of the cliff. But I was high up and it did not bother me much, though it stung my eyes and I rubbed them with my knuckles.

Old Marrow-Bone was the first to be smoked out. A light fan of air drifted the smoke away at the time so that I saw clearly. He broke out through the smoke, stepping on a burning coal and screaming with the sudden hurt of it, and essayed to climb up the cliff. The arrows showered about him. He came to a pause on a ledge, clutching a knob of rock for support, gasping and sneezing and shaking his head. He swayed back and forth. The feathered ends of a dozen arrows were sticking out of him. He was an old man, and he did not want to die. He swayed wider and wider, his knees giving under him, and as he swayed he wailed most plaintively. His hand released its grip and he lurched outward to the fall. His old bones must have been sadly broken. He groaned and strove feebly to rise, but a Fire-Man rushed in upon him and brained him with a club.

And as it happened with Marrow-Bone, so it happened with many of the Folk. Unable to endure the smoke-suffocation, they rushed out to fall beneath the arrows. Some of the women and children remained in the caves to strangle to death, but the majority met death outside.

When the Fire-Men had in this fashion cleared the first tier of caves, they began making arrangements to duplicate the operation on the second tier of caves. It was while they were climbing up with their grass and wood, that Red-Eye, followed by his wife, with the baby holding to her tightly, made a successful flight up the cliff. The Fire-Men must have concluded that in the interval between the smoking-out operations we would remain in our caves; so that they were unprepared, and their arrows did not begin to fly till Red-Eye and his wife were well up the wall. When he reached the top, he turned about and glared down at them, roaring and beating his chest. They arched their arrows at him, and though he was untouched he fled on.

I watched a third tier smoked out, and a fourth. A few of the Folk escaped up the cliff, but most of them were shot off the face of it as they strove to climb. I remember Long-Lip. He got as far as my ledge, crying piteously, an arrow clear through his chest, the feathered shaft sticking out behind, the bone head sticking out before, shot through the back as he climbed. He sank down on my ledge bleeding profusely at the mouth.

It was about this time that the upper tiers seemed to empty themselves spontaneously. Nearly all the Folk not yet smoked out stampeded up the cliff at the same time. This was the saving of many. The Fire People could not shoot arrows fast enough. They filled the air with arrows, and scores of the stricken Folk came tumbling down; but still there were a few who reached the top and got away.

The impulse of flight was now stronger in me than curiosity. The arrows had ceased flying. The last of the Folk seemed gone, though there may have been a few still hiding in the upper caves. The Swift One and I started to make a scramble for the cliff-top. At sight of us a great cry went up from the Fire People. This was not caused by me, but by the Swift One. They were chattering excitedly and pointing her out to one another. They did not try to shoot her. Not an arrow was discharged. They began calling softly and coaxingly. I stopped and looked down. She was afraid, and whimpered and urged me on. So we went up over the top and plunged into the trees.

This event has often caused me to wonder and speculate. If she were really of their kind, she must have been lost from them at a time when she was too young to remember, else would she not have been afraid of them. On the other hand, it may well have been that while she was their kind she had never been lost from them; that she had been born in the wild forest far from their haunts, her father maybe a renegade Fire-Man, her mother maybe one of my own kind, one of the Folk. But who shall say? These things are beyond me, and the Swift One knew no more about them than did I.

We lived through a day of terror. Most of the survivors fled toward the blueberry swamp and took refuge in the forest in that neighborhood. And all day hunting parties of the Fire People ranged the forest, killing us wherever they found us. It must have been a deliberately executed plan. Increasing beyond the limits of their own territory, they had decided on making a conquest of ours. Sorry the conquest! We had no chance against them. It was slaughter, indiscriminate slaughter, for they spared none, killing old and young, effectively ridding the land of our presence.

It was like the end of the world to us. We fled to the trees as a last refuge, only to be surrounded and killed, family by family. We saw much of this during that day, and besides, I wanted to see. The Swift One and I never remained long in one tree, and so escaped being surrounded. But there seemed no place to go. The Fire-Men were everywhere, bent on their task of extermination. Every way we turned we encountered them, and because of this we saw much of their handiwork.

I did not see what became of my mother, but I did see the Chatterer shot down out of the old home-tree. And I am afraid that at the sight I did a bit of joyous teetering. Before I leave this portion of my narrative, I must tell of Red-Eye. He was caught with his wife in a tree down by the blueberry swamp. The Swift One and I stopped long enough in our flight to see. The Fire-Men were too intent upon their work to notice us, and, furthermore, we were well screened by the thicket in which we crouched.

Fully a score of the hunters were under the tree, discharging arrows into it. They always picked up their arrows when they fell back to earth. I could not see Red-Eye, but I could hear him howling from somewhere in the tree.

After a short interval his howling grew muffled. He must have crawled into a hollow in the trunk. But his wife did not win this shelter. An arrow brought her to the ground. She was severely hurt, for she made no effort to get away. She crouched in a sheltering way over her baby (which clung tightly to her), and made pleading signs and sounds to the Fire-Men. They gathered about her and laughed at her -- even as Lop-Ear and I had laughed at the old Tree-Man. And even as we had poked him with twigs and sticks, so did the Fire-Men with Red-Eye's wife. They poked her with the ends of their bows, and prodded her in the ribs. But she was poor fun. She would not fight. Nor, for that matter, would she get angry. She continued to crouch over her baby and to plead. One of the Fire-Men stepped close to her. In his hand was a club. She saw and understood, but she made only the pleading sounds until the blow fell.

Red-Eye, in the hollow of the trunk, was safe from their arrows. They stood together and debated for a while, then one of them climbed into the tree. What happened up there I could not tell, but I heard him yell and saw the excitement of those that remained beneath. After several minutes his body crashed down to the ground. He did not move. They looked at him and raised his head, but it fell back limply when they let go. Red-Eye had accounted for himself.

They were very angry. There was an opening into the trunk close to the ground. They gathered wood and grass and built a fire. The Swift One and I, our arms around each other, waited and watched in the thicket. Sometimes they threw upon the fire green branches with many leaves, whereupon the smoke became very thick.

We saw them suddenly swerve back from the tree. They were not quick enough. Red-Eye's flying body landed in the midst of them.

He was in a frightful rage, smashing about with his long arms right and left. He pulled the face off one of them, literally pulled it off with those gnarly fingers of his and those tremendous muscles. He bit another through the neck. The Fire-Men fell back with wild fierce yells, then rushed upon him. He managed to get hold of a club and began crushing heads like eggshells. He was too much for them, and they were compelled to fall back again. This was his chance, and he turned his back upon them and ran for it, still howling wrathfully. A few arrows sped after him, but he plunged into a thicket and was gone.

The Swift One and I crept quietly away, only to run foul of another party of Fire-Men. They chased us into the blueberry swamp, but we knew the tree-paths across the farther morasses where they could not follow on the ground, and so we escaped. We came out on the other side into a narrow strip of forest that separated the blueberry swamp from the great swamp that extended westward.

Here we met Lop-Ear. How he had escaped I cannot imagine, unless he had not slept the preceding night at the caves.

Here, in the strip of forest, we might have built tree-shelters and settled down; but the Fire People were performing their work of extermination thoroughly. In the afternoon, Hair-Face and his wife fled out from among the trees to the east, passed us, and were gone. They fled silently and swiftly, with alarm in their faces. In the direction from which they had come we heard the cries and yells of the hunters, and the screeching of some one of the Folk. The Fire People had found their way across the swamp.

The Swift One, Lop-Ear, and I followed on the heels of Hair-Face and his wife. When we came to the edge of the great swamp, we stopped. We did not know its paths. It was outside our territory, and it had been always avoided by the Folk. None had ever gone into it -- at least, to return. In our minds it represented mystery and fear, the terrible unknown. As I say, we stopped at the edge of it. We were afraid. The cries of the Fire-Men were drawing nearer. We looked at one another. Hair-Face ran out on the quaking morass and gained the firmer footing of a grass-hummock a dozen yards away.

His wife did not follow. She tried to, but shrank back from the treacherous surface and cowered down.

The Swift One did not wait for me, nor did she pause till she had passed beyond Hair-Face a hundred yards and gained a much larger hummock. By the time Lop-Ear and I had caught up with her, the Fire-Men appeared among the trees. Hair-Face's wife, driven by them into panic terror, dashed after us. But she ran blindly, without caution, and broke through the crust. We turned and watched, and saw them shoot her with arrows as she sank down in the mud. The arrows began falling about us. Hair-Face had now joined us, and the four of us plunged on, we knew not whither, deeper and deeper into the swamp.

Chapter 18

Of our wanderings in the great swamp I have no clear knowledge. When I strive to remember, I have a riot of unrelated impressions and a loss of time-value. I have no idea of how long we were in that vast everglade, but it must have been for weeks. My memories of what occurred invariably take the form of nightmare. For untold ages, oppressed by protean fear, I am aware of wandering, endlessly wandering, through a dank and soggy wilderness, where poisonous snakes struck at us, and animals roared around us, and the mud quaked under us and sucked at our heels.

I know that we were turned from our course countless times by streams and lakes and slimy seas. Then there were storms and risings of the water over great areas of the low-lying lands; and there were periods of hunger and misery when we were kept prisoners in the trees for days and days by these transient floods.

Very strong upon me is one picture. Large trees are about us, and from their branches hang gray filaments of moss, while great creepers, like monstrous serpents, curl around the trunks and writhe in tangles through the air. And all about is the mud, soft mud, that bubbles forth gases, and that heaves and sighs with internal agitations. And in the midst of all this are a dozen of us. We are lean and wretched, and our bones show through our tight-stretched skins. We do not sing and chatter and laugh. We play no pranks. For once our volatile and exuberant spirits are hopelessly subdued. We make plaintive, querulous noises, look at one another, and cluster close together. It is like the meeting of the handful of survivors after the day of the end of the world.

This event is without connection with the other events in the swamp. How we ever managed to cross it, I do not know, but at last we came out where a low range of hills ran down to the bank of the river. It was our river emerging like ourselves from the great swamp. On the south bank, where the river had broken its way through the hills, we found many sand-stone caves. Beyond, toward the west, the ocean boomed on the bar that lay across the river's mouth. And here, in the caves, we settled down in our abiding-place by the sea.

There were not many of us. From time to time, as the days went by, more of the Folk appeared. They dragged themselves from the swamp singly, and in twos and threes, more dead than alive, mere perambulating skeletons, until at last there were thirty of us. Then no more came from the swamp, and Red-Eye was not among us. It was noticeable that no children had survived the frightful journey.

I shall not tell in detail of the years we lived by the sea. It was not a happy abiding-place. The air was raw and chill, and we suffered continually from coughing and colds. We could not survive in such an environment. True, we had children; but they had little hold on life and died early, while we died faster than new ones were born. Our number steadily diminished.

Then the radical change in our diet was not good for us. We got few vegetables and fruits, and became fish-eaters. There were mussels and abalones and clams and rock-oysters, and great ocean-crabs that were thrown upon the beaches in stormy weather. Also, we found several kinds of seaweed that were good to eat. But the change in diet caused us stomach troubles, and none of us ever waxed fat. We were all lean and dyspeptic-looking. It was in getting the big abalones that Lop-Ear was lost. One of them closed upon his fingers at low-tide, and then the flood-tide came in and drowned him. We found his body the next day, and it was a lesson to us. Not another one of us was ever caught in the closing shell of an abalone.

The Swift One and I managed to bring up one child, a boy -- at least we managed to bring him along for several years. But I am quite confident he could never have survived that terrible climate. And then, one day, the Fire People appeared again. They had come down the river, not on a catamaran, but in a rude dug-out. There were three of them that paddled in it, and one of them was the little wizened old hunter. They landed on our beach, and he limped across the sand and examined our caves.

They went away in a few minutes, but the Swift One was badly scared. We were all frightened, but none of us to the extent that she was. She whimpered and cried and was restless all that night. In the morning she took the child in her arms, and by sharp cries, gestures, and example, started me on our second long flight. There were eight of the Folk (all that was left of the horde) that remained behind in the caves. There was no hope for them. Without doubt, even if the Fire People did not return, they must soon have perished. It was a bad climate down there by the sea. The Folk were not constituted for the coast-dwelling life.

We travelled south, for days skirting the great swamp but never venturing into it. Once we broke back to the westward, crossing a range of mountains and coming down to the coast. But it was no place for us. There were no trees -- only bleak headlands, a thundering surf, and strong winds that seemed never to cease from blowing. We turned back across the mountains, travelling east and south, until we came in touch with the great swamp again.

Soon we gained the southern extremity of the swamp, and we continued our course south and east. It was a pleasant land. The air was warm, and we were again in the forest. Later on we crossed a low-lying range of hills and found ourselves in an even better forest country. The farther we penetrated from the coast the warmer we found it, and we went on and on until we came to a large river that seemed familiar to the Swift One. It was where she must have come during the four years' absence from the horde. This river we crossed on logs, landing on side at the large bluff. High up on the bluff we found our new home most difficult of access and quite hidden from any eye beneath.

There is little more of my tale to tell. Here the Swift One and I lived and reared our family. And here my memories end. We never made another migration. I never dream beyond our high, inaccessible cave. And here must have been born the child that inherited the stuff of my dreams, that had moulded into its being all the impressions of my life -- or of the life of Big-Tooth, rather, who is my other-self, and not my real self, but who is so real to me that often I am unable to tell what age I am living in.

I often wonder about this line of descent. I, the modern, am incontestably a man; yet I, Big-Tooth, the primitive, am not a man. Somewhere, and by straight line of descent, these two parties to my dual personality were connected. Were the Folk, before their destruction, in the process of becoming men? And did I and mine carry through this process? On the other hand, may not some descendant of mine have gone in to the Fire People and become one of them? I do not know. There is no way of learning. One thing only is certain, and that is that Big-Tooth did stamp into the cerebral constitution of one of his progeny all the impressions of his life, and stamped them in so indelibly that the hosts of intervening generations have failed to obliterate them.

There is one other thing of which I must speak before I close. It is a dream that I dream often, and in point of time the real event must have occurred during the period of my living in the high, inaccessible cave. I remember that I wandered far in the forest toward the east. There I came upon a tribe of Tree People. I crouched in a thicket and watched them at play. They were holding a laughing council, jumping up and down and screeching rude choruses.

Suddenly they hushed their noise and ceased their capering. They shrank down in fear, and quested anxiously about with their eyes for a way of retreat. Then Red-Eye walked in among them. They cowered away from him. All were frightened. But he made no attempt to hurt them. He was one of them. At his heels, on stringy bended legs, supporting herself with knuckles to the ground on either side, walked an old female of the Tree People, his latest wife. He sat down in the midst of the circle. I can see him now, as I write this, scowling, his eyes inflamed, as he peers about him at the circle of the Tree People. And as he peers he crooks one monstrous leg and with his gnarly toes scratches himself on the stomach. He is Red-Eye, the atavism.

Stories

The Scarlet Plague

1

The way led along upon what had once been the embankment of a railroad. But no train had run upon it for many years. The forest on either side swelled up the slopes of the embankment and crested across it in a green wave of trees and bushes. The trail was as narrow as a man's body, and was no more than a wild-animal runway.

Occasionally, a piece of rusty iron, showing through the forest-mold, advertised that the rail and the ties still remained. In one place, a ten-inch tree, bursting through at a connection, had lifted the end of a rail clearly into view. The tie had evidently followed the rail, held to it by the spike long enough for its bed to be filled with gravel and rotten leaves, so that now the crumbling, rotten timber thrust itself up at a curious slant. Old as the road was, it was manifest that it had been of the mono-rail type.

An old man and a boy travelled along this runway. They moved slowly, for the old man was very old, a touch of palsy made his movements tremulous, and he leaned heavily upon his staff. A rude skull-cap of goatskin protected his head from the sun. From beneath this fell a scant fringe of stained and dirty-white hair. A visor, ingeniously made from a large leaf, shielded his eyes, and from under this he peered at the way of his feet on the trail. His beard, which should have been snow-white but which showed the same weather-wear and camp-stain as his hair, fell nearly to his waist in a great tangled mass. About his chest and shoulders hung a single, mangy garment of goatskin. His arms and legs, withered and skinny, betokened extreme age, as well as did their sunburn and scars and scratches betoken long years of exposure to the elements.

The boy, who led the way, checking the eagerness of his muscles to the slow progress of the elder, likewise wore a single garment -- a ragged-edged piece of bearskin, with a hole in the middle through which he had thrust his head. He could not have been more than twelve years old.

Tucked coquettishly over one ear was the freshly severed tail of a pig.

In one hand he carried a medium-sized bow and an arrow. On his back was a quiverful of arrows. From a sheath hanging about his neck on a thong, projected the battered handle of a hunting knife. He was as brown as a berry, and walked softly, with almost a catlike tread. In marked contrast with his sunburned skin were his eyes -- blue, deep blue, but keen and sharp as a pair of gimlets. They seemed to bore into all about him in a way that was habitual. As he went along he smelled things, as well, his distended, quivering nostrils carrying to his brain an endless series of messages from the outside world. Also, his hearing was acute, and had been so trained that it operated automatically. Without conscious effort, he heard all the slight sounds in the apparent quiet -- heard, and differentiated, and classified these sounds -- whether they were of the wind rustling the leaves, of the humming of bees and gnats, of the distant rumble of the sea that drifted to him only in lulls, or of the gopher, just under his foot, shoving a pouchful of earth into the entrance of his hole.

Suddenly he became alertly tense. Sound, sight, and odor had given him a simultaneous warning. His hand went back to the old man, touching him, and the pair stood still. Ahead, at one side of the top of the embankment, arose a crackling sound, and the boy's gaze was fixed on the tops of the agitated bushes. Then a large bear, a grizzly, crashed into view, and likewise stopped abruptly, at sight of the humans. He did not like them, and growled querulously.

Slowly the boy fitted the arrow to the bow, and slowly he pulled the bowstring taut. But he never removed his eyes from the bear. The old man peered from under his green leaf at the danger, and stood as quietly as the boy. For a few seconds this mutual scrutinizing went on; then, the bear betraying a growing irritability, the boy, with a movement of his head, indicated that the old man must step aside from the trail and go down the embankment. The boy followed, going backward, still holding the bow taut and ready. They waited till a crashing among the bushes from the opposite side of the embankment told them the bear had gone on. The boy grinned as he led back to the trail.

"A big un, Granser," he chuckled.

The old man shook his head.

"They get thicker every day," he complained in, a thin, undependable falsetto. "Who'd have thought I'd live to see the time when a man would be afraid of his life on the way to the Cliff House? When I was a boy, Edwin, men and women and little babies used to come out here from San Francisco by tens of thousands on a nice day. And there weren't any bears then. No, sir. They used to pay money to look at them in cages, they were that rare."

"What is money, Granser?"

Before the old man could answer, the boy recollected and triumphantly shoved his hand into a pouch under his bearskin and pulled forth a battered and tarnished silver dollar. The old man's eyes glistened, as he held the coin close to them.

"I can't see," he muttered. "You look and see if you can make out the date, Edwin."

The boy laughed.

"You're a great Granser," he cried delightedly, "always making believe them little marks mean something."

The old man manifested an accustomed chagrin as he brought the coin back again close to his own eyes.

"2012," he shrilled, and then fell to cackling grotesquely. "That was the year Morgan the Fifth was appointed President of the United States by the Board of Magnates. It must have been one of the last coins minted, for the Scarlet Death came in 2013. Lord! Lord! -- think of it! Sixty years ago, and I am the only person alive to-day that lived in those times. Where did you find it, Edwin?"

The boy, who had been regarding him with the tolerant curiousness one accords to the prattlings of the feeble-minded, answered promptly.

"I got it off of Hoo-Hoo. He found it when we was herdin' goats down near San Jose last spring. Hoo-Hoo said it was money. Ain't you hungry, Granser?"

The ancient caught his staff in a tighter grip and urged along the trail, his old eyes shining greedily.

"I hope Hare-Lip's found a crab.....or two," he mumbled. "They're good eating, crabs, mighty good eating when you've no more teeth and you've got grandsons that love their old grandsire and make a point of catching crabs for him. When I was a boy -- "

But Edwin, suddenly stopped by what he saw, was drawing the bowstring on a fitted arrow. He had paused on the brink of a crevasse in the embankment. An ancient culvert had here washed out, and the stream, no longer confined, had cut a passage through the fill. On the opposite side, the end of a rail projected and overhung. It showed rustily through the creeping vines which overran it. Beyond, crouching by a bush, a rabbit looked across at him in trembling hesitancy. Fully fifty feet was the distance, but the arrow flashed true; and the transfixed rabbit, crying out in sudden fright and hurt, struggled painfully away into the brush. The boy himself was a flash of brown skin and flying fur as he bounded down the steep wall of the gap and up the other side. His lean muscles were springs of steel that released into graceful and efficient action. A hundred feet beyond, in a tangle of bushes, he overtook the wounded creature, knocked its head on a convenient tree-trunk, and turned it over to Granser to carry.

"Rabbit is good, very good," the ancient quavered, "but when it comes to a toothsome delicacy I prefer crab. When I was a boy -- "

"Why do you say so much that ain't got no sense?" Edwin impatiently interrupted the other's threatened garrulousness.

The boy did not exactly utter these words, but something that remotely resembled them and that was more guttural and explosive and economical of qualifying phrases. His speech showed distant kinship with that of the old man, and the latter's speech was approximately an English that had gone through a bath of corrupt usage.

"What I want to know," Edwin continued, "is why you call crab 'toothsome delicacy'? Crab is crab, ain't it? No one I never heard calls it such funny things."

The old man sighed but did not answer, and they moved on in silence.

The surf grew suddenly louder, as they emerged from the forest upon a stretch of sand dunes bordering the sea. A few goats were browsing among the sandy hillocks, and a skin-clad boy, aided by a wolfish-looking dog that was only faintly reminiscent of a collie, was watching them. Mingled with the roar of the surf was a continuous, deep-throated barking or bellowing, which came from a cluster of jagged rocks a hundred yards out from shore. Here huge sea-lions hauled themselves up to lie in the sun or battle with one another. In the immediate foreground arose the smoke of a fire, tended by a third savage-looking boy. Crouched near him were several wolfish dogs similar to the one that guarded the goats.

The old man accelerated his pace, sniffing eagerly as he neared the fire.

"Mussels!" He muttered ecstatically. "Mussels! And ain't that a crab, Hoo-Hoo? Ain't that a crab? My, my, you boys are good to your old grandsire."

Hoo-Hoo, who was apparently of the same age as Edwin, grinned.

"All you want, Granser. I got four."

The old man's palsied eagerness was pitiful. Sitting down in the sand as quickly as his stiff limbs would let him, he poked a large rock-mussel from out of the coals. The heat had forced its shells apart, and the meat, salmon-colored, was thoroughly cooked. Between thumb and forefinger, in trembling haste, he caught the morsel and carried it to his mouth. But it was too hot, and the next moment was violently ejected. The old man spluttered with the pain, and tears ran out of his eyes and down his cheeks.

The boys were true savages, possessing only the cruel humor of the savage. To them the incident was excruciatingly funny, and they burst into loud laughter. Hoo-Hoo danced up and down, while Edwin rolled gleefully on the ground. The boy with the goats came running to join in the fun.

"Set 'em to cool, Edwin, set 'em to cool," the old man besought, in the midst of his grief, making no attempt to wipe away the tears that flowed from his eyes. "And cool a crab, Edwin, too. You know your grandsire likes crabs."

From the coals arose a great sizzling, which proceeded from the many mussels bursting open their shells and exuding their moisture. They were large shellfish, running from three to six inches in length. The boys raked them out with sticks and placed them on a large piece of driftwood to cool.

"When I was a boy, we did not laugh at our elders; we respected them."

The boys took no notice, and Granser continued to babble an incoherent flow of complaint and censure. But this time he was more careful, and did not burn his mouth. All began to eat, using nothing but their hands and making loud mouth-noises and lip-smackings. The third boy, who was called Hare-Lip, slyly deposited a pinch of sand on a mussel the ancient was carrying to his mouth; and when the grit of it bit into the old fellow's mucous membrane and gums, the laughter was again uproarious. He was unaware that a joke had been played on him, and spluttered and spat until Edwin, relenting, gave him a gourd of fresh water with which to wash out his mouth.

"Where's them crabs, Hoo-Hoo?" Edwin demanded. "Granser's set upon having a snack."

Again Granser's eyes burned with greediness as a large crab was handed to him. It was a shell with legs and all complete, but the meat had long since departed. With shaky fingers and babblings of anticipation, the old man broke off a leg and found it filled with emptiness.

"The crabs, Hoo-Hoo?" He wailed. "The crabs?"

"I was foolin', Granser. They ain't no crabs. I never found one."

The boys were overwhelmed with delight at sight of the tears of senile disappointment that dribbled down the old man's cheeks.

Then, unnoticed, Hoo-Hoo replaced the empty shell with a fresh-cooked crab. Already dismembered, from the cracked legs the white meat sent forth a savory steam. This attracted amazement.

The change of his mood to one of joy was immediate. He snuffled and muttered and mumbled, making almost a croon of delight, as he began to eat. Of this the boys took little notice, for it was an accustomed spectacle. Nor did they notice his occasional exclamations and utterances of phrases which meant nothing to them, as, for instance, when he smacked his lips and champed his gums while muttering: "Mayonnaise! Just think -- mayonnaise! And it's sixty years since the last was ever made! Two generations and never a smell of it! Why, in those days it was served in every restaurant with crab."

When he could eat no more, the old man sighed, wiped his hands on his naked legs, and gazed out over the sea. With the content of a full stomach, he waxed reminiscent.

"To think of it! I've seen this beach alive with men, women, and children on a pleasant Sunday. And there weren't any bears to eat them up, either. And right up there on the cliff was a big restaurant where you could get anything you wanted to eat. Four million people lived in San Francisco then. And now, in the whole city and county there aren't forty all told. And out there on the sea were ships and ships always to be seen, going in for the Golden Gate or coming out.

And airships in the air -- dirigibles and flying machines. They could travel two hundred miles an hour. The mail contracts with the New York and San Francisco Limited demanded that for the minimum.

There was a chap, a Frenchman, I forget his name, who succeeded in making three hundred; but the thing was risky, too risky for conservative persons. But he was on the right clue, and he would have managed it if it hadn't been for the Great Plague. When I was a boy, there were men alive who remembered the coming of the first aeroplanes, and now I have lived to see the last of them, and that sixty years ago."

The old man babbled on, unheeded by the boys, who were long accustomed to his garrulousness, and whose vocabularies, besides, lacked the greater portion of the words he used. It was noticeable that in these rambling soliloquies his English seemed to recrudesce into better construction and phraseology. But when he talked directly with the boys it lapsed, largely, into their own uncouth and simpler forms.

"But there weren't many crabs in those days," the old man wandered on. "They were fished out, and they were great delicacies. The open season was only a month long, too. And now crabs are accessible the whole year around. Think of it -- catching all the crabs you want, any time you want, in the surf of the Cliff House beach!"

A sudden commotion among the goats brought the boys to their feet.

The dogs about the fire rushed to join their snarling fellow who guarded the goats, while the goats themselves stampeded in the direction of their human protectors. A half dozen forms, lean and gray, glided about on the sand hillocks or faced the bristling dogs.

Edwin arched an arrow that fell short. But Hare-Lip, with a sling such as David carried into battle against Goliath, hurled a stone through the air that whistled from the speed of its flight. It fell squarely among the wolves and caused them to slink away toward the dark depths of the eucalyptus forest.

The boys laughed and lay down again in the sand, while Granser sighed ponderously. He had eaten too much, and, with hands clasped on his paunch, the fingers interlaced, he resumed his maunderings.

"'The fleeting systems lapse like foam,'" he mumbled what was evidently a quotation. "That's it -- foam, and fleeting. All man's toil upon the planet was just so much foam. He domesticated the serviceable animals, destroyed the hostile ones, and cleared the land of its wild vegetation. And then be passed, and the flood of primordial life rolled back again, sweeping his handiwork away-the weeds and the forest inundated his fields, the beasts of prey swept over his flocks, and now there are wolves on the Cliff House beach." He was appalled by the thought. "Where four million people disported themselves, the wild wolves roam to-day, and the savage progeny of our loins, with prehistoric weapons, defend themselves against the fanged despoilers. Think of it! And all because of the Scarlet Death -- "

The adjective had caught Hare-Lip's ear.

"He's always saying that," he said to Edwin. "What is scarlet?"

"'The scarlet of the maples can shake me like the cry of bugles going by,'" the old man quoted.

"It's red," Edwin answered the question. "And you don't know it because you come from the Chauffeur Tribe. They never did know nothing, none of them. Scarlet is red -- I know that."

"Red is red, ain't it?" Hare-Lip grumbled. "Then what's the good of gettin' cocky and calling it scarlet?"

"Granser, what for do you always say so much what nobody knows?" He asked. "Scarlet ain't anything, but red is red. Why don't you say red, then?"

"Red is not the right word," was the reply. "The plague was scarlet. The whole face and body turned scarlet in a hour's time. Don't I know? Didn't I see enough of it? And I am telling you it was scarlet because -- well, because it was scarlet. There is no other word for it."

"Red is good enough for me," Hare-Lip muttered obstinately. "My dad calls red red, and he ought to know. He says everybody died of the Red Death."

"Your dad is a common fellow, descended from a common fellow," Granser retorted heatedly. "Don't I know the beginnings of the Chauffeurs? Your grandsire was a chauffeur, a servant, and without education. He worked for other persons. But your grandmother was of good stock, only the children did not take after her. Don't I remember when I first met them catching fish at Lake Temescal?"

"What is education?" Edwin asked.

"Calling red scarlet," Hare-Lip sneered, then returned to the attack on Granser. "My dad told me, an' he got it from his dad afore he croaked, that your wife was a Santa Rosan, an' that she was sure no account. He said she was a hash-slinger before the Red Death, though I don't know what a hash-slinger is. You can tell me, Edwin."

But Edwin shook his head in token of ignorance.

"It is true, she was a waitress," Granser acknowledged. "But she was a good woman, and your mother was her daughter. Women were very scarce in the days after the Plague. She was the only wife I could find, even if she was a hash-slinger, as your father calls it. But it is not nice to talk about our progenitors that way."

"Dad says that the wife of the first Chauffeur was a lady -- "

"What's a lady?" Hoo-Hoo demanded.

"A Lady's a Chauffeur squaw," was the quick reply of Hare-Lip.

"The first Chauffeur was Bill, a common fellow, as I said before," the old man expounded; "but his wife was a lady, a great lady. Before the Scarlet Death she was the wife of Van Warden. He was President of the Board of Industrial Magnates, and was one of the dozen men who ruled America. He was worth one billion, eight hundred millions of dollars -- coins like you have there in your pouch, Edwin. And then came the Scarlet Death, and his wife became the wife of Bill, the first Chauffeur. He used to beat her, too. I have seen it myself."

Hoo-Hoo, lying on his stomach and idly digging his toes in the sand, cried out and investigated, first, his toe-nail, and next, the small hole he had dug. The other two boys joined him, excavating the sand rapidly with their hands till there lay three skeletons exposed. Two were of adults, the third being that of a part-grown child. The old man nudged along on the ground and peered at the find.

"Plague victims," he announced. "That's the way they died everywhere in the last days. This must have been a family, running away from the contagion and perishing here on the Cliff House beach. They -- what are you doing, Edwin?"

This question was asked in sudden dismay, as Edwin, using the back of his hunting knife, began to knock out the teeth from the jaws of one of the skulls.

"Going to string 'em," was the response.

The three boys were now hard at it; and quite a knocking and hammering arose, in which Granser babbled on unnoticed.

"You are true savages. Already has begun the custom of wearing human teeth. In another generation you will be perforating your noses and ears and wearing ornaments of bone and shell. I know. The human race is doomed to sink back farther and farther into the primitive night ere again it begins its bloody climb upward to civilization. When we increase and feel the lack of room, we will proceed to kill one another.

And then I suppose you will wear human scalp-locks at your waist, as well -- as you, Edwin, who are the gentlest of my grandsons, have already begun with that vile pigtail. Throw it away, Edwin, boy; throw it away."

"What a gabble the old geezer makes," Hare-Lip remarked, when, the teeth all extracted, they began an attempt at equal division. They were very quick and abrupt in their actions, and their speech, in moments of hot discussion over the allotment of the choicer teeth, was truly a gabble. They spoke in monosyllables and short jerky sentences that was more a gibberish than a language. And yet, through it ran hints of grammatical construction, and appeared vestiges of the conjugation of some superior culture. Even the speech of Granser was so corrupt that were it put down literally it would be almost so much nonsense to the reader. This, however, was when he talked with the boys. When he got into the full swing of babbling to himself, it slowly purged itself into pure English. The sentences grew longer and were enunciated with a rhythm and ease that was reminiscent of the lecture platform.

"Tell us about the Red Death, Granser," Hare-Lip demanded, when the teeth affair had been satisfactorily concluded.

"The Scarlet Death," Edwin corrected.

"An' don't work all that funny lingo on us," Hare-Lip went on. "Talk sensible, Granser, like a Santa Rosan ought to talk. Other Santa Rosans don't talk like you."

2

The old man showed pleasure in being thus called upon. He cleared his throat and began.

"Twenty or thirty years ago my story was in great demand. But in these days nobody seems interested -- "

"There you go!" Hare-Lip cried hotly. "Cut out the funny stuff and talk sensible. What's interested? You talk like a baby that don't know how."

"Let him alone," Edwin urged, "or he'll get mad and won't talk at all. Skip the funny places. We'll catch on to some of what he tells us."

"Let her go, Granser," Hoo-Hoo encouraged; for the old man was already maundering about the disrespect for elders and the reversion to cruelty of all humans that fell from high culture to primitive conditions.

The tale began.

"There were very many people in the world in those days. San Francisco alone held four millions -- "

"What is millions?" Edwin interrupted.

Granser looked at him kindly.

"I know you cannot count beyond ten, so I will tell you. Hold up your two hands. On both of them you have altogether ten fingers and thumbs. Very well. I now take this grain of sand -- you hold it, Hoo-Hoo." He dropped the grain of sand into the lad's palm and went on. "Now that grain of sand stands for the ten fingers of Edwin. I add another grain. That's ten more fingers. And I add another, and another, and another, until I have added as many grains as Edwin has fingers and thumbs. That makes what I call one hundred. Remember that word-one hundred. Now I put this pebble in Hare-Lip's hand. It stands for ten grains of sand, or ten tens of fingers, or one hundred fingers. I put in ten pebbles. They stand for a thousand fingers. I take a mussel-shell, and it stands for ten pebbles, or one hundred grains of sand, or one thousand fingers...."

And so on, laboriously, and with much reiteration, he strove to build up in their minds a crude conception of numbers. As the quantities increased, he had the boys holding different magnitudes in each of their hands. For still higher sums, he laid the symbols on the log of driftwood; and for symbols he was hard put, being compelled to use the teeth from the skulls for millions, and the crab-shells for billions.

It was here that he stopped, for the boys were showing signs of becoming tired.

"There were four million people in San Francisco -- four teeth."

The boys' eyes ranged along from the teeth and from hand to hand, down through the pebbles and sand-grains to Edwin's fingers. And back again they ranged along the ascending series in the effort to grasp such inconceivable numbers.

"That was a lot of folks, Granser," Edwin at last hazarded.

"Like sand on the beach here, like sand on the beach, each grain of sand a man, or woman, or child. Yes, my boy, all those people lived right here in San Francisco. And at one time or another all those people came out on this very beach -- more people than there are grains of sand. More -- more -- more. And San Francisco was a noble city. And across the bay -- where we camped last year, even more people lived, clear from Point Richmond, on the level ground and on the hills, all the way around to San Leandro -- one great city of seven million people. -- Seven teeth ... there, that's it, seven millions."

Again the boys' eyes ranged up and down from Edwin's fingers to the teeth on the log.

"The world was full of people. The census of 2010 gave eight billions for the whole world -- eight crab-shells, yes, eight billions. It was not like today. Mankind knew a great deal more about getting food. And the more food there was, the more people there were. In the year 1800, there were one hundred and seventy millions in Europe alone. One hundred years later -- a grain of sand, Hoo-Hoo -- one hundred years later, at 1900, there were five hundred millions in Europe-five grains of sand, Hoo-Hoo, and this one tooth. This shows how easy was the getting of food, and how men increased. And in the year 2000, there were fifteen hundred millions in Europe. And it was the same all over the rest of the world. Eight crab-shells there, yes, eight billion people were alive on the earth when the Scarlet Death began.

"I was a young man when the Plague came-twenty-seven years old; and I lived on the other side of San Francisco Bay, in Berkeley. You remember those great stone houses, Edwin, when we came down the hills from Contra Costa? That was where I lived, in those stone houses. I was a professor of English literature."

Much of this was over the heads of the boys, but they strove to comprehend dimly this tale of the past.

"What was them stone houses for?" Hare-Lip queried.

"You remember when your dad taught you to swim?" The boy nodded. "Well, in the University of California -- that is the name we had for the houses -- we taught young men and women how to think, just as I have taught you now, by sand and pebbles and shells, to know how many people lived in those days. There was very much to teach. The young men and women we taught were called students. We had large rooms in which we taught. I talked to them, forty or fifty at a time, just as I am talking to you now. I told them about the books other men had written before their time, and even, sometimes, in their time -- "

"Was that all you did? -- just talk, talk, talk?" Hoo-Hoo demanded.

"Who hunted your meat for you? And milked the goats? And caught the fish?"

"A sensible question, Hoo-Hoo, a sensible question. As I have told you, in those days food-getting was easy. We were very wise. A few men got the food for many men. The other men did other things. As you say, I talked. I talked all the time, and for this food was given me-much food, fine food, beautiful food, food that I have not tasted in sixty years and shall never taste again. I sometimes think the most wonderful achievement of our tremendous civilization was food -- its inconceivable abundance, its infinite variety, its marvellous delicacy. Oh my grandsons, life was life in those days, when we had such wonderful things to eat."

This was beyond the boys, and they let it slip by, words and thoughts, as a mere senile wandering in the narrative.

"Our food-getters were called freemen. This was a joke. We of the ruling classes owned all the land, all the machines, everything. These food-getters were our slaves. We took almost all the food they got, and left them a little so that they might eat, and work, and get us more food -- "

"I'd have gone into the forest and got food for myself," Hare-Lip announced; "and if any man tried to take it away from me, I'd have killed him"

The old man laughed.

"Did I not tell you that we of the ruling class owned all the land, all the forest, everything? Any food-getter who would not get food for us, him we punished or compelled to starve to death. And very few did that. They preferred to get food for us, and make clothes for us, and prepare and administer to us a thousand -- a mussel-shell, Hoo-Hoo -- a thousand satisfactions and delights. And I was Professor Smith in those days -- Professor James Howard Smith. And my lecture courses were very popular -- that is, very many of the young men and women liked to hear me talk about the books other men had written.

"And I was very happy, and I had beautiful things to eat. And my hands were soft, because I did no work with them, and my body was clean all over and dressed in the softest garments -- " He surveyed his mangy goatskin with disgust. "We did not wear such things in those days. Even the slaves had better garments. And we were most clean. We washed our faces and hands often every day. You boys never wash unless you fall into the water or go in swimming."

"Neither do you, Granser," Hoo-Hoo retorted.

"I know, I know. I am a filthy old man. But times have changed. Nobody washes these days, and there are no conveniences. It is sixty years since I have seen a piece of soap. You do not know what soap is, and I shall not tell you, for I am telling the story of the Scarlet Death. You know what sickness is. We called it a disease. Very many of the diseases came from what we called germs. Remember that word-germs. A germ is a very small thing. It is like a wood tick, such as you find on the dogs in the spring of the year when they run in the forest. Only the germ is very small. It is so small that you cannot see it -- "

Hoo-Hoo began to laugh.

"You're a queer un, Granser, talking about things you can't see. If you can't see 'em, how do you know they are? That's what I want to know. How do you know anything you can't see?"

"A good question, a very good question, Hoo-Hoo. But we did see some of them. We had what we called microscopes and ultramicroscopes, and we put them to our eyes and looked through them, so that we saw things larger than they really were, and many things we could not see without the microscopes at all. Our best ultramicroscopes could make a germ look forty thousand times larger.

A mussel-shell is a thousand fingers like Edwin's. Take forty mussel-shells, and by as many times larger was the germ when we looked at it through a microscope. And after that, we had other ways, by using what we called moving pictures, of making the forty-thousand-times germ many, many thousand times larger still.

And thus we saw all these things which our eyes of themselves could not see. Take a grain of sand. Break it into ten pieces. Take one piece and break it into ten. Break one of those pieces into ten, and one of those into ten, and one of those into ten, and one of those into ten, and do it all day, and maybe, by sunset, you will have a piece as small as one of the germs."

The boys were openly incredulous. Hare-Lip sniffed and sneered and Hoo-Hoo snickered, until Edwin nudged them to be silent.

"The wood tick sucks the blood of the dog, but the germ, being so very small, goes right into the blood of the body, and there it has many children. In those days there would be as many as a billion -- a crab-shell, please -- as many as that crab-shell in one man's body. We called germs micro-organisms. When a few million, or a billion, of them were in a man, in all the blood of a man, he was sick. These germs were a disease. There were many different kinds of them-more different kinds than there are grains of sand on this beach. We knew only a few of the kinds. The micro-organic world was an invisible world, a world we could not see, and we knew very little about it.

Yet we did know something. There was the *bacillus anthracis*; there was the *micrococcus*; there was the *bacterium termo*, and the *bacterium lactis* -- that's what turns the goat milk sour even to this day, Hare-Lip; and there were *schizomycetes* without end. And there were many others...."

Here the old man launched into a disquisition on germs and their natures, using words and phrases of such extraordinary length and meaninglessness, that the boys grinned at one another and looked out over the deserted ocean till they forgot the old man was babbling on.

"But the Scarlet Death, Granser," Edwin at last suggested.

Granser recollected himself, and with a start tore himself away from the rostrum of the lecture-hall, where, to another-world audience, he had been expounding the latest theory, sixty years gone, of germs and germ-diseases.

"Yes, yes, Edwin; I had forgotten. Sometimes the memory of the past is very strong upon me, and I forget that I am a dirty old man, clad in goatskin, wandering with my savage grandsons who are goatherds in the primeval wilderness. 'The fleeting systems lapse like foam,' and so lapsed our glorious, colossal civilization. I am Granser, a tired old man. I belong to the tribe of Santa Rosans. I married into that tribe.

My sons and daughters married into the Chauffeurs, the Sacramentos, and the Palo-Altos. You, Hare-Lip, are of the Chauffeurs. You, Edwin, are of the Sacramentos. And you, Hoo-Hoo, are of the Palo-Altos. Your tribe takes its name from a town that was near the seat of another great institution of learning. It was called Stanford University. Yes, I remember now. It is perfectly clear. I was telling you of the Scarlet Death. Where was I in my story?"

"You was telling about germs, the things you can't see but which make men sick," Edwin prompted.

"Yes, that's where I was. A man did not notice at first when only a few of these germs got into his body. But each germ broke in half and became two germs, and they kept doing this very rapidly so that in a short time there were many millions of them in the body. Then the man was sick. He had a disease, and the disease was named after the kind of germ that was in him. It might be measles, it might be influenza, it might be yellow fever; it might be any of thousands and thousands of kinds of diseases.

"Now this is the strange thing about these germs. There were always new ones coming to live in men's bodies. Long and long and long ago, when there were only a few men in the world, there were few diseases. But as men increased and lived closely together in great cities and civilizations, new diseases arose, new kinds of germs entered their bodies. Thus were countless millions and billions of human beings killed. And the more thickly men packed together, the more terrible were the new diseases that came to be. Long before my time, in the middle ages, there was the Black Plague that swept across Europe. It swept across Europe many times. There was tuberculosis, that entered into men wherever they were thickly packed. A hundred years before my time there was the bubonic plague. And in Africa was the sleeping sickness. The bacteriologists fought all these sicknesses and destroyed them, just as you boys fight the wolves away from your goats, or squash the mosquitoes that light on you. The bacteriologists -- "

"But, Granser, what is a what-you-call-it?" Edwin interrupted.

"You, Edwin, are a goatherd. Your task is to watch the goats. You know a great deal about goats. A bacteriologist watches germs. That's his task, and he knows a great deal about them. So, as I was saying, the bacteriologists fought with the germs and destroyed them -- sometimes. There was leprosy, a horrible disease. A hundred years before I was born, the bacteriologists discovered the germ of leprosy. They knew all about it. They made pictures of it. I have seen those pictures. But they never found a way to kill it.

But in 1984, there was the Pantoblast Plague, a disease that broke out in a country called Brazil and that killed millions of people. But the bacteriologists found it out, and found the way to kill it, so that the Pantoblast Plague went no farther. They made what they called a serum, which they put into a man's body and which killed the pantoblast germs without killing the man. And in 1910, there was pellagra, and also the hookworm. These were easily killed by the bacteriologists. But in 1947 there arose a new disease that had never been seen before. It got into the bodies of babies of only ten months old or less, and it made them unable to move their hands and feet, or to eat, or anything; and the bacteriologists were eleven years in discovering how to kill that particular germ and save the babies.

"In spite of all these diseases, and of all the new ones that continued to arise, there were more and more men in the world. This was because it was easy to get food. The easier it was to get food, the more men there were; the more men there were, the more thickly were they packed together on the earth; and the more thickly they were packed, the more new kinds of germs became diseases. There were warnings. Soldervetzsky, as early as 1929, told the bacteriologists that they had no guaranty against some new disease, a thousand times more deadly than any they knew, arising and killing by the hundreds of millions and even by the billion. You see, the micro-organic world remained a mystery to the end. They knew there was such a world, and that from time to time armies of new germs emerged from it to kill men. And that was all they knew about it. For all they knew, in that invisible micro-organic world there might be as many different kinds of germs as there are grains of sand on this beach. And also, in that same invisible world it might well be that new kinds of germs came to be. It might be there that life originated-the 'abysmal fecundity,' Soldervetzsky called it, applying the words of other men who had written before him. . . ."

It was at this point that Hare-Lip rose to his feet, an expression of huge contempt on his face.

"Granser," he announced, "you make me sick with your gabble. Why don't you tell about the Red Death? If you ain't going to, say so, an' we'll start back for camp."

The old man looked at him and silently began to cry. The weak tears of age rolled down his cheeks, and all the feebleness of his eighty-seven years showed in his grief-stricken countenance.

"Sit down," Edwin counselled soothingly. "Granser's all right. He's just gettin' to the Scarlet Death, ain't you, Granser? He's just goin' to tell us about it right now. Sit down, Hare-Lip. Go ahead, Granser."

3

The old man wiped the tears away on his grimy knuckles and took up the tale in a tremulous, piping voice that soon strengthened as he got the swing of the narrative.

"It was in the summer of 2013 that the Plague came. I was twenty-seven years old, and well do I remember it. Wireless dispatches -- "

Hare-Lip spat loudly his disgust, and Granser hastened to make amends.

"We talked through the air in those days, thousands and thousands of miles. And the word came of a strange disease that had broken out in New York. There were seventeen millions of people living then in that noblest city of America. Nobody thought anything about the news. It was only a small thing. There had been only a few deaths. It seemed, though that they had died very quickly, and that one of the first signs of the disease was the turning red of the face and all the body. Within twenty-four hours came the report of the first case in Chicago. And on the same day, it was made public that London, the greatest city in the world, next to Chicago, had been secretly fighting the plague for two weeks and censoring the news dispatches -- that is, not permitting the word to go forth to the rest of the world that London had the plague.

"It looked serious, but we in California, like everywhere else, were not alarmed. We were sure that the bacteriologists would find a way to overcome this new germ, just as they had overcome other germs in the past. But the trouble was the astonishing quickness with which this germ destroyed human beings, and the fact that it inevitably killed any human body it entered. No one ever recovered. There was the old Asiatic cholera, when you might eat dinner with a well man in the evening, and the next morning, if you got up early enough, you would see him being hauled by your window in the death-cart. But this new plague was quicker than that -- much quicker. From the moment of the first signs of it, a man would be dead in an hour. Some lasted for several hours. Many died within ten or fifteen minutes of the appearance of the first signs.

"The heart began to beat faster and the heat of the body to increase. Then came the scarlet rash, spreading like wildfire over the face and body. Most persons never noticed the increase in heat and heart-beat, and the first they knew was when the scarlet rash came out. Usually, they had convulsions at the time of the appearance of the rash. But these convulsions did not last long and were not very severe. If one lived through them, he became perfectly quiet, and only then did he feel a numbness swiftly creeping up his body from the feet. The heels became numb first, then the legs, and hips, and when the numbness reached as high as his heart he died. They did not rave or sleep. Their minds always remained cool and calm up to the moment their heart numbed and stopped. And another strange thing was the rapidity of decomposition. No sooner was a person dead than the body seemed to fall to pieces, to fly apart, to melt away even as you looked at it. That was one of the reasons the plague spread so rapidly. All the billions of germs in a corpse were so immediately released.

"And it was because of all this that the bacteriologists had so little chance in fighting the germs. They were killed in their laboratories even as they studied the germ of the Scarlet Death. They were heroes. As fast as they perished, others stepped forth and took their places. It was in London that they first isolated it. The news was telegraphed everywhere. Trask was the name of the man who succeeded in this, but within thirty hours he was dead. Then came the struggle in all the laboratories to find something that would kill the plague germs. All drugs failed. You see, the problem was to get a drug, or serum, that would kill the germs in the body and not kill the body. They tried to fight it with other germs, to put into the body of a sick man germs that were the enemies of the plague germs -- "

"And you can't see these germ-things, Granser," Hare-Lip objected, "and here you gabble, gabble, gabble about them as if they was anything, when they're nothing at all. Anything you can't see, ain't, that's what. Fighting things that ain't with things that ain't! They must have been all fools in them days. That's why they croaked. I ain't goin' to believe in such rot, I tell you that."

Granser promptly began to weep, while Edwin hotly took up his defense.

"Look here, Hare-Lip, you believe in lots of things you can't see."

Hare-Lip shook his head.

"You believe in dead men walking about. You never seen one dead man walk about."

"I tell you I seen 'em, last winter, when I was wolf-hunting with dad."

"Well, you always spit when you cross running water," Edwin challenged.

"That's to keep off bad luck," was Hare-Lip's defence.

"You believe in bad luck?"

"Sure."

"An' you ain't never seen bad luck," Edwin concluded triumphantly.

"You're just as bad as Granser and his germs. You believe in what you don't see. Go on, Granser."

Hare-Lip, crushed by this metaphysical defeat, remained silent, and the old man went on. Often and often, though this narrative must not be clogged by the details, was Granser's tale interrupted while the boys squabbled among themselves. Also, among themselves they kept up a constant, low-voiced exchange of explanation and conjecture, as they strove to follow the old man into his unknown and vanished world.

"The Scarlet Death broke out in San Francisco. The first death came on a Monday morning. By Thursday they were dying like flies in Oakland and San Francisco. They died everywhere -- in their beds, at their work, walking along the street. It was on Tuesday that I saw my first death -- Miss Colibran, one of my students, sitting right there before my eyes, in my lecture-room. I noticed her face while I was talking. It had suddenly turned scarlet. I ceased speaking and could only look at her, for the first fear of the plague was already on all of us and we knew that it had come. The young women screamed and ran out of the room. So did the young men run out, all but two. Miss Colibran's convulsions were very mild and lasted less than a minute. One of the young men fetched her a glass of water. She drank only a little of it, and cried out:

"'My feet! All sensation has left them.'

"After a minute she said, 'I have no feet. I am unaware that I have any feet. And my knees are cold. I can scarcely feel that I -- have knees.'

"She lay on the floor, a bundle of notebooks under her head. And we could do nothing. The coldness and the numbness crept up past her hips to her heart, and when it reached her heart she was dead. In fifteen minutes, by the clock -- I timed it -- she was dead, there, in my own classroom, dead. And she was a very beautiful, strong, healthy young woman. And from the first sign of the plague to her death only fifteen minutes elapsed. That will show you how swift was the Scarlet Death.

"Yet in those few minutes I remained with the dying woman in my classroom, the alarm had spread over the university; and the students, by thousands, all of them, had deserted the lecture-rooms and laboratories. When I emerged, on my way to make report to the President of the Faculty, I found the university deserted. Across the campus were several stragglers hurrying for their homes. Two of them were running.

"President Hoag I found in his office, all alone, looking very old and very gray, with a multitude of wrinkles in his face that I had never seen before. At the sight of me, he pulled himself to his feet and tottered away to the inner office, banging the door after him and locking it. You see, he knew I had been exposed, and he was afraid. He shouted to me through the door to go away. I shall never forget my feelings as I walked down the silent corridors and out across that deserted campus. I was not afraid. I had been exposed, and I looked upon myself as already dead. It was not that, but a feeling of awful depression that impressed me. Everything had stopped. It was like the end of the world to me -- my world. I had been born within sight and sound of the university. It had been my predestined career. My father had been a professor there before me, and his father before him. For a century and a half had this university, like a splendid machine, been running steadily on. And now, in an instant, it had stopped. It was like seeing the sacred flame die down on some thrice-sacred altar. I was shocked, unutterably shocked.

"When I arrived home, my housekeeper screamed as I entered, and fled away. And when I rang, I found the housemaid had likewise fled. I investigated. In the kitchen I found the cook on the point of departure. But she screamed, too, and in her haste dropped a suitcase of her personal belongings and ran out of the house and across the grounds, still screaming. I can hear her scream to this day. You see, we did not act in this way when ordinary diseases smote us. We were always calm over such things, and sent for the doctors and nurses who knew just what to do. But this was different. It struck so suddenly, and killed so swiftly, and never missed a stroke. When the scarlet rash appeared on a person's face, that person was marked by death. There was never a known case of a recovery.

"I was alone in my big house. As I have told you often before, in those days we could talk with one another over wires or through the air. The telephone bell rang, and I found my brother talking to me. He told me that he was not coming home for fear of catching the plague from me, and that he had taken our two sisters to stop at Professor Bacon's home. He advised me to remain where I was, and wait to find out whether or not I had caught the plague.

"To all of this I agreed, staying in my house and for the first time in my life attempting to cook. And the plague did not come out on me. By means of the telephone I could talk with whomsoever I pleased and get the news. Also, there were the newspapers, and I ordered all of them to be thrown up to my door so that I could know what was happening with the rest of the world.

"New York City and Chicago were in chaos. And what happened with them was happening in all the large cities. A third of the New York police were dead. Their chief was also dead, likewise the mayor. All law and order had ceased. The bodies were lying in the streets unburied. All railroads and vessels carrying food and such things into the great city had ceased running, and mobs of the hungry poor were pillaging the stores and warehouses. Murder and robbery and drunkenness were everywhere. Already the people had fled from the city by millions -- at first the rich, in their private motor-cars and dirigibles, and then the great mass of the population, on foot, carrying the plague with them, themselves starving and pillaging the farmers and all the towns and villages on the way.

"The man who sent this news, the wireless operator, was alone with his instrument on the top of a lofty building. The people remaining in the city -- he estimated them at several hundred thousand-had gone mad from fear and drink, and on all sides of him great fires were raging. He was a hero, that man who stayed by his post -- an obscure newspaperman, most likely.

"For twenty-four hours, he said, no transatlantic airships had arrived, and no more messages were coming from England. He did state, though, that a message from Berlin -- that's in Germany -- announced that Hoffmeyer, a bacteriologist of the Metchnikoff School, had discovered the serum for the plague. That was the last word, to this day, that we of America ever received from Europe. If Hoffmeyer discovered the serum, it was too late, or otherwise, long ere this, explorers from Europe would have come looking for us.

We can only conclude that what happened in America happened in Europe, and that, at the best, some several score may have survived the Scarlet Death on that whole continent.

"For one day longer the dispatches continued to come from New York. Then they, too, ceased. The man who had sent them, perched in his lofty building, had either died of the plague or been consumed in the great conflagrations he had described as raging around him. And what had occurred in New York had been duplicated in all the other cities. It was the same in San Francisco, and Oakland, and Berkeley. By Thursday the people were dying so rapidly that their corpses could not be handled, and dead bodies lay everywhere. Thursday night the panic outrush for the country began. Imagine, my grandsons, people, thicker than the salmon-run you have seen on the Sacramento River, pouring out of the cities by millions, madly over the country, in vain attempt to escape the ubiquitous death. You see, they carried the germs with them. Even the airships of the rich, fleeing for mountain and desert fastnesses, carried the germs.

"Hundreds of these airships escaped to Hawaii, and not only did they bring the plague with them, but they found the plague already there before them. This we learned by the dispatches, until all order in San Francisco vanished, and there were no operators left at their posts to receive or send. It was amazing, astounding, this loss of communication with the world. It was exactly as if the world had ceased, been blotted out. For sixty years that world has no longer existed for me. I know there must be such places as New York, Europe, Asia, and Africa; but not one word has been heard of them-not in sixty years. With the coming of the Scarlet Death the world fell apart, absolutely, irretrievably. Ten thousand years of culture and civilization ceased in the twinkling of an eye, 'lapsed like foam.'

"I was telling about the airships of the rich. They carried the plague with them and no matter where they fled, they died. I never encountered but one survivor of any of them -- Mungerson. He was afterwards a Santa Rosan, and he married my eldest daughter.

He came into the tribe eight years after the plague. He was then nineteen years old, and he was compelled to wait twelve years more before he could marry. You see, there were no unmarried women, and some of the older daughters of the Santa Rosans were already bespoken. So he was forced to wait until my Mary had grown to sixteen years. It was his son, Gimp-Leg, who was killed last year by the mountain lion.

"Mungerson was eleven years old at the time of the plague. His father was one of the Industrial Magnates, a very wealthy, powerful man. It was on his airship, the Condor, that they were fleeing, with all the family, for the wilds of British Columbia, which is far to the north of here. But there was some accident, and they were wrecked near Mount Shasta. You have heard of that mountain. It is far to the north. The plague broke out amongst them, and this boy of eleven was the only survivor. For eight years he was alone, wandering over a deserted land and looking vainly for his own kind. And at last, travelling south, he picked up with us, the Santa Rosans.

"But I am ahead of my story. When the great exodus from the cities around San Francisco Bay began, and while the telephones were still working, I talked with my brother. I told him this flight from the cities was insanity, that there were no symptoms of the plague in me, and that the thing for us to do was to isolate ourselves and our relatives in some safe place. We decided on the Chemistry Building, at the university, and we planned to lay in a supply of provisions, and by force of arms to prevent any other persons from forcing their presence upon us after we had retired to our refuge.

"All this being arranged, my brother begged me to stay in my own house for at least twenty-four hours more, on the chance of the plague developing in me. To this I agreed, and he promised to come for me next day. We talked on over the details of the provisioning and the defending of the Chemistry Building until the telephone died. It died in the midst of our conversation. That evening there were no electric lights, and I was alone in my house in the darkness. No more newspapers were being printed, so I had no knowledge of what was taking place outside. I heard sounds of rioting and of pistol shots, and from my windows I could see the glare in the sky of some conflagration in the direction of Oakland. It was a night of terror. I did not sleep a wink. A man -- why and how I do not know -- was killed on the sidewalk in front of the house. I heard the rapid reports of an automatic pistol, and a few minutes later the wounded wretch crawled up to my door, moaning and crying out for help. Arming myself with two automatics, I went to him. By the light of a match I ascertained that while he was dying of the bullet wounds, at the same time the plague was on him. I fled indoors, whence I heard him moan and cry out for half an hour longer.

"In the morning, my brother came to me. I had gathered into a handbag what things of value I purposed taking, but when I saw his face I knew that he would never accompany me to the Chemistry Building. The plague was on him. He intended shaking my hand, but I went back hurriedly before him.

"'Look at yourself in the mirror,' I commanded.

"He did so, and at sight of his scarlet face, the color deepening as he looked at it, he sank down nervelessly in a chair.

"'My God!' He said. 'I've got it. Don't come near me. I am a dead man.'

"Then the convulsions seized him. He was two hours in dying, and he was conscious to the last, complaining about the coldness and loss of sensation in his feet, his calves, his thighs, until at last it was his heart and he was dead.

"That was the way the Scarlet Death slew. I caught up my handbag and fled. The sights in the streets were terrible. One stumbled on bodies everywhere. Some were not yet dead. And even as you looked, you saw men sink down with the death fastened upon them. There were numerous fires burning in Berkeley, while Oakland and San Francisco were apparently being swept by vast conflagrations. The smoke of the burning filled the heavens, so that the mid-day was as a gloomy twilight, and, in the shifts of wind, sometimes the sun shone through dimly, a dull red orb. Truly, my grandsons, it was like the last days of the end of the world.

"There were numerous stalled motor-cars, showing that the gasoline and the engine supplies of the garages had given out. I remember one such car. A man and a woman lay back dead in the seats, and on the pavement near it were two more women and a child. Strange and terrible sights there were on every hand. People slipped by silently, furtively, like ghosts -- white-faced women carrying infants in their arms; fathers leading children by the hand; singly, and in couples, and in families -- all fleeing out of the city of death. Some carried supplies of food, others blankets and valuables, and there were many who carried nothing.

"There was a grocery store -- a place where food was sold. The man to whom it belonged -- I knew him well -- a quiet, sober, but stupid and obstinate fellow, was defending it. The windows and doors had been broken in, but he, inside, hiding behind a counter, was discharging his pistol at a number of men on the sidewalk who were breaking in. In the entrance were several bodies -- of men, I decided, whom he had killed earlier in the day. Even as I looked on from a distance, I saw one of the robbers break the windows of the adjoining store, a place where shoes were sold, and deliberately set fire to it. I did not go to the groceryman's assistance. The time for such acts had already passed. Civilization was crumbling, and it was each for himself."

4

"I went away hastily, down a cross-street, and at the first corner I saw another tragedy. Two men of the working class had caught a man and a woman with two children, and were robbing them. I knew the man by sight though I had never been introduced to him. He was a poet whose verses I had long admired. Yet I did not go to his help, for at the moment I came upon the scene there was a pistol shot, and I saw him sinking to the ground. The woman screamed, and she was felled with a fist-blow by one of the brutes. I cried out threateningly, whereupon they discharged their pistols at me and I ran away around the corner. Here I was blocked by an advancing conflagration. The buildings on both sides were burning, and the street was filled with smoke and flame. From somewhere in that murk came a woman's voice calling shrilly for help. But I did not go to her. A man's heart turned to iron amid such scenes, and one heard all too many appeals for help.

"Returning to the corner, I found the two robbers were gone. The poet and his wife lay dead on the pavement. It was a shocking sight. The two children had vanished -- whither I could not tell. And I knew, now, why it was that the fleeing persons I encountered slipped along so furtively and with such white faces. In the midst of our civilization, down in our slums and labor-ghettos, we had bred a race of barbarians, of savages; and now, in the time of our calamity, they turned upon us like the wild beasts they were and destroyed us. And they destroyed themselves as well. They inflamed themselves with strong drink and committed a thousand atrocities, quarreling and killing one another in the general madness. One group of workingmen I saw, of the better sort, who had banded together, and, with their women and children in their midst, the sick and aged in litters and being carried, and with a number of horses pulling a truck-load of provisions, they were fighting their way out of the city. They made a fine spectacle as they came down the street through the drifting smoke, though they nearly shot me when I first appeared in their path. As they went by, one of their leaders shouted out to me in apologetic explanation. He said they were killing the robbers and looters on sight, and that they had thus banded together as the only means by which to escape the prowlers.

"It was here that I saw for the first time what I was soon to see so often. One of the marching men had suddenly shown the unmistakable mark of the plague. Immediately those about him drew away, and he, without a remonstrance, stepped out of his place to let them pass on. A woman, most probably his wife, attempted to follow him. She was leading a little boy by the hand. But the husband commanded her sternly to go on, while others laid hands on her and restrained her from following him. This I saw, and I saw the man also, with his scarlet blaze of face, step into a doorway on the opposite side of the street. I heard the report of his pistol, and saw him sink lifeless to the ground.

"After being turned aside twice again by advancing fires, I succeeded in getting through to the university. On the edge of the campus I came upon a party of university folk who were going in the direction of the Chemistry Building. They were all family men, and their families were with them, including the nurses and the servants. Professor Badminton greeted me, and I had difficulty in recognizing him. Somewhere he had gone through flames, and his beard was singed off. About his head was a bloody bandage, and his clothes were filthy. He told me he had been cruelly beaten by prowlers, and that his brother had been killed the previous night, in the defence of their dwelling.

"Midway across the campus, he pointed suddenly to Mrs. Swinton's face. The unmistakable scarlet was there. Immediately all the other women set up a screaming and began to run away from her. Her two children were with a nurse, and these also ran with the women. But her husband, Doctor Swinton, remained with her.

"'Go on, Smith,' he told me. 'Keep an eye on the children. As for me, I shall stay with my wife. I know she is as already dead, but I can't leave her. Afterwards, if I escape, I shall come to the Chemistry Building, and do you watch for me and let me in.'

"I left him bending over his wife and soothing her last moments, while I ran to overtake the party. We were the last to be admitted to the Chemistry Building. After that, with our automatic rifles we maintained our isolation. By our plans, we had arranged for a company of sixty to be in this refuge. Instead, every one of the number originally planned had added relatives and friends and whole families until there were over four hundred souls. But the Chemistry Building was large, and, standing by itself, was in no danger of being burned by the great fires that raged everywhere in the city.

"A large quantity of provisions had been gathered, and a food committee took charge of it, issuing rations daily to the various families and groups that arranged themselves into messes. A number of committees were appointed, and we developed a very efficient organization. I was on the committee of defence, though for the first day no prowlers came near. We could see them in the distance, however, and by the smoke of their fires knew that several camps of them were occupying the far edge of the campus. Drunkenness was rife, and often we heard them singing ribald songs or insanely shouting. While the world crashed to ruin about them and all the air was filled with the smoke of its burning, these low creatures gave rein to their bestiality and fought and drank and died. And after all, what did it matter? Everybody died anyway, the good and the bad, the efficients and the weaklings, those that loved to live and those that scorned to live. They passed. Everything passed.

"When twenty-four hours had gone by and no signs of the plague were apparent, we congratulated ourselves and set about digging a well. You have seen the great iron pipes which in those days carried water to all the city-dwellers. We feared that the fires in the city would burst the pipes and empty the reservoirs. So we tore up the cement floor of the central court of the Chemistry Building and dug a well. There were many young men, undergraduates, with us, and we worked night and day on the well. And our fears were confirmed. Three hours before we reached water, the pipes went dry.

"A second twenty-four hours passed, and still the plague did not appear among us. We thought we were saved. But we did not know what I afterwards decided to be true, namely, that the period of the incubation of the plague germs in a human's body was a matter of a number of days. It slew so swiftly when once it manifested itself, that we were led to believe that the period of incubation was equally swift. So, when two days had left us unscathed, we were elated with the idea that we were free of the contagion.

"But the third day disillusioned us. I can never forget the night preceding it. I had charge of the night guards from eight to twelve, and from the roof of the building I watched the passing of all man's glorious works. So terrible were the local conflagrations that all the sky was lighted up. One could read the finest print in the red glare. All the world seemed wrapped in flames. San Francisco spouted smoke and fire from a score of vast conflagrations that were like so many active volcanoes. Oakland, San Leandro, Haywards - all were burning; and to the northward, clear to Point Richmond, other fires were at work. It was an awe-inspiring spectacle. Civilization, my grandsons, civilization was passing in a sheet of flame and a breath of death. At ten o'clock that night, the great powder magazines at Point Pinole exploded in rapid succession. So terrific were the concussions that the strong building rocked as in an earthquake, while every pane of glass was broken. It was then that I left the roof and went down the long corridors, from room to room, quieting the alarmed women and telling them what had happened.

"An hour later, at a window on the ground floor, I heard pandemonium break out in the camps of the prowlers. There were cries and screams, and shots from many pistols. As we afterward conjectured, this fight had been precipitated by an attempt on the part of those that were well to drive out those that were sick. At any rate, a number of the plague-stricken prowlers escaped across the campus and drifted against our doors. We warned them back, but they cursed us and discharged a fusillade from their pistols. Professor Merryweather, at one of the windows, was instantly killed, the bullet striking him squarely between the eyes. We opened fire in turn, and all the prowlers fled away with the exception of three. One was a woman. The plague was on them and they were reckless. Like foul fiends, there in the red glare from the skies, with faces blazing, they continued to curse us and fire at us. One of the men I shot with my own hand. After that the other man and the woman, still cursing us, lay down under our windows, where we were compelled to watch them die of the plague.

"The situation was critical. The explosions of the powder magazines had broken all the windows of the Chemistry Building, so that we were exposed to the germs from the corpses. The sanitary committee was called upon to act, and it responded nobly. Two men were required to go out and remove the corpses, and this meant the probable sacrifice of their own lives, for, having performed the task, they were not to be permitted to re-enter the building. One of the professors, who was a bachelor, and one of the undergraduates volunteered. They bade goodbye to us and went forth. They were heroes. They gave up their lives that four hundred others might live. After they had performed their work, they stood for a moment, at a distance, looking at us wistfully. Then they waved their hands in farewell and went away slowly across the campus toward the burning city.

"And yet it was all useless. The next morning the first one of us was smitten with the plague -- a little nurse-girl in the family of Professor Stout. It was no time for weak-kneed, sentimental policies. On the chance that she might be the only one, we thrust her forth from the building and commanded her to be gone. She went away slowly across the campus, wringing her hands and crying pitifully. We felt like brutes, but what were we to do? There were four hundred of us, and individuals had to be sacrificed.

"In one of the laboratories three families had domiciled themselves, and that afternoon we found among them no less than four corpses and seven cases of the plague in all its different stages.

"Then it was that the horror began. Leaving the dead lie, we forced the living ones to segregate themselves in another room. The plague began to break out among the rest of us, and as fast as the symptoms appeared, we sent the stricken ones to these segregated rooms. We compelled them to walk there by themselves, so as to avoid laying hands on them. It was heartrending. But still the plague raged among us, and room after room was filled with the dead and dying. And so we who were yet clean retreated to the next floor and to the next, before this sea of the dead, that, room by room and floor by floor, inundated the building.

"The place became a charnel house, and in the middle of the

night the survivors fled forth, taking nothing with them except arms and ammunition and a heavy store of tinned foods. We camped on the opposite side of the campus from the prowlers, and, while some stood guard, others of us volunteered to scout into the city in quest of horses, motor-cars, carts, and wagons, or anything that would carry our provisions and enable us to emulate the banded workingmen I had seen fighting their way out to the open country.

"I was one of these scouts; and Doctor Hoyle, remembering that his motor-car had been left behind in his home garage, told me to look for it. We scouted in pairs, and Dombey, a young undergraduate, accompanied me. We had to cross half a mile of the residence portion of the city to get to Doctor Hoyle's home. Here the buildings stood apart, in the midst of trees and grassy lawns, and here the fires had played freaks, burning whole blocks, skipping blocks and often skipping a single house in a block. And here, too, the prowlers were still at their work. We carried our automatic pistols openly in our hands, and looked desperate enough, forsooth, to keep them from attacking us. But at Doctor Hoyle's house the thing happened. Untouched by fire, even as we came to it the smoke of flames burst forth.

"The miscreant who had set fire to it staggered down the steps and out along the driveway. Sticking out of his coat pockets were bottles of whiskey, and he was very drunk. My first impulse was to shoot him, and I have never ceased regretting that I did not. Staggering and maundering to himself, with bloodshot eyes, and a raw and bleeding slash down one side of his bewhiskered face, he was altogether the most nauseating specimen of degradation and filth I had ever encountered. I did not shoot him, and he leaned against a tree on the lawn to let us go by. It was the most absolute, wanton act. Just as we were opposite him, he suddenly drew a pistol and shot Dombey through the head. The next instant I shot him. But it was too late. Dombey expired without a groan, immediately. I doubt if he even knew what had happened to him.

"Leaving the two corpses, I hurried on past the burning house to the garage, and there found Doctor Hoyle's motor-car. The tanks were filled with gasoline, and it was ready for use. And it was in this car that I threaded the streets of the ruined city and came back to the survivors on the campus. The other scouts returned, but none had been so fortunate. Professor Fairmead had found a Shetland pony, but the poor creature, tied in a stable and abandoned for days, was so weak from want of food and water that it could carry no burden at all. Some of the men were for turning it loose, but I insisted that we should lead it along with us, so that, if we got out of food, we would have it to eat.

"There were forty-seven of us when we started, many being women and children. The President of the Faculty, an old man to begin with, and now hopelessly broken by the awful happenings of the past week, rode in the motor-car with several young children and the aged mother of Professor Fairmead. Wathope, a young professor of English, who had a grievous bullet-wound in his leg, drove the car. The rest of us walked, Professor Fairmead leading the pony.

"It was what should have been a bright summer day, but the smoke from the burning world filled the sky, through which the sun shone murkily, a dull and lifeless orb, blood-red and ominous. But we had grown accustomed to that blood-red sun. With the smoke it was different. It bit into our nostrils and eyes, and there was not one of us whose eyes were not bloodshot. We directed our course to the southeast through the endless miles of suburban residences, travelling along where the first swells of low hills rose from the flat of the central city. It was by this way, only, that we could expect to gain the country.

"Our progress was painfully slow. The women and children could not walk fast. They did not dream of walking, my grandsons, in the way all people walk to-day. In truth, none of us knew how to walk. It was not until after the plague that I learned really to walk. So it was that the pace of the slowest was the pace of all, for we dared not separate on account of the prowlers. There were not so many now of these human beasts of prey. The plague had already well diminished their numbers, but enough still lived to be a constant menace to us. Many of the beautiful residences were untouched by fire, yet smoking ruins were everywhere. The prowlers, too, seemed to have got over their insensate desire to burn, and it was more rarely that we saw houses freshly on fire.

"Several of us scouted among the private garages in search of motor-cars and gasoline. But in this we were unsuccessful. The first great flights from the cities had swept all such utilities away. Calgan, a fine young man, was lost in this work. He was shot by prowlers while crossing a lawn. Yet this was our only casualty, though, once, a drunken brute deliberately opened fire on all of us. Luckily, he fired wildly, and we shot him before he had done any hurt.

"At Fruitvale, still in the heart of the magnificent residence section of the city, the plague again smote us. Professor Fairmead was the victim. Making signs to us that his mother was not to know, he turned aside into the grounds of a beautiful mansion. He sat down forlornly on the steps of the front veranda, and I, having lingered, waved him a last farewell. That night, several miles beyond Fruitvale and still in the city, we made camp. And that night we shifted camp twice to get away from our dead. In the morning there were thirty of us. I shall never forget the President of the Faculty. During the morning's march his wife, who was walking, betrayed the fatal symptoms, and when she drew aside to let us go on, he insisted on leaving the motor-car and remaining with her. There was quite a discussion about this, but in the end we gave in. It was just as well, for we knew not which ones of us, if any, might ultimately escape.

"That night, the second of our march, we camped beyond Haywards in the first stretches of country. And in the morning there were eleven of us that lived. Also, during the night, Wathope, the professor with the wounded leg, deserted us in the motor-car. He took with him his sister and his mother and most of our tinned provisions. It was that day, in the afternoon, while resting by the wayside, that I saw the last airship I shall ever see. The smoke was much thinner here in the country, and I first sighted the ship drifting and veering helplessly at an elevation of two thousand feet. What had happened I could not conjecture, but even as we looked we saw her bow dip down lower and lower. Then the bulkheads of the various gas-chambers must have burst, for, quite perpendicular, she fell like a plummet to the earth. And from that day to this I have not seen another airship. Often and often, during the next few years, I scanned the sky for them hoping against hope that somewhere in the world civilization had survived. But it was not to be. What happened with us in California must have happened with everybody everywhere.

"Another day, and at Niles there were three of us. Beyond Niles, in the middle of the highway, we found Wathope. The motor-car had broken down, and there, on the rugs which they had spread on the ground, lay the bodies of his sister, his mother, and himself.

"Wearied by the unusual exercise of continual walking, that night I slept heavily. In the morning I was alone in the world. Canfield and Parsons, my last companions, were dead of the plague. Of the four hundred that sought shelter in the Chemistry Building, and of the forty-seven that began the march, I alone remained -- I and the Shetland pony. Why this should be so there is no explaining. I did not catch the plague, that is all. I was immune. I was merely the one lucky man in a million -- just as every survivor was one in a million, or, rather, in several millions, for the proportion was at least that."

5

"For two days I sheltered in a pleasant grove where there had been no deaths. In those two days, while badly depressed and believing that my turn would come at any moment, nevertheless I rested and recuperated. So did the pony. And on the third day, putting what small store of tinned provisions I possessed on the pony's back, I started on across a very lonely land. Not a live man, woman, child, did I encounter, though the dead were everywhere. Food, however, was abundant. The land then was not as it is now.

It was all cleared of trees and brush, and it was cultivated. The food for millions of mouths was growing, ripening, and going to waste. From the fields and orchards I gathered vegetables, fruits, and berries. Around the deserted farmhouses I got eggs and caught chickens. And frequently I found supplies of tinned provisions in the store-rooms.

"A strange thing was what was taking place with all the domestic animals. Everywhere they were going wild and preying on one another. The chickens and ducks were the first to be destroyed, while the pigs were the first to go wild, followed by the cats. Nor were the dogs long in adapting themselves to the changed conditions. There was a veritable plague of dogs. They devoured the corpses, barked and howled during the nights, and in the daytime slunk about in the distance. As the time went by, I noticed a change in their behavior. At first they were apart from one another, very suspicious and very prone to fight. But after a not very long while they began to come together and run in packs. The dog, you see, always was a social animal, and this was true before ever he came to be domesticated by man. In the last days of the world before the plagues there were many, many very different kinds of dogs -- dogs without hair and dogs with warm fur, dogs so small that they would make scarcely a mouthful for other dogs that were as large as mountain lions. Well, all the small dogs, and the weak types were killed by their fellows. Also, the very large ones were not adapted for the wild life -- it had been bred out. As a result, the many different kinds of dogs disappeared, and there remained, running in packs, the medium-sized wolfish dogs that you know today."

"But the cats don't run in packs, Granser," Hoo-Hoo objected.

"The cat was never a social animal. As one writer in the nineteenth century said, the cat walks by himself. He always walked by himself, from before the time he was tamed by man, down through the long ages of domestication, to to-day when once more he is wild.

"The horses also went wild, and all the fine breeds we had degenerated into the small mustang horse you know today. The cows likewise went wild, as did the pigeons and the sheep. And that a few of the chickens survived you know yourself. But the wild chicken of to-day is quite a different thing from the chickens we had in those days.

"But I must go on with my story. I travelled through a deserted land. As the time went by I began to yearn more and more for human beings. But I never found one, and I grew lonelier and lonelier. I crossed Livermore Valley and the mountains between it and the great valley of the San Joaquin. You have never seen that valley, but it is very large and it is the home of the wild horse. There are great droves there, thousands and tens of thousands. I revisited it thirty years after, so I know. You think there are lots of wild horses down here in the coast valleys, but they are as nothing compared with those of the San Joaquin. Strange to say, the cows, when they went wild, went back into the lower mountains. Evidently they were better able to protect themselves there.

"In the country districts the ghouls and prowlers had been less in evidence, for I found many villages and towns untouched by fire. But they were filled by the pestilential dead, and I passed by without exploring them. It was near Lathrop that, out of my loneliness, I picked up a pair of collie dogs that were so newly free that they were urgently willing to return to their allegiance to man. These collies accompanied me for many years, and the strains of them are in those very dogs there that you boys have today. But in sixty years the collie strain has worked out. These brutes are more like domesticated wolves than anything else."

Hare-Lip rose to his feet, glanced to see that the goats were safe, and looked at the sun's position in the afternoon sky, advertising impatience at the prolixity of the old man's tale. Urged to hurry by Edwin, Granser went on.

"There is little more to tell. With my two dogs and my pony, and riding a horse I had managed to capture, I crossed the San Joaquin and went on to a wonderful valley in the Sierras called Yosemite. In the great hotel there I found a prodigious supply of tinned provisions. The pasture was abundant, as was the game, and the river that ran through the valley was full of trout. I remained there three years in an utter loneliness that none but a man who has once been highly civilized can understand. Then I could stand it no more. I felt that I was going crazy. Like the dog, I was a social animal and I needed my kind. I reasoned that since I had survived the plague, there was a possibility that others had survived. Also, I reasoned that after three years the plague germs must all be gone and the land be clean again.

"With my horse and dogs and pony, I set out. Again I crossed the San Joaquin Valley, the mountains beyond, and came down into Livermore Valley. The change in those three years was amazing. All the land had been splendidly tilled, and now I could scarcely recognize it, such was the sea of rank vegetation that had overrun the agricultural handiwork of man. You see, the wheat, the vegetables, and orchard trees had always been cared for and nursed by man, so that they were soft and tender. The weeds and wild bushes and such things, on the contrary, had always been fought by man, so that they were tough and resistant. As a result, when the hand of man was removed, the wild vegetation smothered and destroyed practically all the domesticated vegetation. The coyotes were greatly increased, and it was at this time that I first encountered wolves, straying in twos and threes and small packs down from the regions where they had always persisted.

"It was at Lake Temescal, not far from the one-time city of Oakland, that I came upon the first live human beings. Oh, my grandsons, how can I describe to you my emotion, when, astride my horse and dropping down the hillside to the lake, I saw the smoke of a campfire rising through the trees. Almost did my heart stop beating. I felt that I was going crazy. Then I heard the cry of a babe -- a human babe. And dogs barked, and my dogs answered. I did not know but what I was the one human alive in the whole world. It could not be true that here were others -- smoke and the cry of a babe!

"Emerging on the lake, there, before my eyes, not a hundred yards away, I saw a man, a large man. He was standing on an outjutting rock and fishing. I was overcome. I stopped my horse. I tried to call out but could not. I waved my hand. It seemed to me that the man looked at me, but he did not appear to wave. Then I laid my head on my arms there in the saddle. I was afraid to look again, for I knew it was an hallucination, and I knew that if I looked the man would be gone. And so precious was the hallucination, that I wanted it to persist yet a little while. I knew, too, that as long as I did not look it would persist.

"Thus I remained, until I heard my dogs snarling, and a man's voice. What do you think the voice said? I will tell you. It said: 'Where in hell did you come from?'

"Those were the words, the exact words. That was what your other grandfather said to me, Hare-Lip, when he greeted me there on the shore of Lake Temescal fifty-seven years ago. And they were the most ineffable words I have ever heard. I opened my eyes, and there he stood before me, a large, dark, hairy man, heavy jawed, slant-browed, fierce-eyed. How I got off my horse I do not know. But it seemed that the next I knew I was clasping his hand with both of mine and crying. I would have embraced him, but he was ever a narrow-minded, suspicious man, and he drew away from me. Yet did I cling to his hand and cry."

Granser's voice faltered and broke at the recollection, and the weak tears streamed down his cheeks while the boys looked on and giggled.

"Yet did I cry," he continued, "and desire to embrace him, though the Chauffeur was a brute, a perfect brute -- the most abhorrent man I have ever known. His name was . . . strange, how I have forgotten his name. Everybody called him Chauffeur -- it was the name of his occupation, and it stuck. That is how, to this day, the tribe he founded is called the Chauffeur Tribe.

"He was a violent, unjust man. Why the plague germs spared him I can never understand. It would seem, in spite of our old metaphysical notions about absolute justice, that there is no justice in the universe. Why did he live? -- an iniquitous, moral monster, a blot on the face of nature, a cruel, relentless, bestial cheat as well. All he could talk about was motor-cars, machinery, gasoline, and garages -- and especially, and with huge delight, of his mean pilferings and sordid swindlings of the persons who had employed him in the days before the coming of the plague. And yet he was spared, while hundreds of millions, yea, billions, of better men were destroyed.

"I went on with him to his camp, and there I saw her, Vesta, the one woman. It was glorious and . . . pitiful. There she was, Vesta Van Warden, the young wife of John Van Warden, clad in rags, with marred and scarred and toil-calloused hands, bending over the campfire and doing scullion work -- she, Vesta, who had been born to the purple, to greatest baronage of wealth the world has ever known. John Van Warden, her husband, worth one billion, eight hundred millions and President of the Board of Industrial Magnates, had been the ruler of America. Also, sitting on the International Board of Control, he had been one of the seven men who ruled the world. And she herself had come of equally noble stock. Her father, Philip Saxon, had been President of the Board of Industrial Magnates up to the time of his death. This office was in process of becoming hereditary, and had Philip Saxon had a son that son would have succeeded him. But his only child was Vesta, the perfect flower of generations of the highest culture this planet has ever produced. It was not until the engagement between Vesta and Van Warden took place, that Saxon indicated the latter as his successor. It was, I am sure, a political marriage. I have reason to believe that Vesta never really loved her husband in the mad passionate way of which the poets used to sing. It was more like the marriages that obtained among crowned heads in the days before they were displaced by the Magnates.

"And there she was, boiling fish-chowder in a soot-covered pot, her glorious eyes inflamed by the acrid smoke of the open fire. Hers was a sad story. She was the one survivor in a million, as I had been, as the Chauffeur had been. On a crowning eminence of the Alameda Hills, overlooking San Francisco Bay, Van Warden had built a vast summer palace. It was surrounded by a park of a thousand acres. When the plague broke out, Van Warden sent her there. Armed guards patrolled the boundaries of the park, and nothing entered in the way of provisions or even mail matter that was not first fumigated. And yet did the plague enter, killing the guards at their posts, the servants at their tasks, sweeping away the whole army of retainers -- or, at least, all of them who did not flee to die elsewhere. So it was that Vesta found herself the sole living person in the palace that had become a charnel house.

"Now the Chauffeur had been one of the servants that ran away. Returning, two months afterward, he discovered Vesta in a little summer pavilion where there had been no deaths and where she had established herself. He was a brute. She was afraid, and she ran away and hid among the trees. That night, on foot, she fled into the mountains -- she, whose tender feet and delicate body had never known the bruise of stones nor the scratch of briars. He followed, and that night he caught her. He struck her. Do you understand? He beat her with those terrible fists of his and made her his slave. It was she who had to gather the firewood, build the fires, cook, and do all the degrading camp-labor -- she, who had never performed a menial act in her life. These things he compelled her to do, while he, a proper savage, elected to lie around camp and look on. He did nothing, absolutely nothing, except on occasion to hunt meat or catch fish."

"Good for Chauffeur," Hare-Lip commented in an undertone to the other boys. "I remember him before he died. He was a corker. But he did things, and he made things go. You know, Dad married his daughter, an' you ought to see the way he knocked the spots outa Dad. The Chauffeur was a son-of-a-gun. He made us kids stand around. Even when he was croakin', he reached out for me, once, an' laid my head open with that long stick he kept always beside him."

Hare-Lip rubbed his bullet head reminiscently, and the boys returned to the old man, who was maundering ecstatically about Vesta, the squaw of the founder of the Chauffeur Tribe.

"And so I say to you that you cannot understand the awfulness of the situation. The Chauffeur was a servant, understand, a servant. And he cringed, with bowed head, to such as she. She was a lord of life, both by birth and by marriage. The destinies of millions, such as he, she carried in the hollow of her pink-white hand. And, in the days before the plague, the slightest contact with such as he would have been pollution. Oh, I have seen it. Once, I remember, there was Mrs. Goldwin, wife of one of the great magnates. It was on a landing stage, just as she was embarking in her private dirigible, that she dropped her parasol. A servant picked it up and made the mistake of handing it to her -- to her, one of the greatest royal ladies of the land! She shrank back, as though he were a leper, and indicated her secretary to receive it. Also, she ordered her secretary to ascertain the creature's name and to see that he was immediately discharged from service. And such a woman was Vesta Van Warden. And her the Chauffeur beat and made his slave.

"Bill -- that was it; Bill, the Chauffeur. That was his name. He was a wretched, primitive man, wholly devoid of the finer instincts and chivalrous promptings of a cultured soul. No, there is no absolute justice, for to him fell that wonder of womanhood, Vesta Van Warden. The grievousness of this you will never understand, my grandsons; for you are yourselves primitive little savages, unaware of aught else but savagery. Why should Vesta not have been mine? I was a man of culture and refinement, a professor in a great university. Even so, in the time before the plague, such was her exalted position, she would not have deigned to know that I existed. Mark, then, the abysmal degradation to which she fell at the hands of the Chauffeur. Nothing less than the destruction of all mankind had made it possible that I should know her, look in her eyes, converse with her, touch her hand -- ay, and love her and know that her feelings toward me were very kindly. I have reason to believe that she, even she, would have loved me, there being no other man in the world except the Chauffeur. Why, when it destroyed eight billions of souls, did not the plague destroy just one more man, and that man the Chauffeur?

"Once, when the Chauffeur was away fishing, she begged me to kill him. With tears in her eyes she begged me to kill him. But he was a strong and violent man, and I was afraid. Afterwards, I talked with him. I offered him my horse, my pony, my dogs, all that I possessed, if he would give Vesta to me. And he grinned in my face and shook his head. He was very insulting. He said that in the old days he had been a servant, had been dirt under the feet of men like me and of women like Vesta, and that now he had the greatest lady in the land to be servant to him and cook his food and nurse his brats. 'You had your day before the plague,' he said; 'but this is my day, and a damned good day it is. I wouldn't trade back to the old times for anything.' Such words he spoke, but they are not his words. He was a vulgar, low minded man, and vile oaths fell continually from his lips.

"Also, he told me that if he caught me making eyes at his woman he'd wring my neck and give her a beating as well. What was I to do? I was afraid. He was a brute. That first night, when I discovered the camp, Vesta and I had great talk about the things of our vanished world. We talked of art, and books, and poetry; and the Chauffeur listened and grinned and sneered. He was bored and angered by our way of speech which he did not comprehend, and finally he spoke up and said: 'And this is Vesta Van Warden, one-time wife of Van Warden the Magnate -- a high and stuck-up beauty, who is now my squaw. Eh, Professor Smith, times is changed, times is changed. Here, you, woman, take off my moccasins, and lively about it. I want Professor Smith to see how well I have you trained.'

"I saw her clench her teeth, and the flame of revolt rise in her face. He drew back his gnarled fist to strike, and I was afraid, and sick at heart. I could do nothing to prevail against him. So I got up to go, and not be witness to such indignity. But the Chauffeur laughed and threatened me with a beating if I did not stay and behold. And I sat there, perforce, by the campfire on the shore of lake Temescal, and saw Vesta, Vesta Van Warden, kneel and remove the moccasins of that grinning, hairy, ape-like human brute.

"Oh, you do not understand, my grandsons. You have never known anything else, and you do not understand.

"'Halter-broke and bridle-wise,' the Chauffeur gloated, while she performed that dreadful, menial task. 'A trifle balky at times, Professor, a trifle balky; but a clout alongside the jaw makes her as meek and gentle as a lamb.'

"And another time he said: 'We've got to start all over and replenish the earth and multiply. You're handicapped, Professor. You ain't got no wife, and we're up against a regular Garden-of-Eden proposition. But I ain't proud. I'll tell you what, Professor.' He pointed at their little infant, barely a year old. 'There's your wife, though you'll have to wait till she grows up. It's rich, ain't it? We're all equals here, and I'm the biggest toad in the splash. But I ain't stuck up -- not I. I do you the honor, Professor Smith, the very great honor of betrothing to you my and Vesta Van Warden's daughter. Ain't it cussed bad that Van Warden ain't here to see?

6

"I lived three weeks of infinite torment there in the Chauffeur's camp. And then, one day, tiring of me, or of what to him was my bad effect on Vesta, he told me that the year before, wandering through the Contra Costa Hills to the Straits of Carquinez, across the Straits he had seen a smoke. This meant that there were still other human beings, and that for three weeks he had kept this inestimably precious information from me. I departed at once, with my dogs and horses, and journeyed across the Contra Costa Hills to the Straits. I saw no smoke on the other side, but at Port Costa discovered a small steel barge on which I was able to embark my animals. Old canvas which I found served me for a sail, and a southerly breeze fanned me across the Straits and up to the ruins of Vallejo. Here, on the outskirts of the city, I found evidences of a recently occupied camp. Many clam-shells showed me why these humans had come to the shores of the Bay. This was the Santa Rosa Tribe, and I followed its track along the old railroad right of way across the salt marshes to Sonoma Valley. Here, at the old brickyard at Glen Ellen, I came upon the camp. There were eighteen souls all told. Two were old men, one of whom was Jones, a banker. The other was Harrison, a retired pawnbroker, who had taken for wife the matron of the State Hospital for the Insane at Napa. Of all the persons of the city of Napa, and of all the other towns and villages in that rich and populous valley, she had been the only survivor. Next, there were the three young men -- Cardiff and Hale, who had been farmers, and Wainwright, a common day-laborer. All three had found wives. To Hale, a crude, illiterate farmer, had fallen Isadore, the greatest prize, next to Vesta, of the women who came through the plague. She was one of the world's most noted singers, and the plague had caught her at San Francisco. She has talked with me for hours at a time, telling me of her adventures, until, at last, rescued by Hale in the Mendocino Forest Reserve, there had remained nothing for her to do but become his wife. But Hale was a good fellow, in spite of his illiteracy. He had a keen sense of justice and right-dealing, and she was far happier with him than was Vesta with the Chauffeur.

"The wives of Cardiff and Wainwright were ordinary women, accustomed to toil, with strong constitutions just the type for the wild new life which they were compelled to live. In addition were two adult idiots from the feeble-minded home at Eldredge, and five or six young children and infants born after the formation of the Santa Rosa Tribe. Also, there was Bertha. She was a good woman, Hare-Lip, in spite of the sneers of your father. Her I took for wife. She was the mother of your father, Edwin, and of yours, Hoo-Hoo. And it was our daughter, Vera, who married your father, Hare-Lip -- your father, Sandow, who was the oldest son of Vesta Van Warden and the Chauffeur.

"And so it was that I became the nineteenth member of the Santa Rosa Tribe. There were only two outsiders added after me. One was Mungerson, descended from the Magnates, who wandered alone in the wilds of Northern California for eight years before he came south and joined us. He it was who waited twelve years more before he married my daughter, Mary. The other was Johnson, the man who founded the Utah Tribe. That was where he came from,

Utah, a country that lies very far away from here, across the great deserts, to the east. It was not until twenty-seven years after the plague that Johnson reached California. In all that Utah region he reported but three survivors, himself one, and all men. For many years these three men lived and hunted together, until at last, desperate, fearing that with them the human race would perish utterly from the planet, they headed westward on the possibility of finding women survivors in California. Johnson alone came through the great desert, where his two companions died. He was forty-six years old when he joined us, and he married the fourth daughter of Isadore and Hale, and his eldest son married your aunt, Hare-Lip, who was the third daughter of Vesta and the Chauffeur Johnson was a strong man, with a will of his own. And it was because of this that he seceded from the Santa Rosans and formed the Utah Tribe at San Jose. It is a small tribe-there are only nine in it; but, though he is dead, such was his influence and the strength of his breed, that it will grow into a strong tribe and play a leading part in the re-civilization of the planet.

"There are oily two other tribes that we know of -- the Los Angelitos and the Carmelitos. The latter started from one man and woman. He was called Lopez, and he was descended from the ancient Mexicans and was very black. He was a cowherd in the ranges beyond Carmel, and his wife was a maidservant in the great Del Monte Hotel. It was seven years before we first got in touch with the Los Angelitos. They have a good country down there, but it is too warm. I estimate the present population of the world at between three hundred and fifty and four hundred -- provided, of course, that there are no scattered little tribes elsewhere in the world. If there be such, we have not heard from them. Since Johnson crossed the desert from Utah, no word nor sign has come from the East or anywhere else. The great world which I knew in my boyhood and early manhood is gone. It has ceased to be. I am the last man who was alive in the days of the plague and who knows the wonders of that far-off time. We, who mastered the planet its earth, and sea, and sky -- and who were as very gods, now live in primitive savagery along the water courses of this California country.

"But we are increasing rapidly -- your sister, Hare-Lip, already has four children. We are increasing rapidly and making ready for a new climb toward civilization. In time, pressure of population will compel us to spread out, and a hundred generations from now we may expect our descendants to start across the Sierras, oozing slowly along, generation by generation, over the great continent to the colonization of the East -- a new Aryan drift around the world.

"But it will be slow, very slow; we have so far to climb. We fell so hopelessly far. If only one physicist or one chemist had survived! But it was not to be, and we have forgotten everything. The Chauffeur started working in iron. He made the forge which we use to this day. But he was a lazy man, and when he died he took with him all he knew of metals and machinery. What was I to know of such things? I was a classical scholar, not a chemist. The other men who survived were not educated. Only two things did the Chauffeur accomplish -- the brewing of strong drink and the growing of tobacco. It was while he was drunk, once, that he killed Vesta. I firmly believe that he killed Vesta in a fit of drunken cruelty though he always maintained that she fell into the lake and was drowned.

"And, my grandsons, let me warn you against the medicine-men. They call themselves doctors, travestying what was once a noble profession, but in reality they are medicine-men, devil-devil men, and they make for superstition and darkness. They are cheats and liars. But so debased and degraded are we, that we believe their lies. They, too, will increase in numbers as we increase, and they will strive to rule us. Yet are they liars and charlatans. Look at young Cross-Eyes, posing as a doctor, selling charms against sickness, giving good hunting, exchanging promises of fair weather for good meat and skins, sending the death stick, performing a thousand abominations. Yet I say to you, that when he says he can do these things, he lies. I, Professor Smith, Professor James Howard Smith, say that he lies. I have told him so to his teeth. Why has he not sent me the death-stick? Because he knows that with me it is without avail. But you, Hare-Lip, so deeply are you sunk in black superstition that did you awake this night and find the death-stick beside you, you would surely die. And you would die, not because of any virtues in the stick, but because you are a savage with the dark and clouded mind of a savage.

"The doctors must be destroyed, and all that was lost must be discovered over again. Wherefore, earnestly, I repeat unto you certain things which you must remember and tell to your children after you. You must tell them that when water is made hot by fire, there resides in it a wonderful thing called steam, which is stronger than ten thousand men and which can do all man's work for him. There are other very useful things. In the lightning flash resides a similarly strong servant of man, which was of old his slave and which some day will be his slave again.

"Quite a different thing is the alphabet. It is what enables me to know the meaning of fine markings, whereas you boys know only rude picture-writing. In that dry cave on Telegraph Hill, where you see me often go when the tribe is down by the sea, I have stored many books. In them is great wisdom Also, with them, I have placed a key to the alphabet, so that one who knows picture-writing may also know print. Some day men will read again; and then, if no accident has befallen my cave, they will know that Professor James Howard Smith once lived and saved for them the knowledge of the ancients.

"There is another little device that men inevitably will rediscover. It is called gunpowder. It was what enabled us to kill surely and at long distances. Certain things which are found in the ground, when combined in the right proportions, will make this gunpowder. What these things are, I have forgotten, or else I never knew. But I wish I did know. Then would I make powder, and then would I certainly kill Cross-Eyes and rid the land of superstition."

"After I am man-grown I am going to give Cross-Eyes all the goats, and meat, and skins I can get, so that he'll teach me to be a doctor," Hoo-Hoo asserted. "And when I know, I'll make everybody else sit up and take notice. They'll get down in the dirt to me, you bet."

The old man nodded his head solemnly, and murmured: "Strange it is to hear the vestiges and remnants of the complicated Aryan speech falling from the lips of a filthy little skin-clad savage. All the world is topsy-turvy. And it has been topsy-turvy ever since the plague."

"You won't make me sit up," Hare-Lip boasted to the would-be medicine-man. "If I paid you for a sending of the death-stick and it didn't work, I'd bust in your head -- understand, you Hoo-Hoo, you?"

"I'm going to get Granser to remember this here gunpowder stuff," Edwin said softly, "and then I'll have you all on the run. You, Hare-Lip, will do my fighting for me and get my meat for me, and you, Hoo-Hoo, will send the death-stick for me and make everybody afraid. And if I catch Hare-Lip trying to bust your head, Hoo-Hoo, I'll fix him with that same gunpowder. Granser ain't such a fool as you think, and I'm going to listen to him and some day I'll be boss over the whole bunch of you."

The old man shook his head sadly, and said: "The gunpowder will come. Nothing can stop it -- the same old story over and over. Man will increase, and men will fight. The gunpowder will enable men to kill millions of men, and in this way only, by fire and blood, will a new civilization, in some remote day, be evolved. And of what profit will it be? Just as the old civilization passed, so will the new. It may take fifty thousand years to build, but it will pass. All things pass.

"Only remain cosmic force and matter, ever in flux, ever acting and reacting and realizing the eternal types-the priest, the soldier, and the king. Out of the mouths of babes comes the wisdom of all the ages. Some will fight, some will rule, some will pray; and all the rest will toil and suffer sore while on their bleeding carcasses is reared again, and yet again, without end, the amazing beauty and surpassing wonder of the civilized state. It were just as well that I destroyed those cave-stored books -- whether they remain or perish, all their old truths will be discovered, their old lies lived and handed down. What is the profit -- "

Hare-Lip leaped to his feet, giving a quick glance at the pasturing goats and the afternoon sun. "Gee!" He muttered to Edwin. "The old geezer gets more long-winded every day. Let's pull for camp."

While the other two, aided by the dogs, assembled the goats and started them for the trail through the forest, Edwin stayed by the old man and guided him in the same direction. When they reached the old right of way, Edwin stopped suddenly and looked back. Hare-Lip and Hoo-Hoo and the dogs and the goats passed on.

Edwin was looking at a small herd of wild horses which had come down on the hard sand. There were at least twenty of them, young colts and yearlings and mares, led by a beautiful stallion which stood in the foam at the edge of the surf, with arched neck and bright wild eyes, sniffing the salt air from off the sea.

"What is it?" Granser queried.

"Horses," was the answer. "First time I ever seen 'em on the beach. It's the mountain lions getting thicker and thicker and driving 'em down."

The low sun shot red shafts of light, fan shaped, up from a cloud-tumbled horizon. And close at hand, in the white waste of shore-lashed waters, the sea-lions, bellowing their old primeval chant, hauled up out of the sea on the black rocks and fought and loved.

"Come on, Granser," Edwin prompted.

And old man and boy, skin-clad and barbaric, turned and went along the right of way into the forest in the wake of the goats.

A Relic of the Pliocene

I wash my hands of him at the start. I cannot father his tales, nor will I be responsible for them. I make these preliminary reservations, observe, as a guard upon my own integrity. I possess a certain definite position in a small way, also a wife; and for the good name of the community that honours my existence with its approval, and for the sake of her posterity and mine, I cannot take the chances I once did, nor foster probabilities with the careless improvidence of youth. So, I repeat, I wash my hands of him, this Nimrod, this mighty hunter, this homely, blue-eyed, freckle-faced Thomas Stevens.

Having been honest to myself, and to whatever prospective olive branches my wife may be pleased to tender me, I can now afford to be generous. I shall not criticize the tales told me by Thomas Stevens, and, further, I shall withhold my judgment. If it be asked why, I can only add that judgment I have none. Long have I pondered, weighed, and balanced, but never have my conclusions been twice the same -- forsooth! because Thomas Stevens is a greater man than I. If he have told truths, well and good; if untruths, still well and good. For who can prove? Or who disprove? I eliminate myself from the proposition, while those of little faith may do as I have done -- go find the same Thomas Stevens, and discuss to his face the various matters which, if fortune serve, I shall relate. As to where he may be found? The directions are simple: anywhere between 53 north latitude and the Pole, on the one hand; and, on the other, the likeliest hunting grounds that lie between the east coast of Siberia and farthermost Labrador. That he is there, somewhere, within that clearly defined territory, I pledge the word of an honourable man whose expectations entail straight speaking and right living.

Thomas Stevens may have toyed prodigiously with truth, but when we first met (it were well to mark this point), he wandered into my camp when I thought myself a thousand miles beyond the outermost post of civilization. At the sight of his human face, the first in weary months, I could have sprung forward and folded him in my arms (and I am not by any means a demonstrative man); but to him his visit seemed the most casual thing under the sun. He just strolled into the light of my camp, passed the time of day after the custom of men on beaten trails, threw my snowshoes the one way and a couple of dogs the other, and so made room for himself by the fire. Said he'd just dropped in to borrow a pinch of soda and to see if I had any decent tobacco. He plucked forth an ancient pipe, loaded it with painstaking care, and, without as much as by your leave, whacked half the tobacco of my pouch into his. Yes, the stuff was fairly good. He sighed with the contentment of the just, and literally absorbed the smoke from the crisping yellow flakes, and it did my smoker's heart good to behold him.

Hunter? Trapper? Prospector? He shrugged his shoulders No; just sort of knocking round a bit. Had come up from the Great Slave some time since, and was thinking of traipsing over into the Yukon country. The Factor of Koshim had spoken about the discoveries on the Klondike, and he was of a mind to run over for a peep. I noticed that he spoke of the Klondike in the archaic vernacular, calling it the Reindeer River -- a conceited custom that the Old Timers employ against the *che-cha-quas* and all tenderfeet in general. But he did it so naively and as such a matter of course, that there was no sting, and I forgave him. He also had it in view, he said, before he crossed the divide into the Yukon, to make a little run up Fort o' Good Hope way.

Now Fort o' Good Hope is a far journey to the north, over and beyond the Circle, in a place where the feet of few men have trod; and when a nondescript ragamuffin comes in out of the night, from nowhere in particular, to sit by one's fire and discourse on such in terms of "traipsing" and "a little run," it is fair time to rouse up and shake off the dream. Wherefore I looked about me; saw the fly and, underneath, the pine boughs spread for the sleeping furs; saw the grub sacks, the camera, the frosty breaths of the dogs circling on the edge of the light; and, above, a great streamer of the aurora, bridging the zenith from south-east to north-west. I shivered. There is a magic in the Northland night, that steals in on one like fevers from malarial marshes. You are clutched and downed before you are aware. Then I looked to the snowshoes, lying prone and crossed where he had flung them. Also I had an eye to my tobacco pouch. Half, at least, of its goodly store had vamoosed. That settled it. Fancy had not tricked me after all.

Crazed with suffering, I thought, looking steadfastly at the man -- one of those wild stampeders, strayed far from his bearings and wandering like a lost soul through great vastnesses and unknown deeps. Oh, well, let his moods slip on, until, mayhap, he gathers his tangled wits together. Who knows? -- the mere sound of a fellow-creature's voice may bring all straight again.

So I led him on in talk, and soon I marvelled, for he talked of game and the ways thereof. He had killed the Siberian wolf of westernmost Alaska, and the chamois in the secret Rockies. He averred he knew the haunts where the last buffalo still roamed; that he had hung on the flanks of the caribou when they ran by the hundred thousand, and slept in the Great Barrens on the musk-ox's winter trail.

And I shifted my judgment accordingly (the first revision, but by no account the last), and deemed him a monumental effigy of truth. Why it was I know not, but the spirit moved me to repeat a tale told to me by a man who had dwelt in the land too long to know better. It was of the great bear that hugs the steep slopes of St. Elias, never descending to the levels of the gentler inclines. Now God so constituted this creature for its hillside habitat that the legs of one side are all of a foot longer than those of the other. This is mighty convenient, as will be reality admitted. So I hunted this rare beast in my own name, told it in the first person, present tense, painted the requisite locale, gave it the necessary garnishings and touches of verisimilitude, and looked to see the man stunned by the recital.

Not he. Had he doubted, I could have forgiven him. Had he objected, denying the dangers of such a hunt by virtue of the animal's inability to turn about and go the other way -- had he done this, I say, I could have taken him by the hand for the true sportsman that he was. Not he. He sniffed, looked on me, and sniffed again; then gave my tobacco due praise, thrust one foot into my lap, and bade me examine the gear. It was a *muclu*c of the Innuit pattern, sewed together with sinew threads, and devoid of beads or furbelows. But it was the skin itself that was remarkable. In that it was all of half an inch thick, it reminded me of walrus-hide; but there the resemblance ceased, for no walrus ever bore so marvellous a growth of hair. On the side and ankles this hair was well-nigh worn away, what of friction with underbrush and snow; but around the top and down the more sheltered back it was coarse, dirty black, and very thick. I parted it with difficulty and looked beneath for the fine fur that is common with northern animals, but found it in this case to be absent. This, however, was compensated for by the length. Indeed, the tufts that had survived wear and tear measured all of seven or eight inches.

I looked up into the man's face, and he pulled his foot down and asked, "Find hide like that on your St. Elias bear?"

I shook my head. "Nor on any other creature of land or sea," I answered candidly. The thickness of it, and the length of the hair, puzzled me.

"That," he said, and said without the slightest hint of impressiveness, "that came from a mammoth."

"Nonsense!" I exclaimed, for I could not forbear the protest of my unbelief. "The mammoth, my dear sir, long ago vanished from the earth. We know it once existed by the fossil remains that we have unearthed, and by a frozen carcase that the Siberian sun saw fit to melt from out the bosom of a glacier; but we also know that no living specimen exists. Our explorers -- "

At this word he broke in impatiently. "Your explorers? Pish! A weakly breed. Let us hear no more of them. But tell me, O man, what you may know of the mammoth and his ways."

Beyond contradiction, this was leading to a yarn; so I baited my hook by ransacking my memory for whatever data I possessed on the subject in hand. To begin with, I emphasized that the animal was prehistoric, and marshalled all my facts in support of this. I mentioned the Siberian sand-bars that abounded with ancient mammoth bones; spoke of the large quantities of fossil ivory purchased from the Innuits by the Alaska Commercial Company; and acknowledged having myself mined six and eight foot tusks from the pay gravel of the Klondike creeks. "All fossils," I concluded, "found in the midst of debris deposited through countless ages."

"I remember when I was a kid," Thomas Stevens sniffed (he had a most confounded way of sniffing), "that I saw a petrified water-melon. Hence, though mistaken persons sometimes delude themselves into thinking that they are really raising or eating them, there are no such things as extant water-melons?"

"But the question of food," I objected, ignoring his point, which was puerile and without bearing. "The soil must bring forth vegetable life in lavish abundance to support so monstrous creations. Nowhere in the North is the soil so prolific. Ergo, the mammoth cannot exist."

"I pardon your ignorance concerning many matters of this Northland, for you are a young man and have travelled little; but, at the same time, I am inclined to agree with you on one thing. The mammoth no longer exists. How do I know? I killed the last one with my own right arm."

Thus spake Nimrod, the mighty Hunter. I threw a stick of firewood at the dogs and bade them quit their unholy howling, and waited. Undoubtedly this liar of singular felicity would open his mouth and requite me for my St. Elias bear.

"It was this way," he at last began, after the appropriate silence had intervened. "I was in camp one day -- "

"Where?" I interrupted.

He waved his hand vaguely in the direction of the north-east, where stretched a *terra incognita* into which vastness few men have strayed and fewer emerged. "I was in camp one day with Klooch. Klooch was as handsome a little *kamooks* as ever whined betwixt the traces or shoved nose into a camp kettle. Her father was a full-blood Malemute from Russian Pastilik on Bering Sea, and I bred her, and with understanding, out of a clean-legged bitch of the Hudson Bay stock. I tell you, O man, she was a corker combination. And now, on this day I have in mind, she was brought to pup through a pure wild wolf of the woods -- grey, and long of limb, with big lungs and no end of staying powers. Say! Was there ever the like? It was a new breed of dog I had started, and I could look forward to big things.

"As I have said, she was brought neatly to pup, and safely delivered. I was squatting on my hams over the litter -- seven sturdy, blind little beggars -- when from behind came a bray of trumpets and crash of brass. There was a rush, like the wind-squall that kicks the heels of the rain, and I was midway to my feet when knocked flat on my face. At the same instant I heard Klooch sigh, very much as a man does when you've planted your fist in his belly. You can stake your sack I lay quiet, but I twisted my head around and saw a huge bulk swaying above me. Then the blue sky flashed into view and I got to my feet. A hairy mountain of flesh was just disappearing in the underbrush on the edge of the open. I caught a rear-end glimpse, with a stiff tail, as big in girth as my body, standing out straight behind. The next second only a tremendous hole remained in the thicket, though I could still hear the sounds as of a tornado dying quickly away, underbrush ripping and tearing, and trees snapping and crashing.

"I cast about for my rifle. It had been lying on the ground with the muzzle against a log; but now the stock was smashed, the barrel out of line, and the working-gear in a thousand bits. Then I looked for the slut, and -- and what do you suppose?"

I shook my head.

"May my soul burn in a thousand hells if there was anything left of her! Klooch, the seven sturdy, blind little beggars -- gone, all gone. Where she had stretched was a slimy, bloody depression in the soft earth, all of a yard in diameter, and around the edges a few scattered hairs."

I measured three feet on the snow, threw about it a circle, and glanced at Nimrod.

"The beast was thirty long and twenty high," he answered, "and its tusks scaled over six times three feet. I couldn't believe, myself, at the time, for all that it had just happened. But if my senses had played me, there was the broken gun and the hole in the brush. And there was -- or, rather, there was not -- Klooch and the pups. O man, it makes me hot all over now when I think of it. Klooch! Another Eve! The mother of a new race! And a rampaging, ranting, old bull mammoth, like a second flood, wiping them, root and branch, off the face of the earth! Do you wonder that the blood-soaked earth cried out to high God? Or that I grabbed the hand-axe and took the trail?"

"The hand-axe?" I exclaimed, startled out of myself by the picture. "The hand-axe, and a big bull mammoth, thirty feet long, twenty feet -- "

Nimrod joined me in my merriment, chuckling gleefully. "Wouldn't it kill you?" He cried. "Wasn't it a beaver's dream? Many's the time I've laughed about it since, but at the time it was no laughing matter, I was that danged mad, what of the gun and Klooch. Think of it, O man! A brand-new, unclassified, uncopyrighted breed, and wiped out before ever it opened its eyes or took out its intention papers! Well, so be it. Life's full of disappointments, and rightly so. Meat is best after a famine, and a bed soft after a hard trail.

"As I was saying, I took out after the beast with the hand-axe, and hung to its heels down the valley; but when he circled back toward the head, I was left winded at the lower end. Speaking of grub, I might as well stop long enough to explain a couple of points. Up thereabouts, in the midst of the mountains, is an almighty curious formation. There is no end of little valleys, each like the other much as peas in a pod, and all neatly tucked away with straight, rocky walls rising on all sides. And at the lower ends are always small openings where the drainage or glaciers must have broken out. The only way in is through these mouths, and they are all small, and some smaller than others. As to grub -- you've slushed around on the rain-soaked islands of the Alaskan coast down Sitka way, most likely, seeing as you're a traveller. And you know how stuff grows there -- big, and juicy, and jungly. Well, that's the way it was with those valleys. Thick, rich soil, with ferns and grasses and such things in patches higher than your head. Rain three days out of four during the summer months; and food in them for a thousand mammoths, to say nothing of small game for man.

"But to get back. Down at the lower end of the valley I got winded and gave over. I began to speculate, for when my wind left me my dander got hotter and hotter, and I knew I'd never know peace of mind till I dined on roasted mammoth-foot. And I knew, also, that that stood for *skookum mamook pukapuk* -- excuse Chinook, I mean there was a big fight coming. Now the mouth of my valley was very narrow, and the walls steep. High up on one side was one of those big pivot rocks, or balancing rocks, as some call them, weighing all of a couple of hundred tons. Just the thing. I hit back for camp, keeping an eye open so the bull couldn't slip past, and got my ammunition. It wasn't worth anything with the rifle smashed; so I opened the shells, planted the powder under the rock, and touched it off with slow fuse. Wasn't much of a charge, but the old boulder tilted up lazily and dropped down into place, with just space enough to let the creek drain nicely. Now I had him."

"But how did you have him?" I queried. "Who ever heard of a man killing a mammoth with a hand-axe? And, for that matter, with anything else?"

"O man, have I not told you I was mad?" Nimrod replied, with a slight manifestation of sensitiveness. "Mad clean through, what of Klooch and the gun. Also, was I not a hunter? And was this not new and most unusual game? A hand-axe? Pish! I did not need it. Listen, and you shall hear of a hunt, such as might have happened in the youth of the world when cavemen rounded up the kill with hand-axe of stone. Such would have served me as well. Now is it not a fact that man can out walk the dog or horse? That he can wear them out with the intelligence of his endurance?"

I nodded.

"Well?"

The light broke in on me, and I bade him continue.

"My valley was perhaps five miles around. The mouth was closed. There was no way to get out. A timid beast was that bull mammoth, and I had him at my mercy. I got on his heels again hollered like a fiend, pelted him with cobbles, and raced him around the valley three times before I knocked off for supper. Don't you see? A race-course! A man and a mammoth! A hippodrome, with sun, moon, and stars to referee!

"It took me two months to do it, but I did it. And that's no beaver dream. Round and round I ran him, me travelling on the inner circle, eating jerked meat and salmon berries on the run, and snatching winks of sleep between. Of course, he'd get desperate at times and turn. Then I'd head for soft ground where the creek spread out, and lay anathema upon him and his ancestry, and dare him to come on. But he was too wise to bog in a mud puddle. Once he pinned me in against the walls, and I crawled back into a deep crevice and waited. Whenever he felt for me with his trunk, I'd belt him with the hand-axe till he pulled out, shrieking fit to split my ear drums, he was that mad. He knew he had me and didn't have me, and it near drove him wild. But he was no man's fool. He knew he was safe as long as I stayed in the crevice, and he made up his mind to keep me there. And he was dead right, only he hadn't figured on the commissary. There was neither grub nor water around that spot, so on the face of it he couldn't keep up the siege. He'd stand before the opening for hours, keeping an eye on me and flapping mosquitoes away with his big blanket ears. Then the thirst would come on him and he'd ramp round and roar till the earth shook, calling me every name he could lay tongue to. This was to frighten me, of course; and when he thought I was sufficiently impressed, he'd back away softly and try to make a sneak for the creek. Sometimes I'd let him get almost there -- only a couple of hundred yards away it was -- when out I'd pop and back he'd come, lumbering along like the old landslide he was. After I'd done this a few times, and he'd figured it out, he changed his tactics. Grasped the time element, you see. Without a word of warning, away he'd go, tearing for the water like mad, scheming to get there and back before I ran away. Finally, after cursing me most horribly, he raised the siege and deliberately stalked off to the water-hole.

"That was the only time he penned me -- three days of it -- but after that the hippodrome never stopped. Round, and round, and round, like a six days' go-as-I-please, for he never pleased. My clothes went to rags and tatters, but I never stopped to mend, till at last I ran naked as a son of the earth, with nothing but the old hand-axe in one hand and a cobble in the other. In fact, I never stopped, save for peeps of sleep in the crannies and ledges of the cliffs. As for the bull, he got perceptibly thinner and thinner -- must have lost several tons at least -- and as nervous as a school-marm on the wrong side of matrimony. When I'd come up with him and yell, or lain him with a rock at long range, he'd jump like a skittish colt and tremble all over. Then he'd pull out on the run, tail and trunk waving stiff, head over one shoulder and wicked eyes blazing, and the way he'd swear at me was something dreadful. A most immoral beast he was, a murderer, and a blasphemer.

"But towards the end he quit all this, and fell to whimpering and crying like a baby. His spirit broke and he became a quivering jelly-mountain of misery. He'd get attacks of palpitation of the heart, and stagger around like a drunken man, and fall down and bark his shins. And then he'd cry, but always on the run. O man, the gods themselves would have wept with him, and you yourself or any other man. It was pitiful, and there was so much of it, but I only hardened my heart and hit up the pace. At last I wore him clean out, and he lay down, broken-winded, broken-hearted, hungry, and thirsty. When I found he wouldn't budge, I hamstrung him, and spent the better part of the day wading into him with the hand-axe, he a-sniffing and sobbing till I worked in far enough to shut him off. Thirty feet long he was, and twenty high, and a man could sling a hammock between his tusks and sleep comfortably. Barring the fact that I had run most of the juices out of him, he was fair eating, and his four feet, alone, roasted whole, would have lasted a man a twelvemonth. I spent the winter there myself."

"And where is this valley?" I asked

He waved his hand in the direction of the north-east, and said: "Your tobacco is very good. I carry a fair share of it in my pouch, but I shall carry the recollection of it until I die. In token of my appreciation, and in return for the moccasins on your own feet, I will present to you these *muclucs*. They commemorate Klooch and the seven blind little beggars. They are also souvenirs of an unparalleled event in history, namely, the destruction of the oldest breed of animal on earth, and the youngest. And their chief virtue lies in that they will never wear out."

Having effected the exchange, he knocked the ashes from his pipe, gripped my hand good-night, and wandered off through the snow. Concerning this tale, for which I have already disclaimed responsibility, I would recommend those of little faith to make a visit to the Smithsonian Institute. If they bring the requisite credentials and do not come in vacation time, they will undoubtedly gain an audience with Professor Dolvidson. The *muclucs* are in his possession, and he will verify, not the manner in which they were obtained, but the material of which they are composed. When he states that they are made from the skin of the mammoth, the scientific world accepts his verdict. What more would you have?

When the World Was Young

He was a very quiet, self-possessed sort of man, sitting a moment on top of the wall to sound the damp darkness for warnings of the dangers it might conceal. But the plummet of his hearing brought nothing to him save the moaning of wind through invisible trees and the rustling of leaves on swaying branches. A heavy fog drifted and drove before the wind, and though he could not see this fog, the wet of it blew upon his face, and the wall on which he sat was wet.

Without noise he had climbed to the top of the wall from the outside, and without noise he dropped to the ground on the inside. From his pocket he drew an electric night-stick, but he did not use it. Dark as the way was, he was not anxious for light. Carrying the night-stick in his hand, his finger on the button, he advanced through the darkness. The ground was velvety and springy to his feet, being carpeted with dead pine-needles and leaves and mold which evidently bad been undisturbed for years. Leaves and branches brushed against his body, but so dark was it that he could not avoid them. Soon he walked with his hand stretched out gropingly before him, and more than once the hand fetched up against the solid trunks of massive trees. All about him he knew were these trees; he sensed the loom of them everywhere; and he experienced a strange feeling of microscopic smallness in the midst of great bulks leaning toward him to crush him. Beyond, he knew, was the house, and he expected to find some trail or winding path that would lead easily to it.

Once, he found himself trapped. On every side he groped against trees and branches, or blundered into thickets of underbrush, until there seemed no way out. Then he turned on his light, circumspectly, directing its rays to the ground at his feet. Slowly and carefully he moved it about him, the white brightness showing in sharp detail all the obstacles to his progress. He saw, an opening between huge-trunked trees, and advanced through it, putting out the light and treading on dry footing as yet protected from the drip of the fog by the dense foliage overhead. His sense of direction was good, and he knew he was going toward the house.

And then the thing happened -- the thing unthinkable and unexpected. His descending foot came down upon something that was soft and alive, and that arose with a snort under the weight of his body. He sprang clear, and crouched for another spring, anywhere, tense and expectant, keyed for the onslaught of the unknown. He waited a moment, wondering what manner of animal it was that had arisen from under his foot and that now made no sound nor movement and that must be crouching and waiting just as tensely and expectantly as he. The strain became unbearable. Holding the night-stick before him, he pressed the button, saw, and screamed aloud in terror. He was prepared for anything, from a frightened calf or fawn to a belligerent lion, but he was not prepared for what he saw. In that instant his tiny searchlight, sharp and white, had shown him what a thousand years would not enable him to forget -- a man, huge and blond, yellow-haired and yellow-bearded, naked except for soft-tanned moccasins and what seemed a goat-skin about his middle. Arms and legs were bare, as were his shoulders and most of his chest. The skin was smooth and hairless, but browned by sun and wind, while under it heavy muscles were knotted like fat snakes.

Still, this alone, unexpected as it well was, was not what had made the man scream out. What had caused his terror was the unspeakable ferocity of the face, the wild-animal glare of the blue eyes scarcely dazzled by the light, the pine-needles matted and clinging in the beard and hair, and the whole formidable body crouched and in the act of springing at him. Practically in the instant he saw all this, and while his scream still rang, the thing leaped, he flung his night-stick full at it, and threw himself to the ground. He felt its feet and shins strike against his ribs, and he bounded up and away while the thing itself hurled onward in a heavy crashing fall into the underbrush.

As the noise of the fall ceased, the man stopped and on hands and knees waited. He could hear the thing moving about, searching for him, and he was afraid to advertise his location by attempting further flight. He knew that inevitably he would crackle the underbrush and be pursued. Once he drew out his revolver, then changed his mind. He had recovered his composure and hoped to get away without noise. Several times he heard the thing beating up the thickets for him, and there were moments when it, too, remained still and listened. This gave an idea to the man. One of his hands was resting on a chunk of dead wood. Carefully, first feeling about him in the darkness to know that the full swing of his arm was clear, he raised the chunk of wood and threw it. It was not a large piece, and it went far, landing noisily in a bush. He heard the thing bound into the bush, and at the same time himself crawled steadily away. And on hands and knees, slowly and cautiously, he crawled on, till his knees were wet on the soggy mold, When he listened he heard naught but the moaning wind and the drip-drip of the fog from the branches. Never abating his caution, he stood erect and went on to the stone wall, over which he climbed and dropped down to the road outside.

Feeling his way in a clump of bushes, he drew out a bicycle and prepared to mount. He was in the act of driving the gear around with his foot for the purpose of getting the opposite pedal in position, when he heard the thud of a heavy body that landed lightly and evidently on its feet. He did not wait for more, but ran, with hands on the handles of his bicycle, until he was able to vault astride the saddle, catch the pedals, and start a spurt. Behind he could hear the quick thud-thud of feet on the dust of the road, but he drew away from it and lost it.

Unfortunately, he had started away from the direction of town and was heading higher up into the hills. He knew that on this particular road there were no cross roads. The only way back was past that terror, and he could not steel himself to face it. At the end of half an hour, finding himself on an ever increasing grade, he dismounted. For still greater safety, leaving the wheel by the roadside, he climbed through a fence into what he decided was a hillside pasture, spread a newspaper on the ground, and sat down.

"Gosh!" He said aloud, mopping the sweat and fog from his face.

And "Gosh!" He said once again, while rolling a cigarette and as he pondered the problem of getting back.

But he made no attempt to go back. He was resolved not to face that road in the dark, and with head bowed on knees, he dozed, waiting for daylight.

How long afterward he did not know, he was awakened by the yapping bark of a young coyote. As he looked about and located it on the brow of the hill behind him, he noted the change that had come over the face of the night. The fog was gone; the stars and moon were out; even the wind had died down. It had transformed into a balmy California summer night. He tried to doze again, but the yap of the coyote disturbed him. Half asleep, he heard a wild and eerie chant. Looking about him, he noticed that the coyote had ceased its noise and was running away along the crest of the hill, and behind it, in full pursuit, no longer chanting, ran the naked creature he had encountered in the garden. It was a young coyote, and it was being overtaken when the chase passed from view. The man trembled as with a chill as he started to his feet, clambered over the fence, and mounted his wheel. But it was his chance and he knew it. The terror was no longer between him and Mill Valley.

He sped at a breakneck rate down the hill, but in the turn at the bottom, in the deep shadows, he encountered a chuck-hole and pitched headlong over the handle bar.

"It's sure not my night," he muttered, as he examined the broken fork of the machine.

Shouldering the useless wheel, he trudged on. In time he came to the stone wall, and, half disbelieving his experience, he sought in the road for tracks, and found them -- moccasin tracks, large ones, deep-bitten into the dust at the toes. It was while bending over them, examining, that again he heard the eerie chant. He had seen the thing pursue the coyote, and he knew he had no chance on a straight run. He did not attempt it, contenting himself with hiding in the shadows on the off side of the road.

And again he saw the thing that was like a naked man, running swiftly and lightly and singing as it ran. Opposite him it paused, and his heart stood still. But instead of coming toward his hiding-place, it leaped into the air, caught the branch of a roadside tree, and swung swiftly upward, from limb to limb, like an ape. It swung across the wall, and a dozen feet above the top, into the branches of another tree, and dropped out of sight to the ground. The man waited a few wondering minutes, then started on.

2

Dave Slotter leaned belligerently against the desk that barred the way to the private office of James Ward, senior partner of the firm of Ward, Knowles & Co. Dave was angry. Every one in the outer office had looked him over suspiciously, and the man who faced him was excessively suspicious.

"You just tell Mr. Ward it's important," he urged.

"I tell you he is dictating and cannot be disturbed," was the answer. "Come tomorrow."

"Tomorrow will be too late. You just trot along and tell Mr. Ward it's a matter of life and death."

The secretary hesitated and Dave seized the advantage.

"You just tell him I was across the bay in Mill Valley last night, and that I want to put him wise to something."

"What name?" Was the query.

"Never mind the name. He don't know me."

When Dave was shown into the private office, he was still in the belligerent frame of mind, but when he saw a large fair man whirl in a revolving chair from dictating to a stenographer to face him, Dave's demeanor abruptly changed. He did not know why it changed, and he was secretly angry with himself.

"You are Mr. Ward?" Dave asked with a fatuousness that still further irritated him. He had never intended it at all.

"Yes," came the answer.

"And who are you?"

"Harry Bancroft," Dave lied. "You don't know me, and my name don't matter."

"You sent in word that you were in Mill Valley last night?"

"You live there, don't you?" Dave countered, looking suspiciously at the stenographer.

"Yes. What do you mean to see me about? I am very busy."

"I'd like to see you alone, sir."

Mr. Ward gave him a quick, penetrating look, hesitated, then made up his mind.

"That will do for a few minutes, Miss Potter."

The girl arose, gathered her notes together, and passed out. Dave looked at Mr. James Ward wonderingly, until that gentleman broke his train of inchoate thought.

"Well?"

"I was over in Mill Valley last night," Dave began confusedly.

"I've heard that before. What do you want?"

And Dave proceeded in the face of a growing conviction that was unbelievable. "I was at your house, or in the grounds, I mean."

"What were you doing there?"

"I came to break in," Dave answered in all frankness.

"I heard you lived all alone with a Chinaman for cook, and it looked good to me. Only I didn't break in. Something happened that prevented. That's why I'm here. I come to warn you. I found a wild man loose in your grounds -- a regular devil. He could pull a guy like me to pieces. He gave me the run of my life. He don't wear any clothes to speak of, he climbs trees like a monkey, and he runs like a deer. I saw him chasing a coyote, and the last I saw of it, by God, he was gaining on it."

Dave paused and looked for the effect that would follow his words. But no effect came. James Ward was quietly curious, and that was all.

"Very remarkable, very remarkable," he murmured. "A wild man, you say. Why have you come to tell me?"

"To warn you of your danger. I'm something of a hard proposition myself, but I don't believe in killing people . . . that is, unnecessarily. I realized that you was in danger. I thought I'd warn you. Honest, that's the game. Of course, if you wanted to give me anything for my trouble, I'd take it. That was in my mind, too. But I don't care whether you give me anything or not. I've warned you any way, and done my duty."

Mr. Ward meditated and drummed on the surface of his desk. Dave noticed they were large, powerful hands, withal well-cared for despite their dark sunburn. Also, he noted what had already caught his eye before -- a tiny strip of flesh-colored courtplaster on the forehead over one eve. And still the thought that forced itself into his mind was unbelievable.

Mr. Ward took a wallet from his inside coat pocket, drew out a greenback, and passed it to Dave, who noted as he pocketed it that it was for twenty dollars.

"Thank you," said Mr. Ward, indicating that the interview was at an end.

"I shall have the matter investigated. A wild man running loose *is* dangerous."

But so quiet a man was Mr. Ward, that Dave's courage returned. Besides, a new theory had suggested itself. The wild man was evidently Mr. Ward's brother, a lunatic privately confined. Dave had heard of such things. Perhaps Mr. Ward wanted it kept quiet. That was why he had given him the twenty dollars.

"Say," Dave began, "now I come to think of it that wild man looked a lot like you -- "

That was as far as Dave got, for at that moment he witnessed a transformation and found himself gazing into the same unspeakably ferocious blue eyes of the night before, at the same clutching talon-like hands, and at the same formidable bulk in the act of springing upon him. But this time Dave had no night-stick to throw, and he was caught by the biceps of both arms in a grip so terrific that it made him groan with pain. He saw the large white teeth exposed, for all the world as a dog's about to bite. Mr. Ward's beard brushed his face as the teeth went in for the grip on his throat. But the bite was not given. Instead, Dave felt the other's body stiffen as with an iron restraint, and then he was flung aside, without effort but with such force that only the wall stopped his momentum and dropped him gasping to the floor.

"What do you mean by coming here and trying to blackmail me?" Mr. Ward was snarling at him. "Here, give me back that money."

Dave passed the bill back without a word.

"I thought you came here with good intentions. I know you now. Let me see and hear no more of you, or I'll put you in prison where you belong. Do you understand?"

"Yes, sir," Dave gasped.

"Then go."

And Dave went, without further word, both his biceps aching intolerably from the bruise of that tremendous grip. As his hand rested on the door knob, he was stopped.

"You were lucky," Mr. Ward was saying, and Dave noted that his face and eyes were cruel and gloating and proud.

"You were lucky. Had I wanted, I could have torn your muscles out of your arms and thrown them in the waste basket there."

"Yes, sir," said Dave; and absolute conviction vibrated in his voice.

He opened the door and passed out. The secretary looked at him interrogatively.

"Gosh!" Was all Dave vouchsafed, and with this utterance passed out of the offices and the story.

3

James G. Ward was forty years of age, a successful business man, and very unhappy. For forty years he had vainly tried to solve a problem that was really himself and that with increasing years became more and more a woeful affliction. In himself he was two men, and, chronologically speaking, these men were several thousand years or so apart. He had studied the question of dual personality probably more profoundly than any half dozen of the leading specialists in that intricate and mysterious psychological field. In himself he was a different case from any that had been recorded. Even the most fanciful flights of the fiction-writers had not quite hit upon him. He was not a Dr. Jekyll and Mr. Hyde, nor was he like the unfortunate young man in Kipling's "Greatest Story in the World." His two personalities were so mixed that they were practically aware of themselves and of each other all the time.

His other self he had located as a savage and a barbarian living under the primitive conditions of several thousand years before. But which self was he, and which was the other, he could never tell. For he was both selves, and both selves all the time. Very rarely indeed did it happen that one self did not know what the other was doing. Another thing was that he had no visions nor memories of the past in which that early self had lived. That early self lived in the present; but while it lived in the present, it was under the compulsion to live the way of life that must have been in that distant past.

In his childhood he had been a problem to his father and mother, and to the family doctors, though never had they come within a thousand miles of hitting upon the clue to his erratic, conduct. Thus, they could not understand his excessive somnolence in the forenoon, nor his excessive activity at night. When they found him wandering along the hallways at night, or climbing over giddy roofs, or running in the hills, they decided he was a somnambulist. In reality he was wide-eyed awake and merely under the night-roaming compulsion of his early self. Questioned by an obtuse medico, he once told the truth and suffered the ignominy of having the revelation contemptuously labeled and dismissed as "dreams."

The point was, that as twilight and evening came on he became wakeful. The four walls of a room were an irk and a restraint. He heard a thousand voices whispering to him through the darkness. The night called to him, for he was, for that period of the twenty-four hours, essentially a night-prowler. But nobody understood, and never again did he attempt to explain. They classified him as a sleep-walker and took precautions accordingly -- precautions that very often were futile. As his childhood advanced, he grew more cunning, so that the major portion of all his nights were spent in the open at realizing his other self. As a result, he slept in the forenoons. Morning studies and schools were impossible, and it was discovered that only in the afternoons, under private teachers, could he be taught anything. Thus was his modern self educated and developed.

But a problem, as a child, he ever remained. He was known as a little demon, of insensate cruelty and viciousness. The family medicos privately adjudged him a mental monstrosity and degenerate. Such few boy companions as he had, hailed him as a wonder, though they were all afraid of him. He could outclimb, outswim, outrun, outdevil any of them; while none dared fight with him. He was too terribly strong, madly furious.

When nine years of age he ran away to the hills, where he flourished, night-prowling, for seven weeks before he was discovered and brought home. The marvel was how he had managed to subsist and keep in condition during that time. They did not know, and he never told them, of the rabbits he had killed, of the quail, young and old, he had captured and devoured, of the farmers' chicken-roosts he had raided, nor of the cave-lair he had made and carpeted with dry leaves and grasses and in which he had slept in warmth and comfort through the forenoons of many days.

At college he was notorious for his sleepiness and stupidity during the morning lectures and for his brilliance in the afternoon. By collateral reading and by borrowing the notebook of his fellow students he managed to scrape through the detestable morning courses, while his afternoon courses were triumphs. In football he proved a giant and a terror, and, in almost every form of track athletics, save for strange Berserker rages that were sometimes displayed, he could be depended upon to win. But his fellows were afraid to box with him, and he signalized his last wrestling bout by sinking his teeth into the shoulder of his opponent.

After college, his father, in despair, sent him among the cow-punchers of a Wyoming ranch. Three months later the doughty cow-men confessed he was too much for them and telegraphed his father to come and take the wild man away. Also, when the father arrived to take him away, the cowmen allowed that they would vastly prefer chumming with howling cannibals, gibbering lunatics, cavorting gorillas, grizzly bears, and man-eating tigers than with this particular young college product with hair parted in the middle.

There was one exception to the lack of memory of the life of his early self, and that was language. By some quirk of atavism, a certain portion of that early self's language had come down to him as a racial memory. In moments of happiness, exaltation, or battle, he was prone to burst out in wild barbaric songs or chants. It was by this means that he located in time and space that strayed half of him who should have been dead and dust for thousands of years. He sang, once, and deliberately, several of the ancient chants in the presence of Professor Wertz, who gave courses in old Saxon and who was a philologist of repute and passion. At the first one, the professor pricked up his ears and demanded to know what mongrel tongue or hog-German it was.

When the second chant was rendered, the professor was highly excited. James Ward then concluded the performance by giving a song that always irresistibly rushed to his lips when he was engaged in fierce struggling or fighting. Then it was that Professor Wertz proclaimed it no hog-German, but early German, or early Teuton, of a date that must far precede anything that had ever been discovered and handed down by the scholars. So early was it that it was beyond him; yet it was filled with haunting reminiscences of word-forms he knew and which his trained intuition told him were true and real. He demanded the source of the songs, and asked to borrow the precious book that contained them. Also, he demanded to know why young Ward had always posed as being profoundly ignorant of the German language. And Ward could neither explain his ignorance nor lend the book. Whereupon, after pleadings and entreaties that extended through weeks, Professor Wertz took a dislike to the young man, believed him a liar, and classified him as a man of monstrous selfishness for not giving him a glimpse of this wonderful screed that was older than the oldest any philologist had ever known or dreamed.

But little good did it do this much-mixed young man to know that half of him was late American and the other half early Teuton. Nevertheless, the late American in him was no weakling, and he (if he were a he and had a shred of existence outside of these two) compelled an adjustment or compromise between his one self that was a night-prowling savage that kept his other self sleepy of mornings, and that other self that was cultured and refined and that wanted to be normal and live and love and prosecute business like other people. The afternoons and early evenings he gave to the one, the nights to the other; the forenoons and parts of the nights were devoted to sleep for the twain. But in the mornings he slept in bed like a civilized man. In the night time he slept like a wild animal, as he had slept Dave Slotter stepped on him in the woods.

Persuading his father to advance the capital, he went into business and keen and successful business he made of it, devoting his afternoons whole-souled to it, while his partner devoted the mornings. The early evenings he spent socially, but, as the hour grew to nine or ten, an irresistible restlessness overcame him and he disappeared from the haunts of men until the next afternoon. Friends and acquaintances thought that he spent much of his time in sport. And they were right, though they never would have dreamed of the nature of the sport, even if they had seen him running coyotes in night-chases over the hills of Mill Valley. Neither were the schooner captains believed when they reported seeing, on cold winter mornings, a man swimming in the tide-rips of Raccoon Straits or in the swift currents between Goat island and Angel Island miles from shore.

In the bungalow at Mill Valley he lived alone, save for Lee Sing, the Chinese cook and factotum, who knew much about the strangeness of his master, who was paid well for saying nothing, and who never did say anything. After the satisfaction of his nights, a morning's sleep, and a breakfast of Lee Sing's, James Ward crossed the bay to San Francisco on a midday ferryboat and went to the club and on to his office, as normal and conventional a man of business as could be found in the city. But as the evening lengthened, the night called to him. There came a quickening of all his perceptions and a restlessness. His hearing was suddenly acute; the myriad night-noises told him a luring and familiar story; and, if alone, he would begin to pace up and down the narrow room like any caged animal from the wild.

Once, he ventured to fall in love. He never permitted himself that diversion again. He was afraid. And for many a day the young lady, scared at least out of a portion of her young ladyhood, bore on her arms and shoulders and wrists divers black-and-blue bruises -- tokens of caresses which he had bestowed in all fond gentleness but too late at night. There was the mistake. Had he ventured love-making in the afternoon, all would have been well, for it would have been as the quiet gentleman that he would have made love -- but at night it was the uncouth, wife-stealing savage of the dark German forests. Out of his wisdom, he decided that afternoon love-making could be prosecuted successfully; but out of the same wisdom he was convinced that marriage as would prove a ghastly failure. He found it appalling to imagine being married and encountering his wife after dark.

So he had eschewed all love-making, regulated his dual life, cleaned up a million in business, fought shy of match-making mamas and bright-eyed and eager young ladies of various ages, met Lilian Gersdale and made it a rigid observance never to see her later than eight o'clock in the evening, run of nights after his coyotes, and slept in forest lairs -- and through it all had kept his secret safe save Lee Sing . . . and now, Dave Slotter. It was the latter's discovery of both his selves that frightened him. In spite of the counter fright he had given the burglar, the latter might talk. And even if he did not, sooner or later he would be found out by someone else.

Thus it was that James Ward made a fresh and heroic effort to control the Teutonic barbarian that was half of him. So well did he make it a point to see Lilian in the afternoons, that the time came when she accepted him for better or worse, and when he prayed privily and fervently that it was not for worse. During this period no prize-fighter ever trained more harshly and faithfully for a contest than he trained to subdue the wild savage in him. Among other things, he strove to exhaust himself during the day, so that sleep would render him deaf to the call of the night. He took a vacation from the office and went on long hunting trips, following the deer through the most inaccessible and rugged country he could find -- and always in the daytime. Night found him indoors and tired. At home he installed a score of exercise machines, and where other men might go through a particular movement ten times, he went hundreds. Also, as a compromise, he built a sleeping porch on the second story. Here he at least breathed the blessed night air. Double screens prevented him from escaping into the woods, and each night Lee Sing locked him in and each morning let him out.

The time came, in the month of August, when he engaged additional servants to assist Lee Sing and dared a house party in his Mill Valley bungalow. Lilian, her mother and brother, and half a dozen mutual friends, were the guests. For two days and nights all went well. And on the third night, playing bridge till eleven o'clock, he had reason to be proud of himself. His restlessness fully hid, but as luck would have it, Lilian Gersdale was his opponent on his right. She was a frail delicate flower of a woman, and in his night-mood her very frailty incensed him. Not that he loved her less, but that he felt almost irresistibly impelled to reach out and paw and maul her. Especially was this true when she was engaged in playing a winning hand against him.

He had one of the deer-hounds brought in and, when it seemed he must fly to pieces with the tension, a caressing hand laid on the animal brought him relief. These contacts with the hairy coat gave him instant easement and enabled him to play out the evening. Nor did anyone guess the whole terrible struggle their host was making, while he laughed so carelessly and played so keenly and deliberately.

When they separated for the night, he saw to it that he parted from Lilian in the presence of the others. Once on his sleeping porch and safely locked in, he doubled and tripled and even quadrupled his exercises until, exhausted, he lay down on the couch to woo sleep and to ponder two problems that especially troubled him. One was this matter of exercise. It was a paradox. The more he exercised in this excessive fashion, the stronger he became. While it was true that he thus quite tired out his night-running Teutonic self, it seemed that he was merely setting back the fatal day when his strength would be too much for him and overpower him, and then it would be a strength more terrible than he had yet known. The other problem was that of his marriage and of the stratagems he must employ in order to avoid his wife after dark. And thus, fruitlessly pondering, he fell asleep.

Now, where the huge grizzly bear came from that night was long a mystery, while the people of the Springs Brothers' Circus, showing at Sausalito, searched long and vainly for "Big Ben, the Biggest Grizzly in Captivity." But Big Ben escaped, and, out of the mazes of half a thousand bungalows and country estates, selected the grounds of James J. Ward for visitation. The first Mr. Ward knew was when he found him on his feet, quivering and tense, a surge of battle in his breast and on his lips the old war-chant. From without came a wild baying and bellowing of the hounds. And sharp as a knife-thrust through the pandemonium came the agony of a stricken dog -- his dog, he knew.

Not stopping for slippers, pajama-clad, he burst through the door Lee Sing had so carefully locked, and sped down the stairs and out into the night. As his naked feet struck the graveled driveway, he stopped abruptly, reached under the steps to a hiding-place he knew well, and pulled forth a huge knotty club -- his old companion on many a mad night adventure on the hills. The frantic hullabaloo of the dogs was coming nearer, and, swinging the club, he sprang straight into the thickets to meet it.

The aroused household assembled on the wide veranda. Somebody turned on the electric lights, but they could see nothing but one another's frightened faces. Beyond the brightly illuminated driveway the trees formed a wall of impenetrable blackness. Yet somewhere in that blackness a terrible struggle was going on. There was an infernal outcry of animals, a great snarling and growling, the sound of blows being struck and a smashing and crashing of underbrush by heavy bodies.

The tide of battle swept out from among the trees and upon the driveway just beneath the onlookers. Then they saw. Mrs. Gersdale cried out and clung fainting to her son. Lilian, clutching the railing so spasmodically that a bruising hurt was left in her finger-ends for days, gazed horror-stricken at a yellow-haired, wild-eyed giant whom she recognized as the man who was to be her husband. He was swinging a great club, and fighting furiously and calmly with a shaggy monster that was bigger than any bear she had ever seen. One rip of the beast's claws had dragged away Ward's pajama-coat and streaked his flesh with blood.

While most of Lilian Gersdale's fright was for the man beloved, there was a large portion of it due to the man himself. Never had she dreamed so formidable and magnificent a savage lurked under the starched shirt and conventional garb of her betrothed. And never had she had any conception of how a man battled. Such a battle was certainly not modern; nor was she there beholding a modern man, though she did not know it. For this was not Mr. James J. Ward, the San Francisco business man, but one, unnamed and unknown, a crude, rude savage creature who, by some freak of chance, lived again after thrice a thousand years.

The hounds, ever maintaining their mad uproar, circled about the fight, or dashed in and out, distracting the bear. When the animal turned to meet such flanking assaults, the man leaped in and the club came down. Angered afresh by every such blow, the bear would rush, and the man, leaping and skipping, avoiding the dogs, went backwards or circled to one side or the other. Whereupon the dogs, taking advantage of the opening, would again spring in and draw the animal's wrath to them.

The end came suddenly. Whirling, the grizzly caught a hound with a wide sweeping cuff that sent the brute, its ribs caved in and its back broken, hurtling twenty feet. Then the human brute went mad. A foaming rage flecked the lips that parted with a wild inarticulate cry, as it sprang in, swung the club mightily in both hands, and brought it down full on the head of the uprearing grizzly. Not even the skull of a grizzly could withstand the crushing force of such a blow, and the animal went down to meet the worrying of the hounds. And through their scurrying leaped the man, squarely upon the body, where, in the white electric light, resting on his club, he chanted a triumph in an unknown tongue -- a song so ancient that Professor Wertz would have given ten years of his life for it.

His guests rushed to possess him and acclaim him, but James Ward, suddenly looking out of the eyes of the early Teuton, saw the fair frail Twentieth Century girl he loved, and felt something snap in his brain. He staggered weakly toward her, dropped the club, and nearly fell. Something had gone wrong with him. Inside his brain was an intolerable agony. It seemed as if the soul of him were flying asunder. Following the excited gaze of the others, he glanced back and saw the carcass of the bear. The sight filled him with fear. He uttered a cry and would have fled, had they not restrained him and led him into the bungalow.

. . . . . .

James J. Ward is still at the head of the firm of Ward, Knowles & Co. But he no longer lives in the country; nor does he run of nights after the coyotes under the moon. The early Teuton in him died the night of the Mill Valley fight with the bear. James J. Ward is now wholly James J. Ward, and he shares no part of his being with any vagabond anachronism from the younger world. And so wholly is James J. Ward modern, that he knows in all its bitter fullness the curse of civilized fear. He is now afraid of the dark, and night in the forest is to him a thing of abysmal terror. His city house is of the spick and span order, and he evinces a great interest in burglar-proof devices. His home is a tangle of electric wires, and after bed-time a guest can scarcely breathe without setting off an alarm. Also, he had invented a combination keyless door-lock that travelers may carry in their vest pockets and apply immediately and successfully under all circumstances. But his wife does not deem him a coward. She knows better. And, like any hero, he is content to rest on his laurels. His bravery is never questioned by those friends who are aware of the Mill Valley episode.

The Red One

There it was! The abrupt liberation of sound! As he timed it with his watch, Bassett likened it to the trump of an archangel. Walls of cities, he meditated, might well fall down before so vast and compelling a summons. For the thousandth time vainly he tried to analyse the tone-quality of that enormous peal that dominated the land far into the strong-holds of the surrounding tribes. The mountain gorge which was its source rang to the rising tide of it until it brimmed over and flooded earth and sky and air. With the wantonness of a sick man's fancy, he likened it to the mighty cry of some Titan of the Elder World vexed with misery or wrath. Higher and higher it arose, challenging and demanding in such profounds of volume that it seemed intended for ears beyond the narrow confines of the solar system. There was in it, too, the clamour of protest in that there were no ears to hear and comprehend its utterance.

Such the sick man's fancy. Still he strove to analyse the sound. Sonorous as thunder was it, mellow as a golden bell, thin and sweet as a thrummed taut cord of silver -- no; it was none of these, nor a blend of these. There were no words nor semblances in his vocabulary and experience with which to describe the totality of that sound.

Time passed. Minutes merged into quarters of hours, and quarters of hours into half-hours, and still the sound persisted, ever changing from its initial vocal impulse yet never receiving fresh impulse -- fading, dimming, dying as enormously as it had sprung into being. It became a confusion of troubled mutterings and babblings and colossal whisperings. Slowly it withdrew, sob by sob, into whatever great bosom had birthed it, until it whimpered deadly whispers of wrath and as equally seductive whispers of delight, striving still to be heard, to convey some cosmic secret, some understanding of infinite import and value. It dwindled to a ghost of sound that had lost its menace and promise, and became a thing that pulsed on in the sick man's consciousness for minutes after it had ceased. When he could hear it no longer, Bassett glanced at his watch. An hour had elapsed ere that archangel's trump had subsided into tonal nothingness.

Was this, then, *his* dark tower? -- Bassett pondered, remembering his Browning and gazing at his skeleton-like and fever-wasted hands. And the fancy made him smile -- of Childe Roland bearing a slug-horn to his lips with an arm as feeble as his was. Was it months, or years, he asked himself, since he first heard that mysterious call on the beach at Ringmanu? To save himself he could not tell. The long sickness had been most long. In conscious count of time he knew of months, many of them; but he had no way of estimating the long intervals of delirium and stupor. And how fared Captain Bateman of the blackbirder *Nari*? he wondered; and had Captain Bateman's drunken mate died of delirium tremens yet?

From which vain speculations, Bassett turned idly to review all that had occurred since that day on the beach of Ringmanu when he first heard the sound and plunged into the jungle after it. Sagawa had protested. He could see him yet, his queer little monkeyish face eloquent with fear, his back burdened with specimen cases, in his hands Bassett's butterfly net and naturalist's shot-gun, as he quavered, in Beche-de-mer English: "Me fella too much fright along bush. Bad fella boy, too much stop'm along bush."

Bassett smiled sadly at the recollection. The little New Hanover boy had been frightened, but had proved faithful, following him without hesitancy into the bush in the quest after the source of the wonderful sound. No fire-hollowed tree-trunk, that, throbbing war through the jungle depths, had been Bassett's conclusion. Erroneous had been his next conclusion, namely, that the source or cause could not be more distant than an hour's walk, and that he would easily be back by mid-afternoon to be picked up by the *Nari's* whale-boat.

"That big fella noise no good, all the same devil-devil," Sagawa had adjudged. And Sagawa had been right. Had he not had his head hacked off within the day? Bassett shuddered. Without doubt Sagawa had been eaten as well by the "bad fella boys too much" that stopped along the bush. He could see him, as he had last seen him, stripped of the shot-gun and all the naturalist's gear of his master, lying on the narrow trail where he had been decapitated barely the moment before. Yes, within a minute the thing had happened. Within a minute, looking back, Bassett had seen him trudging patiently along under his burdens. Then Bassett's own trouble had come upon him. He looked at the cruelly healed stumps of the first and second fingers of his left hand, then rubbed them softly into the indentation in the back of his skull. Quick as had been the flash of the long handled tomahawk, he had been quick enough to duck away his head and partially to deflect the stroke with his up-flung hand. Two fingers and a hasty scalp-wound had been the price he paid for his life. With one barrel of his ten-gauge shot-gun he had blown the life out of the bushman who had so nearly got him; with the other barrel he had peppered the bushmen bending over Sagawa, and had the pleasure of knowing that the major portion of the charge had gone into the one who leaped away with Sagawa's head. Everything had occurred in a flash. Only himself, the slain bushman, and what remained of Sagawa, were in the narrow, wild-pig run of a path. From the dark jungle on either side came no rustle of movement or sound of life. And he had suffered distinct and dreadful shock. For the first time in his life he had killed a human being, and he knew nausea as he contemplated the mess of his handiwork.

Then had begun the chase. He retreated up the pig-run before his hunters, who were between him and the beach. How many there were, he could not guess. There might have been one, or a hundred, for aught he saw of them. That some of them took to the trees and travelled along through the jungle roof he was certain; but at the most he never glimpsed more than an occasional flitting of shadows. No bow-strings twanged that he could hear; but every little while, whence discharged he knew not, tiny arrows whispered past him or struck tree-boles and fluttered to the ground beside him. They were bone-tipped and feather shafted, and the feathers, torn from the breasts of humming-birds, iridesced like jewels.

Once -- and now, after the long lapse of time, he chuckled gleefully at the recollection -- he had detected a shadow above him that came to instant rest as he turned his gaze upward. He could make out nothing, but, deciding to chance it, had fired at it a heavy charge of number five shot. Squalling like an infuriated cat, the shadow crashed down through tree-ferns and orchids and thudded upon the earth at his feet, and, still squalling its rage and pain, had sunk its human teeth into the ankle of his stout tramping boot. He, on the other hand, was not idle, and with his free foot had done what reduced the squalling to silence. So inured to savagery has Bassett since become, that he chuckled again with the glee of the recollection.

What a night had followed! Small wonder that he had accumulated such a virulence and variety of fevers, he thought, as he recalled that sleepless night of torment, when the throb of his wounds was as nothing compared with the myriad stings of the mosquitoes. There had been no escaping them, and he had not dared to light a fire. They had literally pumped his body full of poison, so that, with the coming of day, eyes swollen almost shut, he had stumbled blindly on, not caring much when his head should be hacked off and his carcass started on the way of Sagawa's to the cooking fire. Twenty-four hours had made a wreck of him -- of mind as well as body. He had scarcely retained his wits at all, so maddened was he by the tremendous inoculation of poison he had received. Several times he fired his shot-gun with effect into the shadows that dogged him. Stinging day insects and gnats added to his torment, while his bloody wounds attracted hosts of loathsome flies that clung sluggishly to his flesh and had to be brushed off and crushed off.

Once, in that day, he heard again the wonderful sound, seemingly more distant, but rising imperiously above the nearer war-drums in the bush. Right there was where he had made his mistake.

Thinking that he had passed beyond it and that, therefore, it was between him and the beach of Ringmanu, he had worked back toward it when in reality he was penetrating deeper and deeper into the mysterious heart of the unexplored island. That night, crawling in among the twisted roots of a banyan tree, he had slept from exhaustion while the mosquitoes had had their will of him.

Followed days and nights that were vague as nightmares in his memory. One clear vision he remembered was of suddenly finding himself in the midst of a bush village and watching the old men and children fleeing into the jungle. All had fled but one. From close at hand and above him, a whimpering as of some animal in pain and terror had startled him. And looking up he had seen her -- a girl, or young woman rather, suspended by one arm in the cooking sun. Perhaps for days she had so hung. Her swollen, protruding tongue spoke as much. Still alive, she gazed at him with eyes of terror. Past help, he decided, as he noted the swellings of her legs which advertised that the joints had been crushed and the great bones broken. He resolved to shoot her, and there the vision terminated. He could not remember whether he had or not, any more than could he remember how he chanced to be in that village, or how he succeeded in getting away from it.

Many pictures, unrelated, came and went in Bassett's mind as he reviewed that period of his terrible wanderings. He remembered invading another village of a dozen houses and driving all before him with his shot-gun save, for one old man, too feeble to flee, who spat at him and whined and snarled as he dug open a ground-oven and from amid the hot stones dragged forth a roasted pig that steamed its essence deliciously through its green-leaf wrappings. It was at this place that a wantonness of savagery had seized upon him. Having feasted, ready to depart with a hind-quarter of the pig in his hand, he deliberately fired the grass thatch of a house with his burning glass.

But seared deepest of all in Bassett's brain, was the dank and noisome jungle. It actually stank with evil, and it was always twilight. Rarely did a shaft of sunlight penetrate its matted roof a hundred feet overhead. And beneath that roof was an aerial ooze of vegetation, a monstrous, parasitic dripping of decadent life-forms that rooted in death and lived on death. And through all this he drifted, ever pursued by the flitting shadows of the anthropophagi, themselves ghosts of evil that dared not face him in battle but that knew that, soon or late, they would feed on him. Bassett remembered that at the time, in lucid moments, he had likened himself to a wounded bull pursued by plains' coyotes too cowardly to battle with him for the meat of him, yet certain of the inevitable end of him when they would be full gorged. As the bull's horns and stamping hoofs kept off the coyotes, so his shot-gun kept off these Solomon Islanders, these twilight shades of bushmen of the island of Guadalcanal.

Came the day of the grass lands. Abruptly, as if cloven by the sword of God in the hand of God, the jungle terminated. The edge of it, perpendicular and as black as the infamy of it, was a hundred feet up and down. And, beginning at the edge of it, grew the grass -- sweet, soft, tender, pasture grass that would have delighted the eyes and beasts of any husbandman and that extended, on and on, for leagues and leagues of velvet verdure, to the backbone of the great island, the towering mountain range flung up by some ancient earth-cataclysm, serrated and gullied but not yet erased by the erosive tropic rains. But the grass! He had crawled into it a dozen yards, buried his face in it, smelled it, and broken down in a fit of involuntary weeping.

And, while he wept, the wonderful sound had pealed forth -- if by *peal*, he had often thought since, an adequate description could be given of the enunciation of so vast a sound melting sweet. Sweet it was, as no sound ever heard. Vast it was, of so mighty a resonance that it might have proceeded from some brazen-throated monster. And yet it called to him across that leagues-wide savannah, and was like a benediction to his long-suffering, pain racked spirit.

He remembered how he lay there in the grass, wet-cheeked but no longer sobbing, listening to the sound and wondering that he had been able to hear it on the beach of Ringmanu. Some freak of air pressures and air currents, he reflected, had made it possible for the sound to carry so far. Such conditions might not happen again in a thousand days or ten thousand days, but the one day it had happened had been the day he landed from the *Nari* for several hours' collecting. Especially had he been in quest of the famed jungle butterfly, a foot across from wing-tip to wing-tip, as velvet-dusky of lack of colour as was the gloom of the roof, of such lofty arboreal habits that it resorted only to the jungle roof and could be brought down only by a dose of shot. It was for this purpose that Sagawa had carried the ten-gauge shot-gun.

Two days and nights he had spent crawling across that belt of grass land. He had suffered much, but pursuit had ceased at the jungle- edge. And he would have died of thirst had not a heavy thunderstorm revived him on the second day.

And then had come Balatta. In the first shade, where the savannah yielded to the dense mountain jungle, he had collapsed to die. At first she had squealed with delight at sight of his helplessness, and was for beating his brain out with a stout forest branch. Perhaps it was his very utter helplessness that had appealed to her, and perhaps it was her human curiosity that made her refrain. At any rate, she had refrained, for he opened his eyes again under the impending blow, and saw her studying him intently. What especially struck her about him were his blue eyes and white skin. Coolly she had squatted on her hams, spat on his arm, and with her finger-tips scrubbed away the dirt of days and nights of muck and jungle that sullied the pristine whiteness of his skin.

And everything about her had struck him especially, although there was nothing conventional about her at all. He laughed weakly at the recollection, for she had been as innocent of garb as Eve before the fig-leaf adventure. Squat and lean at the same time, asymmetrically limbed, string-muscled as if with lengths of cordage, dirt-caked from infancy save for casual showers, she was as unbeautiful a prototype of woman as he, with a scientist's eye, had ever gazed upon. Her breasts advertised at the one time her maturity and youth; and, if by nothing else, her sex was advertised by the one article of finery with which she was adorned, namely a pig's tail, thrust though a hole in her left ear-lobe. So lately had the tail been severed, that its raw end still oozed blood that dried upon her shoulder like so much candle-droppings. And her face! A twisted and wizened complex of apish features, perforated by up-turned, sky-open, Mongolian nostrils, by a mouth that sagged from a huge upper-lip and faded precipitately into a retreating chin, by peering querulous eyes that blinked as blink the eyes of denizens of monkey-cages.

Not even the water she brought him in a forest-leaf, and the ancient and half-putrid chunk of roast pig, could redeem in the slightest the grotesque hideousness of her. When he had eaten weakly for a space, he closed his eyes in order not to see her, although again and again she poked them open to peer at the blue of them. Then had come the sound. Nearer, much nearer, he knew it to be; and he knew equally well, despite the weary way he had come, that it was still many hours distant. The effect of it on her had been startling. She cringed under it, with averted face, moaning and chattering with fear. But after it had lived its full life of an hour, he closed his eyes and fell asleep with Balatta brushing the flies from him.

When he awoke it was night, and she was gone. But he was aware of renewed strength, and, by then too thoroughly inoculated by the mosquito poison to suffer further inflammation, he closed his eyes and slept an unbroken stretch till sun-up. A little later Balatta had returned, bringing with her a half-dozen women who, unbeautiful as they were, were patently not so unbeautiful as she. She evidenced by her conduct that she considered him her find, her property, and the pride she took in showing him off would have been ludicrous had his situation not been so desperate.

Later, after what had been to him a terrible journey of miles, when he collapsed in front of the devil-devil house in the shadow of the breadfruit tree, she had shown very lively ideas on the matter of retaining possession of him. Ngurn, whom Bassett was to know afterward as the devil-devil doctor, priest, or medicine man of the village, had wanted his head. Others of the grinning and chattering monkey-men, all as stark of clothes and bestial of appearance as Balatta, had wanted his body for the roasting oven. At that time he had not understood their language, if by *language* might be dignified the uncouth sounds they made to represent ideas. But Bassett had thoroughly understood the matter of debate, especially when the men pressed and prodded and felt of the flesh of him as if he were so much commodity in a butcher's stall.

Balatta had been losing the debate rapidly, when the accident happened. One of the men, curiously examining Bassett's shot-gun, managed to cock and pull a trigger. The recoil of the butt into the pit of the man's stomach had not been the most sanguinary result, for the charge of shot, at a distance of a yard, had blown the head of one of the debaters into nothingness.

Even Balatta joined the others in flight, and, ere they returned, his senses already reeling from the oncoming fever-attack, Bassett had regained possession of the gun. Whereupon, although his teeth chattered with the ague and his swimming eyes could scarcely see, he held on to his fading consciousness until he could intimidate the bushmen with the simple magics of compass, watch, burning glass, and matches. At the last, with due emphasis, of solemnity and awfulness, he had killed a young pig with his shot-gun and promptly fainted.

Bassett flexed his arm-muscles in quest of what possible strength might reside in such weakness, and dragged himself slowly and totteringly to his feet. He was shockingly emaciated; yet, during the various convalescences of the many months of his long sickness, he had never regained quite the same degree of strength as this time. What he feared was another relapse such as he had already frequently experienced. Without drugs, without even quinine, he had managed so far to live through a combination of the most pernicious and most malignant of malarial and black-water fevers. But could he continue to endure? Such was his everlasting query. For, like the genuine scientist he was, he would not be content to die until he had solved the secret of the sound.

Supported by a staff, he staggered the few steps to the devil-devil house where death and Ngurn reigned in gloom. Almost as infamously dark and evil-stinking as the jungle was the devil-devil house -- in Bassett's opinion. Yet therein was usually to be found his favourite crony and gossip, Ngurn, always willing for a yarn or a discussion, the while he sat in the ashes of death and in a slow smoke shrewdly revolved curing human heads suspended from the rafters. For, through the months' interval of consciousness of his long sickness, Bassett had mastered the psychological simplicities and lingual difficulties of the language of the tribe of Ngurn and Balatta and Vngngn -- the latter the addle-headed young chief who was ruled by Ngurn, and who, whispered intrigue had it, was the son of Ngurn.

"Will the Red One speak to-day?" Bassett asked, by this time so accustomed to the old man's gruesome occupation as to take even an interest in the progress of the smoke-curing.

With the eye of an expert Ngurn examined the particular head he was at work upon.

"It will be ten days before I can say 'finish,'" he said. "Never has any man fixed heads like these."

Bassett smiled inwardly at the old fellow's reluctance to talk with him of the Red One. It had always been so. Never, by any chance, had Ngurn or any other member of the weird tribe divulged the slightest hint of any physical characteristic of the Red One. Physical the Red One must be, to emit the wonderful sound, and though it was called the Red One, Bassett could not be sure that red represented the colour of it. Red enough were the deeds and powers of it, from what abstract clues he had gleaned. Not alone, had Ngurn informed him, was the Red One more bestial powerful than the neighbour tribal gods, ever athirst for the red blood of living human sacrifices, but the neighbour gods themselves were sacrificed and tormented before him. He was the god of a dozen allied villages similar to this one, which was the central and commanding village of the federation. By virtue of the Red One many alien villages had been devastated and even wiped out, the prisoners sacrificed to the Red One. This was true to-day, and it extended back into old history carried down by word of mouth through the generations. When he, Ngurn, had been a young man, the tribes beyond the grass lands had made a war raid. In the counter raid, Ngurn and his fighting folk had made many prisoners. Of children alone over five score living had been bled white before the Red One, and many, many more men and women.

The Thunderer was another of Ngurn's names for the mysterious deity. Also at times was he called The Loud Shouter, The God- Voiced, The Bird-Throated, The One with the Throat Sweet as the Throat of the Honey-Bird, The Sun Singer, and The Star-Born.

Why The Star-Born? In vain Bassett interrogated Ngurn. According to that old devil-devil doctor, the Red One had always been, just where he was at present, for ever singing and thundering his will over men. But Ngurn's father, wrapped in decaying grass-matting and hanging even then over their heads among the smoky rafters of the devil-devil house, had held otherwise. That departed wise one had believed that the Red One came from out of the starry night, else why -- so his argument had run -- had the old and forgotten ones passed his name down as the Star-Born? Bassett could not but recognize something cogent in such argument. But Ngurn affirmed the long years of his long life, wherein he had gazed upon many starry nights, yet never had he found a star on grass land or in jungle depth -- and he had looked for them. True, he had beheld shooting stars (this in reply to Bassett's contention); but likewise had he beheld the phosphorescence of fungoid growths and rotten meat and fireflies on dark nights, and the flames of wood-fires and of blazing candle-nuts; yet what were flame and blaze and glow when they had flamed and blazed and glowed? Answer: memories, memories only, of things which had ceased to be, like memories of matings accomplished, of feasts forgotten, of desires that were the ghosts of desires, flaring, flaming, burning, yet unrealized in achievement of easement and satisfaction. Where was the appetite of yesterday? The roasted flesh of the wild pig the hunter's arrow failed to slay? The maid, unwed and dead ere the young man knew her?

A memory was not a star, was Ngurn's contention. How could a memory be a star? Further, after all his long life he still observed the starry night-sky unaltered. Never had he noted the absence of a single star from its accustomed place. Besides, stars were fire, and the Red One was not fire -- which last involuntary betrayal told Bassett nothing.

"Will the Red One speak tomorrow?" He queried.

Ngurn shrugged his shoulders as who should say.

"And the day after? -- and the day after that?" Bassett persisted.

"I would like to have the curing of your head," Ngurn changed the subject. "It is different from any other head. No devil-devil has a head like it. Besides, I would cure it well. I would take months and months. The moons would come and the moons would go, and the smoke would be very slow, and I should myself gather the materials for the curing smoke. The skin would not wrinkle. It would be as smooth as your skin now."

He stood up, and from the dim rafters, grimed with the smoking of countless heads, where day was no more than a gloom, took down a matting-wrapped parcel and began to open it.

"It is a head like yours," he said, "but it is poorly cured."

Bassett had pricked up his ears at the suggestion that it was a white man's head; for he had long since come to accept that these jungle-dwellers, in the midmost centre of the great island, had never had intercourse with white men. Certainly he had found them without the almost universal beche-de-mer English of the west South Pacific. Nor had they knowledge of tobacco, nor of gunpowder. Their few precious knives, made from lengths of hoop-iron, and their few and more precious tomahawks from cheap trade hatchets, he had surmised they had captured in war from the bushmen of the jungle beyond the grass lands, and that they, in turn, had similarly gained them from the salt-water men who fringed the coral beaches of the shore and had contact with the occasional white men.

"The folk in the out beyond do not know how to cure heads," old Ngurn explained, as he drew forth from the filthy matting and placed in Bassett's hands an indubitable white man's head.

Ancient it was beyond question; white it was as the blond hair attested. He could have sworn it once belonged to an Englishman, and to an Englishman of long before by token of the heavy gold circlets still threaded in the withered ear-lobes.

"Now your head . . ." the devil-devil doctor began on his favourite topic.

"I'll tell you what," Bassett interrupted, struck by a new idea. "When I die I'll let you have my head to cure, if, first, you take me to look upon the Red One."

"I will have your head anyway when you are dead," Ngurn rejected the proposition. He added, with the brutal frankness of the savage: "Besides, you have not long to live. You are almost a dead man now. You will grow less strong. In not many months I shall have you here turning and turning in the smoke. It is pleasant, through the long afternoons, to turn the head of one you have known as well as I know you. And I shall talk to you and tell you the many secrets you want to know. Which will not matter, for you will be dead."

"Ngurn," Bassett threatened in sudden anger. "You know the Baby Thunder in the Iron that is mine." (This was in reference to his all-potent and all-awful shotgun.) "I can kill you any time, and then you will not get my head."

"Just the same, will Vngngn, or some one else of my folk get it," Ngurn complacently assured him. "And just the same will it turn and turn here in the devil-devil house in the smoke. The quicker you slay me with your Baby Thunder, the quicker will your head turn in the smoke."

And Bassett knew he was beaten in the discussion.

What was the Red One? Bassett asked himself a thousand times in the succeeding week, while he seemed to grow stronger. What was the source of the wonderful sound? What was this Sun Singer, this Star-Born One, this mysterious deity, as bestial-conducted as the black and kinky-headed and monkey-like human beasts who worshipped it, and whose silver-sweet, bull-mouthed singing and commanding he had heard at the taboo distance for so long?

Ngurn had he failed to bribe with the inevitable curing of his head when he was dead. Vngngn, imbecile and chief that he was, was too imbecilic, too much under the sway of Ngurn, to be considered. Remained Balatta, who, from the time she found him and poked his blue eyes open to recrudescence of her grotesque female hideousness, had continued his adorer. Woman she was, and he had long known that the only way to win from her treason of her tribe was through the woman's heart of her.

Bassett was a fastidious man. He had never recovered from the initial horror caused by Balatta's female awfulness. Back in England, even at best the charm of woman, to him, had never been robust. Yet now, resolutely, as only a man can do who is capable of martyring himself for the cause of science, he proceeded to violate all the fineness and delicacy of his nature by making love to the unthinkably disgusting bushwoman.

He shuddered, but with averted face hid his grimaces and swallowed his gorge as he put his arm around her dirt-crusted shoulders and felt the contact of her rancid, oily and kinky hair with his neck and chin. But he nearly screamed when she succumbed to that caress so at the very first of the courtship and mowed and gibbered and squealed little, queer, pig-like gurgly noises of delight. It was too much. And the next he did in the singular courtship was to take her down to the stream and give her a vigorous scrubbing.

From then on he devoted himself to her like a true swain as frequently and for as long at a time as his will could override his repugnance. But marriage, which she ardently suggested, with due observance of tribal custom, he balked at. Fortunately, taboo rule was strong in the tribe. Thus, Ngurn could never touch bone, or flesh, or hide of crocodile. This had been ordained at his birth. Vngngn was denied ever the touch of woman. Such pollution, did it chance to occur, could be purged only by the death of the offending female. It had happened once, since Bassett's arrival, when a girl of nine, running in play, stumbled and fell against the sacred chief. And the girl-child was seen no more. In whispers, Balatta told Bassett that she had been three days and nights in dying before the Red One. As for Balatta, the breadfruit was taboo to her. For which Bassett was thankful. The taboo might have been water.

For himself, he fabricated a special taboo. Only could he marry, he explained, when the Southern Cross rode highest in the sky. Knowing his astronomy, he thus gained a reprieve of nearly nine months; and he was confident that within that time he would either be dead or escaped to the coast with full knowledge of the Red One and of the source of the Red One's wonderful voice. At first he had fancied the Red One to be some colossal statue, like Memnon, rendered vocal under certain temperature conditions of sunlight. But when, after a war raid, a batch of prisoners was brought in and the sacrifice made at night, in the midst of rain, when the sun could play no part, the Red One had been more vocal than usual, Bassett discarded that hypothesis.

In company with Balatta, sometimes with men and parties of women, the freedom of the jungle was his for three quadrants of the compass. But the fourth quadrant, which contained the Red One's abiding place, was taboo. He made more thorough love to Balatta -- also saw to it that she scrubbed herself more frequently. Eternal female she was, capable of any treason for the sake of love. And, though the sight of her was provocative of nausea and the contact of her provocative of despair, although he could not escape her awfulness in his dream-haunted nightmares of her, he nevertheless was aware of the cosmic verity of sex that animated her and that made her own life of less value than the happiness of her lover with whom she hoped to mate. Juliet or Balatta? Where was the intrinsic difference? The soft and tender product of ultra- civilization, or her bestial prototype of a hundred thousand years before her? -- there was no difference.

Bassett was a scientist first, a humanist afterward. In the jungle-heart of Guadalcanal he put the affair to the test, as in the laboratory he would have put to the test any chemical reaction. He increased his feigned ardour for the bushwoman, at the same time increasing the imperiousness of his will of desire over her to be led to look upon the Red One face to face. It was the old story, he recognized, that the woman must pay, and it occurred when the two of them, one day, were catching the unclassified and unnamed little black fish, an inch long, half-eel and half-scaled, rotund with salmon-golden roe, that frequented the fresh water, and that were esteemed, raw and whole, fresh or putrid, a perfect delicacy. Prone in the muck of the decaying jungle-floor, Balatta threw herself, clutching his ankles with her hands kissing his feet and making slubbery noises that chilled his backbone up and down again. She begged him to kill her rather than exact this ultimate love- payment. She told him of the penalty of breaking the taboo of the Red One -- a week of torture, living, the details of which she yammered out from her face in the mire until he realized that he was yet a tyro in knowledge of the frightfulness the human was capable of wreaking on the human.

Yet did Bassett insist on having his man's will satisfied, at the woman's risk, that he might solve the mystery of the Red One's singing, though she should die long and horribly and screaming. And Balatta, being mere woman, yielded. She led him into the forbidden quadrant. An abrupt mountain, shouldering in from the north to meet a similar intrusion from the south, tormented the stream in which they had fished into a deep and gloomy gorge. After a mile along the gorge, the way plunged sharply upward until they crossed a saddle of raw limestone which attracted his geologist's eye. Still climbing, although he paused often from sheer physical weakness, they scaled forest-clad heights until they emerged on a naked mesa or tableland. Bassett recognized the stuff of its composition as black volcanic sand, and knew that a pocket magnet could have captured a full load of the sharply angular grains he trod upon.

And then holding Balatta by the hand and leading her onward, he came to it -- a tremendous pit, obviously artificial, in the heart of the plateau. Old history, the South Seas Sailing Directions, scores of remembered data and connotations swift and furious, surged through his brain. It was Mendana who had discovered the islands and named them Solomon's, believing that he had found that monarch's fabled mines. They had laughed at the old navigator's child-like credulity; and yet here stood himself, Bassett, on the rim of an excavation for all the world like the diamond pits of South Africa.

But no diamond this that he gazed down upon. Rather was it a pearl, with the depth of iridescence of a pearl; but of a size all pearls of earth and time, welded into one, could not have totalled; and of a colour undreamed of in any pearl, or of anything else, for that matter, for it was the colour of the Red One. And the Red One himself Bassett knew it to be on the instant. A perfect sphere, full two hundred feet in diameter, the top of it was a hundred feet below the level of the rim. He likened the colour quality of it to lacquer. Indeed, he took it to be some sort of lacquer, applied by man, but a lacquer too marvellously clever to have been manufactured by the bush-folk. Brighter than bright cherry-red, its richness of colour was as if it were red builded upon red. It glowed and iridesced in the sunlight as if gleaming up from underlay under underlay of red.

In vain Balatta strove to dissuade him from descending. She threw herself in the dirt; but, when he continued down the trail that spiralled the pit-wall, she followed, cringing and whimpering her terror. That the red sphere had been dug out as a precious thing, was patent. Considering the paucity of members of the federated twelve villages and their primitive tools and methods, Bassett knew that the toil of a myriad generations could scarcely have made that enormous excavation.

He found the pit bottom carpeted with human bones, among which, battered and defaced, lay village gods of wood and stone.

Some, covered with obscene totemic figures and designs, were carved from solid tree trunks forty or fifty feet in length. He noted the absence of the shark and turtle gods, so common among the shore villages, and was amazed at the constant recurrence of the helmet motive. What did these jungle savages of the dark heart of Guadalcanal know of helmets? Had Mendana's men-at-arms worn helmets and penetrated here centuries before? And if not, then whence had the bush-folk caught the motive?

Advancing over the litter of gods and bones, Balatta whimpering at his heels, Bassett entered the shadow of the Red One and passed on under its gigantic overhang until he touched it with his finger- tips. No lacquer that. Nor was the surface smooth as it should have been in the case of lacquer. On the contrary, it was corrugated and pitted, with here and there patches that showed signs of heat and fusing. Also, the substance of it was metal, though unlike any metal, or combination of metals, he had ever known. As for the colour itself, he decided it to be no application. It was the intrinsic colour of the metal itself.

He moved his finger-tips, which up to that had merely rested, along the surface, and felt the whole gigantic sphere quicken and live and respond. It was incredible! So light a touch on so vast a mass! Yet did it quiver under the finger-tip caress in rhythmic vibrations that became whisperings and rustlings and mutterings of sound -- but of sound so different; so elusively thin that it was shimmeringly sibilant; so mellow that it was maddening sweet, piping like an elfin horn, which last was just what Bassett decided would be like a peal from some bell of the gods reaching earthward from across space.

He looked at Balatta with swift questioning; but the voice of the Red One he had evoked had flung her face downward and moaning among the bones. He returned to contemplation of the prodigy. Hollow it was, and of no metal known on earth, was his conclusion. It was right-named by the ones of old-time as the Star-Born. Only from the stars could it have come, and no thing of chance was it. It was a creation of artifice and mind. Such perfection of form, such hollowness that it certainly possessed, could not be the result of mere fortuitousness. A child of intelligences, remote and unguessable, working corporally in metals, it indubitably was. He stared at it in amazement, his brain a racing wild-fire of hypotheses to account for this far-journeyer who had adventured the night of space, threaded the stars, and now rose before him and above him, exhumed by patient anthropophagi, pitted and lacquered by its fiery bath in two atmospheres.

But was the colour a lacquer of heat upon some familiar metal? Or was it an intrinsic quality of the metal itself? He thrust in the blue-point of his pocket-knife to test the constitution of the stuff. Instantly the entire sphere burst into a mighty whispering, sharp with protest, almost twanging goldenly, if a whisper could possibly be considered to twang, rising higher, sinking deeper, the two extremes of the registry of sound threatening to complete the circle and coalesce into the bull-mouthed thundering he had so often heard beyond the taboo distance.

Forgetful of safety, of his own life itself, entranced by the wonder of the unthinkable and unguessable thing, he raised his knife to strike heavily from a long stroke, but was prevented by Balatta. She upreared on her own knees in an agony of terror, clasping his knees and supplicating him to desist. In the intensity of her desire to impress him, she put her forearm between her teeth and sank them to the bone.

He scarcely observed her act, although he yielded automatically to his gentler instincts and withheld the knife-hack. To him, human life had dwarfed to microscopic proportions before this colossal portent of higher life from within the distances of the sidereal universe. As had she been a dog, he kicked the ugly little bushwoman to her feet and compelled her to start with him on an encirclement of the base. Part way around, he encountered horrors. Even, among the others, did he recognize the sun-shrivelled remnant of the nine-years girl who had accidentally broken Chief Vngngn's personality taboo. And, among what was left of these that had passed, he encountered what was left of one who had not yet passed. Truly had the bush-folk named themselves into the name of the Red One, seeing in him their own image which they strove to placate and please with such red offerings.

Farther around, always treading the bones and images of humans and gods that constituted the floor of this ancient charnel-house of sacrifice, he came upon the device by which the Red One was made to send his call singing thunderingly across the jungle-belts and grass-lands to the far beach of Ringmanu. Simple and primitive was it as was the Red One's consummate artifice. A great king-post, half a hundred feet in length, seasoned by centuries of superstitious care, carven into dynasties of gods, each superimposed, each helmeted, each seated in the open mouth of a crocodile, was slung by ropes, twisted of climbing vegetable parasites, from the apex of a tripod of three great forest trunks, themselves carved into grinning and grotesque adumbrations of man's modern concepts of art and god. From the striker king-post, were suspended ropes of climbers to which men could apply their strength and direction. Like a battering ram, this king-post could be driven end-onward against the mighty red-iridescent sphere.

Here was where Ngurn officiated and functioned religiously for himself and the twelve tribes under him. Bassett laughed aloud, almost with madness, at the thought of this wonderful messenger, winged with intelligence across space, to fall into a bushman stronghold and be worshipped by ape-like, man-eating and head-hunting savages. It was as if God's World had fallen into the muck mire of the abyss underlying the bottom of hell; as if Jehovah's Commandments had been presented on carved stone to the monkeys of the monkey cage at the Zoo; as if the Sermon on the Mount had been preached in a roaring bedlam of lunatics.

The slow weeks passed. The nights, by election, Bassett spent on the ashen floor of the devil-devil house, beneath the ever-swinging, slow-curing heads. His reason for this was that it was taboo to the lesser sex of woman, and therefore, a refuge for him from Balatta, who grew more persecutingly and perilously loverly as the Southern Cross rode higher in the sky and marked the imminence of her nuptials. His days Bassett spent in a hammock swung under the shade of the great breadfruit tree before the devil-devil house. There were breaks in this programme, when, in the comas of his devastating fever-attacks, he lay for days and nights in the house of heads. Ever he struggled to combat the fever, to live, to continue to live, to grow strong and stronger against the day when he would be strong enough to dare the grass-lands and the belted jungle beyond, and win to the beach, and to some labour-recruiting, black-birding ketch or schooner, and on to civilization and the men of civilization, to whom he could give news of the message from other worlds that lay, darkly worshipped by beastmen, in the black heart of Guadalcanal's midmost centre.

On the other nights, lying late under the breadfruit tree, Bassett spent long hours watching the slow setting of the western stars beyond the black wall of jungle where it had been thrust back by the clearing for the village. Possessed of more than a cursory knowledge of astronomy, he took a sick man's pleasure in speculating as to the dwellers on the unseen worlds of those incredibly remote suns, to haunt whose houses of light, life came forth, a shy visitant, from the rayless crypts of matter. He could no more apprehend limits to time than bounds to space. No subversive radium speculations had shaken his steady scientific faith in the conservation of energy and the indestructibility of matter. Always and forever must there have been stars. And surely, in that cosmic ferment, all must be comparatively alike, comparatively of the same substance, or substances, save for the freaks of the ferment. All must obey, or compose, the same laws that ran without infraction through the entire experience of man. Therefore, he argued and agreed, must worlds and life be appanages to all the suns as they were appanages to the particular of his own solar system.

Even as he lay here, under the breadfruit tree, an intelligence that stared across the starry gulfs, so must all the universe be exposed to the ceaseless scrutiny of innumerable eyes, like his, though grantedly different, with behind them, by the same token, intelligences that questioned and sought the meaning and the construction of the whole. So reasoning, he felt his soul go forth in kinship with that august company, that multitude whose gaze was forever upon the arras of infinity.

Who were they, what were they, those far distant and superior ones who had bridged the sky with their gigantic, red-iridescent, heaven-singing message? Surely, and long since, had they, too, trod the path on which man had so recently, by the calendar of the cosmos, set his feet. And to be able to send a message across the pit of space, surely they had reached those heights to which man, in tears and travail and bloody sweat, in darkness and confusion of many counsels, was so slowly struggling. And what were they on their heights? Had they won Brotherhood? Or had they learned that the law of love imposed the penalty of weakness and decay? Was strife, life? Was the rule of all the universe the pitiless rule of natural selection? And, and most immediately and poignantly, were their far conclusions, their long-won wisdoms, shut even then in the huge, metallic heart of the Red One, waiting for the first earth-man to read? Of one thing he was certain: No drop of red dew shaken from the lion-mane of some sun in torment, was the sounding sphere. It was of design, not chance, and it contained the speech and wisdom of the stars.

What engines and elements and mastered forces, what lore and mysteries and destiny-controls, might be there! Undoubtedly, since so much could be enclosed in so little a thing as the foundation stone of a public building, this enormous sphere should contain vast histories, profounds of research achieved beyond man's wildest guesses, laws and formulae that, easily mastered, would make man's life on earth, individual and collective, spring up from its present mire to inconceivable heights of purity and power. It was Time's greatest gift to blindfold, insatiable, and sky-aspiring man. And to him, Bassett, had been vouchsafed the lordly fortune to be the first to receive this message from man's interstellar kin!

No white man, much less no outland man of the other bush-tribes, had gazed upon the Red One and lived. Such the law expounded by Ngurn to Bassett. There was such a thing as blood brotherhood. Bassett, in return, had often argued in the past. But Ngurn had stated solemnly no. Even the blood brotherhood was outside the favour of the Red One. Only a man born within the tribe could look upon the Red One and live. But now, his guilty secret known only to Balatta, whose fear of immolation before the Red One fast-sealed her lips, the situation was different. What he had to do was to recover from the abominable fevers that weakened him, and gain to civilization. Then would he lead an expedition back, and, although the entire population of Guadalcanal he destroyed, extract from the heart of the Red One the message of the world from other worlds.

But Bassett's relapses grew more frequent, his brief convalescences less and less vigorous, his periods of coma longer, until he came to know, beyond the last promptings of the optimism inherent in so tremendous a constitution as his own, that he would never live to cross the grass lands, perforate the perilous coast jungle, and reach the sea. He faded as the Southern Cross rose higher in the sky, till even Balatta knew that he would be dead ere the nuptial date determined by his taboo. Ngurn made pilgrimage personally and gathered the smoke materials for the curing of Bassett's head, and to him made proud announcement and exhibition of the artistic perfectness of his intention when Bassett should be dead. As for himself, Bassett was not shocked. Too long and too deeply had life ebbed down in him to bite him with fear of its impending extinction. He continued to persist, alternating periods of unconsciousness with periods of semi-consciousness, dreamy and unreal, in which he idly wondered whether he had ever truly beheld the Red One or whether it was a nightmare fancy of delirium.

Came the day when all mists and cob-webs dissolved, when he found his brain clear as a bell, and took just appraisement of his body's weakness. Neither hand nor foot could he lift. So little control of his body did he have, that he was scarcely aware of possessing one. Lightly indeed his flesh sat upon his soul, and his soul, in its briefness of clarity, knew by its very clarity that the black of cessation was near. He knew the end was close; knew that in all truth he had with his eyes beheld the Red One, the messenger between the worlds; knew that he would never live to carry that message to the world -- that message, for aught to the contrary, which might already have waited man's hearing in the heart of Guadalcanal for ten thousand years. And Bassett stirred with resolve, calling Ngurn to him, out under the shade of the breadfruit tree, and with the old devil-devil doctor discussing the terms and arrangements of his last life effort, his final adventure in the quick of the flesh.

"I know the law, O Ngurn," he concluded the matter. "Whoso is not of the folk may not look upon the Red One and live. I shall not live anyway. Your young men shall carry me before the face of the Red One, and I shall look upon him, and hear his voice, and thereupon die, under your hand, O Ngurn. Thus will the three things be satisfied: the law, my desire, and your quicker possession of my head for which all your preparations wait."

To which Ngurn consented, adding:

"It is better so. A sick man who cannot get well is foolish to live on for so little a while. Also is it better for the living that he should go. You have been much in the way of late. Not but what it was good for me to talk to such a wise one. But for moons of days we have held little talk. Instead, you have taken up room in the house of heads, making noises like a dying pig, or talking much and loudly in your own language which I do not understand. This has been a confusion to me, for I like to think on the great things of the light and dark as I turn the heads in the smoke. Your much noise has thus been a disturbance to the long-learning and hatching of the final wisdom that will be mine before I die. As for you, upon whom the dark has already brooded, it is well that you die now. And I promise you, in the long days to come when I turn your head in the smoke, no man of the tribe shall come in to disturb us. And I will tell you many secrets, for I am an old man and very wise, and I shall be adding wisdom to wisdom as I turn your head in the smoke."

So a litter was made, and, borne on the shoulders of half a dozen of the men, Bassett departed on the last little adventure that was to cap the total adventure, for him, of living. With a body of which he was scarcely aware, for even the pain had been exhausted out of it, and with a bright clear brain that accommodated him to a quiet ecstasy of sheer lucidness of thought, he lay back on the lurching litter and watched the fading of the passing world, beholding for the last time the breadfruit tree before the devil-devil house, the dim day beneath the matted jungle roof, the gloomy gorge between the shouldering mountains, the saddle of raw limestone, and the mesa of black volcanic sand.

Down the spiral path of the pit they bore him, encircling the sheening, glowing Red One that seemed ever imminent to iridesce from colour and light into sweet singing and thunder. And over bones and logs of immolated men and gods they bore him, past the horrors of other immolated ones that yet lived, to the three-king- post tripod and the huge king-post striker.

Here Bassett, helped by Ngurn and Balatta, weakly sat up, swaying weakly from the hips, and with clear, unfaltering, all-seeing eyes gazed upon the Red One.

"Once, O Ngurn," he said, not taking his eyes from the sheening, vibrating surface whereon and wherein all the shades of cherry-red played unceasingly, ever a-quiver to change into sound, to become silken rustlings, silvery whisperings, golden thrummings of cords, velvet pipings of elfland, mellow distances of thunderings.

"I wait," Ngurn prompted after a long pause, the long-handled tomahawk unassumingly ready in his hand.

"Once, O Ngurn," Bassett repeated, "let the Red One speak so that I may see it speak as well as hear it. Then strike, thus, when I raise my hand; for, when I raise my hand, I shall drop my head forward and make place for the stroke at the base of my neck. But, O Ngurn, I, who am about to pass out of the light of day for ever, would like to pass with the wonder-voice of the Red One singing greatly in my ears."

"And I promise you that never will a head be so well cured as yours," Ngurn assured him, at the same time signalling the tribesmen to man the propelling ropes suspended from the king-post striker. "Your head shall be my greatest piece of work in the curing of heads."

Bassett smiled quietly to the old one's conceit, as the great carved log, drawn back through two-score feet of space, was released. The next moment he was lost in ecstasy at the abrupt and thunderous liberation of sound. But such thunder! Mellow it was with preciousness of all sounding metals. Archangels spoke in it; it was magnificently beautiful before all other sounds; it was invested with the intelligence of supermen of planets of other suns; it was the voice of God, seducing and commanding to be heard. And -- the everlasting miracle of that interstellar metal! Bassett, with his own eyes, saw colour and colours transform into sound till the whole visible surface of the vast sphere was a-crawl and titillant and vaporous with what he could not tell was colour or was sound. In that moment the interstices of matter were his, and the interfusings and intermating transfusings of matter and force.

Time passed. At the last Bassett was brought back from his ecstasy by an impatient movement of Ngurn. He had quite forgotten the old devil-devil one. A quick flash of fancy brought a husky chuckle into Bassett's throat. His shot-gun lay beside him in the litter. All he had to do, muzzle to head, was to press the trigger and blow his head into nothingness.

But why cheat him? was Bassett's next thought. Head-hunting, cannibal beast of a human that was as much ape as human, nevertheless Old Ngurn had, according to his lights, played squarer than square. Ngurn was in himself a forerunner of ethics and contract, of consideration, and gentleness in man. No, Bassett decided; it would be a ghastly pity and an act of dishonour to cheat the old fellow at the last. His head was Ngurn's, and Ngurn's head to cure it would be.

And Bassett, raising his hand in signal, bending forward his head as agreed so as to expose cleanly the articulation to his taut spinal cord, forgot Balatta, who was merely a woman, a woman merely and only and undesired. He knew, without seeing, when the razor-edged hatchet rose in the air behind him. And for that instant, ere the end, there fell upon Bassett the shadows of the Unknown, a sense of impending marvel of the rending of walls before the imaginable. Almost, when he knew the blow had started and just ere the edge of steel bit the flesh and nerves it seemed that he gazed upon the serene face of the Medusa, Truth -- And, simultaneous with the bite of the steel on the onrush of the dark, in a flashing instant of fancy, he saw the vision of his head turning slowly, always turning, in the devil-devil house beside the breadfruit tree.

Planchette

"It is my right to know," the girl said.

Her voice was firm-fibred with determination. There was no hint of pleading in it, yet it was the determination that is reached through a long period of pleading. But in her case it had been pleading, not of speech, but of personality. Her lips had been ever mute, but her face and eyes, and the very attitude of her soul, had been for a long time eloquent with questioning. This the man had known, but he had never answered; and now she was demanding by the spoken word that he answer.

"It is my right," the girl repeated.

"I know it," he answered, desperately and helplessly.

She waited, in the silence which followed, her eyes fixed upon the light that filtered down through the lofty boughs and bathed the great redwood trunks in mellow warmth. This light, subdued and colored, seemed almost a radiation from the trunks themselves, so strongly did they saturate it with their hue. The girl saw without seeing, as she heard, without hearing, the deep gurgling of the stream far below on the canyon bottom.

She looked down at the man. "Well?" She asked, with the firmness which feigns belief that obedience will be forthcoming.

She was sitting upright, her back against a fallen tree-trunk, while he lay near to her, on his side, an elbow on the ground and the hand supporting his head.

"Dear, dear Lute," he murmured.

She shivered at the sound of his voice -- not from repulsion, but from struggle against the fascination of its caressing gentleness. She had come to know well the lure of the man -- the wealth of easement and rest that was promised by every caressing intonation of his voice, by the mere touch of hand on hand or the faint impact of his breath on neck or cheek. The man could not express himself by word nor look nor touch without weaving into the expression, subtly and occultly, the feeling as of a hand that passed and that in passing stroked softly and soothingly. Nor was this all-pervading caress a something that cloyed with too great sweetness; nor was it sickly sentimental; nor was it maudlin with love's madness. It was vigorous, compelling, masculine. For that matter, it was largely unconscious on the man's part. He was only dimly aware of it. It was a part of him, the breath of his soul as it were, involuntary and unpremeditated.

But now, resolved and desperate, she steeled herself against him. He tried to face her, but her gray eyes looked out to him, steadily, from under cool, level brows, and he dropped his head upon her knee. Her hand strayed into his hair softly, and her face melted into solicitude and tenderness. But when he looked up again, her gray eyes were steady, her brows cool and level.

"What more can I tell you?" The man said. He raised his head and met her gaze. "I cannot marry you. I cannot marry any woman. I love you -- you know that -- better than my own life. I weigh you in the scales against all the dear things of living, and you outweigh everything. I would give everything to possess you, yet I may not. I cannot marry you. I can never marry you."

Her lips were compressed with the effort of control. His head was sinking back to her knee, when she checked him.

"You are already married, Chris?"

"No! no!" He cried vehemently. "I have never been married. I want to marry only you, and I cannot!"

"Then -- "

"Don't!" He interrupted. "Don't ask me!"

"It is my right to know," she repeated.

"I know it," he again interrupted. "But I cannot tell you."

"You have not considered me, Chris," she went on gently.

"I know, I know," he broke in.

"You cannot have considered me. You do not know what I have to bear from my people because of you."

"I did not think they felt so very unkindly toward me," he said bitterly.

"It is true. They can scarcely tolerate you. They do not show it to you, but they almost hate you. It is I who have had to bear all this. It was not always so, though. They liked you at first as . . . as I liked you. But that was four years ago. The time passed by -- a year, two years; and then they began to turn against you. They are not to be blamed. You spoke no word. They felt that you were destroying my life. It is four years, now, and you have never once mentioned marriage to them. What were they to think? What they have thought, that you were destroying my life."

As she talked, she continued to pass her fingers caressingly through his hair, sorrowful for the pain that she was inflicting.

"They did like you at first. Who can help liking you? You seem to draw affection from all living things, as the trees draw the moisture from the ground. It comes to you as it were your birthright. Aunt Mildred and Uncle Robert thought there was nobody like you. The sun rose and set in you. They thought I was the luckiest girl alive to win the love of a man like you. 'For it looks very much like it,' Uncle Robert used to say, wagging his head wickedly at me. Of course they liked you. Aunt Mildred used to sigh, and look across teasingly at Uncle, and say, 'When I think of Chris, it almost makes me wish I were younger myself.' And Uncle would answer, 'I don't blame you, my dear, not in the least.' And then the pair of them would beam upon me their congratulations that I had won the love of a man like you.

"And they knew I loved you as well. How could I hide it? -- this great, wonderful thing that had entered into my life and swallowed up all my days! For four years, Chris, I have lived only for you. Every moment was yours. Waking, I loved you. Sleeping, I dreamed of you. Every act I have performed was shaped by you, by the thought of you. Even my thoughts were moulded by you, by the invisible presence of you. I had no end, petty or great, that you were not there for me."

"I had no idea of imposing such slavery," he muttered.

"You imposed nothing. You always let me have my own way. It was you who were the obedient slave. You did for me without offending me. You forestalled my wishes without the semblance of forestalling; them, so natural and inevitable was everything you did for me. I said, without offending me. You were no dancing puppet. You made no fuss. Don't you see? You did not seem to do things at all. Somehow they were always there, just done, as a matter of course.

"The slavery was love's slavery. It was just my love for you that made you swallow up all my days. You did not force yourself into my thoughts. You crept in, always, and you were there always -- how much, you will never know.

"But as time went by, Aunt Mildred and Uncle grew to dislike you. They grew afraid. What was to become of me? You were destroying my life. My music? You know how my dream of it has dimmed away. That spring, when I first met you -- I was twenty, and I was about to start for Germany. I was going to study hard. That was four years ago, and I am still here in California.

"I had other lovers. You drove them away -- No! no! I don't mean that. It was I that drove them away. What did I care for lovers, for anything, when you were near? But as I said, Aunt Mildred and Uncle grew afraid. There has been talk -- friends, busybodies, and all the rest. The time went by. You did not speak. I could only wonder, wonder. I knew you loved me. Much was said against you by Uncle at first, and then by Aunt Mildred. They were father and mother to me, you know. I could not defend you. Yet I was loyal to you. I refused to discuss you. I closed up. There was half-estrangement in my home -- Uncle Robert with a face like an undertaker, and Aunt Mildred's heart breaking. But what could I do, Chris? What could I do?"

The man, his head resting on her knee again, groaned, but made no other reply.

"Aunt Mildred was mother to me, yet I went to her no more with my confidences. My childhood's book was closed. It was a sweet book, Chris. The tears come into my eyes sometimes when I think of it. But never mind that. Great happiness has been mine as well. I am glad I can talk frankly of my love for you. And the attaining of such frankness has been very sweet. I do love you, Chris. I love you . . . I cannot tell you how. You are everything to me, and more besides. You remember that Christmas tree of the children? -- when we played blindman's buff? And you caught me by the arm so, with such a clutching of fingers that I cried out with the hurt? I never told you, but the arm was badly bruised. And such sweet pleasure I got of it you could never guess. There, black and blue, was the imprint of your fingers -- your fingers, Chris, your fingers. It was the touch of you made visible. It was there a week, and I kissed the marks -- oh, so often! I hated to see them go; I wanted to rebruise the arm and make them linger. I was jealous of the returning white that drove the bruise away. Somehow, -- oh! I cannot explain, but I loved you so!"

In the silence that fell, she continued her caressing of his hair, while she idly watched a great gray squirrel, boisterous and hilarious, as it scampered back and forth in a distant vista of the redwoods. A crimson-crested woodpecker, energetically drilling a fallen trunk, caught and transferred her gaze. The man did not lift his head. Rather, he crushed his face closer against her knee, while his heaving shoulders marked the hardness with which he breathed.

"You must tell me, Chris," the girl said gently. "This mystery -- it is killing me. I must know why we cannot be married. Are we always to be this way? -- merely lovers, meeting often, it is true, and yet with the long absences between the meetings? Is it all the world holds for you and me, Chris? Are we never to be more to each other? Oh, it is good just to love, I know -- you have made me madly happy; but one does get so hungry at times for something more! I want more and more of you, Chris. I want all of you. I want all our days to be together. I want all the companionship, the comradeship, which cannot be ours now, and which will be ours when we are married -- " She caught her breath quickly. "But we are never to be married. I forgot. And you must tell me why."

The man raised his head and looked her in the eyes. It was a way he had with whomever he talked, of looking them in the eyes.

"I have considered you, Lute," he began doggedly. "I did consider you at the very first. I should never have gone on with it. I should have gone away. I knew it. And I considered you in the light of that knowledge, and yet . . . I did not go away. My God! What was I to do? I loved you. I could not go away. I could not help it. I stayed. I resolved, but I broke my resolves. I was like a drunkard. I was drunk of you. I was weak, I know. I failed. I could not go away. I tried. I went away -- you will remember, though you did not know why. You know now. I went away, but I could not remain away. Knowing that we could never marry, I came back to you. I am here, now, with you. Send me away, Lute. I have not the strength to go myself."

"But why should you go away?" She asked. "Besides, I must know why, before I can send you away."

"Don't ask me."

"Tell me," she said, her voice tenderly imperative.

"Don't, Lute; don't force me," the man pleaded, and there was appeal in his eyes and voice.

"But you must tell me," she insisted. "It is justice you owe me."

The man wavered. "If I do . . ." he began. Then he ended with determination, "I should never be able to forgive myself. No, I cannot tell you. Don't try to compel me, Lute. You would be as sorry as I."

"If there is anything . . . if then are, obstacles . . . if this mystery does really prevent . . ." She was speaking slowly, with long pauses, seeking the more delicate ways of speech for the framing of her thought. "Chris, I do love you. I love you as deeply as it is possible for any woman to love, I am sure. If you were to say to me now 'Come,' I would go with you. I would follow wherever you led. I would be your page, as in the days of old when ladies went with their knights to far lands. You are my knight, Chris, and you can do no wrong. Your will is my wish. I was once afraid of the censure of the world. Now that you have come into my life I am no longer afraid. I would laugh at the world and its censure for your sake -- for my sake too. I would laugh, for I should have you, and you are more to me than the good will and approval of the world. If you say 'Come,' I will -- "

"Don't! Don't!" He cried. "It is impossible! Marriage or not, I cannot even say 'Come.' I dare not. I'll show you. I'll tell you."

He sat up beside her, the action stamped with resolve. He took her hand in his and held it closely. His lips moved to the verge of speech. The mystery trembled for utterance. The air was palpitant with its presence. As if it were an irrevocable decree, the girl steeled herself to hear. But the man paused, gazing straight out before him. She felt his hand relax in hers, and she pressed it sympathetically, encouragingly. But she felt the rigidity going out of his tensed body, and she knew that spirit and flesh were relaxing together. His resolution was ebbing. He would not speak -- she knew it; and she knew, likewise, with the sureness of faith, that it was because he could not.

She gazed despairingly before her, a numb feeling at her heart, as though hope and happiness had died. She watched the sun flickering down through the warm-trunked redwoods. But she watched in a mechanical, absent way. She looked at the scene as from a long way off, without interest, herself an alien, no longer an intimate part of the earth and trees and flowers she loved so well.

So far removed did she seem, that she was aware of a curiosity, strangely impersonal, in what lay around her. Through a near vista she looked at a buckeye tree in full blossom as though her eyes encountered it for the first time. Her eyes paused and dwelt upon a yellow cluster of Diogenes' lanterns that grew on the edge of an open space. It was the way of flowers always to give her quick pleasure-thrills, but no thrill was hers now. She pondered the flower slowly and thoughtfully, as a hasheesh-eater, heavy with the drug, might ponder some whim-flower that obtruded on his vision. In her ears was the voice of the stream -- a hoarse-throated, sleepy old giant, muttering and mumbling his somnolent fancies. But her fancy was not in turn aroused, as was its wont; she knew the sound merely for water rushing over the rocks of the deep canyon-bottom, that and nothing more.

Her gaze wandered on beyond the Diogenes' lanterns into the open space. Knee-deep in the wild oats of the hillside grazed two horses, chestnut-sorrels the pair of them, perfectly matched, warm and golden in the sunshine, their spring-coats a sheen of highlights shot through with color flashes that glowed like fiery jewels. She recognized, almost with a shock, that one of them was hers, Dolly, the companion of her girlhood and womanhood, on whose neck she had sobbed her sorrows and sung her joys. A moistness welled into her eyes at the sight, and she came back from the remoteness of her mood, quick with passion and sorrow, to be part of the world again.

The man sank forward from the hips, relaxing entirely, and with a groan dropped his head on her knee. She leaned over him and pressed her lips softly and lingeringly to his hair.

"Come, let us go," she said, almost in a whisper.

She caught her breath in a half-sob, then tightened her lips as she rose. His face was white to ghastliness, so shaken was he by the struggle through which he had passed. They did not look at each other, but walked directly to the horses. She leaned against Dolly's neck while he tightened the girths. Then she gathered the reins in her hand and waited. He looked at her as he bent down, an appeal for forgiveness in his eyes; and in that moment her own eyes answered. Her foot rested in his hands, and from there she vaulted into the saddle. Without speaking, without further looking at each other, they turned the horses' heads and took the narrow trail that wound down through the sombre redwood aisles and across the open glades to the pasture-lands below. The trail became a cow-path, the cow-path became a wood-road, which later joined with a hay-road; and they rode down through the low-rolling, tawny California hills to where a set of bars let out on the county road which ran along the bottom of the valley. The girl sat her horse while the man dismounted and began taking down the bars.

"No -- wait!" She cried, before he had touched the two lower bars.

She urged the mare forward a couple of strides, and then the animal lifted over the bars in a clean little jump. The man's eyes sparkled, and he clapped his hands.

"You beauty! You beauty!" The girl cried, leaning forward impulsively in the saddle and pressing her cheek to the mare's neck where it burned flame-color in the sun.

"Let's trade horses for the ride in," she suggested, when he had led his horse through and finished putting up the bars. "You've never sufficiently appreciated Dolly."

"No, no," he protested.

"You think she is too old, too sedate," Lute insisted. "She's only sixteen, and she can outrun nine colts out of ten. Only she never cuts up. She's too steady, and you don't approve of her -- no, don't deny it, sir. I know. And I know also that she can outrun your vaunted Washoe Ban. There! I challenge you! And furthermore, you may ride her yourself. You know what Ban can do; so you must ride Dolly and see for yourself what she can do."

They proceeded to exchange the saddles on the horses, glad of the diversion and making the most of it.

"I'm glad I was born in California," Lute remarked, as she swung astride of Ban. "It's an outrage both to horse and woman to ride in a sidesaddle."

"You look like a young Amazon," the man said approvingly, his eyes passing tenderly over the girl as she swung the horse around.

"Are you ready?" She asked.

"All ready!"

"To the old mill," she called, as the horses sprang forward. "That's less than a mile."

"To a finish?" He demanded.

She nodded, and the horses, feeling the urge of the reins, caught the spirit of the race. The dust rose in clouds behind as they tore along the level road. They swung around the bend, horses and riders tilted at sharp angles to the ground, and more than once the riders ducked low to escape the branches of outreaching and overhanging trees. They clattered over the small plank bridges, and thundered over the larger iron ones to an ominous clanking of loose rods.

They rode side by side, saving the animals for the rush at the finish, yet putting them at a pace that drew upon vitality and staying power. Curving around a clump of white oaks, the road straightened out before them for several hundred yards, at the end of which they could see the ruined mill.

"Now for it!" The girl cried.

She urged the horse by suddenly leaning forward with her body, at the same time, for an instant, letting the rein slack and touching the neck with her bridle hand. She began to draw away from the man.

"Touch her on the neck!" She cried to him.

With this, the mare pulled alongside and began gradually to pass the girl. Chris and Lute looked at each other for a moment, the mare still drawing ahead, so that Chris was compelled slowly to turn his head. The mill was a hundred yards away.

"Shall I give him the spurs?" Lute shouted.

The man nodded, and the girl drove the spurs in sharply and quickly, calling upon the horse for its utmost, but watched her own horse forge slowly ahead of her.

"Beaten by three lengths!" Lute beamed triumphantly, as they pulled into a walk. "Confess, sir, confess! You didn't think the old mare had it in her."

Lute leaned to the side and rested her hand for a moment on Dolly's wet neck.

"Ban's a sluggard alongside of her," Chris affirmed. "Dolly's all right, if she is in her Indian Summer."

Lute nodded approval. "That's a sweet way of putting it -- Indian Summer. It just describes her. But she's not lazy. She has all the fire and none of the folly. She is very wise, what of her years."

"That accounts for it," Chris demurred. "Her folly passed with her youth. Many's the lively time she's given you."

"No," Lute answered. "I never knew her really to cut up. I think the only trouble she ever gave me was when I was training her to open gates. She was afraid when they swung back upon her -- the animal's fear of the trap, perhaps. But she bravely got over it. And she never was vicious. She never bolted, nor bucked, nor cut up in all her life -- never, not once."

The horses went on at a walk, still breathing heavily from their run. The road wound along the bottom of the valley, now and again crossing the stream. From either side rose the drowsy purr of mowing-machines, punctuated by occasional sharp cries of the men who were gathering the hay-crop. On the western side of the valley the hills rose green and dark, but the eastern side was already burned brown and tan by the sun.

"There is summer, here is spring," Lute said. "Oh, beautiful Sonoma Valley!"

Her eyes were glistening and her face was radiant with love of the land. Her gaze wandered on across orchard patches and sweeping vineyard stretches, seeking out the purple which seemed to hang like a dim smoke in the wrinkles of the hills and in the more distant canyon gorges. Far up, among the more rugged crests, where the steep slopes were covered with manzanita, she caught a glimpse of a clear space where the wild grass had not yet lost its green.

"Have you ever heard of the secret pasture?" She asked, her eyes still fixed on the remote green.

A snort of fear brought her eyes back to the man beside her. Dolly, upreared, with distended nostrils and wild eyes, was pawing the air madly with her fore legs. Chris threw himself forward against her neck to keep her from falling backward, and at the same time touched her with the spurs to compel her to drop her fore feet to the ground in order to obey the go-ahead impulse of the spurs.

"Why, Dolly, this is most remarkable," Lute began reprovingly.

But, to her surprise, the mare threw her head down, arched her back as she went up in the air, and, returning, struck the ground stiff-legged and bunched.

"A genuine buck!" Chris called out, and the next moment the mare was rising under him in a second buck.

Lute looked on, astounded at the unprecedented conduct of her mare, and admiring her lover's horsemanship. He was quite cool, and was himself evidently enjoying the performance. Again and again, half a dozen times, Dolly arched herself into the air and struck, stiffly bunched. Then she threw her head straight up and rose on her hind legs, pivoting about and striking with her fore feet. Lute whirled into safety the horse she was riding, and as she did so caught a glimpse of Dolly's eyes, with the look in them of blind brute madness, bulging until it seemed they must burst from her head. The faint pink in the white of the eyes was gone, replaced by a white that was like dull marble and that yet flashed as from some inner fire.

A faint cry of fear, suppressed in the instant of utterance, slipped past Lute's lips. One hind leg of the mare seemed to collapse, and for a moment the whole quivering body, upreared and perpendicular, swayed back and forth, and there was uncertainty as to whether it would fall forward or backward. The man, half-slipping sidewise from the saddle, so as to fall clear if the mare toppled backward, threw his weight to the front and alongside her neck. This overcame the dangerous teetering balance, and the mare struck the ground on her feet again.

But there was no let-up. Dolly straightened out so that the line of the face was almost a continuation of the line of the stretched neck; this position enabled her to master the bit, which she did by bolting straight ahead down the road.

For the first time Lute became really frightened. She spurred Washoe Ban in pursuit, but he could not hold his own with the mad mare, and dropped gradually behind. Lute saw Dolly check and rear in the air again, and caught up just as the mare made a second bolt. As Dolly dashed around a bend, she stopped suddenly, stiff-legged. Lute saw her lover torn out of the saddle, his thigh-grip broken by the sudden jerk. Though he had lost his seat, he had not been thrown, and as the mare dashed on Lute saw him clinging to the side of the horse, a hand in the mane and a leg across the saddle. With a quick cavort he regained his seat and proceeded to fight with the mare for control.

But Dolly swerved from the road and dashed down a grassy slope yellowed with innumerable mariposa lilies. An ancient fence at the bottom was no obstacle. She burst through as though it were filmy spider-web and disappeared in the underbrush. Lute followed unhesitatingly, putting Ban through the gap in the fence and plunging on into the thicket. She lay along his neck, closely, to escape the ripping and tearing of the trees and vines. She felt the horse drop down through leafy branches and into the cool gravel of a stream's bottom. From ahead came a splashing of water, and she caught a glimpse of Dolly, dashing up the small bank and into a clump of scrub-oaks, against the trunks of which she was trying to scrape off her rider.

Lute almost caught up amongst the trees, but was hopelessly out-distanced on the fallow field adjoining, across which the mare tore with a fine disregard for heavy ground and gopher-holes. When she turned at a sharp angle into the thicket-land beyond, Lute took the long diagonal, skirted the ticket, and reined in Ban at the other side. She had arrived first. From within the thicket she could hear a tremendous crashing of brush and branches. Then the mare burst through and into the open, falling to her knees, exhausted, on the soft earth. She arose and staggered forward, then came limply to a halt. She was in lather-sweat of fear, and stood trembling pitiably.

Chris was still on her back. His shirt was in ribbons. The backs of his hands were bruised and lacerated, while his face was streaming blood from a gash near the temple. Lute had controlled herself well, but now she was aware of a quick nausea and a trembling of weakness.

"Chris!" She said, so softly that it was almost a whisper. Then she sighed, "Thank God."

"Oh, I'm all right," he cried to her, putting into his voice all the heartiness he could command, which was not much, for he had himself been under no mean nervous strain.

He showed the reaction he was undergoing, when he swung down out of the saddle. He began with a brave muscular display as he lifted his leg over, but ended, on his feet, leaning against the limp Dolly for support. Lute flashed out of her saddle, and her arms were about him in an embrace of thankfulness.

"I know where there is a spring," she said, a moment later.

They left the horses standing untethered, and she led her lover into the cool recesses of the thicket to where crystal water bubbled from out the base of the mountain.

"What was that you said about Dolly's never cutting up?" He asked, when the blood had been stanched and his nerves and pulse-beats were normal again.

"I am stunned," Lute answered. "I cannot understand it. She never did anything like it in all her life. And all animals like you so -- it's not because of that. Why, she is a child's horse. I was only a little girl when I first rode her, and to this day -- "

"Well, this day she was everything but a child's horse," Chris broke in. "She was a devil. She tried to scrape me off against the trees, and to batter my brains out against the limbs. She tried all the lowest and narrowest places she could find. You should have seen her squeeze through. And did you see those bucks?"

Lute nodded.

"Regular bucking-bronco proposition."

"But what should she know about bucking?" Lute demanded. "She was never known to buck -- never."

He shrugged his shoulders. "Some forgotten instinct, perhaps, long-lapsed and come to life again."

The girl rose to her feet determinedly. "I'm going to find out," she said.

They went back to the horses, where they subjected Dolly to a rigid examination that disclosed nothing. Hoofs, legs, bit, mouth, body -- everything was as it should be. The saddle and saddle-cloth were innocent of bur or sticker; the back was smooth and unbroken. They searched for sign of snake-bite and sting of fly or insect, but found nothing.

"Whatever it was, it was subjective, that much is certain," Chris said.

"Obsession," Lute suggested.

They laughed together at the idea, for both were twentieth-century products, healthy-minded and normal, with souls that delighted in the butterfly-chase of ideals but that halted before the brink where superstition begins.

"An evil spirit," Chris laughed; "but what evil have I done that I should be so punished?"

"You think too much of yourself, sir," she rejoined. "It is more likely some evil, I don't know what, that Dolly has done. You were a mere accident. I might have been on her back at the time, or Aunt Mildred, or anybody."

As she talked, she took hold of the stirrup-strap and started to shorten it.

"What are you doing?" Chris demanded.

"I'm going to ride Dolly in."

"No, you're not," he announced. "It would be bad discipline. After what has happened I am simply compelled to ride her in myself."

But it was a very weak and very sick mare he rode, stumbling and halting, afflicted with nervous jerks and recurring muscular spasms -- the aftermath of the tremendous orgasm through which she had passed.

"I feel like a book of verse and a hammock, after all that has happened," Lute said, as they rode into camp.

It was a summer camp of city-tired people, pitched in a grove of towering redwoods through whose lofty boughs the sunshine trickled down, broken and subdued to soft light and cool shadow. Apart from the main camp were the kitchen and the servants' tents; and midway between was the great dining hall, walled by the living redwood columns, where fresh whispers of air were always to be found, and where no canopy was needed to keep the sun away.

"Poor Dolly, she is really sick," Lute said that evening, when they had returned from a last look at the mare. "But you weren't hurt, Chris, and that's enough for one small woman to be thankful for. I thought I knew, but I really did not know till today, how much you meant to me. I could hear only the plunging and struggle in the thicket. I could not see you, nor know how it went with you."

"My thoughts were of you," Chris answered, and felt the responsive pressure of the hand that rested on his arm.

She turned her face up to his and met his lips.

"Goodnight," she said.

"Dear Lute, dear Lute," he caressed her with his voice as she moved away among the shadows.

***

"Who's going for the mail?" Called a woman's voice through the trees.

Lute closed the book from which they had been reading, and sighed.

"We weren't going to ride today," she said.

"Let me go," Chris proposed. "You stay here. I'll be down and back in no time."

She shook her head.

"Who's going for the mail?" The voice insisted.

"Where's Martin?" Lute called, lifting; her voice in answer.

"I don't know," came the voice. "I think Robert took him along somewhere -- horse-buying, or fishing, or I don't know what. There's really nobody left but Chris and you. Besides, it will give you an appetite for dinner. You've been lounging in the hammock all day. And Uncle Robert must have his newspaper."

"All right, Aunty, we're starting," Lute called back, getting out of the hammock.

A few minutes later, in riding-clothes, they were saddling the horses. They rode out on to the county road, where blazed the afternoon sun, and turned toward Glen Ellen. The little town slept in the sun, and the somnolent storekeeper and postmaster scarcely kept his eyes open long enough to make up the packet of letters and newspapers.

An hour later Lute and Chris turned aside from the road and dipped along a cow-path down the high bank to water the horses, before going into camp.

"Dolly looks as though she'd forgotten all about yesterday," Chris said, as they sat their horses knee-deep in the rushing water. "Look at her."

The mare had raised her head and cocked her ears at the rustling of a quail in the thicket. Chris leaned over and rubbed around her ears. Dolly's enjoyment was evident, and she drooped her head over against the shoulder of his own horse.

"Like a kitten," was Lute's comment.

"Yet I shall never be able wholly to trust her again," Chris said. "Not after yesterday's mad freak."

"I have a feeling myself that you are safer on Ban," Lute laughed. "It is strange. My trust in Dolly is as implicit as ever. I feel confident so far as I am concerned, but I should never care to see you on her back again. Now with Ban, my faith is still unshaken. Look at that neck! Isn't he handsome! He'll be as wise as Dolly when he is as old as she."

"I feel the same way," Chris laughed back. "Ban could never possibly betray me."

They turned their horses out of the stream. Dolly stopped to brush a fly from her knee with her nose, and Ban urged past into the narrow way of the path. The space was too restricted to make him return, save with much trouble, and Chris allowed him to go on. Lute, riding behind, dwelt with her eyes upon her lover's back, pleasuring in the lines of the bare neck and the sweep out to the muscular shoulders.

Suddenly she reined in her horse. She could do nothing but look, so brief was the duration of the happening. Beneath and above was the almost perpendicular bank. The path itself was barely wide enough for footing. Yet Washoe Ban, whirling and rearing at the same time, toppled for a moment in the air and fell backward off the path.

So unexpected and so quick was it, that the man was involved in the fall. There had been no time for him to throw himself to the path. He was falling ere he knew it, and he did the only thing possible -- slipped the stirrups and threw his body into the air, to the side, and at the same time down. It was twelve feet to the rocks below. He maintained an upright position, his head up and his eyes fixed on the horse above him and falling upon him.

Chris struck like a cat, on his feet, on the instant making a leap to the side. The next instant Ban crashed down beside him. The animal struggled little, but sounded the terrible cry that horses sometimes sound when they have received mortal hurt. He had struck almost squarely on his back, and in that position he remained, his head twisted partly under, his hind legs relaxed and motionless, his fore legs futilely striking the air.

Chris looked up reassuringly.

"I am getting used to it," Lute smiled down to him. "Of course I need not ask if you are hurt. Can I do anything?"

He smiled back and went over to the fallen beast, letting go the girths of the saddle and getting the head straightened out.

"I thought so," he said, after a cursory examination. "I thought so at the time. Did you hear that sort of crunching snap?"

She shuddered.

"Well, that was the punctuation of life, the final period dropped at the end of Ban's usefulness." He started around to come up by the path. "I've been astride of Ban for the last time. Let us go home."

At the top of the bank Chris turned and looked down.

"Goodbye, Washoe Ban!" He called out. "Goodbye, old fellow."

The animal was struggling to lift its head. There were tears in Chris's eyes as he turned abruptly away, and tears In Lute's eyes as they met his. She was silent in her sympathy, though the pressure of her hand was firm in his as he walked beside her horse down the dusty road.

"It was done deliberately," Chris burst forth suddenly. "There was no warning. He deliberately flung himself over backward."

"There was no warning," Lute concurred. "I was looking. I saw him. He whirled and threw himself at the same time, just as if you had done it yourself, with a tremendous jerk and backward pull on the bit."

"It was not my hand, I swear it. I was not even thinking of him. He was going up with a fairly loose rein, as a matter of course."

"I should have seen it, had you done it," Lute said. "But it was all done before you had a chance to do anything. It was not your hand, not even your unconscious hand."

"Then it was some invisible hand, reaching out from I don't know where."

He looked up whimsically at the sky and smiled at the conceit.

Martin stepped forward to receive Dolly, when they came into the stable end of the grove, but his face expressed no surprise at sight of Chris coming in on foot. Chris lingered behind Lute for moment.

"Can you shoot a horse?" He asked.

The groom nodded, then added, "Yes, sir," with a second and deeper nod.

"How do you do it?"

"Draw a line from the eyes to the ears -- I mean the opposite ears, sir. And where the lines cross -- "

"That will do," Chris interrupted. "You know the watering place at: the second bend. You'll find Ban there with a broken back."

★★★

"Oh, here you are, sir. I have been looking for you everywhere since dinner. You are wanted immediately."

Chris tossed his cigar away, then went over and pressed his foot on its glowing; fire.

"You haven't told anybody about it? -- Ban?" He queried.

Lute shook her head. "They'll learn soon enough. Martin will mention it to Uncle Robert tomorrow."

"But don't feel too bad about it," she said, after a moment's pause, slipping her hand into his.

"He was my colt," he said. "Nobody has ridden him but you. I broke him myself. I knew him from the time he was born. I knew every bit of him, every trick, every caper, and I would have staked my life that it was impossible for him to do a thing like this. There was no warning, no fighting for the bit, no previous unruliness. I have been thinking it over. He didn't fight for the bit, for that matter. He wasn't unruly, nor disobedient. There wasn't time. It was an impulse, and he acted upon it like lightning. I am astounded now at the swiftness with which it took place. Inside the first second we were over the edge and falling.

"It was deliberate -- deliberate suicide. And attempted murder. It was a trap. I was the victim. He had me, and he threw himself over with me. Yet he did not hate me. He loved me . . . as much as it is possible for a horse to love. I am confounded. I cannot understand it any more than you can understand Dolly's behavior yesterday."

"But horses go insane, Chris," Lute said. "You know that. It's merely coincidence that two horses in two days should have spells under you."

"That's the only explanation," he answered, starting off with her. "But why am I wanted urgently?"

"Planchette."

"Oh, I remember. It will be a new experience to me. Somehow I missed it when it was all the rage long ago."

"So did all of us," Lute replied, "except Mrs. Grantly. It is her favorite phantom, it seems."

"A weird little thing," he remarked. "Bundle of nerves and black eyes. I'll wager she doesn't weigh ninety pounds, and most of that's magnetism."

"Positively uncanny . . . at times." Lute shivered involuntarily. "She gives me the creeps."

"Contact of the healthy with the morbid," he explained dryly. "You will notice it is the healthy that always has the creeps. The morbid never has the creeps. It gives the creeps. That's its function. Where did you people pick her up, anyway?"

"I don't know -- yes, I do, too. Aunt Mildred met her in Boston, I think -- oh, I don't know. At any rate, Mrs. Grantly came to California, and of course had to visit Aunt Mildred. You know the open house we keep.

They halted where a passageway between two great redwood trunks gave entrance to the dining room. Above, through lacing boughs, could be seen the stars. Candles lighted the tree-columned space. About the table, examining the Planchette contrivance, were four persons. Chris's gaze roved over them, and he was aware of a guilty sorrow-pang as he paused for a moment on Lute's Aunt Mildred and Uncle Robert, mellow with ripe middle age and genial with the gentle buffets life had dealt them. He passed amusedly over the black-eyed, frail-bodied Mrs. Grantly, and halted on the fourth person, a portly, massive-headed man, whose gray temples belied the youthful solidity of his face.

"Who's that?" Chris whispered.

"A Mr. Barton. The train was late. That's why you didn't see him at dinner. He's only a capitalist -- water-power-long-distance-electricity-transmitter, or something like that."

"Doesn't look as though he could give an ox points on imagination."

"He can't. He inherited his money. But he knows enough to hold on to it and hire other men's brains. He is very conservative."

"That is to be expected," was Chris's comment. His gaze went back to the man and woman who had been father and mother to the girl beside him. "Do you know," he said, "it came to me with a shock yesterday when you told me that they had turned against me and that I was scarcely tolerated. I met them afterwards, last evening, guiltily, in fear and trembling -- and today, too. And yet I could see no difference from of old."

"Dear man," Lute sighed. "Hospitality is as natural to them as the act of breathing. But it isn't that, after all. It is all genuine in their dear hearts. No matter how severe the censure they put upon you when you are absent, the moment they are with you they soften and are all kindness and warmth. As soon as their eyes rest on you, affection and love come bubbling up. You are so made. Every animal likes you. All people like you. They can't help it. You can't help it. You are universally lovable, and the best of it is that you don't know it. You don't know it now. Even as I tell it to you, you don't realize it, you won't realize it -- and that very incapacity to realize it is one of the reasons why you are so loved. You are incredulous now, and you shake your head; but I know, who am your slave, as all people know, for they likewise are your slaves.

"Why, in a minute we shall go in and join them. Mark the affection, almost maternal, that will well up in Aunt Mildred's eyes. Listen to the tones of Uncle Robert's voice when he says, 'Well, Chris, my boy?' Watch Mrs. Grantly melt, literally melt, like a dewdrop in the sun.

"Take Mr. Barton, there. You have never seen him before. Why, you will invite him out to smoke a cigar with you when the rest of us have gone to bed -- you, a mere nobody, and he a man of many millions, a man of power, a man obtuse and stupid like the ox; and he will follow you about, smoking; the cigar, like a little dog, your little dog, trotting at your back. He will not know he is doing it, but he will be doing it just the same. Don't I know, Chris? Oh, I have watched you, watched you, so often, and loved you for it, and loved you again for it, because you were so delightfully and blindly unaware of what you were doing."

"I'm almost bursting with vanity from listening to you," he laughed, passing his arm around her and drawing her against him.

"Yes," she whispered, "and in this very moment, when you are laughing at all that I have said, you, the feel of you, your soul, -- call it what you will, it is you, -- is calling for all the love that is in me."

She leaned more closely against him, and sighed as with fatigue. He breathed a kiss into her hair and held her with firm tenderness.

Aunt Mildred stirred briskly and looked up from the Planchette board.

"Come, let us begin," she said. "It will soon grow chilly. Robert, where are those children?"

"Here we are," Lute called out, disengaging herself.

"Now for a bundle of creeps," Chris whispered, as they started in.

Lute's prophecy of the manner in which her lover would be received was realized. Mrs. Grantly, unreal, unhealthy, scintillant with frigid magnetism, warmed and melted as though of truth she were dew and he sun. Mr. Barton beamed broadly upon him, and was colossally gracious. Aunt Mildred greeted him with a glow of fondness and motherly kindness, while Uncle Robert genially and heartily demanded, "Well, Chris, my boy, and what of the riding?"

But Aunt Mildred drew her shawl more closely around her and hastened them to the business in hand. On the table was a sheet of paper. On the paper, rifling on three supports, was a small triangular board. Two of the supports were easily moving casters. The third support, placed at the apex of the triangle, was a lead pencil.

"Who's first?" Uncle Robert demanded.

There was a moment's hesitancy, then Aunt Mildred placed her hand on the board, and said: "Some one has always to be the fool for the delectation of the rest."

"Brave woman," applauded her husband. "Now, Mrs. Grantly, do your worst."

"I?" That lady queried. "I do nothing. The power, or whatever you care to think it, is outside of me, as it is outside of all of you. As to what that power is, I will not dare to say. There is such a power. I have had evidences of it. And you will undoubtedly have evidences of it. Now please be quiet, everybody. Touch the board very lightly, but firmly, Mrs. Story; but do nothing of your own volition."

Aunt Mildred nodded, and stood with her hand on Planchette; while the rest formed about her in a silent and expectant circle. But nothing happened. The minutes ticked away, and Planchette remained motionless.

"Be patient," Mrs. Grantly counselled. "Do not struggle against any influences you may feel working on you. But do not do anything yourself. The influence will take care of that. You will feel impelled to do things, and such impulses will be practically irresistible."

"I wish the influence would hurry up," Aunt Mildred protested at the end of five motionless minutes.

"Just a little longer, Mrs. Story, just a little longer," Mrs. Grantly said soothingly.

Suddenly Aunt Mildred's hand began to twitch into movement. A mild concern showed in her face as she observed the movement of her hand and heard the scratching of the pencil-point at the apex of Planchette.

For another five minutes this continued, when Aunt Mildred withdrew her hand with an effort, and said, with a nervous laugh:

"I don't know whether I did it myself or not. I do know that I was growing nervous, standing there like a psychic fool with all your solemn faces turned upon me."

"Hen-scratches," was Uncle Robert's judgement, when he looked over the paper upon which she had scrawled.

"Quite illegible," was Mrs. Grantly's dictum. "It does not resemble writing at all. The influences have not got to working yet. You try it, Mr. Barton."

That gentleman stepped forward, ponderously willing to please, and placed his hand on the board. And for ten solid, stolid minutes he stood there, motionless, like a statue, the frozen personification of the commercial age. Uncle Robert's face began to work. He blinked, stiffened his mouth, uttered suppressed, throaty sounds, deep down; finally he snorted, lost his self-control, and broke out in a roar of laughter. All joined in this merriment, including Mrs. Grantly. Mr. Barton laughed with them, but he was vaguely nettled.

"You try it, Story," he said.

Uncle Robert, still laughing, and urged on by Lute and his wife, took the board. Suddenly his face sobered. His hand had begun to move, and the pencil could be heard scratching across the paper.

"By George!" He muttered. "That's curious. Look at it. I'm not doing it. I know I'm not doing it. Look at that hand go! Just look at it!"

"Now, Robert, none of your ridiculousness," his wife warned him.

"I tell you I'm not doing it," he replied indignantly. "The force has got hold of me. Ask Mrs. Grantly. Tell her to make it stop, if you want it to stop. I can't stop it. By George! Look at that flourish. I didn't do that. I never wrote a flourish in my life."

"Do try to be serious," Mrs. Grantly warned them. "An atmosphere of levity does not conduce to the best operation of Planchette."

"There, that will do, I guess," Uncle Robert said as he took his hand away. "Now let's see."

He bent over and adjusted his glasses. "It's handwriting at any rate, and that's better than the rest of you did. Here, Lute, your eyes are young."

"Oh, what flourishes!" Lute exclaimed, as she looked at the paper. "And look there, there are two different handwritings."

She began to read: "This is the first lecture. Concentrate on this sentence: 'I am a positive spirit and not negative to any condition.' Then follow with concentration on positive love. After that peace and harmony will vibrate through and around your body. Your soul -- The other writing breaks right in. This is the way it goes: Bullfrog 95, Dixie 16, Golden Anchor 65, Gold Mountain 13, Jim Butler 70, Jumbo 75, North Star 42, Rescue 7, Black Butte 75, Brown Hope 16, Iron Top 3."

"Iron Top's pretty low," Mr. Barton murmured.

"Robert, you've been dabbling again!" Aunt Mildred cried accusingly.

"No, I've not," he denied. "I only read the quotations. But how the devil -- I beg your pardon -- they got there on that piece of paper I'd like to know."

"Your subconscious mind," Chris suggested. "You read the quotations in today's paper."

"No, I didn't; but last week I glanced over the column."

"A day or a year is all the same in the subconscious mind," said Mrs. Grantly. "The subconscious mind never forgets. But I am not saying that this is due to the subconscious mind. I refuse to state to what I think it is due."

"But how about that other stuff?" Uncle Robert demanded. "Sounds like what I'd think Christian Science ought to sound like."

"Or theosophy," Aunt Mildred volunteered. "Some message to a neophyte."

"Go on, read the rest," her husband commanded.

"This puts you in touch with the mightier spirits," Lute read. "You shall become one with us, and your name shall be 'Arya,' and you shall -- Conqueror 20, Empire 12, Columbia Mountain 18, Midway 140 -- and, and that is all. Oh, no! Here's a last flourish, Arya, from Kandor -- that must surely be the Mahatma."

"I'd like to have you explain that theosophy stuff on the basis of the subconscious mind, Chris," Uncle Robert challenged.

Chris shrugged his shoulders. "No explanation. You must have got a message intended for someone else."

"Lines were crossed, eh?" Uncle Robert chuckled. "Multiplex spiritual wireless telegraphy, I'd call it."

"It *is* nonsense," Mrs. Grantly said. "I never knew Planchette to behave so outrageously. There are disturbing influences at work. I felt them from the first. Perhaps it is because you are all making too much fun of it. You are too hilarious."

"A certain befitting gravity should grace the occasion," Chris agreed, placing his hand on Planchette. "Let me try. And not one of you must laugh or giggle, or even think 'laugh' or 'giggle.' And if you dare to snort, even once, Uncle Robert, there is no telling what occult vengeance may be wreaked upon you."

"I'll be good," Uncle Robert rejoined. "But if I really must snort, may I silently slip away?"

Chris nodded. His hand had already begun to work. There had been no preliminary twitchings nor tentative essays at writing. At once his hand had started off, and Planchette was moving swiftly and smoothly across the paper.

"Look at him," Lute whispered to her aunt. "See how white he is."

Chris betrayed disturbance at the sound of her voice, and thereafter silence was maintained. Only could be heard the steady scratching of the pencil. Suddenly, as though it had been stung, he jerked his hand away. With a sigh and a yawn he stepped back from the table, then glanced with the curiosity of a newly awakened man at their faces.

"I think I wrote something," he said.

"I should say you did," Mrs. Grantly remarked with satisfaction, holding up the sheet of paper and glancing at it.

"Read it aloud," Uncle Robert said.

"Here it is, then. It begins with 'beware' written three times, and in much larger characters than the rest of the writing. BEWARE! BEWARE! BEWARE! Chris Dunbar, I intend to destroy you. I have already made two attempts upon your life, and failed. I shall yet succeed. So sure am I that I shall succeed that I dare to tell you. I do not need to tell you why. In your own heart you know. The wrong you are doing -- And here it abruptly ends."

Mrs. Grantly laid the paper down on the table and looked at Chris, who had already become the centre of all eyes, and who was yawning as from an overpowering drowsiness.

"Quite a sanguinary turn, I should say," Uncle Robert remarked.

"I have already made two attempts upon your life," Mrs. Grantly read from the paper, which she was going over a second time.

"On my life?" Chris demanded between yawns. "Why, my life hasn't been attempted even once. My! I am sleepy!"

"Ah, my boy, you are thinking of flesh-and-blood men," Uncle Robert laughed. "But this is a spirit. Your life has been attempted by unseen things. Most likely ghostly hands have tried to throttle you in your sleep."

"Oh, Chris!" Lute cried impulsively. "This afternoon! The hand you said must have seized your rein!"

"But I was joking," he objected.

"Nevertheless . . ."Lute left her thought unspoken.

Mrs. Grantly had become keen on the scent. "What was that about this afternoon? Was your life in danger?"

Chris's drowsiness had disappeared. "I'm becoming interested myself," he acknowledged. "We haven't said anything about it. Ban broke his back this afternoon. He threw himself off the bank, and I ran the risk of being caught underneath."

"I wonder, I wonder," Mrs. Grantly communed aloud. "There is something in this. . . . It is a warning . . . Ah! You were hurt yesterday riding Miss Story's horse! That makes the two attempts!"

She looked triumphantly at them. Planchette had been vindicated.

"Nonsense," laughed Uncle Robert, but with a slight hint of irritation in his manner. "Such things do not happen these days. This is the twentieth century, my dear madam. The thing, at the very latest, smacks of mediaevalism."

"I have had such wonderful tests with Planchette," Mrs. Grantly began, then broke off suddenly to go to the table and place her hand on the board.

"Who are you?" She asked. "What is your name?"

The board immediately began to write. By this time all heads, with the exception of Mr. Barton's, were bent over the table and following the pencil.

"It's Dick," Aunt Mildred cried, a note of the mildly hysterical in her voice.

Her husband straightened up, his face for the first time grave.

"It's Dick's signature," he said. "I'd know his fist in a thousand."

"'Dick Curtis,'" Mrs. Grantly read aloud. "Who is Dick Curtis?"

"By Jove, that's remarkable!" Mr. Barton broke in. "The handwriting in both instances is the same. Clever, I should say, really clever," he added admiringly.

"Let me see," Uncle Robert demanded, taking the paper and examining it. "Yes, it is Dick's handwriting."

"But who is Dick?" Mrs. Grantly insisted. "Who is this Dick Curtis?"

"Dick Curtis, why, he was Captain Richard Curtis," Uncle Robert answered.

"He was Lute's father," Aunt Mildred supplemented. "Lute took our name. She never saw him. He died when she was a few weeks old. He was my brother."

"Remarkable, most remarkable." Mrs. Grantly was revolving the message in her mind. "There were two attempts on Mr. Dunbar's life. The subconscious mind cannot explain that, for none of us knew of the accident today."

"I knew," Chris answered, "and it was I that operated Planchette. The explanation is simple."

"But the handwriting," interposed Mr. Barton. "What you wrote and what Mrs. Grantly wrote are identical."

Chris bent over and compared the handwriting.

"Besides," Mrs. Grantly cried, "Mr. Story recognizes the handwriting."

She looked at him for verification.

He nodded his head. "Yes, it is Dick's fist. I'll swear to that."

But to Lute had come a visioning;. While the rest argued pro and con and the air was filled with phrases, -- "psychic phenomena," "self-hypnotism," "residuum of unexplained truth," and "spiritism," -- she was reviving mentally the girlhood pictures she had conjured of this soldier-father she had never seen. She possessed his sword, there were several old-fashioned daguerreotypes, there was much that had been said of him, stories told of him -- and all this had constituted the material out of which she had builded him in her childhood fancy.

"There is the possibility of one mind unconsciously suggesting to another mind," Mrs. Grantly was saying; but through Lute's mind was trooping her father on his great roan war-horse. Now he was leading his men. She saw him on lonely scouts, or in the midst of the yelling, Indians at Salt Meadows, when of his command he returned with one man in ten. And in the picture she had of him, in the physical semblance she had made of him, was reflected his spiritual nature, reflected by her worshipful artistry in form and feature and expression -- his bravery, his quick temper, his impulsive championship, his madness of wrath in a righteous cause, his warm generosity and swift forgiveness, and his chivalry that epitomized codes and ideals primitive as the days of knighthood. And first, last, and always, dominating all, she saw in the face of him the hot passion and quickness of deed that had earned for him the name "Fighting Dick Curtis."

"Let me put it to the test," she heard Mrs. Grantly saying;. "Let Miss Story try Planchette. There may be a further message."

"No, no, I beg of you," Aunt Mildred interposed. "It is too uncanny. It surely is wrong to tamper with the dead. Besides, I am nervous. Or, better, let me go to bed, leaving you to go on with your experiments. That will be the best way, and you can tell me in the morning." Mingled with the "Good-nights," were half-hearted protests from Mrs. Grantly, as Aunt Mildred withdrew.

"Robert can return," she called back, "as soon as he has seen me to my tent."

"It would be a shame to give it up now," Mrs. Grantly said. "There is no telling what we are on the verge of. Won't you try it, Miss Story?"

Lute obeyed, but when she placed her hand on the board she was conscious of a vague and nameless fear at this toying with the supernatural. She was twentieth-century, and the thing in essence, as her uncle had said, was mediaeval. Yet she could not shake off the instinctive fear that arose in her -- man's inheritance from the wild and howling ages when his hairy, apelike prototype was afraid of the dark and personified the elements into things of fear.

But as the mysterious influence seized her hand and sent it meriting across the paper, all the unusual passed out of the situation and she was unaware of more than a feeble curiosity. For she was intent on another visioning -- this time of her mother, who was also unremembered in the flesh. Not sharp and vivid like that of her father, but dim and nebulous was the picture she shaped of her mother -- a saint's head in an aureole of sweetness and goodness and meekness, and withal, shot through with a hint of reposeful determination, of will, stubborn and unobtrusive, that in life had expressed itself mainly in resignation.

Lute's hand had ceased moving, and Mrs. Grantly was already reading the message that had been written.

"It is a different handwriting," she said. "A woman's hand. 'Martha,' it is signed. Who is Martha?"

Lute was not surprised. "It is my mother," she said simply. "What does she say?"

She had not been made sleepy, as Chris had; but the keen edge of her vitality had been blunted, and she was experiencing a sweet and pleasing lassitude. And while the message was being read, in her eyes persisted the vision of her mother.

"Dear child," Mrs. Grantly read, "do not mind him. He was ever quick of speech and rash. Be no niggard with your love. Love cannot hurt you. To deny love is to sin. Obey your heart and you can do no wrong. Obey worldly considerations, obey pride, obey those that prompt you against your heart's prompting, and you do sin. Do not mind your father. He is angry now, as was his way in the earth-life; but he will come to see the wisdom of my counsel, for this, too, was his way in the earth-life. Love, my child, and love well. -- Martha."

"Let me see it," Lute cried, seizing the paper and devouring the handwriting with her eyes. She was thrilling with unexpressed love for the mother she had never seen, and this written speech from the grave seemed to give more tangibility to her having ever existed, than did the vision of her.

"This *is* remarkable," Mrs. Grantly was reiterating. "There was never anything like it. Think of it, my dear, both your father and mother here with us tonight."

Lute shivered. The lassitude was gone, and she was her natural self again, vibrant with the instinctive fear of things unseen. And it was offensive to her mind that, real or illusion, the presence or the memorized existences of her father and mother should he touched by these two persons who were practically strangers -- Mrs. Grantly, unhealthy and morbid, and Mr. Barton, stolid and stupid with a grossness both of the flesh and the spirit. And it further seemed a trespass that these strangers should thus enter into the intimacy between her and Chris.

She could hear the steps of her uncle approaching, and the situation flashed upon her, luminous and clear. She hurriedly folded the sheet of paper and thrust it into her bosom.

"Don't say anything to him about this second message, Mrs. Grantly, please, and Mr. Barton. Nor to Aunt Mildred. It would only cause them irritation and needless anxiety."

In her mind there was also the desire to protect her lover, for she knew that the strain of his present standing with her aunt and uncle would be added to, unconsciously in their minds, by the weird message of Planchette.

"And please don't let us have any more Planchette," Lute continued hastily. "Let us forget all the nonsense that has occurred."

"'Nonsense,' my dear child?" Mrs. Grantly was indignantly protesting when Uncle Robert strode into the circle.

"Hello!" He demanded. "What's being done?"

"Too late," Lute answered lightly. "No more stock quotations for you. Planchette is adjourned, and we're just winding up the discussion of the theory of it. Do you know how late it is?"

★★★

"Well, what did you do last night after we left?"

"Oh, took a stroll," Chris answered.

Lute's eyes were quizzical as she asked with a tentativeness that was palpably assumed, "With -- a -- with Mr. Barton?"

"Why, yes."

"And a smoke?"

"Yes; and now what's it all about?"

Lute broke into merry laughter. "Just as I told you that you would do. Am I not a prophet? But I knew before I saw you that my forecast had come true. I have just left Mr. Barton, and I knew he had walked with you last night, for he is vowing by all his fetishes and idols that you are a perfectly splendid young man. I could see it with my eyes shut. The Chris Dunbar glamour has fallen upon him. But I have not finished the catechism by any means. Where have you been all morning?"

"Where I am going to take you this afternoon."

"You plan well without knowing my wishes."

"I knew well what your wishes are. It is to see a horse I have found."

Her voice betrayed her delight, as she cried, "Oh, good!"

"He is a beauty," Chris said.

But her face had suddenly gone grave, and apprehension brooded in her eyes.

"He's called Comanche," Chris went on. "A beauty, a regular beauty, the perfect type of the Californian cow-pony. And his lines -- why, what's the matter?"

Don't let us ride any more," Lute said, "at least for a while. Really, I think I am a tiny bit tired of it, too."

He was looking at her in astonishment, and she was bravely meeting his eyes.

"I see hearses and flowers for you," he began, "and a funeral oration; I see the end of the world, and the stars falling out of the sky, and the heavens rolling up as a scroll; I see the living and the dead gathered together for the final judgement, the sheep and the goats, the lambs and the rams and all the rest of it, the white-robed saints, the sound of golden harps, and the lost souls howling as they fall into the Pit -- all this I see on the day that you, Lute Story, no longer care to ride a horse. A horse, Lute! A horse!"

"For a while, at least," she pleaded.

"Ridiculous!" He cried. "What's the matter? Aren't you well? -- you who are always so abominably and adorably well!"

"No, it's not that," she answered. "I know it is ridiculous, Chris, I know it, but the doubt will arise. I cannot help it. You always say I am so sanely rooted to the earth and reality and all that, but -- perhaps it's superstition, I don't know -- but the whole occurrence, the messages of Planchette, the possibility of my father's hand, I know not how, reaching, out to Ban's rein and hurling him and you to death, the correspondence between my father's statement that he has twice attempted your life and the fact that in the last two days your life has twice been endangered by horses -- my father was a great horseman -- all this, I say, causes the doubt to arise in my mind. What if there be something in it? I am not so sure. Science may be too dogmatic in its denial of the unseen. The forces of the unseen, of the spirit, may well be too subtle, too sublimated, for science to lay hold of, and recognize, and formulate. Don't you see, Chris, that there is rationality in the very doubt? It may be a very small doubt -- oh, so small; but I love you too much to run even that slight risk. Besides, I am a woman, and that should in itself fully account for my predisposition toward superstition.

"Yes, yes, I know, call it unreality. But I've heard you paradoxing upon the reality of the unreal -- the reality of delusion to the mind that is sick. And so with me, if you will; it is delusion and unreal, but to me, constituted as I am, it is very real -- is real as a nightmare is real, in the throes of it, before one awakes."

"The most logical argument for illogic I have ever heard," Chris smiled. "It is a good gaming proposition, at any rate. You manage to embrace more chances in your philosophy than do I in mine. It reminds me of Sam -- the gardener you had a couple of years ago. I overheard him and Martin arguing in the stable. You know what a bigoted atheist Martin is. Well, Martin had deluged Sam with floods of logic. Sam pondered awhile, and then he said, 'Foh a fack, Mis' Martin, you jis' tawk like a house afire; but you ain't got de show I has.' 'How's that?' Martin asked. 'Well, you see, Mis' Martin, you has one chance to mah two.' 'I don't see it,' Martin said. 'Mis' Martin, it's dis way. You has jis' de chance, lak you say, to become worms foh de fruitification of de cabbage garden. But I's got de chance to lif' mah voice to de glory of de Lawd as I go paddin' dem golden streets -- along 'ith de chance to be jis' worms along 'ith you, Mis' Martin.'"

"You refuse to take me seriously," Lute said, when she had laughed her appreciation.

"How can I take that Planchette rigmarole seriously?" He asked.

"You don't explain it -- the handwriting of my father, which Uncle Robert recognized -- oh, the whole thing, you don't explain it."

"I don't know all the mysteries of mind," Chris answered. " But I believe such phenomena will all yield to scientific explanation in the not distant future."

"Just the same, I have a sneaking desire to find out some more from Planchette," Lute confessed. "The board is still down in the dining room. We could try it now, you and I, and no one would know."

Chris caught her hand, crying: "Come on! It will be a lark."

Hand in hand they ran down the path to the tree-pillared room.

"The camp is deserted," Lute said, as she placed Planchette on the table. "Mrs. Grantly and Aunt Mildred are lying down, and Mr. Barton has gone off with Uncle Robert. There is nobody to disturb us." She placed her hand on the board. "Now begin."

For a few minutes nothing happened. Chris started to speak, but she hushed him to silence. The preliminary twitchings had appeared in her hand and arm. Then the pencil began to write. They read the message, word by word, as it was written:

There is wisdom greater than the wisdom of reason. Love proceeds not out of the dry-as-dust way of the mind. Love is of the heart, and is beyond all reason, and logic, and philosophy. Trust your own heart, my daughter. And if your heart bids you have faith in your lover, then laugh at the mind and its cold wisdom, and obey your heart, and have faith in your lover. -- Martha.

"But that whole message is the dictate of your own heart," Chris cried. "Don't you see, Lute? The thought is your very own, and your subconscious mind has expressed it there on the paper."

"But there is one thing I don't see," she objected.

"And that?"

"Is the handwriting. Look at it. It does not resemble mine at all. It is mincing, it is old-fashioned, it is the old-fashioned feminine of a generation ago."

"But you don't mean to tell me that you really believe that this is a message from the dead?" He interrupted.

"I don't know, Chris," she wavered. "I am sure I don't know."

"It is absurd!" He cried. "These are cobwebs of fancy. When one dies, he is dead. He is dust. He goes to the worms, as Martin says. The dead? I laugh at the dead. They do not exist. They are not. I defy the powers of the grave, the men dead and dust and gone!

"And what have you to say to that?" He challenged, placing his hand on Planchette.

On the instant his hand began to write. Both were startled by the suddenness of it. The message was brief:

BEWARE! BEWARE! BEWARE!

He was distinctly sobered, but he laughed. "It is like a miracle play. Death we have, speaking to us from the grave. But Good Deeds, where art thou? And Kindred? And Joy? And Household Goods? And Friendship? And all the goodly company?"

But Lute did not share his bravado. Her fright showed itself in her face. She laid her trembling hand on his arm.

"Oh, Chris, let us stop. I am sorry we began it. Let us leave the quiet dead to their rest. It is wrong. It must be wrong. I confess I am affected by it. I cannot help it. As my body is trembling, so is my soul. This speech of the grave, this dead man reaching out from the mould of a generation to protect me from you. There is reason in it. There is the living mystery that prevents you from marrying me. Were my father alive, he would protect me from you. Dead, he still strives to protect me. His hands, his ghostly hands, are against your life!"

"Do be calm," Chris said soothingly. "Listen to me. It is all a lark. We are playing with the subjective forces of our own being, with phenomena which science has not yet explained, that is all. Psychology is so young a science. The subconscious mind has just been discovered, one might say. It is all mystery as yet; the laws of it are yet to he formulated. This is simply unexplained phenomena. But that is no reason that we should immediately account for it by labelling it spiritism. As yet we do not know, that is all. As for Planchette -- "

He abruptly ceased, for at that moment, to enforce his remark, he had placed his hand on Planchette, and at that moment his hand had been seized, as by a paroxysm, and sent dashing, willy-nilly, across the paper, writing as the hand of an angry person would write.

"No, I don't care for any more of it," Lute said, when the message was completed. "It is like witnessing a fight between you and my father in the flesh. There is the savor in it of struggle and blows."

She pointed out a sentence that read: "You cannot escape me nor the just punishment that is yours!"

"Perhaps I visualize too vividly for my own comfort, for I can see his hands at your throat. I know that he is, as you say, dead and dust, but for all that, I can see him as a man that is alive and walks the earth; I see the anger in his face, the anger and the vengeance, and I see it all directed against you."

She crumpled up the scrawled sheets of paper, and put Planchette away.

"We won't bother with it any more," Chris said. "I didn't think it would affect you so strongly. But it's all subjective, I'm sure, with possibly a bit of suggestion thrown in -- that and nothing more. And the whole strain of our situation has made conditions unusually favorable for striking phenomena."

"And about our situation," Lute said, as they went slowly up the path they had run down. "What we are to do, I don't know. Are we to go on, as we have gone on? What is best? Have you thought of anything?"

He debated for a few steps. "I have thought of telling your uncle and aunt."

"What you couldn't tell me?" She asked quickly.

"No," he answered slowly; "but just as much as I have told you. I have no right to tell them more than I have told you."

This time it was she that debated. "No, don't tell them," she said finally. "They wouldn't understand. I don't understand, for that matter, but I have faith in you, and in the nature of things they

are not capable of this same Implicit faith. You raise up before me a mystery that prevents our marriage, and I believe you; but they could not believe you without doubts arising as to the wrong and ill-nature of the mystery. Besides, it would but make their anxieties greater."

"I should go away, I know I should go away," he said, half under his breath. "And I can. I am no weakling. Because I have failed to remain away once, is no reason that I shall fail again."

She caught her breath with a quick gasp. "It is like a bereavement to hear you speak of going away and remaining away. I should never see you again. It is too terrible. And do not reproach yourself for weakness. It is I who am to blame. It is I who prevented you from remaining away before, I know. I wanted you so. I want you so.

"There is nothing to be done, Chris, nothing to be done but to go on with it and let it work itself out somehow. That is one thing we are sure of: it will work out somehow."

"But it would be easier if I went away," he suggested.

"I am happier when you are here."

"The cruelty of circumstance," he muttered savagely.

"Go or stay -- that will be part of the working out. But I do not want you to go, Chris; you know that. And now no more about it. Talk cannot mend it. Let us never mention it again -- unless . . . unless some time, some wonderful, happy time, you can come to me and say: 'Lute, all is well with me. The mystery no longer binds me. I am free.' Until that time let us bury it, along with Planchette and all the rest, and make the most of the little that is given us.

"And now, to show you how prepared I am to make the most of that little, I am even ready to go with you this afternoon to see the horse -- though I wish you wouldn't ride any more . . . for a few days, anyway, or for a week. What did you say was his name?"

"Comanche," he answered. "I know you will like him."

***

Chris lay on his back, his head propped by the bare jutting wall of stone, his gaze attentively directed across the canyon to the opposing tree-covered slope. There was a sound of crashing through underbrush, the ringing of steel-shod hoofs on stone, and an occasional and mossy descent of a dislodged boulder that bounded from the hill and fetched up with a final splash in the torrent that rushed over a wild chaos of rocks beneath him. Now and again he caught glimpses, framed in green foliage, of the golden brown of Lute's corduroy riding-habit and of the bay horse that moved beneath her.

She rode out into an open space where a loose earth-slide denied lodgement to trees and grass. She halted the horse at the brink of the slide and glanced down it with a measuring eye. Forty feet beneath, the slide terminated in a small, firm-surfaced terrace, the banked accumulation of fallen earth and gravel.

"It's a good test," she called across the canyon. "I'm going to put him down it."

The animal gingerly launched himself on the treacherous footing, irregularly losing and gaining his hind feet, keeping his fore legs stiff, and steadily and calmly, without panic or nervousness, extricating the fore feet as fast as they sank too deep into the sliding earth that surged along in a wave before him. When the firm footing at the bottom was reached, he strode out on the little terrace with a quickness and springiness of gait and with glintings of muscular fires that gave the lie to the calm deliberation of his movements on the slide

"Bravo!" Chris shouted across the canyon, clapping his hands.

"The wisest-footed, clearest-headed horse I ever saw," Lute called back, as she turned the animal to the side and dropped down a broken slope of rubble and into the trees again.

Chris followed her by the sound of her progress, and by occasional glimpses where the foliage was more open, as she zig-zagged down the steep and trailless descent. She emerged below him at the rugged rim of the torrent, dropped the horse down a three-foot wall, and halted to study the crossing.

Four feet out in the stream, a narrow ledge thrust above the surface of the water. Beyond the ledge boiled an angry pool. But to the left, from the ledge, and several feet lower, was a bed of gravel. A giant boulder prevented direct access to the gravel bed. The only way to gain it was by first leaping to the ledge of rock. She studied it carefully, and the tightening of her bridle-arm advertised that she had made up her mind.

Chris, in his anxiety, had sat up to observe more closely what she meditated.

"Don't tackle it," he called.

"I have faith in Comanche," she called in return.

"He can't make that side-jump to the gravel," Chris warned. "He'll never keep his legs. He'll topple over into the pool. Not one horse in a thousand could do that stunt."

"And Comanche is that very horse," she answered. "Watch him."

She gave the animal his head, and he leaped cleanly and accurately to the ledge, striking with feet close together on the narrow space. On the instant he struck, Lute lightly touched his neck with the rein, impelling him to the left; and in that instant, tottering on the insecure footing, with front feet slipping over into the pool beyond, he lifted on his hind legs, with a half turn, sprang to the left, and dropped squarely down to the tiny gravel bed. An easy jump brought him across the stream, and Lute angled him up the bank and halted before her lover.

"Well?" She asked.

"I am all tense," Chris answered. "I was holding my breath."

"Buy him, by all means," Lute said, dismounting. "He is a bargain. I could dare anything on him. I never in my life had such confidence in a horse's feet."

"His owner says that he has never been known to lose his feet, that it is impossible to get him down."

"Buy him, buy him at once," she counselled, "before the man changes his mind. If you don't, I shall. Oh, such feet! I feel such confidence in them that when I am on him I don't consider he has feet at all. And he's quick as a cat, and instantly obedient. Bridlewise is no name for it! You could guide him with silken threads.

Oh, I know I'm enthusiastic, but if you don't buy him, Chris. I shall. Remember, I've second refusal."

Chris smiled agreement as he changed the saddles. Meanwhile she compared the two horses.

"Of course he doesn't match Dolly the way Ban did," she concluded regretfully; "but his coat is splendid just the same. And think of the horse that is under the coat!"

Chris gave her a hand into the saddle, and followed her up the slope to the county road. She reined in suddenly, saying:

"We won't go straight back to camp."

"You forget dinner," he said.

"But I remember Comanche," she retorted. "We'll ride directly over to the ranch and buy him. Dinner will keep."

"But the cook won't," Chris laughed. "She's already threatened to leave, what of our late-comings."

"Even so," was the answer. "Aunt Mildred may have to get another cook, but at any rate we shall have got Comanche."

They turned the horses in the other direction, and took the climb of the Nun Canyon road that led over the divide and down into the Napa Valley. But the climb was hard, the going was slow. Sometimes they topped the bed of the torrent by hundreds of feet, and again they dipped down and crossed and recrossed it twenty times in twice as many rods. They rode through the deep shade of clean-bunked maples and towering redwoods, to emerge on open stretches of mountain shoulder where the earth lay dry and cracked under the sun.

On one such shoulder they emerged, where the road stretched level before them, for a quarter of a mile. On one side rose the huge bulk of the mountain. On the other side the steep wall of the canyon fell away in impossible slopes and sheer drops to the torrent at the bottom. It was an abyss of green beauty and shady depths, pierced by vagrant shafts of the sun and mottled here and there by the sun's broader blazes. The sound of rushing water ascended on the windless air, and there was a hum of mountain bees.

The horses broke into an easy lope. Chris rode on the outside, looking down into the great depths and pleasuring with his eyes in what he saw. Dissociating itself from the murmur of the bees, a murmur arose of falling water. It grew louder with every stride of the horses.

"Look!" He cried.

Lute leaned well out from her horse to see. Beneath them the water slid foaming down a smooth-faced rock to the lip, whence it leaped clear -- a pulsating ribbon of white, a-breath with movement, ever falling and ever remaining, changing its substance but never its form, an aerial waterway as immaterial as gauze and as permanent as the hills, that spanned space and the free air from the lip of the rock to the tops of the trees far below, into whose green screen it disappeared to fall into a secret pool.

They had flashed past. The descending water became a distant murmur that merged again into the murmur of the bees and ceased. Swayed by a common impulse, they looked at each other.

"Oh, Chris, it is good to be alive . . . and to have you here by my side!"

He answered her by the warm light in his eyes.

All things tended to key them to an exquisite pitch -- the movement of their bodies, at one with the moving bodies of the animals beneath them; the gently stimulated blood caressing the flesh through and through with the soft vigors of health; the warm air fanning their faces, flowing over the skin with balmy and tonic touch, permeating them and bathing them, subtly, with faint, sensuous delight; and the beauty of the world, more subtly still, flowing upon them and bathing them in the delight that is of the spirit and is personal and holy, that is inexpressible yet communicable by the flash of an eye and the dissolving of the veils of the soul.

So looked they at each other, the horses bounding beneath them, the spring of the world and the spring of their youth astir in their blood, the secret of being trembling in their eyes to the brink of disclosure, as if about to dispel, with one magic word, all the irks and riddles of existence.

The road curved before them, so that the upper reaches of the canyon could be seen, the distant bed of it towering high above their heads. They were rounding the curve, leaning toward the inside, gazing before them at the swift-growing picture. There was no sound of warning. She heard nothing, but even before the horse went down she experienced the feeling that the unison of the two leaping animals was broken. She turned her head, and so quickly that she saw Comanche fall. It was not a stumble nor a trip. He fell as though, abruptly, in mid-leap, he had died or been struck a stunning blow.

And in that moment she remembered Planchette; it seared her brain as a lightning-flash of all-embracing memory. Her horse was back on its haunches, the weight of her body on the reins; but her head was turned and her eyes were on the falling Comanche. He struck the road-bed squarely, with his legs loose and lifeless beneath him.

It all occurred in one of those age-long seconds that embrace an eternity of happening. There was a slight but perceptible rebound from the impact of Comanche's body with the earth. The violence with which he struck forced the air from his great lungs in an audible groan. His momentum swept him onward and over the edge. The weight of the rider on his neck turned him over head first as he pitched to the fall.

She was off her horse, she knew not how, and to the edge. Her lover was out of the saddle and clear of Comanche, though held to the animal by his right foot, which was caught in the stirrup. The slope was too steep for them to come to a stop. Earth and small stones, dislodged by their struggles, were rolling down with them and before them in a miniature avalanche. She stood very quietly, holding one hand against her heart and gazing down. But while she saw the real happening, in her eyes was also the vision of her father dealing the spectral blow that had smashed Comanche down in mid-leap and sent horse and rider hurtling over the edge.

Beneath horse and man the steep terminated in an up-and-down wall, from the base of which, in turn, a second slope ran down to a second wall. A third slope terminated in a final wall that based itself on the canyon-bed four hundred feet beneath the point where the girl stood and watched. She could see Chris vainly kicking his leg to free the foot from the trap of the stirrup. Comanche fetched up hard against an outputting point of rock. For a fraction of a second his fall was stopped, and in the slight interval the man managed to grip hold of a young shoot of manzanita. Lute saw him complete the grip with his other hand. Then Comanche's fall began again. She saw the stirrup-strap draw taut, then her lover's body and arms. The manzanita shoot yielded its roots, and horse and man plunged over the edge and out of sight.

They came into view on the next slope, together and rolling over and over, with sometimes the man under and sometimes the horse. Chris no longer struggled, and together they dashed over to the third slope. Near the edge of the final wall, Comanche lodged on a buttock of stone. He lay quietly, and near him, still attached to him by the stirrup, face downward, lay his rider.

"If only he will lie quietly," Lute breathed aloud, her mind at work on the means of rescue.

But she saw Comanche begin to struggle again, and clear on her vision, it seemed, was the spectral arm of her father clutching the reins and dragging the animal over. Comanche floundered across the hummock, the inert body following, and together, horse and man, they plunged from sight. They did not appear again. They had fetched bottom.

Lute looked about her. She stood alone on the world. Her lover was gone. There was naught to show of his existence, save the marks of Comanche's hoofs on the road and of his body where it had slid over the brink.

"Chris!" She called once, and twice; but she called hopelessly.

Out of the depths, on the windless air, arose only the murmur of bees and of running water

"Chris!" She called yet a third time, and sank slowly down in the dust of the road.

She felt the touch of Dolly's muzzle on her arm, and she leaned her head against the mare's neck and waited. She knew not why she waited, nor for what, only there seemed nothing else but waiting left for her to do.

A Thousand Deaths

I had been in the water about an hour, and cold, exhausted, with a terrible cramp in my right calf, it seemed as though my hour had come. Fruitlessly struggling against the strong ebb tide, I had beheld the maddening procession of the water-front lights slip by, but now I gave up attempting to breast the stream and contended myself with the bitter thoughts of a wasted career, now drawing to a close.

It had been my luck to come of good, English stock, but of parents whose account with the bankers far exceeded their knowledge of child-nature and the rearing of children. While born with a silver spoon in my mouth, the blessed atmosphere of the home circle was to me unknown. My father, a very learned man and a celebrated antiquarian, gave no thought to his family, being constantly lost in the abstractions of his study; while my mother, noted far more for her good looks than her good sense, sated herself with the adulation of the society in which she was perpetually plunged. I went through the regular school and college routine of a boy of the English bourgeoisie, and as the years brought me increasing strength and passions, my parents suddenly became aware that I was possessed of an immortal soul, and endeavoured to draw the curb. But it was too late; I perpetrated the wildest and most audacious folly, and was disowned by my people, ostracised by the society I had so long outraged, and with the thousand pounds my father gave me, with the declaration that he would neither see me again nor give me more, I took a first-class passage to Australia.

Since then my life had been one long peregrination -- from the Orient to the Occident, from the Arctic to the Antarctic -- to find myself at last, an able seaman at thirty, in the full vigour of my manhood, drowning in San Francisco bay because of a disastrously successful attempt to desert my ship.

My right leg was drawn up by the cramp, and I was suffering the keenest agony. A slight breeze stirred up a choppy sea, which washed into my mouth and down my throat, nor could I prevent it. Though I still contrived to keep afloat, it was merely mechanical, for I was rapidly becoming unconscious. I have a dim recollection of drifting past the sea-wall, and of catching a glimpse of an up-river steamer's starboard light; then everything became a blank.

* * *

I heard the low hum of insect life, and felt the balmy air of a spring morning fanning my cheek. Gradually it assumed a rhythmic flow, to whose soft pulsations my body seemed to respond. I floated on the gentle bosom of a summer's sea, rising and falling with dreamy pleasure on each crooning wave. But the pulsations grew stronger; the humming, louder; the waves, larger, fiercer -- I was dashed about on a stormy sea. A great agony fastened upon me. Brilliant, intermittent sparks of light flashed athwart my inner consciousness; in my ears there was the sound of many waters; then a sudden snapping of an intangible something, and I awoke.

The scene, of which I was protagonist, was a curious one. A glance sufficed to inform me that I lay on the cabin floor of some gentleman's yacht, in a most uncomfortable posture. On either side, grasping my arms and working them up and down like pump handles, were two peculiarly clad, dark-skinned creatures. Though conversant with most aboriginal types, I could not conjecture their nationality. Some attachment had been fastened about my head, which connected my respiratory organs with the machine I shall next describe. My nostrils, however, had been closed, forcing me to breathe through my mouth. Foreshortened by the obliquity of my line of vision, I beheld two tubes, similar to small hosing but of different composition, which emerged from my mouth and went off at an acute angle from each other. The first came to an abrupt termination and lay on the floor beside me; the second traversed the floor in numerous coils, connecting with the apparatus I have promised to describe.

In the days before my life had become tangential, I had dabbled not a little in science, and, conversant with the appurtenances and general paraphernalia of the laboratory, I appreciated the machine I now beheld. It was composed chiefly of glass, the construction being of that crude sort which is employed for experimentative purposes. A vessel of water was surrounded by an air chamber, to which was fixed a vertical tube, surmounted by a globe. In the centre of this was a vacuum gauge. The water in the tube moved upwards and downwards, creating alternate inhalations and exhalations, which were in turn communicated to me through the hose. With this, and the aid of the men who pumped my arms, so vigorously, had the process of breathing been artificially carried on, my chest rising and falling and my lungs expanding and contracting, till nature could be persuaded to again take up her wonted labour.

As I opened my eyes the appliance about my head, nostrils and mouth was removed. Draining a stiff three fingers of brandy, I staggered to my feet to thank my preserver, and confronted -- my father. But long years of fellowship with danger had taught me self-control, and I waited to see if he would recognise me. Not so; he saw in me no more than a runaway sailor and treated me accordingly.

Leaving me to the care of the blackies, he fell to revising the notes he had made on my resuscitation. As I ate of the handsome fare served up to me, confusion began on deck, and from the chanteys of the sailors and the rattling of blocks and tackles I surmised that we were getting under way. What a lark! Off on a cruise with my recluse father into the wide Pacific! Little did I realise, as I laughed to myself, which side the joke was to be on. Aye, had I known, I would have plunged overboard and welcomed the dirty fo'c'sle from which I had just escaped.

I was not allowed on deck till we had sunk the Farallones and the last pilot boat. I appreciated this forethought on the part of my father and made it a point to thank him heartily, in my bluff seaman's manner. I could not suspect that he had his own ends in view, in thus keeping my presence secret to all save the crew. He told me briefly of my rescue by his sailors, assuring me that the obligation was on his side, as my appearance had been most opportune. He had constructed the apparatus for the vindication of a theory concerning certain biological phenomena, and had been waiting for an opportunity to use it.

"You have proved it beyond all doubt," he said; then added with a sigh, "But only in the small matter of drowning." But, to take a reef in my yarn -- he offered me an advance of two pounds on my previous wages to sail with him, and this I considered handsome, for he really did not need me. Contrary to my expectations, I did not join the sailor' mess, for'ard, being assigned to a comfortable stateroom and eating at the captain's table. He had perceived that I was no common sailor, and I resolved to take this chance for reinstating myself in his good graces. I wove a fictitious past to account for my education and present position, and did my best to come in touch with him. I was not long in disclosing a predilection for scientific pursuits, nor he in appreciating my aptitude. I became his assistant, with a corresponding increase in wages, and before long, as he grew confidential and expounded his theories, I was as enthusiastic as himself.

The days flew quickly by, for I was deeply interested in my new studies, passing my waking hours in his well-stocked library, or listening to his plans and aiding him in his laboratory work. But we were forced to forego many enticing experiments, a rolling ship not being exactly the proper place for delicate or intricate work. He promised me, however, many delightful hours in the magnificent laboratory for which we were bound. He had taken possession of an uncharted South Sea island, as he said, and turned it into a scientific paradise.

We had not been on the island long, before I discovered the horrible mare's nest I had fallen into. But before I describe the strange things which came to pass, I must briefly outline the causes which culminated in as startling an experience as ever fell to the lot of man.

Late in life, my father had abandoned the musty charms of antiquity and succumbed to the more fascinating ones embraced under the general head of biology. Having been thoroughly grounded during his youth in the fundamentals, he rapidly explored all the higher branches as far as the scientific world had gone, and found himself on the no man's land of the unknowable. It was his intention to pre-empt some of this unclaimed territory, and it was at this stage of his investigations that we had been thrown together. Having a good brain, though I say it myself, I had mastered his speculations and methods of reasoning, becoming almost as mad as himself. But I should not say this. The marvellous results we afterwards obtained can only go to prove his sanity. I can but say that he was the most abnormal specimen of cold-blooded cruelty I have ever seen.

After having penetrated the dual mysteries of physiology and psychology, his thought had led him to the verge of a great field, for which, the better to explore, he began studies in higher organic chemistry, pathology, toxicology and other sciences and sub-sciences rendered kindred as accessories to his speculative hypotheses. Starting from the proposition that the direct cause of the temporary and permanent arrest of vitality was due to the coagulation of certain elements and compounds in the protoplasm, he had isolated and subjected these various substances to innumerable experiments. Since the temporary arrest of vitality in an organism brought coma, and a permanent arrest death, he held that by artificial means this coagulation of the protoplasm could be retarded, prevented, and even overcome in the extreme states of solidification. Or, to do away with the technical nomenclature, he argued that death, when not violent and in which none of the organs had suffered injury, was merely suspended vitality; and that, in such instances, life could be induced to resume its functions by the use of proper methods. This, then, was his idea: To discover the method -- and by practical experimentation prove the possibility -- of renewing vitality in a structure from which life had seemingly fled. Of course, he recognised the futility of such endeavour after decomposition had set in; he must have organisms which but the moment, the hour, or the day before, had been quick with life. With me, in a crude way, he had proved this theory. I was really drowned, really dead, when picked from the water of San Francisco bay -- but the vital spark had been renewed by means of his aerotherapeutical apparatus, as he called it.

Now to his dark purpose concerning me. He first showed me how completely I was in his power. He had sent the yacht away for a year, retaining only his two blackies, who were utterly devoted to him. He then made an exhaustive review of his theory and outlined the method of proof he had adopted, concluding with the startling announcement that I was to be his subject.

I had faced death and weighed my chances in many a desperate venture, but never in one of this nature. I can swear I am no coward, yet this proposition of journeying back and forth across the borderland of death put the yellow fear upon me. I asked for time, which he granted, at the same time assuring me that but the one course was open -- I must submit. Escape from the Island was out of the question; escape by suicide was not to be entertained, though really preferable to what it seemed I must undergo; my only hope was to destroy my captors. But this latter was frustrated through the precautions taken by my father. I was subjected to a constant surveillance, even in my sleep being guarded by one or the other of the blacks.

Having pleaded in vain, I announced and proved that I was his son. It was my last card, and I had played all my hopes upon it. But he was inexorable; he was not a father but a scientific machine. I wonder yet how it ever came to pass that he married my mother or begat me, for there was not the slightest grain of emotion in his make-up. Reason was all in all to him, nor could he understand such things as love or sympathy in others, except as petty weaknesses which should be overcome. So he informed me that in the beginning he had given me life, and who had better right to take it away than he? Such, he said, was not his desire, however; he merely wished to borrow it occasionally, promising to return it punctually at the appointed time. Of course, there was a liability of mishaps, but I could do no more than take the chances, since the affairs of men were full of such.

The better to insure success, he wished me to be in the best possible condition, so I was dieted and trained like a great athlete before a decisive contest. What could I do? If I had to undergo the peril, it were best to be in good shape. In my intervals of relaxation he allowed me to assist in the arranging of the apparatus and in the various subsidiary experiments. The interest I took in all such operations can be imagined. I mastered the work as thoroughly as he, and often had the pleasure of seeing some of my suggestions or alterations put into effect. After such events I would smile grimly, conscious of officiating at my own funeral.

He began by inaugurating a series of experiments in toxicology. When all was ready, I was killed by a stiff dose of strychnine and allowed to lie dead for some twenty hours. During that period my body was dead, absolutely dead. All respiration and circulation ceased; but the frightful part of it was, that while the protoplasmic coagulation proceeded, I retained consciousness and was enabled to study it in all its ghastly details.

The apparatus to bring me back to life was an air-tight chamber, fitted to receive my body. The mechanism was simple -- a few valves, a rotary shaft and crank, and an electric motor. When in operation, the interior atmosphere was alternately condenses and rarefied, thus communicating to my lungs an artificial respiration without the agency of the hosing previously used. Though my body was inert, and, for all I knew, in the first stages of decomposition, I was cognisant of everything that transpired. I knew when they placed me in the chamber, and though all my senses were quiescent, I was aware of hypodermic injections of a compound to react upon the coagulatory process. Then the chamber was closed and the machinery started. My anxiety was terrible; but the circulation became gradually restored, the different organs began to carry on their respective functions, and in an hour's time I was eating a hearty dinner.

It cannot be said that I participated in this series, nor in the subsequent ones, with much verve; but after two ineffectual attempts of escape, I began to take quite an interest. Besides, I was becoming accustomed. My father was beside himself at his success, and as the months rolled by his speculations took wilder and yet wilder flights. We ranged through the three great classes of poisons, the neurotics, the gaseous and the irritants, but carefully avoided some of the mineral irritants and passed the whole group of corrosives. During the poison regime I became quite accustomed to dying, and had but one mishap to shake my growing confidence. Scarifying a number of lesser blood vessels in my arm, he introduced a minute quantity of that most frightful of poisons, the arrow poison, or curare. I lost consciousness at the start, quickly followed by the cessation of respiration and circulation, and so far had the solidification of the protoplasm advanced, that he gave up all hope. But at the last moment he applied a discovery he had been working upon, receiving such encouragement as to redouble his efforts.

In a glass vacuum, similar but not exactly like a Crookes' tube, was placed a magnetic field. When penetrated by polarised light, it gave no phenomena of phosphorescence nor the rectilinear projection of atoms, but emitted non-luminous rays, similar to the X ray. While the X ray could reveal opaque objects hidden in dense mediums, this was possessed of far subtler penetration. By this he photographed my body, and found on the negative an infinite number of blurred shadows, due to the chemical and electric motions still going on. This was an infallible proof that the rigor mortis in which I lay was not genuine; that is, those mysterious forces, those delicate bonds which held my soul to my body, were still in action. The resultants of all other poisons were unapparent, save those of mercurial compounds, which usually left me languid for several days.

Another series of delightful experiments was with electricity. We verified Tesla's assertion that high currents were utterly harmless by passing 100,000 volts through my body. As this did not affect me, the current was reduced to 2,500, and I was quickly electrocuted. This time he ventured so far as to allow me to remain dead, or in a state of suspended vitality, for three days. It took four hours to bring me back.

Once, he super-induced lockjaw; but the agony of dying was so great that I positively refused to undergo similar experiments. The easiest deaths were by asphyxiation, such as drowning, strangling, and suffocation by gas; while those by morphine, opium, cocaine and chloroform, were not at all hard.

Another time, after being suffocated, he kept me in cold storage for three months, not permitting me to freeze or decay. This was without my knowledge, and I was in a great fright on discovering the lapse of time. I became afraid of what he might do with me when I lay dead, my alarm being increased by the predilection he was beginning to betray towards vivisection. The last time I was resurrected, I discovered that he had been tampering with my breast. Though he had carefully dressed and sewed the incisions up, they were so severe that I had to take to my bed for some time. It was during this convalescence that I evolved the plan by which I ultimately escaped.

While feigning unbounded enthusiasm in the work, I asked and received a vacation from my moribund occupation. During this period I devoted myself to laboratory work, while he was too deep in the vivisection of the many animals captured by the blacks to take notice of my work.

It was on these two propositions that I constructed my theory: First, electrolysis, or the decomposition of water into its constituent gases by means of electricity; and, second, by the hypothetical existence of a force, the converse of gravitation, which Astor has named "apergy". Terrestrial attraction, for instance, merely draws objects together but does not combine them; hence, apergy is merely repulsion. Now, atomic or molecular attraction not only draws objects together but integrates them; and it was the converse of this, or a disintegrative force, which I wished to not only discover and produce, but to direct at will. Thus, the molecules of hydrogen and oxygen reacting on each other, separate and create new molecules, containing both elements and forming water. Electrolysis causes these molecules to split up and resume their original condition, producing the two gases separately. The force I wished to find must not only do this with two, but with all elements, no matter in what compounds they exist. If I could then entice my father within its radius, he would be instantly disintegrated and sent flying to the four quarters, a mass of isolated elements.

It must not be understood that this force, which I finally came to control, annihilated matter; it merely annihilated form. Nor, as I soon discovered, had it any effect on inorganic structure; but to all organic form it was absolutely fatal. This partiality puzzled me at first, though had I stopped to think deeper I would have seen through it. Since the number of atoms in organic molecules is far greater than in the most complex mineral molecules, organic compounds are characterised by their instability and the ease with which they are split up by physical forces and chemical reagents.

By two powerful batteries, connected with magnets constructed specially for this purpose, two tremendous forces were projected. Considered apart from each other, they were perfectly harmless; but they accomplished their purpose by focusing at an invisible point in mid-air. After practically demonstrating its success, besides narrowly escaping being blown into nothingness, I laid my trap. Concealing the magnets, so that their force made the whole space of my chamber doorway a field of death, and placing by my couch a button by which I could throw on the current from the storage batteries, I climbed into bed.

The blackies still guarded my sleeping quarters, one relieving the other at midnight. I turned on the current as soon as the first man arrived. Hardly had I begun to doze, when I was aroused by a sharp, metallic tinkle. There, on the mid-threshold, lay the collar of Dan, my father's St. Bernard. My keeper ran to pick it up. He disappeared like a gust of wind, his clothes falling to the floor in a heap. There was a slight wiff of ozone in the air, but since the principal gaseous components of his body were hydrogen, oxygen and nitrogen, which are equally colourless and odourless, there was no other manifestation of his departure. Yet when I shut off the current and removed the garments, I found a deposit of carbon in the form of animal charcoal; also other powders, the isolated, solid elements of his organism, such as sulphur, potassium and iron. Resetting the trap, I crawled back to bed. At midnight I got up and removed the remains of the second black, and then slept peacefully till morning.

I was awakened by the strident voice of my father, who was calling to me from across the laboratory. I laughed to myself. There had been no one to call him and he had overslept. I could hear him as he approached my room with the intention of rousing me, and so I sat up in bed, the better to observe his translation -- perhaps apotheosis were a better term. He paused a moment at the threshold, then took the fatal step. Puff! It was like the wind sighing among the pines. He was gone. His clothes fell in a fantastic heap on the floor. Besides ozone, I noticed the faint, garlic-like odour of phosphorus. A little pile of elementary solids lay among his garments. That was all. The wide world lay before me. My captors were no more.

Goliah

In 1924 — to be precise, on the morning of January 3 — the city of San Francisco awoke to read in one of its daily papers a curious letter, which bad been received by Walter Bassett and which had evidently been written by some crank. Walter Bassett was the greatest captain of industry west of the Rockies, and was one of the small group that controlled the nation in everything but name. As such, he was the recipient of lucubrations from countless cranks; but this particular lucubration was so different from the average ruck of similar letters that, instead of putting it into the waste-basket, he had turned it over to a reporter. It was signed "Goliah," and the superscription gave his address as "Palgrave Island." The letter was as follows: —

"Mr. Walter Bassett,

"Dear Sir:

"I am inviting you, with nine of your fellow captains of industry, to visit me here on my island for the purpose of considering plans for the reconstruction of society upon a more rational basis, Up to the present, social evolution has been a blind and aimless, blundering thing. The time has come for a change. Man has risen from the vitalized slime of the primeval sea to the mastery of matter; but be has not yet mastered society. Man is today as much the slave to his collective stupidity, as a hundred thousand generations ago he was a slave to matter.

"There are two theoretical methods whereby man may become the master of society, and make of society an intelligent and efficacious device for the pursuit and capture of happiness and laughter. The first theory advances the proposition that no government can be wiser or better than the people that compose that government; that reform and development must spring from the individual; that in so far as the individuals become wiser and better, by that much will their government become wiser and better; in short, that the majority of individuals must become wiser and better before their government becomes wiser and better. The mob, the political convention, the abysmal brutality and stupid ignorance, of all concourses of people, give the lie to this theory. In a mob the collective intelligence and mercy is that of the least intelligent and most brutal members that compose the mob. On the other hand, a thousand passengers will surrender themselves to the wisdom and discretion of the captain, when their ship is in a storm on the sea. In such matter, he is the wisest and most experienced among them.

"The second theory advances the proposition that the majority of the people are not pioneers, that they are weighted down by the inertia of the established; that the government that is representative of them represents only their feebleness, and futility, and brutishness; that this blind thing called government is not the serf of their wills, but that they are the serfs of it; in short, speaking always of the great mass, that they do not make government, but that government makes them, and that government is and has been a stupid and awful monster, misbegotten of the glimmerings of intelligence that come from the inertia-crushed mass.

"Personally, I incline to the second theory. Also, I am impatient., For a hundred thousand generations, from the first social groups of our savage forebears, government has remained a monster. Today, the inertia-crushed mass has less laughter in it than ever before. In spite of man's mastery of matter, human suffering and misery and degradation mar the fair world.

"Wherefore I have decided to step in and become captain of this world-ship for a while. I have the intelligence and the wide vision of the skilled expert. Also, I have the power. I shall be obeyed. The men of all the world shall perform my bidding and make governments so that they shall become laughter producers. These modelled governments I have in mind shall not make the people happy, wise, and noble by decree; but they shall give opportunity for the people to become happy, wise, and noble.

"I have spoken. I have invited you, and nine of your fellow captains, to confer with me. On March third the yacht *Energon* will sail from San Francisco. You are requested to be on board the night before. This is serious. The affairs of the world must be handled for a time by a strong hand. Mine is that strong hand. If you fail to obey my summons, you will die. Candidly, I do not expect that you will obey. But your death for failure to obey will cause obedience on the part of those I subsequently summon. You will have served a purpose. And please remember that I have no unscientific sentimentality about the value of human life. I carry always in the background of my consciousness the innumerable billions of lives that are to laugh and be happy in future aeons on the earth.

"Yours for the reconstruction of society,

"Goliah.""

The publication of this letter did not cause even local amusement. Men might have smiled to themselves as they read it, but it was so palpably the handiwork of a crank that it did not merit discussion. Interest did not arouse till next morning. An Associated Press despatch to the Eastern states, followed by interviews by eager-nosed reporters, bad brought out the names of the other nine captains of industry who had received similar letters but who had not thought the matter of sufficient importance to be made public. But the interest aroused was mild, and it would have died out quickly had not Gabberton cartooned a chronic presidential aspirant as "Goliah." Then came the song that was sung hilariously from sea to sea, with the refrain, "Goliah will catch you if you don't watch out."

The weeks passed and the incident was forgotten. Walter Bassett had forgotten it likewise; but on the evening of February 22, he was called to the telephone by the Collector of the Port. "I just wanted to tell you," said the latter, "that the yacht *Energon* has arrived and gone to anchor in the stream off Pier Seven."

What happened that night Walter Bassett has never divulged. But it is known that he rode down in his auto to the water front, chartered one of Crowley's launches, and was put aboard the strange yacht. It is further known that when he, returned to the shore, three hours later, he immediately despatched a sheaf of telegrams to his nine fellow captains of industry who had received letters from Goliah. These telegrams were similarly worded, and read: "The yacht *Energon* has arrived. There is something in this. I advise you to come."

Bassett was laughed at for his pains. It was a huge laugh that went up (for his telegrams had been made public), and the popular song on Goliah revived and became more popular than ever. Goliah and Bassett were cartooned and lampooned unmercifully, the former, as the Old Man of the Sea, riding on the latter's neck. The laugh tittered and rippled through clubs and social circles, was restrainedly merry in the editorial columns, and broke out in loud guffaws in the comic weeklies.. There was a serious side as well, and Bassett's sanity was gravely questioned by many, and especially by his business associates.

Bassett had ever been a short-tempered man, and after he sent the second sheaf of telegrams to his brother captains, and had been laughed at again, he remained silent. In this second sheaf, he had said: "Come, I implore you. As you value your life, come." He arranged all his business affairs for an absence, and on the night of March 2 went on board the *Energon*. The latter, properly cleared, sailed next morning. And next morning the newsboys in every city and town were crying "Extra."

In the slang of the day, Goliah had delivered the goods. The nine captains of industry who had failed to accept his invitation were dead. A sort of violent disintegration of the tissues was the report of the various autopsies held on the bodies of the slain millionnaires; yet the surgeons and physicians (the most highly skilled in the land had participated) would not venture the opinion that the men had been slain. Much less would they venture the conclusion, "at the hands of parties unknown." It was all too mysterious. They were stunned. Their scientific credulity broke down. They had no warrant in the whole domain of science for believing that an anonymous person on Palgrave Island had murdered the poor gentlemen.

One thing was quickly learned, however; namely, that Palgrave Island was no myth. It was charted and well known to all navigators, lying on the line of 160 west longitude, right at its intersection by the tenth parallel north latitude, and only a few miles away from Diana Shoal. Like Midway and Fanning, Palgrave Island was isolated, volcanic and coral in formation. Furthermore, it was uninhabited. A survey ship, in 1887, had visited the place and reported the existence of several springs and of a good harbor that was very dangerous of approach. And, that was all that was known of the tiny speck of land that was soon to have focussed on it the awed attention of the world.

Goliah remained silent till March 24, On the morning of that day, the newspapers published his second letter, copies of which had been received by the ten chief politicians of the United States — ten leading men in the political world who were conventionally known as "statesmen." The letter, with the same superscription as before, was as follows: —

"Dear Sir:

"I have spoken in no uncertain tone. I must be obeyed. You may consider this an invitation or a summons; but if you still wish to tread this earth and laugh, you will be aboard the yacht *Energon*, in San Francisco harbor, not later than the evening of April 5. It is my wish and my will that you confer with me here on Palgrave Island in the matter of reconstructing society upon some rational basis.

"Do not misunderstand me, when I tell you that I am one with a theory. I want to see that theory work, and therefore I call upon your cooperation. In this theory of mine, lives are but pawns; I deal with quantities of lives. I am after laughter, and those that stand in the way of laughter must perish. The game is big. There are fifteen hundred million human lives today on the planet. What is your single life against them ? It is as naught, in my theory. And remember that mine is the power. Remember that I am a scientist, and that one life, or one million of lives, mean nothing to me as arrayed against the countless billions of billions of the lives of the generations to come. It is for their laughter that I seek to reconstruct society now; and against them your own meagre little life is a paltry thing indeed.

"Whoso has power can command his fellows. By virtue of that military device known as the phalanx, Alexander conquered his bit of the world. By virtue of that chemical device, gunpowder, Cortes with his several hundred cutthroats conquered the empire of the Montezumas. Now I am in possession of a device that is all my own. In the course of a century not more than half a dozen fundamental discoveries or inventions are made. I have made such an invention. The possession of it gives me the mastery of the world. I shall use this invention, not for commercial exploitation, but for the good of humanity. For that purpose I want help — willing agents, obedient hands; and I am strong enough to compel the service. I am taking the shortest way, though I am in no hurry. I shall not clutter my speed with haste.

"The incentive of material gain developed man from the savage to the semi-barbarian he is today. This incentive has been a useful device for the development of the human; but it has now fulfilled its function and is ready to be cast aside into the scrap-heap of rudimentary vestiges such as gills in the throat and belief in the divine right of kings. Of course you do not think so; but I do not see that that will prevent you from aiding me to fling the anachronism into the scrap-heap. For I tell you now that the time has come when mere food and shelter and similar sordid things shall be automatic, as free and easy and involuntary of access as the air. I shall make them automatic, what of my discovery and the power that discovery gives me. And with food and shelter automatic, the incentive of material gain passes away from the world forever. With food and shelter automatic, the higher incentives will universally obtain — the spiritual, aesthetic, and intellectual incentives that will tend to develop and make beautiful and noble body, mind, and spirit. Then all the world will be dominated by happiness and laughter. It will be the reign of universal laughter.

"Yours for that day,

"Goliah.""

Still the world would not believe. The ten politicians were at Washington, so that they did not have the opportunity of being convinced that Bassett had had, and not one of them took the trouble to journey out to San Francisco to make the opportunity. As for Goliah, he was hailed by the newspapers as another Tom Lawson with a panacea; and there were specialists in mental disease who, by analysis of Goliah's letters, proved conclusively that he was a lunatic.

The yacht *Energon* arrived in the harbor of San Francisco on the afternoon of April 5, and Bassett came ashore. But the *Energon* did not sail next day, for not one of the ten summoned politicians had elected to make the journey to Palgrave Island. The newsboys, however, called "Extra" that day in all the cities. The ten politicians were dead. The yacht, lying peacefully at anchor in the harbor, became the centre of excited interest. She was surrounded by a flotilla of launches and rowboats, and many tugs and steamboats ran excursions to her. While the rabble was firmly kept off, the proper authorities and even reporters were permitted to board her. The mayor of San Francisco and the chief of police reported that nothing suspicious was to be seen upon her, and the port authorities announced that her papers were correct and in order in every detail. Many photographs and columns of descriptive matter were run in the newspapers.

The crew was reported to be composed principally of Scandinavians, — fair-haired, blue-eyed Swedes, Norwegians afflicted with the temperamental melancholy of their race, stolid Russian Finns, and a slight sprinkling of Americans and English. It was noted that there was nothing mercurial and flyaway about them. They seemed weighty men, oppressed by a sad and stolid bovine-sort of integrity. A sober seriousness and enormous certitude characterized all of them. They appeared men without nerves and without fear, as though upheld by some overwhelming power or carried in the hollow of some superhuman hand. The captain, a sad-eyed, strong-featured American, was cartooned in the papers as "Gloomy Gus" (the pessimistic hero, of the comic supplement).

Some sea-captain recognized the *Energon* as the yacht Scud, once owned by Merrivale of the New York Yacht Club. With this clew it was soon ascertained that the Scud had disappeared several years before. The agent who sold her reported the purchaser to be merely another agent, a man he had seen neither before nor since. The yacht had been reconstructed at Duffey's Shipyard in New Jersey. The change in her name and registry occurred at that time and had been legally executed. Then the *Energon* had disappeared in the shroud of mystery.

In the meantime, Basset was going crazy-at least his friends and business associates said so. He kept away from, his vast business enterprises and said that he must hold his hands until the other masters of the world could join with him in the reconstruction of society — proof indubitable that Goliah's bee had entered his bonnet. To reporters he had little to say. He was not at liberty, he said, to relate what he had seen on Palgrave Island; but he could assure them that the matter was serious, the most serious thing that had ever happened. His final word was that the world was on the verge of a turnover, for good or ill he did not know, but, one way or the other, he was absolutely convinced that the turnover was coming. As for business, business could go hang. He had seen things, he had, and that was all there was to it.

There was a great telegraphing, during this period, between the local Federal officials and the state and war departments at Washington. A secret attempt was made late one afternoon to board the *Energon* and place the captain under arrest — the Attorney General having given the opinion that the captain could be held for the murder of the ten "statesmen." The government launch was seen to leave Meigg's Wharf and steer for the *Energon*, and that was the last ever seen of the launch and the men on board of it. The government tried to keep the affair hushed up, but the cat was slipped out of the bag by the families of the missing men and the papers were filled with monstrous versions of the affair.

The government now proceeded to extreme measures. The battleship Alaska was ordered to capture the strange yacht, or, failing that, to sink her. These were secret instructions; but thousands of eyes, from the water front and from the shipping in the harbor, witnessed what happened that afternoon. The battleship got under way and steamed slowly toward the *Energon*. At half a mile distant the battleship blew up — simply blew up, that was all, her shattered frame sinking to the bottom of the bay, a riff-raff of wreckage and a few survivors strewing the surface. Among the survivors was a young lieutenant who had had charge of the wireless on board the Alaska. The reporters got hold of him first, and he talked. No sooner had the Alaska got under way, he said, than a I message was received from the *Energon*. It was in the international code, and it was a warning to the Alaska to come no nearer than half a mile. He had sent the message, through the speaking tube, immediately to the captain. He did not know anything more, except that the *Energon* twice repeated the message and that five minutes afterward the explosion occurred. The captain of the Alaska had perished with his ship, and nothing more was to be learned.

The *Energon*, however, promptly hoisted anchor and cleared out to sea. A great clamor was raised by the papers; the government was charged with cowardice and vacillation in its dealings with a mere pleasure yacht and a lunatic who called himself "Goliah," and immediate and decisive action was demanded. Also, a great cry went up about the loss of life, especially the wanton killing of the ten "statesmen." Goliah promptly replied. In fact, so prompt was his reply that the experts in wireless telegraphy announced that, since it was impossible to send wireless messages so great a distance, Goliah was in their very midst and not on Palgrave Island. Goliah's letter was delivered to the Associated Press by a messenger boy who had been engaged on the street. The letter was as follows: —

> "What are a few paltry lives? In your insane wars you destroy millions of lives and think nothing of it. In your fratricidal commercial struggle you kill countless babes, women, and men, and you triumphantly call the shambles 'individualism.' I call it anarchy. I am going to put a stop to your wholesale destruction of human beings. I want laughter, not slaughter. Those of you who stand in the way of laughter will get slaughter.
>
> "Your government is trying to delude you into believing that the destruction of the Alaska was an accident. Know here and now that it was by my orders that the Alaska was destroyed. In a few short months, all battleships on all seas will be destroyed or flung to the scrap-heap, and all nations shall disarm; fortresses shall be dismantled, armies disbanded, and warfare shall cease from the earth. Mine is the power. I am the will of God. The whole world shall be in vassalage to me, but it shall be a vassalage of peace.
>
> "I am "Goliah"."

"Blow Palgrave Island out of the water! " was the head-line retort of the newspapers. The government was of the same frame of mind, and the assembling of the fleets began. Walter Bassett broke out in ineffectual protest, but was swiftly silenced by the threat of a lunacy commission. Goliah remained silent. Against Palgrave Island five great fleets were hurled — the Asiatic Squadron, the South Pacific Squadron, the North Pacific Squadron, the Caribbean Squadron, and half of the North Atlantic Squadron, the two latter coming through the Panama Canal.

"I have the honor to report that we sighted Palgrave Island on the evening of April 29," ran the report of Captain Johnson, of the battleship *North Dakota* to the Secretary of the Navy. "The Asiatic Squadron was delayed and did not arrive until the morning of April 30. A council of the admirals was held, and it was decided to attack early, next morning. The destroyer, *Swift VII*, crept in, unmolested, and reported no warlike preparations on the island. It noted several small merchant steamers in the harbor, and the existence of a small village in a hopelessly exposed position that could be swept by our fire.

"It had been decided that all the vessels should rush in, scattered, upon the island, opening fire at three miles, and continuing to the edge of the reef, there to retain loose formation and engage. Palgrave Island repeatedly warned us, by wireless, in the international code, to keep outside the ten-mile limit; but no heed was paid to the warnings.

"The *North Dakota* did not take part in the movement of the morning of May 1. This was due to a slight accident of the preceding night that temporarily disabled our steering-gear. The morning of May 1 broke clear and calm. There was a slight breeze from the southwest that quickly died away. The *North Dakota* lay twelve miles off the island. At the signal the squadrons charged in upon the island, from all sides, at full speed. Our wireless receiver continued to tick off warnings from the island. The ten-mile limit was passed, and nothing happened. I watched through my glasses. At five, miles nothing happened; at four miles nothing happened; at three miles, the *New York*, in the lead on our side of the island, opened fire. She fired only one shot. Then she blew up. The rest of the vessels never fired a shot. They began to blow up, everywhere, before our eyes. Several swerved about and started back, but they failed to escape. The destroyer, *Dart XXX*, nearly made the ten-mile limit when she blew up. She was the last survivor. No harm came to the *North Dakota*, and that night, the steering-gear being repaired, I gave orders to sail for San Francisco."

To say that the United States was stunned is but to expose the inadequacy of language. The whole world was stunned. It confronted that blight of the human brain, the unprecedented. Human endeavor was a jest, a monstrous futility, when a lunatic on a lonely island, who owned a yacht and an exposed village, could destroy five of the proudest fleets of Christendom. And how had he done it? Nobody knew. The scientists lay down in the dust of the common road and wailed and gibbered. They did not know. Military experts committed suicide by scores. The mighty fabric of warfare they had fashioned was a gossamer veil rent asunder by a miserable lunatic. It was, too much for their sanity. Mere human reason could not withstand the shock. As the savage is crushed by the sleight-of-hand of the witch-doctor, so was the world crushed by the magic of Goliah. How did he do it ? It was the awful face of the Unknown upon which the world gazed and by which it was frightened out of the memory of its proudest achievements.

But all the world was not stunned. There was the invariable exception — the Island Empire of Japan. Drunken with the wine of success deep-quaffed, without superstition and without faith in aught but its own ascendant star, laughing at the wreckage of science and mad with pride of race, it went forth upon the way of war. America's fleets had been destroyed. From the battlements of heaven the multitudinous ancestral shades of Japan leaned down. The opportunity, God-given, had come. The Mikado was in truth a brother to the gods.

The war-monsters of Japan were loosed in mighty fleets. The Philippines were gathered in as a child gathers a nosegay. It took longer for the battleships to travel to Hawaii, to Panama, and to the Pacific Coast. The United States was panic-stricken, and there arose the powerful party of dishonorable peace. In the midst of the clamor the *Energon* arrived in San Francisco Bay and Goliah spoke once more. There was a little brush as the *Energon* came in, and a few explosions of magazines occurred along the war-tunnelled hills as the coast defences went to smash. Also, the blowing up of the submarine mines in the Golden Gate made a remarkably fine display. Goliah's message to the people of San Francisco, dated as usual from Palgrave Island, was published in the papers. It ran: —

"Peace? Peace be with you. You shall have peace. I have spoken to this purpose before. And give you me peace. Leave my yacht *Energon* alone. Commit one overt act against her and not one stone in San Francisco shall stand upon another.

"Tomorrow let all good citizens go out upon the hills that slope down to the sea. Go with music and laughter and garlands. Make festival for the new age that is dawning. Be like children upon your hills, and witness the passing of war. Do not miss the opportunity. It is your last chance to behold what henceforth you will be compelled to seek in museums of antiquities.

"I promise you a merry day,

"Goliah.""

The madness of magic was in the air. With the people it was as if all their gods had crashed and the heavens still stood. Order and law had passed away from the universe; but the sun still shone, the wind still blew, the flowers still bloomed — that was the amazing thing about it. That water should continue to run downhill was a miracle. All the stabilities of the human mind and human achievement were crumbling. The one stable thing that remained was, Goliah, a madman on an island. And so it was that the whole population of San Francisco went forth next day in colossal frolic upon the hills that overlooked the sea. Brass bands and banners went forth, brewery wagons and Sunday-school picnics — all the strange heterogeneous groupings of swarming metropolitan life.

On the sea-rim rose the smoke from the funnels of a hundred hostile vessels of war, all converging upon the helpless, undefended, Golden Gate. And not all undefended, for out through the Golden Gate moved the *Energon*, a tiny toy of white, rolling like a straw in the stiff sea on the bar where a strong ebb-tide ran in the teeth of the summer sea-breeze. But the Japanese were cautious. Their thirty and forty- thousand-ton battleships slowed down half a dozen miles offshore and maneuvered in ponderous evolutions, while tiny scout-boats (lean, six-funneled destroyers) ran in, cutting blackly the flashing sea like so many sharks. But, compared with the *Energon*, they were leviathans. Compared with them, the *Energon* was as the sword of the archangel Michael, and they the forerunners of the hosts of hell.

But the flashing of the sword, the good people of San Francisco, gathered on her hills, never saw. Mysterious, invisible, it cleaved the air and smote the mightiest blows of combat the world had ever witnessed. The good people of San Francisco saw little and understood less. They saw only a million and a half of tons of brine-cleaving, thunder-flinging fabrics hurled skyward and smashed back in ruin to sink into the sea. It was all over in five minutes. Remained upon the wide expanse of sea only the *Energon*, rolling white and toy-like on the bar.

Goliah spoke to the Mikado and the Elder Statesmen. It was only an ordinary cable message, despatched from San Francisco by the captain of the *Energon*, but it was of sufficient moment to cause the immediate withdrawal of Japan from the Philippines and of her surviving fleets from the sea. Japan the sceptical was converted. She had felt the weight of Goliah's arm. And meekly she obeyed when Goliah commanded her to dismantle her war vessels and to turn the metal into useful appliances for the arts of peace. In all the ports, navy-yards, machine-shops, and foundries of Japan tens of thousands of brown-skinned artisans converted the war-monsters into myriads of useful things, such as ploughshares (Goliah insisted on ploughshares), gasolene engines, bridge-trusses, telephone and telegraph wires, steel rails, locomotives, and rolling stock for railways. It was a world-penance for a world to see, and paltry indeed it made appear that earlier penance, barefooted in the snow, of an emperor to a pope for daring to squabble over temporal power.

Goliah's next summons was to the ten leading scientists of the United States. This time there was no hesitancy in obeying. The savants were ludicrously prompt, some of them waiting in San Francisco for weeks so as not to miss the scheduled sailing-date. They departed on the *Energon* on June 15; and while they were on the sea, on the way to Palgrave Island, Goliah performed another spectacular feat. Germany and France were preparing to fly at each other's throats. Goliah commanded peace. They ignored the command, tacitly agreeing to fight it out on land where it seemed safer for the belligerently inclined. Goliah set the date of June 19 for the cessation of hostile preparations. Both countries mobilized their armies on June 18, and hurled them at the common frontier. And on June 19, Goliah struck. All generals, war-secretaries, and jingo-leaders in the two countries died on that day; and that day two vast armies, undirected, like strayed sheep, walked over each other's frontiers and fraternized. But the great German war lord had escaped — it was learned, afterward, by hiding in the huge safe where were stored the secret archives of his empire. And when he emerged he was a very penitent war lord, and like the Mikado of Japan he was set to work beating his sword-blades into plough-shares and pruning-hooks.

But in the escape of the German Emperor was discovered a great significance. The scientists of the world plucked up courage, got back their nerve. One thing was conclusively evident — Goliah's power was not magic. Law still reigned in the universe. Goliah's power had limitations, else had the German Emperor not escaped by secretly hiding in a steel safe. Many learned articles on the subject appeared in the magazines.

The ten scientists arrived back from Palgrave Island on July 6. Heavy platoons of police protected them from the reporters. No, they had not seen Goliah, they said in the one official interview that was vouchsafed; but they had talked with him, and they had seen things. They were not permitted to state definitely all that they had seen and heard, but they could say that the world was about to be revolutionized. Goliah was in the possession of a tremendous discovery that placed all the world at his mercy, and it was a good thing for the world that Goliah, was merciful. The ten scientists proceeded directly to Washington on a special train, where, for days, they were closeted with the heads of government, while the nation hung breathless on the outcome.

But the outcome was a long time in arriving. From Washington the President issued commands to the masters and leading figures of the nation. Everything was secret. Day by day deputations of bankers, railway lords, captains of industry, and Supreme Court justices arrived; and when they arrived they remained. The weeks dragged on, and then, on August 25, began the famous issuance of proclamations. Congress and the Senate cooperated with the President in this, while the Supreme Court justices gave their sanction and the money lords and the captains of industry agreed. War was declared upon the capitalist masters of the nation. Martial law was declared over, the whole United States. The supreme power was vested in the President.

In one day, child-labor in the whole country was abolished. It was done by decree, and the United States was prepared with its army to enforce its decrees. In the same day all women factory workers were dismissed to their homes, and all the sweatshops were closed. "But we cannot make profits!" wailed the petty capitalists. "Fools!" was the retort of Goliah. "As if the meaning of life were profits! Give up your businesses and your profit-mongering." "But there is nobody to buy our business!" they wailed. "Buy and sell -- is that all the meaning life has for you?" Replied Goliah., "You have nothing to sell. Turn over your little cut-throating, anarchistic businesses to the government so that they may be rationally organized and operated." And the next day, by decree, the government began taking possession of all factories, shops, mines, ships, railroads, and producing lands.

The nationalization of the means of production and distribution went on apace. Here and there were sceptical capitalists of moment. They were made prisoners and hauled to Palgrave Island, and when they returned they always acquiesced in what the government was doing. A little later the journey to Palgrave Island became unnecessary. When objection was made, the reply of the officials was: — "Goliah has spoken" — which was another way of saying, "He must be obeyed."

The captains of industry became heads of departments. It was found that civil engineers, for instance, worked just as well in government employ as, before, they had worked in private employ. It was found that men of high executive ability could not violate their nature. They could not escape exercising their executive ability, any more than a crab could escape crawling or a bird could escape flying. And so it was that all the splendid force of the men who had previously worked for themselves was now put to work for the good of society. The half-dozen great railway chief's cooperated in the organizing of a national system of railways that was amazingly efficacious. Never again was there such a thing as a car shortage. These chiefs were not the Wall Street railway magnates, but they were the men who formerly had done the real work while in the employ of the Wall Street magnates.

Wall Street was dead. There was no more buying and selling and speculating. Nobody had anything to buy or sell. There was nothing in which to speculate. "Put the stock gamblers to work," said Goliah; give those that are young and that so desire, a chance to learn useful trades." "Put the drummers, and salesmen, and advertising agents, and real estate agents to work," said Goliah; and by hundreds of thousands the erstwhile useless middlemen and parasites went into useful occupations. The four hundred thousand idle gentlemen of the country who had lived upon incomes were likewise put to work. Then there were a lot of helpless men in high places who were cleared out, the remarkable thing about this being that they were cleared out by their own fellows. Of this class were the professional politicians, whose wisdom and power consisted of manipulating machine politics and of grafting, There was no longer any graft. Since there were no private interests to purchase special privileges, no bribes were offered to legislators, and legislators for the first time legislated for the people, The result was that men who were efficient, not in corruption, but in direction, found their way into the legislatures.

With this rational organization of society amazing results were brought about. The national day's work was eight hours, and yet production increased. In spite of the great permanent improvements and of the immense amount of energy consumed in systematizing the competitive chaos of society, production doubled and tripled upon itself. The standard of living increased, and still consumption could not keep up with production. The maximum working age was decreased to fifty years, to forty-nine years, and to forty- eight years. The minimum working age went up from sixteen years to eighteen years. The eight-hour day became a seven-hour day, and in a few months the national working day was reduced to five hours.

In the meantime glimmerings were being caught, not of the identity of Goliah, but of how he had worked and prepared for his assuming control of the world. Little things leaked out, clews were followed up, apparently unrelated things were pieced together. Strange stories of blacks stolen from Africa were remembered, of Chinese and Japanese contract coolies who had mysteriously disappeared, of lonely South Sea Islands raided and their inhabitants carried away; stories of yachts and merchant steamers, mysteriously purchased, that had disappeared and the descriptions of which remotely tallied with the crafts that had carried the Orientals and Africans and islanders away. Where had Goliah got the sinews of war? Was the question. And the surmised answer was: By exploiting these stolen laborers. It was they that lived in the exposed village on Palgrave Island. It was the product of their toil that had purchased the yachts and merchant steamers, and Goliah continued to awe and rule the world.

One of the uses of Energon was in wireless telegraphy. It was by its means that Goliah was able to communicate with his agents all over the world. At that time the apparatus required by an agent was so clumsy that it could not be packed in anything less than a fair-sized steamer trunk. Today, thanks to the improvements of Hendsoll, the perfected apparatus can be carried in a coat pocket.

It was in December, 1924, that Goliah sent out his famous "Christmas Letter," part of the text of which, is here given: —

> "So far, while I have kept the rest of the nations from each other's throats, I have devoted myself particularly to the United States. Now I have not given to the people of the United States a rational social organization. What I have done has been to compel them to make that organization themselves. There is more laughter in the United States these days, and there is more sense. Food and shelter are no longer obtained by the anarchistic methods of so-called individualism, but are now well nigh automatic. And the beauty of it is that the people of the United States, have achieved all this for themselves. I did not achieve it, for them. I repeat, they achieved it for themselves. All that I did was to put the fear of death in the hearts of the few that sat in the high places and obstructed the coming of rationality and laughter. The fear of death made those in the high places get out of the way, that was all, and gave the intelligence of man a chance to realize itself socially.
>
> "In the year that is to come I shall devote myself to the rest of the world. I shall put the fear of death in the hearts of all that sit in the high places in all the nations. And they will do as they have done in the United States — get down out of the high places and give the intelligence of man a chance for social rationality. All the nations shall tread the path the United States is now on.
>
> "And when all the nations are well along on that path, I shall have something else for them. But first they must travel that path for themselves. They must demonstrate that the intelligence of mankind today, with the mechanical energy now at its disposal, is capable of organizing society so that food and shelter be made automatic, labor be reduced

to a three-hour day, and joy and laughter be made universal. And when that is accomplished, not by me but by the intelligence of mankind, then I shall make a present to the world of a new mechanical energy. This is my discovery. This Energon is nothing more nor less than the cosmic energy that resides in the solar rays. When it is harnessed by mankind it will do the work of the world. There will be no more multitudes of miners slaving out their lives in the bowels of the earth, no more sooty firemen and greasy engineers. All may dress in white, if they so will. The work of life will have become play and young and old will be the children of joy, and the business of living will become joy; and they will compete, one with another, in achieving ethical concepts and spiritual heights, in fashioning pictures and songs, and stories, in statecraft and beauty craft, in the sweat and the endeavor of the wrestler and the runner and the player of games — all will compete, not for sordid coin and base material reward, but for the joy that shall be theirs in the development and vigor of flesh and in the development and keenness of spirit. All will be joy-smiths, and their task shall be to beat out laughter from the ringing anvil of life.

"And now one word for the immediate future. On New Year's. Day all nations shall disarm, all fortresses and warships shall be dismantled, and all armies shall be disbanded.

"Goliah.""

On New Year's Day all the world disarmed. The millions of soldiers and sailors and workmen in the standing armies, in the navies, and in the countless arsenals, machine-shops, and factories for the manufacture of war machinery, were dismissed to their homes. These many millions of men, as well as their costly war machinery, had hitherto been supported on the back of labor. They now went into useful occupations, and the released labor giant heaved a mighty sigh of relief. The policing of the world was left to the peace officers and was purely social, whereas war had been distinctly anti-social.

Ninety per cent of the crimes against society had, been crimes against private property. With the passing of private property, at least in the means of production, and with the organization of industry that gave every man a chance, the crimes against private property practically ceased. The police forces everywhere were reduced repeatedly and again and again. Nearly all occasional and habitual criminals ceased voluntarily from their depredations. There was no longer any need for them to commit crime. They merely changed with changing conditions. A smaller number of criminals was put into hospitals and cured. And the remnant of the hopelessly criminal and degenerate was segregated. And the courts in all countries were likewise decreased in number again and again. Ninety-five per cent of all civil cases had been squabbles over property, conflicts of, property-rights, lawsuits, contests of wills, breaches of contract, bankruptcies, etc. With the passing of private property, this ninety-five per cent of the cases that cluttered the courts also passed. The courts became shadows, attenuated ghosts, rudimentary vestiges of the anarchistic times that had preceded the coming of Goliah.

The year 1925 was a lively year in the world's history. Goliah ruled the world with a strong hand. Kings and emperors journeyed to Palgrave Island, saw the wonders of Energon, and went away, with the fear of death in their hearts, to abdicate thrones and crowns and hereditary licenses. When Goliah spoke to politicians (so-called "statesmen"), they obeyed . . . or died. He dictated universal reforms, dissolved refractory parliaments, and to the great conspiracy that was formed of mutinous money lords and captains of industry he sent his destroying angels. "The time is past for fooling," he told them. "You are anachronisms. You stand in the way of humanity. To the scrap-heap with you." To those that protested, and they were many, he said: "This is no time for logomachy. You can argue for centuries. It is what you have done in the past. I have no, time for argument. Get out of the way."

With the exception of putting a stop to war, and of indicating the broad general plan, Goliah did nothing. By putting the fear of death into the hearts of those that sat in the high places and obstructed progress, Goliah made the opportunity for the unshackled intelligence of the best social thinkers of the world to exert itself. Goliah left all the multitudinous details of reconstruction to these social thinkers. He wanted them to prove that they were able to do it, and they proved it. It was due to their initiative that the white plague was stamped out from the world. It was due to them, and in spite of a deal of protesting from the sentimentalists, that all the extreme, hereditary inefficients were segregated and denied marriage.

Goliah had nothing whatever to do with the instituting Of the colleges of invention. This idea originated practically simultaneously in the minds of thousands of social thinkers. The time was ripe for the realization of the idea, and everywhere arose the splendid institutions of invention. For the first time the ingenuity of man was loosed upon the problem of simplifying life, instead of upon the making of money-earning devices. The affairs of life, such, as house-cleaning, dish and window-washing, dust-removing, and scrubbing and clothes-washing, and all the endless sordid and necessary details, were simplified by invention until they became automatic. We of today cannot realize the barbarously filthy and slavish lives of those that lived prior to 1925.

The international government of the world was another idea that sprang simultaneously into the minds of thousands. The successful realization of this idea was a surprise to many, but as a surprise it was nothing to that received by the mildly protestant sociologists and biologists when irrefutable facts exploded the doctrine of Malthus. With leisure and joy in the world; with an immensely higher standard of living; and with the enormous spaciousness of opportunity for recreation, development, and pursuit of beauty and nobility and all the higher attributes, the birth-rate fell, and fell astoundingly. People ceased breeding like cattle. And better, than that, it was immediately noticeable that a higher average of children was being born. The doctrine of Malthus was knocked into a cocked hat — or flung to the scrap-heap, as Goliah would have put it.

All that Goliah had predicted that the intelligence of mankind could accomplish with the mechanical energy at its disposal, came to pass. Human dissatisfaction practically disappeared. The elderly people were the great grumblers; but when they were honorably pensioned by society, as they passed the age limit for work, the great majority ceased grumbling. They found themselves better off in their idle old days under the new regime, enjoying vastly more pleasures and comforts than they had in their busy and toilsome youth under the old regime. The younger generation had easily adapted itself to the changed order, and the very young had never known anything else. The sum of human happiness had increased enormously. The world had become gay and sane Even the old fogies of professors of sociology, who had opposed with might and main the coming of the new regime, made no complaint. They were a score of times better remunerated than in the old days, and they were not worked nearly so hard. Besides, they were busy revising sociology and writing new text-books on the subject. Here and there, it is true, there were atavisms, men who yearned for the flesh-pots and cannibal-feasts of the old alleged "individualism," creatures long of teeth and savage of claw who wanted to prey upon their fellow-men; but they were looked upon as diseased, and were treated in hospitals. A small remnant, however, proved incurable, and was confined in asylums and denied marriage. Thus there was no progeny to inherit their atavistic tendencies.

As the years went by, Goliah dropped out of the running of the world. There was nothing for him to run. The world was running itself, and doing it smoothly and beautifully. In 1937, Goliah made his long- promised present of Energon to the world. He himself had devised a thousand ways in which the little giant should do the work of the world — all of which he made public at the same time. But instantly the colleges of invention seized upon Energon and utilized it in a hundred thousand additional ways. In fact, as Goliah confessed in his letter of March, 1938, the colleges of invention cleared up several puzzling features of Energon that had baffled him during the preceding years. With the introduction of the use of Energon the two-hour work-day was cut down almost to nothing. As Goliah had predicted, work indeed became play. And, so tremendous was man's productive capacity, due to Energon and the rational social utilization of it, that the humblest citizen enjoyed leisure and time and opportunity for an immensely greater abundance of living than had the most favored under the old anarchistic system.

Nobody had ever seen Goliah, and all peoples began to clamor for their savior to appear. While the world did not minimize his discovery of Energon, it was decided that greater than that was his wide social vision. He was a superman, a scientific superman; and the curiosity of the world to see him had become well-nigh unbearable. It was in 1941, after much hesitancy on his part, that he finally emerged from Palgrave Island. He arrived on June 6 in San Francisco, and for the first time, since his retirement to Palgrave Island, the world looked upon his face. And the world was disappointed. Its imagination had been touched. An heroic figure had been made out of Goliah. He was the man, or the demigod, rather, who bad turned the planet over. The deeds of Alexander, Caesar, Genghis Khan, and Napoleon we're as the play of babes alongside his colossal achievements.

And ashore in San Francisco and through its streets stepped and rode a little old man, sixty-five years of age, well preserved, with a pink-and-white complexion and a bald spot on his head the size of an apple. He was short-sighted and wore spectacles. But when the spectacles were removed, his were quizzical blue eyes like a child's, filled with mild wonder at the world. Also his eyes had a way of twinkling, accompanied by a screwing up of the face, as if he laughed at the huge joke he had played upon the world, trapping it, in spite of itself, into happiness and laughter.

For a scientific superman and world tyrant, he had remarkable weaknesses. He loved sweets, and was inordinately fond of salted almonds and salted pecans, especially of the latter. He always carried a paper bag of them in his pocket, and he had a way of saying frequently that the chemism of his nature demanded such fare. Perhaps his most astonishing failing was cats. He had an ineradicable aversion to that domestic animal. It will be remembered that he fainted dead away with sudden fright, while speaking in, Brotherhood Palace, when the janitor's cat walked out upon the stage and brushed against his legs.

But no sooner had he revealed himself to the world than he was identified. Old-time friends had no difficulty in recognizing him as Percival Stultz, the German-American who, in 1898, had worked in the Union Iron Works, and who, for two years at that time, had been secretary of Branch 369 of the International Brotherhood of Machinists. It was in 1901, then twenty-five years of age, that he had taken special scientific courses at the University of California, at the same time supporting himself by soliciting what was then known as "life insurance." His records as a student are preserved in the university museum, and they are unenviable. He is remembered by the professors he sat under chiefly for his absent-mindedness. Undoubtedly, even then, he was catching glimpses of the wide visions that later were to be his.

His naming himself "Goliah" and shrouding himself in mystery was his little joke, he later explained. As Goliah, or any other thing like that, he said, he was able to touch the imagination of the world and turn it over; but as Percival Stultz, wearing side-whiskers and spectacles, and weighing one hundred and eighteen pounds, he would have been unable to turn over a pecan — "not even a salted pecan."

But the world quickly got over its disappointment in his personal appearance and antecedents. It knew him and revered him as the master-mind of the ages; and it loved him for himself, for his quizzical shortsighted eyes and the inimitable way in which he screwed up his face when he laughed; it loved him for his simplicity and comradeship and warm humanness, and for his fondness for salted pecans and his aversion to cats. And today, in the wonder-city of Asgard, rises in awful beauty that monument to him that dwarfs the pyramids and all the monstrous blood-stained monuments of antiquity. And on that monument, as all know, is inscribed in imperishable bronze the prophecy and the fulfillment:

**All Will be Joy-Smiths,
and Their Task Shall be to Beat
Out Laughter From the Ringing
Anvil of Life**

EDITORIAL NOTE: — This remarkable production is the work of Harry Beckwith, a student in the Lowell High School of San Francisco, and it is here reproduced chiefly because of the youth of its author. Far be it from our policy to burden our readers with ancient history; and when it is known that Harry Beckwith was only fifteen when the foregoing was written, our motive will be understood. "Goliah" won the Premier for high school composition in 2254, and last year Harry Beckwith took advantage of the privilege earned, by electing to spend six months in Asgard. The wealth of historical detail, the atmosphere of the times, and the mature style of the composition are especially noteworthy in one so young.

A Curious Fragment

[**Editors Note:** The capitalist, or industrial oligarch, Roger Vanderwater, mentioned in the narrative, has been identified as the ninth in the line of the Vanderwaters that controlled for hundreds of years the cotton factories of the South. This Roger Vanderwater flourished in the last decades of the twenty-sixth century after Christ, which was the fifth century of the terrible industrial oligarchy that was reared upon the ruins of the early Republic.

From internal evidences we are convinced that the narrative which follows was not reduced to writing till the twenty-ninth century. Not only was it unlawful to write or print such matter during that period, but the working-class was so illiterate that only in rare instances were its members able to read and write. This was the dark reign of the overman, in whose speech the great mass of the people were characterized as the "herd animals." All literacy was frowned upon and stamped out. From the statute books of the times may be instanced that black law that made it a capital offence for any man, no matter of what class, to teach even the alphabet to a member of the working-class. Such stringent limitation of education to the ruling class was necessary if that class was to continue to rule.

One result of the foregoing was the development of the professional story-tellers. These story-tellers were paid by the oligarchy, and the tales they told were legendary, mythical, romantic, and harmless. But the spirit of freedom never quite died out, and agitators, under the guise of storytellers, preached revolt to the slave class. That the following tale was banned by the oligarchs we have proof from the records of the criminal police court of Ashbury, wherein, on January 27, 2734, one John Tourney, found guilty of telling the tale in a boozing-den of laborers, was sentenced to five years' penal servitude in the borax mines of the Arizona Desert.]

Listen, my brothers, and I will tell you a tale of an arm. It was the arm of Tom Dixon, and Tom Dixon was a weaver of the first class in a factory of that hell-hound and master, Roger Vanderwater. This factory was called "Hell's Bottom" . . . by the slaves who toiled in it, and I guess they ought to know; and it was situated in Kingsbury, at the other end of the town from Vanderwater's summer palace. You do not know where Kingsbury is? There are many things, my brothers, that you do not know, and it is sad. It is because you do not know that you are slaves. When I have told you this tale, I should like to form a class among you for the learning of written and printed speech. Our masters read and write and possess many books, and it is because of that that they are our masters, and live in palaces, and do not work. When the toilers learn to read and write, --all of them, --they will grow strong; then they will use their strength to break their bonds, and there will be no more masters and no more slaves.

Kingsbury, my brothers, is in the old State of Alabama. For three hundred years the Vanderwaters have owned Kingsbury and its slave pens and factories, and slave pens and factories in many other places and States. You have heard of the Vanderwaters, --who has not? --but let me tell you things you do not know about them. The first Vanderwater was a slave, even as you and I. Have you got that? He was a slave, and that was over three hundred years ago. His father was a machinist in the slave pen of Alexander Burrell, and his mother was a washerwoman in the same slave pen. There is no doubt about this. I am telling you truth. It is history. It is printed, every word of it, in the history books of our masters, which you cannot read because your masters will not permit you to learn to read. You can understand why they will not permit you to learn to read, when there are such things in the books. They know, and they are very wise. If you did read such things, you might be wanting in respect to your masters, which would be a dangerous thing . . . to your masters. But I know, for I can read, and I am telling you what I have read with my own eyes in the history books of our masters.

The first Vanderwater's name was not Vanderwater; it was Vange - Bill Vange, the son of Yergis Vange, the machinist, and Laura Carnly, the washerwoman. Young Bill Vange was strong. He might have remained with the slaves and led them to freedom; instead, however, he served the masters and was well rewarded. He began his service, when yet a small child, as a spy in his home slave pen. He is known to have informed on his own father for seditious utterance. This is fact. I have read it with my own eyes in the records. He was too good a slave for the slave pen. Alexander Burrell took him out, while yet a child, and he was taught to read and write. He was taught many things, and he was entered in the secret service of the government. Of course, he no longer wore the slave dress, except for disguise at such times when he sought to penetrate the secrets and plots of the slaves. It was he, when but eighteen years of age, who brought that great hero and comrade, Ralph Jacobus, to trial and execution in the electric chair. Of course, you have all heard the sacred name of Ralph Jacobus, but it is news to you that he was brought to his death by the first Vanderwater, whose name was Vange. I know. I have read it in the books. There are many interesting things like that in the books.

And after Ralph Jacobus died his shameful death, Bill Vange's name began the many changes it was to undergo. He was known as "Sly Vange" far and wide. He rose high in the secret service, and he was rewarded in grand ways, but still he was not a member of the master class. The men were willing that he should become so; it was the women of the master class who refused to have Sly Vange one of them. Sly Vange gave good service to the masters. He had been a slave himself, and he knew the ways of the slaves. There was no fooling him. In those days the slaves were braver than now, and they were always trying for their freedom. And Sly Vange was everywhere, in all their schemes and plans, bringing their schemes and plans to naught and their leaders to the electric chair.

It was in 2255 that his name was next changed for him. It was in that year that the Great Mutiny took place. In that region west of the Rocky Mountains, seventeen millions of slaves strove bravely to overthrow their masters. Who knows, if Sly Vange had not lived, but that they would have succeeded? But Sly Vange was very much alive. The masters gave him supreme command of the situation. In eight months of fighting, one million and three hundred and fifty thousand slaves were killed. Vange, Bill Vange, Sly Vange, killed them, and he broke the Great Mutiny. And he was greatly rewarded, and so red were his hands with the blood of the slaves that thereafter he was called "Bloody Vange." You see, my brothers, what interesting things are to be found in the books when one can read them. And, take my word for it, there are many other things, even more interesting, in the books. And if you will but study with me, in a year's time you can read those books for yourselves -- ay, in six months some of you will be able to read those books for yourselves.

Bloody Vange lived to a ripe old age, and always, to the last, was he received in the councils of the masters; but never was he made a master himself. He had first opened his eyes, you see, in a slave pen. But oh, he was well rewarded! He had a dozen palaces in which to live. He, who was no master, owned thousands of slaves. He had a great pleasure yacht upon the sea that was a floating palace, and he owned a whole island in the sea where toiled ten thousand slaves on his coffee plantations. But in his old age he was lonely, for he lived apart, hated by his brothers, the slaves, and looked down upon by those he had served and who refused to be his brothers. The masters looked down upon him because he had been born a slave. Enormously wealthy he died; but he died horribly, tormented by his conscience, regretting all he had done and the red stain on his name.

But with his children it was different. They had not been born in the slave pen, and by the special ruling of the Chief Oligarch of that time, John Morrison, they were elevated to the master class. And it was then that the name of Vange disappears from the pages of history. It becomes Vanderwater, and Jason Vange, the son of Bloody Vange, becomes Jason Vanderwater, the founder of the Vanderwater line. But that was three hundred years ago, and the Vanderwaters of today forget their beginnings and imagine that somehow the clay of their bodies is different stuff from the clay in your body and mine and in the bodies of all slaves. And I ask you, why should a slave become the master of another slave? And why should the son of a slave become the master of many slaves? I leave these questions for you to answer for yourselves, but do not forget that in the beginning the Vanderwaters were slaves.

And now, my brothers, I come back to the beginning of my tale to tell you of Tom Dixon's arm. Roger Vanderwater's factory in Kingsbury was rightly named "Hell's Bottom," but the men who toiled in it were men, as you shall see. Women toiled there, too, and children, little children. All that toiled there had the regular slave rights under the law, but only under the law, for they were deprived of many of their rights by the two overseers of Hell's Bottom, Joseph Clancy and Adolph Munster.

It is a long story, but I shall not tell all of it to you. I shall tell only about the arm. It happened that, according to the law, a portion of the starvation wage of the slaves was held back each month and put into a fund. This fund was for the purpose of helping such unfortunate fellow-workmen as happened to be injured by accidents or to be overtaken by sickness. As you know with yourselves, these funds are controlled by the overseers. It is the law, and so it was that the fund at Hell's Bottom was controlled by the two overseers of accursed memory.

Now, Clancy and Munster took this fund for their own use. When accidents happened to the workmen, their fellows, as was the custom, made grants from the fund; but the overseers refused to pay over the grants. What could the slaves do? They had their rights under the law, but they had no access to the law. Those that complained to the overseers were punished. You know yourselves what form such punishment takes -- the fines for faulty work that is not faulty; the overcharging of accounts in the Company's store; the vile treatment of one's women and children; and the allotment to bad machines whereon, work as one will, he starves.

Once, the slaves of Hell's Bottom protested to Vanderwater. It was the time of the year when he spent several months in Kingsbury. One of the slaves could write; it chanced that his mother could write, and she had secretly taught him as her mother had secretly taught her. So this slave wrote a round robin, wherein was contained their grievances, and all the slaves signed by mark. And, with proper stamps upon the envelope, the round robin was mailed to Roger Vanderwater. And Roger Vanderwater did nothing, save to turn the round robin over to the two overseers. Clancy and Munster were angered. They turned the guards loose at night on the slave pen. The guards were armed with pick handles. It is said that next day only half of the slaves were able to work in Hell's Bottom. They were well beaten. The slave who could write was so badly beaten that he lived only three months. But before he died, he wrote once more, to what purpose you shall hear.

Four or five weeks afterward, Tom Dixon, a slave, had his arm torn off by a belt in Hell's Bottom. His fellow-workmen, as usual, made a grant to him from the fund, and Clancy and Munster, as usual, refused to pay it over from the fund. The slave who could write, and who even then was dying, wrote anew a recital of their grievances. And this document was thrust into the hand of the arm that had been torn from Tom Dixon's body.

Now it chanced that Roger Vanderwater was lying ill in his palace at the other end of Kingsbury -- not the dire illness that strikes down you and me, brothers; just a bit of biliousness, mayhap, or no more than a bad headache because he had eaten too heartily or drunk too deeply. But it was enough for him, being tender and soft from careful rearing. Such men, packed in cotton wool all their lives, are exceeding tender and soft. Believe me, brothers, Roger Vanderwater felt as badly with his aching head, or thought he felt as badly, as Tom Dixon really felt with his arm torn out by the roots.

It happened that Roger Vanderwater was fond of scientific farming, and that on his farm, three miles outside of Kingsbury, he had managed to grow a new kind of strawberry. He was very proud of that new strawberry of his, and he would have been out to see and pick the first ripe ones, had it not been for his illness. Because of his illness he had ordered the old farm slave to bring in personally the first box of the berries. All this was learned from the gossip of a palace scullion, who slept each night in the slave pen. The overseer of the plantation should have brought in the berries, but he was on his back with a broken leg from trying to break a colt. The scullion brought the word in the night, and it was known that next day the berries would come in. And the men in the slave pen of Hell's Bottom, being men and not cowards, held a council.

The slave who could write, and who was sick and dying from the pick-handle beating, said he would carry Tom Dixon's arm; also, he said he must die anyway, and that it mattered nothing if he died a little sooner. So five slaves stole from the slave pen that night after the guards had made their last rounds. One of the slaves was the man who could write. They lay in the brush by the roadside until late in the morning, when the old farm slave came driving to town with the precious fruit for the master. What of the farm slave being old and rheumatic, and of the slave who could write being stiff and injured from his beating, they moved their bodies about when they walked, very much in the same fashion. The slave who could write put on the other's clothes, pulled the broad-brimmed hat over his eyes, climbed upon the seat of the wagon, and drove on to town. The old farm slave was kept tied all day in the bushes until evening, when the others loosed him and went back to the slave pen to take their punishment for having broken bounds

In the meantime, Roger Vanderwater lay waiting for the berries in his wonderful bedroom -- such wonders and such comforts were there that they would have blinded the eyes of you and me who have never seen such things. The slave who could write said afterward that it was like a glimpse of Paradise. And why not? The labor and the lives of ten thousand slaves had gone to the making of that bedchamber, while they themselves slept in vile lairs like wild beasts. The slave who could write brought in the berries on a silver tray or platter -- you see, Roger Vanderwater wanted to speak with him in person about the berries. The slave who could write tottered his dying body across the wonderful room and knelt by the couch of Vanderwater, holding out before him the tray. Large, green leaves covered the top of the tray, and these the body-servant alongside whisked away so that Vanderwater could see. And Roger Vanderwater, propped upon his elbow, saw. He saw the fresh, wonderful fruit lying there like precious jewels, and in the midst of it the arm of Tom Dixon as it had been torn from his body, well washed, of course, my brothers, and very white against the blood-red fruit. And also he saw, clutched in the stiff, dead fingers, the petition of his slaves who toiled in Hell's Bottom.

"Take and read," said the slave who could write. And even as the master took the petition, the body-servant, who till then had been motionless with surprise, struck with his fist the kneeling slave upon the mouth. The slave was dying anyway, and was very weak, and did not mind. He made no sound, and, having fallen over on his side, he lay there quietly, bleeding from the blow on the mouth. The physician, who had run for the palace guards, came back with them, and the slave was dragged upright upon his feet. But as they dragged him up, his hand clutched Tom Dixon's arm from where it had fallen on the floor.

"He shall be flung alive to the hounds!" The body-servant was crying in great wrath. "He shall be flung alive to the hounds!"

But Roger Vanderwater, forgetting his headache, still leaning on his elbow, commanded silence, and went on reading the petition. And while he read, there was silence, all standing upright, the wrathful body-servant, the physician, the palace guards, and in their midst the slave, bleeding at the mouth and still holding Tom Dixon's arm. And when Roger Vanderwater had done, he turned upon the slave, saying:--

"If in this paper there be one lie, you shall be sorry that you were ever born."

And the slave said, "I have been sorry all my life that I was born."

Roger Vanderwater looked at him closely, and the slave said:--

"You have done your worst to me. I am dying now. In a week I shall be dead."

"What do you with that?" The master asked, pointing to the arm; and the slave made answer:

"I take it back to the pen to give it burial. Tom Dixon was my friend. We worked beside each other at our looms."

There is little more to my tale, brothers. The slave and the arm were sent back in a cart to the pen. Nor were any of the slaves punished for what they had done. Instead, Roger Vanderwater made investigation and punished the two overseers, Joseph Clancy and Adolph Munster. Their freeholds were taken from them. They were branded, each upon the forehead, their right hands were cut off, and they were turned loose upon the highway to wander and beg until they died. And the fund was managed rightfully thereafter for a time -- for a time, only, my brothers; for after Roger Vanderwater came his son, Albert, who was a cruel master and half mad.

Brothers, that slave who carried the arm into the presence of the master was my father. He was a brave man. And even as his mother secretly taught him to read, so did he teach me. Because he died shortly after from the pick-handle beating. Roger Vanderwater took me out of the slave pen and tried to make various better things out of me. I might have become an overseer in Hell's Bottom, but I chose to become a story-teller, wandering over the land and getting close to my brothers, the slaves, everywhere. And I tell you stories like this, secretly, knowing that you will not betray me; for if you did, you know as well as I that my tongue will be torn out and that I shall tell stories no more. And my message is, brothers, that there is a good time coming, when all will be well in the world and there will be neither masters nor slaves. But first you must prepare for that good time by learning to read. There is power in the printed word. And here am I to teach you to read, and as well there are others to see that you get the books when I am gone along upon my way -- the history books wherein you will learn about your masters, and learn to become strong even as they.

[**Editor's Note:** From "Historical Fragments and Sketches," first published in fifty volumes in 4427, and now, after two hundred years, because of its accuracy and value, edited and republished by the National Committee on Historical Research.]

The Rejuvenation of Major Rathbone

Alchemy was a magnificent dream, fascinating, impossible; but before it passed away there sprang from its loins a more marvelous child, none other than chemistry. More marvelous, because it substituted fact for fancy, and immensely widened man's realm of achievement. It has turned probability into possibility, and from the ideal it has fashioned the real. Do you follow me?"

Dover absently hunted for a match, at the same time regarding me with a heavy seriousness which instantly called to my mind Old Doc Frawley, our clinical lecturer of but a few years previous. I nodded assent, and he, having appropriately wreathed himself in smoke, went on with his discourse.

"Alchemy has taught us many things, while not a few of its visions have been realized by us in these latter days. The Elixir of Life was absurd, perpetual youth a rank negation of the very principle of life. But—"

Dover here paused with exasperating solemnity.

"But prolongation of life is too common an incident nowadays for anyone to question. Not so very long ago a *generation* represented thirty-three years, the average duration of human existence. Today, because of the rapid strides of medicine, sanitation, distribution, and so forth, a generation is reckoned at thirty-four years. By the time of our great-grandchildren, it may have increased to forty years. *Quien sabe*? And again, we ourselves may see it actually doubled."

"Ah!" He cried, observing my start. "You see what I am driving at?"

"Yes," I replied. "But—"

"Never mind the "buts"," he burst in autocratically. "You ossified conservatives have always hung back at the coat-tails of science—"

"And as often saved it from breaking its neck," I retaliated.

"Just hold your horses a minute, and let me go on. What is life? Schopenhauer has defined it as the affirmation of the will to live, which is a philosophical absurdity, by the way, but with which we have no concern. Now, what is death? Simply the wearing out, the exhaustion, the breaking down, of the cells, tissues, nerves, bones and muscles of the human organism. Surgeons find great difficulty in knitting the broken bones of elderly people. Why? Because the bone, weakened, approaching the stage of dissolution, is no longer able to cast off the mineral deposits thrust in upon it by the natural functions of the body. And how easily such a bone is fractured! Yet, were it possible to remove the large deposits of phosphate, carbonate of soda, and so forth, the bone would regain the spring and rebound which it possessed in its youth.

"Merely apply this process, in varying measures, to the rest of the anatomy, and you have what? Simply the retardation of the system's break-up, the circumvention of old age, the banishment of senility, and the recapture of giddy youth. If science has prolonged the life of the generation by one year, is it not equally possible that it may prolong that of the individual by many?"

To turn back the dial of life, to reverse the hour-glass of Time and run its golden sands anew—the audacity of it fascinated me. What was to prevent? If one year, why not twenty? Forty?

Pshaw! I was just beginning to smile at my credulity when Dover pulled open the drawer beside him and brought to view a metal-stoppered vial. I confess to a sharp pang of disappointment as I gazed upon the very ordinary liquid it contained—a heavy, almost colorless fluid, with none of the brilliant iridescence one would so naturally expect of such a magic compound. He shook it lovingly, almost caressingly; but there was no manifestation of its occult properties. Then he pressed open a black leather case and nodded suggestively at the hypodermic syringe on its velvet bed. The Brown-Sequard Elixir and Koch's experiments with lymph darted across my mind. I smiled with cheery doubtfulness; but he, divining my thought, made haste to say, "No, they were on the right road, but missed it."

He opened an inner door of the laboratory and called "Hector! Come, old fellow, come on!"

Hector was a superannuated Newfoundland who had for years been utterly worthless for anything save lying around in people's way, and in this he was an admirable success. Conceive my astonishment when a heavy, burly animal rushed in like a whirlwind and upset things generally, till finally quelled by his master. Dover looked eloquently at me, without speaking.

"But that—that isn't Hector!" He cried, doubting against doubt.

He turned up the under side of the animal's ear, and I saw two hard-lipped slits, mementoes of his wild young fighting days, when his master and I were mere lads ourselves. I remembered the wounds perfectly.

"Sixteen years old and as lively as a puppy." Dover beamed triumphantly. "I've been experimenting on him for two months. Nobody knows as yet, but won't they open their eyes when Hector runs abroad again! The plain matter of fact is I've given him a new lease of life with lymph injection—same lymph as that used by earlier investigators, only they failed to clarify their compounds while I have succeeded. What is it? An animal derivative to stay and remove the effects of senility by acting upon the stagnated life-cells of any animal organism. Take the anatomical changes in Hector here, produced by infusion of the lymph compound; in the main they may be characterized as the expulsion from the bones of mineral deposits and an infiltration of the muscular tissues. Of course there are minor considerations; but these I have also overcome, not however, without the unfortunate demise of several of my earlier animal subjects. I could not bring myself to work on Hector till failure had been eliminated from the problem. And now—"

He rose to his feet and paced excitedly up and down. It was some time before he took up his uncompleted thought.

"And now I am prepared to administer this rejuvenator to humans. And I propose, first of all, to work on one who is very dear to me—"

"Not—not—?" I quavered.

"Yes, Uncle Max. That's why I have called in your assistance. I have found discovery capping discovery, till now the process of rejuvenation has become so accelerated that am afraid of myself. Besides, Uncle Max is so very old that the greatest discretion is necessary. Such crucial transformations in the whole organism of an age-weakened body can only be brought about by the most drastic methods, and there is great need to be careful. As I have said, I have grown afraid of myself, and need another mind to hold me in check. Do you understand? Will you help me?"

I have introduced the above conversation with my friend, Dover Wallingford, to show by what means I was led into one of the strangest scientific experiences of my life. Of the utterly unheard of things that followed, the village has not yet ceased to talk upon and wonder. And as the village is unacquainted with the real facts in the case, it has been stirred to its profoundest depths by the untoward happenings. The excitement created was tremendous; three camp meetings ran simultaneously and with marvelous success; there has been much talk of signs and portents, and not a few otherwise normal members of the community have proclaimed the advent of the latter-day miracles, and even yet their ears are patiently alert for the Trump of Doom, and their eyes lifted that they may witness the rolling up of the heavens as a scroll. As for Major Rathbone, otherwise Dover's Uncle Max, why he is looked upon by a certain portion of the village as a second Lazarus raised from the dead, as one who has almost seen God; while another portion of the village is equally set in its belief that he has entered into a league with Lucifer, and that some day he will disappear in a whirlwind of brimstone and hell-fire.

But be this as it may, I shall here state the facts as they really are. It is not my intention, however, to go into the details of the case, except as to the results regarding Major Rathbone. Several contingencies have arisen, which must be seen to before we electrify the sleepy old world with the working formula of our wonderful discovery.

Then we shall convene a synod of the nations, and the rejuvenation of mankind will be placed in the hands of competent boards of experts belonging to the several governments. And we here promise that it shall be as free as the air we breathe or the water we drink. Further, in view of our purely altruistic motives, we ask that our present secrecy be respected and not be made the object of invidious reflections by the world we intend befriending.

Now to work. I at once sent for my traps and took up my residence in one of the suites adjoining Dover's laboratory. Major Rathbone, dazzled by the glittering promise of youth, yielded readily to our solicitations. To the world at large, he was lying sick unto death; but in reality he was waxing heartier and stronger with every day spent upon him. For three months we devoted ourselves to the task—a task fraught with constant danger, yet so absorbing that we hardly noted the flight of time. The color returned to the Major's pallid skin, the muscles filled out, and the wrinkles in part disappeared. He had been no mean athlete in his younger days, and having no organic weaknesses, his strength returned to him in a most miraculous manner. The snap and energy he gathered were surprising, and lusty youth so rioted in his blood that toward the last we were often hard put to restrain him. We who had started out to resuscitate a feeble old man, found upon our hands an impetuous young giant. The remarkable part of it was that his snow-white hair and beard remained unchanged. Try as we would, it resisted every effort. Further, the irascibility which had come with advancing years still remained. And this, allied with the natural stubbornness and truculency of his disposition, became a grievous burden to us.

Sometime in the early part of April, because of a red-tape tangle at the express office regarding a shipment of chemicals, both Dover and myself were forced to be away. We had given Michel, Dover's trusted man, the necessary instructions, so did not apprehend any trouble. But on our return he met us rather shame-facedly at the entrance to the grounds.

"He's gone!" He gasped. "He's gone!" He repeated again and again, in his distress. His right arm hung limp and nerveless at his side, and it required no little patience to finally come to an understanding.

"I told him it was the orders that he mustn't go out. But be bellered like a wild bull, and wanted to know whose orders. And when I told him, he said it was time I should know that be took orders from no man. And when I stood in his way he took me by the arm, so, and just squeezed tight. I'm afraid it's broken, sir. And then he called Hector and went off across the fields to the village."

"Oh, your arm's all right," Dover assured him after due examination. "Just crushed the biceps a little, be kind of stiff and sore for a couple of days, that's all." And then to me, "Come on; we've got to find him."

It was a simple matter to follow him to the village. As we came down the main street, a crowd before the post office attracted our attention, and though we arrived at the climax, we could easily divine what had gone before. A bulldog, belonging to a trio of mill-hands, had picked a quarrel with Hector; and as it had been impossible to balance the second puppyhood of Hector with a new set of teeth, it was patent that he had been at a miserable disadvantage in the fight that followed. It was evident that Major Rathbone had intervened in an endeavor to separate the animals, and that the roughs had resented this. Besides, he was such a harmless-looking old gentleman, with his snow-white hair and patriarchal aspect, that they anticipated having a little fun with him.

"Aw, g'wan," we could hear one of the burly fellows saying, at the same time shoving the Major back as though he were a little boy.

He protested courteously that the dog was his; but they chose to regard him as a joke and refused to listen. The crowd was composed of a low breed of men, anyway, and they jammed in so closely to see the sport that we had hard work in cleaving a passage.

"Now, nibsy," commanded the mill-hand who had shoved Major Rathbone back, "don't yer think you'd better chase yerself home to yer mammy? This ain't no manner o' place fer leetle boys like you."

The Major was a fighter from the word go. And just then he let go. Before one could count three it was over; a swing under the first ruffian's ear, a half-jolt on the point of the second one's chin, and a shrewd block, with fake swing and swift uppercut on the jugular of the third, stretched the three brutes in the muck of the street. The crowd drew back hastily before this ancient prodigy, and we could bear more than one fervently abjuring his eyes.

As he arose from drawing the dogs apart, there was a cheery twinkle in the Major's eye which disconcerted us. We had approached him in the attitude of keepers recovering a patient; but his thorough sanity and perfect composure took us aback.

"Say," he said jovially, "there's a little place just round the corner here—best old rye—a-hem!" And he winked significantly as we linked arms like comrades and passed out through the petrified crowd.

From this moment our control was at an end. He always had been a masterful man, and from now on, he proceeded to demonstrate how capable he was of taking care of himself. His mysterious rejuvenation became, but would not remain, a nine days' wonder, for it grew and grew from day to day. Morning after morning he could be seen tramping home for breakfast across the dewy fields, with a fair-filled game-bag and Dover's shotgun. In previous years he had been a devoted horseman. One afternoon we returned from a trip to the city to find half the village hanging over the paddock fence. On closer inspection we discovered the Major breaking in one of the colts which had hitherto defied the stable-men. It was an edifying spectacle—his gray locks and venerable beard the sport of the wind as he dashed round and round on the maddened animal's back. But conquer the brute he did, till a stable boy led it away, trembling and as abject as a kitten. Another time, taking what had now become his customary afternoon ride, his indomitable spirit was fired by a party of well-mounted young fellows, and he let out with his big black stallion till he gave them his dust all the way down the principal street of the drowsy town.

In short, he took up the reins of life where he had dropped them years before. He was a fiery conservative as regards politics, and the peculiarly distasteful state of affairs then prevailing enticed him again into the arena. A crisis was approaching between the mill-owners and their working men, and a turbulent class of "agitators" had drifted into our midst. Not only did the Major oppose them openly, but he thrashed several of the more offensive leaders, nipped the strike in its incipiency, and in a most exciting campaign swept into the mayoralty. The closeness of the count but served to accentuate how bitter had been the struggle. And in the meantime he presided at indignant mass-meetings, and had the whole community shouting "*Cuba Libre!*" and almost ready to march to her deliverance.

In truth, he rioted about the country like a young Nimrod, and administered the affairs of the town with the wisdom of a Solomon. He snorted like an old war-horse at opposition, and woe to them that ventured to stand up against him. Success only stimulated him to greater activity; but, while such activity would have been commendable in a younger man, in one of his advanced years it seemed so inconsistent and inappropriate that his friends and relatives were shocked beyond measure. Dover and I could but hold our hands in helplessness and watch the antics of our hoary marvel.

His fame, or as we chose to call it, his notoriety spread till there was talk in the district of running him for Congress in the coming elections. Sensational space writers filled columns of Sunday editions with garbled accounts of his doings and of his tremendous vitality. These "yellow-journal" interviewers would have driven us to distraction with their insistent clamor, had not the Major himself taken the matter in hand. For a while it was his custom to occasionally throw an odd one out of the house before breakfast, and invariably, when he returned home in the evening, to attend similarly to the wants of three or four. A pest of curiosity-mongers and learned professors descended upon our quiet neighborhood. Spectacled gentlemen, usually bald-headed and always urbane, came singly, in pairs, in committees and delegations to note the facts and phenomena of this most remarkable of cases. Mystic enthusiasts, long-haired and wild-eyed, and devotees of countless occult systems haunted our front and back doors, and trampled upon the flowers till the gardener threatened to throw up his position in despair. And I veritably believe a saving of ten per cent on the coal bill could have been compassed by the burning up of unsolicited correspondence.

And to cap the whole business, when the United States declared war against Spain, Major Rathbone at once resigned his mayorship and applied to the war department for a commission. In view of his civil war record and his present superb health, it was highly probable that his request would be granted.

"It seems that before we can foist this rejuvenator upon the world, we must also discover an antidote for it—a sort of emasculator to reduce the friskiness attendant upon the return to youth, you know."

We had sat down, though in seemingly hopeless despondency, to discuss the difficulty and to try and find some way out of it.

"You see," Dover went on, "after revivifying an aged person, that person passes wholly out of our power. We can impose no checks, nor in any way can we tone down whatever excess of youthful spontaneity we may have induced. I see, now, that great care must be exercised in the administration of our lymph—the greatest of care if we should wish to avoid all manner of absurdities in the conduct of the patient. But that isn't the question at issue. What are we to do with Uncle Max? I confess, beyond gaining delay through the War Office, that I am at the end of my tether."

For the nonce Dover was so helpless that I felt not a little elation in unfolding the plan I had been considering for some time.

"You spoke of antidotes," I began tentatively.

"Now, as we happen to know, there are antidotes and antidotes, and yet again are there antidotes, some as a remedy for this evil and some for that. Should a babe drink a pint of kerosene, what antidote would you suggest?"

Dover shook his head.

"And since there is no antidote for such an emergency, do we assume that the babe must die? Not at all. We administer an emetic. But of course, an emetic is out of the question in the present case. But again, say for one suffering from uxoriousness, or for an hypochondriac, what remedy should be applied? Certainly, neither of the two I have mentioned will do. Now, for a man, melancholy-mad, what would you prescribe?"

"Change," he replied, instantly. "Something else to withdraw him from himself and his morbid brooding to give him new interest in life, to supply him with a reason for existence."

"Very good," I continued, jubilantly. "You will notice that you have prescribed an antidote, it is true, but instead of a physical or medicinal one, it is intangible and abstract. Now, can you give me a similar remedy for excessive spirits or strength?"

Dover looked puzzled and waited for me to go on.

"Do you remember a certain strong man of the name of Samson? Also Delilah, the fair Philistine? Have you ever noted the significance of "Beauty and the Beast"?" Do you not know that the strength of the strong has been wilted, dynasties been raised or demolished, and countless nations plunged into or rescued from civil strife, all because of the love of woman?"

"There's your antidote," I added modestly, as an afterthought.

"Oh!" His eyes flashed hopefully for an instant, but dismay returned as he shook his head sadly and said, "But the eligibles? There are none."

"Do you recollect a certain romance of the Major's when he was quite a young man, long before the war?"

"You mean Miss Deborah Furbush, your Aunt Debby?"

"Yes; my Aunt Debby. They quarreled, you know, and never made up—"

"Nor spoke to each other since—"

"Oh yes, they have. Ever since his rejuvenation he has called there regularly to pay his respects and ask for her health. Sort of gloats over her, you see. She's been bedridden a year now; have to carry her up and down stairs, and nothing the matter except simple old age."

"If she's strong enough," Dover hazarded.

"Strong enough!" I cried, "I tell you, man, it's genuine senility—nothing in the world to guard against but a very slight valvular weakness of the heart. What d'ye say? Get a couple of month's delay on his commission, and start in on Aunt Debby at once. What say, old man? What say?"

Not only had I grown excited over this solution of our difficulty, but I had at last aroused his enthusiasm. Appreciating the need for haste, we at once gutted the laboratory of all essentials and took up our abode at my home, which, in turn, was just over the way from Aunt Debby's.

By this time we had the whole operation at the ends of our fingers, so were able to proceed with the utmost dispatch. But we were very sly about it, and Major Rathbone had not the slightest idea of what we were up to. A week from the time we began, the Furbush household was startled by Aunt Debby's rising to give her hand to the Major when he made his usual call. A fortnight later, from a point of vantage in my windmill, we saw them strolling about the garden, and noted a certain new gallantry in the Major's carriage. And the rapidity with which Aunt Debby breasted the tide of time was dizzying. She grew visibly younger, day by day, and the roses of youth returned to her cheek, giving her the most beautiful pink and pearl complexion imaginable.

Perhaps ten days after that, he drove up to the door and took her out driving. And how the village talked! Which was nothing to the way it gabbled, when, a month later, the Major's interest in the war abated and he declined his commission. And when the superannuated lovers walked bravely to the altar and then went off on their honeymoon, it seemed that all tongues wagged till they could wag no more.

As I have said, this lymph is a wonderful discovery.

ALSO FROM LEONAUR

AVAILABLE IN SOFTCOVER OR HARDCOVER WITH DUST JACKET

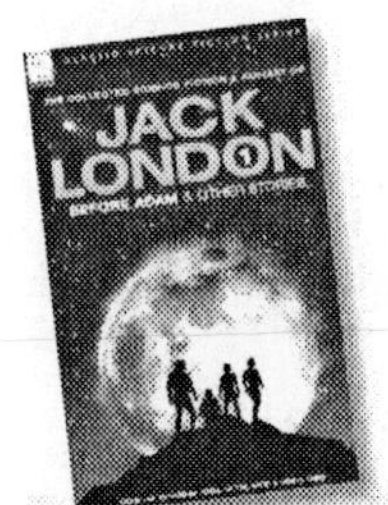

SF1 CLASSIC SCIENCE FICTION SERIES

BEFORE ADAM & Other Stories

by Jack London

Volume 1 of The Collected Science Fiction & Fantasy of Jack London.

SOFTCOVER : **ISBN 1-84677-008-4**
HARDCOVER : **ISBN 1-84677-015-7**

SF2 CLASSIC SCIENCE FICTION SERIES

THE IRON HEEL & Other Stories

by Jack London

Volume 2 of The Collected Science Fiction & Fantasy of Jack London.

SOFTCOVER : **ISBN 1-84677-004-1**
HARDCOVER : **ISBN 1-84677-011-4**

SF3 CLASSIC SCIENCE FICTION SERIES

THE STAR ROVER & Other Stories

by Jack London

Volume 3 of The Collected Science Fiction & Fantasy of Jack London.

SOFTCOVER : **ISBN 1-84677-006-8**
HARDCOVER : **ISBN 1-84677-013-0**

WF1 THE WARFARE FICTION SERIES

NAPOLEONIC WAR STORIES

by Sir Arthur Quiller-Couch

Tales of soldiers, spies, battles & Sieges from the Peninsular & Waterloo campaigns

SOFTCOVER : **ISBN 1-84677-003-3**
HARDCOVER : **ISBN 1-84677-014-9**

Printed in the United Kingdom
by Lightning Source UK Ltd.
119353UK00002B/10